About M...

Bill Walsh worked as a plasterer for nearly thirty years before becoming a full-time writer. He is married, has two adult children and lives in Waterford. *About Matilda* is his first novel.

About Matilda

BILL WALSH

PENGUIN
IRELAND

PENGUIN IRELAND

Published by the Penguin Group
Penguin Ireland, 25 St Stephen's Green, Dublin 2, Ireland
(a division of Penguin Books Ltd)
Penguin Books Ltd, 80 Strand, London WC2R ORL, England
Penguin Group (USA) Inc., 375 Hudson Street, New York, New York 10014, USA
Penguin Group (Australia), 250 Camberwell Road,
Camberwell, Victoria 3124, Australia (a division of Pearson Australia Group Pty Ltd)
Penguin Group (Canada), 90 Eglinton Avenue East, Suite 700, Toronto, Ontario, Canada M4P 2Y3
(a division of Pearson Penguin Canada Inc.)
Penguin Books India Pvt Ltd, 11 Community Centre,
Panchsheel Park, New Delhi – 110 017, India
Penguin Group (NZ), cnr Airborne and Rosedale Roads, Albany,
Auckland 1310, New Zealand (a division of Pearson New Zealand Ltd)
Penguin Books (South Africa) (Pty) Ltd, 24 Sturdee Avenue,
Rosebank, Johannesburg 2196, South Africa

Penguin Books Ltd, Registered Offices: 80 Strand, London WC2R ORL, England

www.penguin.com

First published 2006
1

Set in 12/14.75 pt Monotype Dante
Typeset by Rowland Phototypesetting Ltd, Bury St Edmunds, Suffolk
Printed in Great Britain by Clays Ltd, St Ives plc

A CIP catalogue record for this book is available from the British Library

ISBN-13 978-1-844-88099-7
ISBN-10 1-844-88099-0

For Belita

We are all in the gutter, but some of us are looking at the stars.

Oscar Wilde

I

Grandad parks the car outside a corner house. The front of the house has a window upstairs, and a door and window downstairs, and waiting at the door is a small woman in a green dress with white dots. She's round like a bubble, her hands are in the pocket of her apron. I think she's our Nanny and we might be coming to live with her. At the side of the house there's a building with a flat roof. It has a door and a window out front but the grey blinds are pulled down and I can't see what's in there.

A gang of boys are playing football on the road while girls play hopscotch on the pavement. Maybe we can play with them, if we're good.

As we all get out of the car, a man in a dark coat passes on the pavement and complains about the cold.

Our Grandad, who drove us here, claps his hands and breath puffs from his lips as he says, Shockin' altogether.

The trees in the street bend in the wind as we five children in our black duffle coats follow our Daddy up the garden path towards the woman in the dress with white dots.

Ah, will yeh look at them, she says, and kneels on one knee with her hands clasped in front of her. She opens her arms and calls for us to give our Nanny a hug.

I don't know what to do. Mona looks up at Daddy and he nods towards Nanny. Nanny wraps Mona in her arms so tightly all I can see are Mona's black curls sticking up from Nanny's arms. Nanny hugs Sheamie and Pippa. I think I'd like a hug too but now Nanny is standing up to talk to Daddy.

Let me look, Peter, and see if you've changed.

I don't know what Nanny means because Daddy's hair is still black his eyes are still yellow and his long narrow eyebrows still meet over his eyes.

Nanny says to Daddy, You're looking a bit thin. But never mind that. You're back in Waterford, and that's all matters for now.

Nanny turns to Grandad.

What kept you, Willie? Don't tell me you brought them to the pub?

Well, ah, says Grandad, wiping the black stain from his mouth.

Well, ah, my feckin' arse, says Nanny. She stands with her arms folded for an answer.

'Twas only the one after they got off the train from Dublin. Jasus, Peter didn't have a decent pint since he went to Australia. God, Annie, can't a man have a pint after seven years?

Nanny waves Grandad away.

That's no excuse. The poor children are jaded. Look at their eyes falling out of their sockets.

The two women up the street turn their necks to watch and Nanny says she's not talking about it now. Come inside and don't be perishing here any longer, with the world gawkin' at our business.

As Nanny and Grandad walk ahead of us through a narrow hallway with stairs on one side and a bedroom with a lamp on the other, my little brother Danny reaches for Daddy's hand. I turn to hold Daddy's other hand but Daddy walks past and tells us, Go ahead, there's nothing to be frightened of. I look for another hand to hold but all the hands are on the other side of the door in a room Nanny calls the sitting room. It looks small and smells like other people's dinners but it's warm from a blazing fire and I never saw a fire in a room.

Grandad makes straight for it and when he bends to it to heat his hands his underpants stick up over the back of his trousers. Christ, I'm freezin', he says, and gives himself a little shake. He's a big square man like a wooden box and has a round face like a clock.

Nanny tells us to come nearer the fireplace. Mona, Sheamie and Pippa are there first and I have to squeeze my hands between Mona and Pippa. I feel the cold leaving everywhere but my fingers. My fingers are so cold the heat makes them sore. I'd like to move them away but Nanny said I was to come close. There's a brown sofa and two armchairs in front of the fire and I'd love to sit because my legs are stiff from the plane and train, but when you never saw your grandmother before you can't sit on her chairs unless she tells you.

With her hand on Mona's shoulder, Nanny says, I'd know those freckles anywhere. How old are you now, Mona?

Mona turns all red and shy and I never saw Mona red or shy before. Mona flicks her eyes at Daddy and Daddy nods for Mona to answer.

Eight, Nanny.

Next, Nanny put her hand on Sheamie's head. Hair as red as ever, she says. He was in the pram the last time I saw him.

Sheamie fixes his thick glasses back up his nose and squints at Nanny but he doesn't say anything because he's serious. Maybe he's afraid to say something wrong. Daddy has to say Sheamie is seven now, the years don't be long going, Mammy.

They don't indeed, Peter. Nanny tries to smile but tears run from her old grey eyes. Daddy puts his huge arm around her shoulder and Nanny looks tiny lying against his chest. She says, Last year is after being the longest of my life. Thank God it's over. Let nineteen sixty-nine be a new start for all of us. She lifts her apron to wipe her cheeks and when she lets it drop her cheeks are damp but she's smiling down at Pippa and me.

And tell me, who have I here?

Pippa and me are nervous. We never had a Nanny that wanted to look at us before.

Daddy says, This is Pippa with the blonde hair, and Nanny calls Pippa a little doll. She straightens the green ribbon on Pippa's blonde ponytail. I wish I had a ponytail with a green ribbon so Nanny would straighten mine.

Nanny kisses Pippa on the cheek and Pippa says, I'm six and a half, Nanny, and Nanny says, Sure, God love her. I wonder should I tell Nanny I'm five and a half so she'll say sure, God love her about me?

Daddy taps me on the head and tells Nanny, The black hair is Matilda.

Nanny looks at the grey bear in my arms and wonders, Is that one of them what-ya-ma-call-ums with the sad little faces? A koala? she says.

Nanny is smiling down at me and I don't know what to say. I think I should say something, but it doesn't matter now because I'm too slow. Nanny kneels down to Danny who's clutching Daddy's trouser leg with his chubby fists. Nanny says, Danny is a Kelly, so he is, with those dark brown eyes.

I thought we were all Kellys though my eyes aren't brown, they're blue.

Nanny stands now and looks down at the five of us.

I want yee all to know this is yeer home as long as I'm alive and there's breath in my body. We don't know what to do. Nanny cocks her ear for an answer. Do yee hear?

Daddy says, Did yee hear that? This is yeer home from now on. What do you say? Mona, you're the oldest.

Mona whispers, Thank you, Nanny. Then we all say, Thank you, Nanny, except Danny who's looking under the chairs for something to play with. He's only three.

Grandad says to Nanny, Sure, Annie, you hardly think the

children want to stay with us. Peter will get on his feet quick enough. He'll pull the pieces together.

And why won't they want to stay with us? That's what we agreed.

Is it?

Don't start trouble here today or you'll answer to me. The best thing you can do is make yourself useful and don't be wonderin' how you're going to sneak out to the pub, either. No more pubs today.

Grandad grumbles under his breath as he tucks his shirt inside his trousers and hangs our duffle coats in the closet under the stairs. I look at Nanny's grey hair and wonder how this old woman with whiskers like a wombat will mind the five of us.

Nanny sits on the brown sofa and pats the cushions and tells Mona, Sheamie, Pippa and me to sit beside her, there's nothing to be frightened of. Sheamie sits on one side of Nanny and Mona and Pippa are quick to sit on the other side. There's no room for me. There's an empty armchair beside the television but I think it's Grandad's because there's a hollow in the cushion and a rolled-up newspaper tucked down the side. I sit on the red rug in front of the fire and hope nobody tells me to move, that I'm sitting in everyone's way.

Grandad goes to the kitchen to make tea. That is, he bends over the cooker and wonders, How do I light this gas, Annie? Nanny says, That man, I don't know how he'd survive if I wasn't here. She goes out to light the gas ring for Grandad and when she comes back Mona asks Nanny can she use the dunny.

The what?

Daddy laughs and says Mona is looking for the toilet.

Oh! Nanny laughs. There's no need to ask, Mona.

Mona stares at Nanny's lips and Pippa says, Mona didn't hear, Nanny. She only hears in one ear.

5

Nanny says to Daddy, Mona had two good ears the last time I saw her.

Daddy is sitting in the armchair with Danny on his lap under a blue picture of Jesus, sad because his Crown of Thorns is hurting his head. The veins in Daddy's temples swell, his forehead wrinkles and his yellow eyes glare at Pippa, making her pink cheeks turn red. Her bright blue eyes turn to the floor. Daddy says, Mona got an infection. Sheamie squints at me through his glasses and I lean tighter into the sofa. Daddy has told a lie.

Nanny shows Mona where the bathroom is and when she comes back she sits on the brown sofa again and asks Daddy about our Mum. What in God's name possessed her? she says.

Daddy looks sad like Jesus in the picture. Grandad calls from the kitchen to wait till we have the tea, then Daddy can tell them everything. He brings in cups on a tray and round bits of crusty bread that he calls blaas. The tea is sweet and warm and the blaas are smothered in flour and butter. I hurry mine because I want Daddy to tell about Mum.

Daddy finishes his tea. He curls his long straight fingers around the teacup and flicks at the handle with his thumbnail. Nanny and Grandad sit up on their seats, only Daddy doesn't say anything because now there's a noise in the hallway and everyone looks to the sitting-room door.

When it opens, a man in a suit and squeaky black shoes comes in. He has a round face like Grandad, clumps of curly black hair and eyebrows growing down over his eyes. Nanny says he's our Daddy's brother, Uncle Philip, home from his job in the bank. I wonder does he live here too and will he mind us coming to stay?

He comes right up to ask our names and wants to shake our hands. He has big hands and his skin is soft like a girl's.

Aren't they gorgeous children, he says to Nanny, and listen to that accent.

He stares at each of us. I turn my face away when he smiles at me because I never had an uncle before. Then he goes off to change his clothes. He comes back to shake hands with Daddy again and kiss Nanny on the cheek before he goes out again.

When he's gone Nanny says, I don't know what I'd do without Philip in the house.

Philip is the pet, says Grandad, and winks over at Daddy. Daddy winks back and smiles across at Grandad, but Nanny carries on about Uncle Philip. She won't hear a bad word about him the way he hands up his money every Friday without a bit of bother. He's very involved in the community too. He collects for the St Vincent de Paul. That's because he's going out with a nice girl, Rita, who's very religious. Almost became a nun. Now she works in Grace's supermarket. Two evenings a week he trains the schoolgirls' hockey team. That's where he's gone off to now.

Schoolgirls? Daddy throws his head back and laughs out loud. Grandad laughs too and spews tea from his mouth down the front of his jumper. And that's the last sound I hear. In front of the fire, I fall asleep.

I wake in the dark and there's a sour smell of feet. My teeth clatter so loud, I hear them. I'm in a big soft bed with my brothers and sisters. I'm squashed between Mona and Pippa with my koala on my chest. They're asleep. Sheamie and Danny are at the bottom and Sheamie's toes are in our faces. I'd push them away if I weren't so tired.

There's the clink of a light switch. I see the shape of a door and Nanny coming into the room with the light of the landing behind her. I try not to make any noise but my teeth won't stop their clattering like a ruler on railings.

Nanny is bending over me whispering my name. She tells me she just came to check and why aren't I asleep. I tell her my teeth woke me up and she tells me it's the cold. She moves away and I hear the squeak of a wardrobe door and metal coat hangers slide.

She comes back carrying a long green coat with gold buttons that twinkle in the landing light. As she bends over, spreading it upon me, she whispers, This was Grandad's coat when he sailed the world in the Merchant Navy and it kept him warm many a cold night at sea, so it did. The coat has a strange smell which gets stronger when she takes little white balls from the pockets and holds them in her hand. I ask, Is the smell from the sea and countries all over the world, Nanny? and she says I'm an awful blaggard to be coddin' her like that. She kisses my forehead and it's lovely the way I can feel her warm lips there even after she is gone and the bedroom door closed and the landing light turned out.

In the morning Nanny sends us out to play. But not the front. She says the road is dangerous with motorcars and we wouldn't be used to that after a year in an orphanage. The back garden is far enough for now. And no climbing, she says.

In the garden, there's a black wooden shed that's falling down. In the middle is a long narrow path that we run up and down in our black duffle coats to keep warm, wondering why Nanny lives in a place with no sun. A place where in winter, my Daddy always told us, everything is cold and hard and damp. My Daddy is no fool.

Sheamie wants to climb to the shed roof and we tell him Nanny said no. He stands there looking up at the shed and he looks funny in the long pants the nuns bought him before we

left Australia. Pippa knows Sheamie's going t.
so she stays near the back door keeping wat.
out the corner of one blue eye and shaking her h
what he's going to break this time.

Sheamie has long skinny arms and can easil
of the plain wood fence that runs down the sid
He pulls himself to the top by putting his feet in the cracks in
the boards, stands on the top rail with his arms out from his
sides and walks along like he's walking a tightrope. Pippa turns
her face away because if she doesn't see him fall then it's not
her fault and she can't get blamed. I want to climb too but
Mona scrunches her freckles at me. She's the oldest. Daddy
says she's in charge.

You let Sheamie climb.

He's a boy. He can do what he likes.

Sheamie straightens his glasses and calls to us that he can
see a river. He thinks there's a bridge across it but he's not
sure 'cos he can only see one end. There's a hill in the distance,
he says, and paddocks with pylons and cows in them. Then
he moves along the top of the fence putting one foot in front
of the other, heel to toe. He wobbles a bit. I'm certain he's
going to fall but he keeps going till he's close enough to the
shed to step onto the roof.

There's an empty metal bucket by the door and I carry it
to the fence, turn it upside down and stand on it. My eyes are
in line with the top of the fence. There's a cold wind in my
eyes that stings and makes me blink. Sheamie is now lying on
the roof shooting the cows with a pretend rifle, shouting Bang!
every time his finger pulls the trigger. The soles of his shoes
are caked with wet clay and the hood of his duffle coat is
pulled down so you can see his red hair. Pippa is still at the
back door shaking her blonde fringe at Sheamie. Pippa thinks
pretending is stupid. You either have a gun or you don't.

...shed doesn't look dangerous and Mona has gone inside ...Danny because it's warmer. The bucket makes me high enough to drag myself to the top of the fence the way Sheamie did, and I sit on it like you'd sit on a horse. I slide my bottom towards the shed and soon I'm lying on it myself, seeing the pylons like tall iron men carrying wires on their shoulders across the paddocks. I try to stand up straight but I'm scared. The shed roof has a small slope and is slippery with white stuff. Now Danny is trying to climb the fence too.

He still has all his baby teeth like white needles in his gums. He can't quite manage the climb, so he runs to the other side of the garden with his chubby little legs red from the cold and turns and runs at the fence with his head down and bumps straight into it and falls on his bum. Mona runs from the shed and catches his hand. She tells me to get down. But I can't. I'm stuck.

Danny pulls away from Mona and runs at the fence and bangs his head again.

Sheamie turns around and sits up. He tells me, Just walk slowly, don't straighten up yet, Matilda.

I feel dizzy. I see the clouds moving across Sheamie's thick glasses. I reach for Sheamie, who's sliding towards me on his bum with his hand out. I feel his icy fingertips but before he catches my hand properly I slip and bounce on the footpath beside Mona.

I stand up quick. I don't want to be in trouble. I don't feel pain until Mona pinches my leg.

You were told not to climb.

Danny points at my leg, Look, 'Tilda. He covers his hand with his mouth and says, Bud!

There's blood spouting from my knee. I want my Mum.

I run down the path and in the back door. Nanny is drinking tea at the kitchen table and I run to her.

She jumps up, Jesus, Mary and holy St Joseph!

Mona runs in the back door with Pippa behind her. Pippa yells, She fell off the roof. She fell off the roof.

Nanny fixes her old grey eyes on Pippa. Did you see her climb?

No, Nanny.

Mona says, I told Matilda not to climb.

My leg is cold but the blood is wet and warm and running into my sock and making it squishy.

Nanny rinses a cloth under the tap and holds it to my knee and tells Mona to go upstairs for Grandad. That knee needs stitches.

Daddy comes from the sitting room. He doesn't say anything, just pulls on an overcoat that's hanging on the back of one of the chairs and lifts me in his arms.

I grab hold of his neck and he runs with me out the front door and through the streets. People stop and ask, What's the matter? Daddy rushes past. He tells me I'm a brave girl for not crying. The wind is bitter and I shelter my face in his neck where it's warm and smells of cod liver oil.

At the top of a hill there's a building with tall windows. The corridor is full. There are people on crutches, in wheelchairs, lying on trolleys complaining they'd be better off at home with a glass of water and an aspirin for all the attention they get. But I'm the only one with blood, the only one in her Daddy's arms. He holds me high for all the world to see.

A nurse in a blue veil hurries from behind a desk. She has a fluffy moustache and smells of medicine. She pulls at my knee and I pull my leg away. She says it's nothing a few stitches won't fix. There might be a scar but that can't be helped. Sit and wait.

Daddy pushes her aside, kicks the door open and sends the empty trolley behind it crashing off the wall. Nurses rush from behind bed curtains and patients sit up in their beds. Daddy lays me on an empty bed. Don't move, Matilda, I'll be straight back.

He pulls the white curtain around me and comes back with a man wearing a white coat. The nurse in the blue veil rushes in and tells Daddy he'll have to wait in the queue. Do you hear me?

Daddy keeps his back to her and tells the man in the white coat we arrived from Australia yesterday, and about Mona, Sheamie, Pippa and Danny back in Nanny's. About our mother walking out, about us spending a year in the orphanage and how I'm worn out from three days travelling on planes and trains and he won't have his daughter sitting in a queue. She's been through enough.

The man has a kind face. He smiles at me and tells me I'm a lucky girl to have a Daddy that cares.

The nurse complains to the man in the white coat. We can't have people jumping queues, Doctor. They must wait their turn.

We can make an exception, Sister. Disinfect that child's knee. Give her a tetanus injection. I'll be right back.

Daddy holds my hand when the nurse puts the needle in my bum and, even though the needle is sharp and makes my leg stiff, I don't cry. And I don't cry when the man puts stitches in my knee with a needle and thread and wraps it in a bandage the same colour as my leg. He says I'm a great girl. They must make them tough in Australia. He hands me a lollipop from a glass jar on the windowsill and tells Daddy I'm young, there won't be a scar.

Grandad is waiting outside in the car in his slippers, but slippers or no slippers, he needs a pint after this. What would you think yourself, Peter?

Daddy says he hardly drinks anymore. Yesterday was the

first pint he had in years. Australia isn't like Ireland with a pub on every corner.

No pints? Is it jokin' me yeh are? By Jesus, I'm after hearin' everything now.

A few days later Nanny is sitting at the kitchen table with big tears on her chin that she wipes away with her small white hands. Daddy bends down to kiss her forehead and she hugs him before saying, I'll offer a novena that you uncover some news.

We all go out to the garden. The clouds hurry by and a crow squawks away from the front gate and sails down Gracedieu Road and over the red-brick chimney of a factory at the bottom of the street. Nanny tries to smile as she wraps a scarf around Daddy's neck and tells him to keep himself covered. The Irish Sea is a rough place in January.

Daddy's friend, who he calls Umbilical Bill, has got him a lift to England on a cattle boat. He's going to see our Mum's brother, the bishop, and his own brother James, who's a millionaire. He says he'll let no stone unturned to find our mother. I want to ask Nanny why would Mum be under a stone but she'd probably tell me I'm an awful blaggard to be coddin' her like that.

Daddy kisses us goodbye at the gate and tells us not to cry. He hoists his green canvas bag to his shoulder and tells us to be good for our Nanny.

I watch him step out onto the footpath and down the street. I start to run after him and get the gate open but Nanny chases and clutches my arm. I try to pull away. I scream out, Daddy, come back. But he's too far away.

Nanny says, Shush, he'll be back. Your father won't leave you.

Our Mummy did.

Don't worry about your Daddy, Matilda. Your Daddy had no choice but to put you into that place when your mother left. The man had to work. He had to search for your mother. Your Daddy loves all of you very much.

Nanny's fingers are soft and warm and calm me. I stop wriggling and she strokes my neck with her fingers.

Pippa is at the gate, her bottom lip sticks out and there are tears in her blue eyes and I know Pippa doesn't believe Nanny either when she says, Your father will be back. I lean my head against the top of Nanny's leg where it's soft and say a prayer that Daddy will come back with Mum so I can tell her I'm sorry. She left because I done something wrong even though I don't know what. Daddy has to find her so I can tell her I love her and ask if she'll come home to us again. I'll say my prayers and I'll be good and do what I'm told. We all will. It will be a new start. We'll be happy and forget everything bad that happened. Maybe she'll come tomorrow.

Grandad lifts Danny into his arms and Danny waves after Daddy, even though we can't see Daddy anymore. Sheamie wanders out into the street with his hands in his pockets. Nanny calls him back but Sheamie keeps walking.

Mona says, Don't mind him, Nanny. No matter where Sheamie is he wants to be someplace else.

Nanny says, The poor little boy. He misses his mother.

2

Grandad likes to sit in his car with an oily rag in his hand listening to the radio. When he does come in, he sits in his chair with the hollow and drinks stout from small fat bottles and wonders when dinner will be ready.

It will be ready when it's ready!

Nanny has two voices. The one that never stops talking and the one that barks and makes us hop. Even Grandad hops. He loves Friday nights when the greyhound races come on television. Other than that, he says he wouldn't have television in the house.

Nanny says, That television is going nowhere till she sees what happens to Dr Richard Kimble chasing the one-armed man all over America and running from that awful Inspector Gerard. And what would I do without *The Riordans*?

Couldn't yeh do what yeh always done, Annie?

Put them thoughts out of your head and don't talk like that in front of the children.

I meant the novena.

I know what you meant, all right.

I never know what they're arguing about, but Nanny always wins.

Friday nights, when Uncle Philip goes to the Savoy cinema with his girlfriend Rita, Nanny sends me into the shop for a big bottle of orange and some packets of crisps. Quick, she says, they're starting. She brings Grandad his bottle of stout and sets it beside his ankle.

Batten down the hatches, Annie, says Grandad, and pours his stout into a tall glass.

Nanny tells Sheamie to get the bucket of coal from the yard. Pippa, turn off the sitting-room light. Mona, turn off the kitchen light. Nanny goes out to the hallway herself and takes the key out of the front door and stuffs a sock in the back of the letterbox to keep out the draught. She closes the sitting-room door behind her and sits in the armchair in front of the fire and tells us if we hear a knock, don't answer. They can come back tomorrow. She takes the plastic moneybag from her apron pocket and divides the pennies between us as we take our places on the red rug. Nanny says there're six greyhounds in each race. Everyone pick a dog and put a penny on it to win. Grandad says, Sure, I'll pick an aul dog meself, but Nanny says there're not enough dogs, because there're five of us children and her and only six dogs in each race. Help Danny pick one.

Grandad says to Danny, Come up to me youngfella and we'll show 'em how it's done.

Danny climbs on Grandad's lap and Grandad tickles Danny's face with his chin whiskers until Danny begs him to stop but he's laughing so much he can't get the words out. Grandad calls it the giggilleens and it's torture.

We gather round the fire and open our crisps and scream for our dog. Grandad doesn't mind how loud the crisp bags are because he's shouting louder, Come on, black fella, come on yeh bastard, he's gonna catch him, Danny, look at him, look he's catchin' up he's catchin up look at him look at him, ah, Jasus, who won? Sheamie again. Danny jumps up and down on Grandad's lap clapping his hands and laughing and tormenting Grandad for a sup of his stout till Grandad gives in.

Nanny says, Good man, Sheamie, we won't have a penny left with you. Sheamie has a grin like there's a saucer in his mouth. His long legs are stretched out behind him and he makes stacks of his pennies on the rug and wonders is a penny all he can bet?

When the ads come on television, Nanny says to Grandad, Stay as you are, Willie, I'll get you another drink.

Good girl, Annie.

Grandad lights a cigar and makes big smoke circles for us to poke our fingers through. Sheamie prods the coal fire with the poker and the heat comes out as a pink glow we can see on Grandad's trouser leg. He fills his glass with the stout, takes a sup, belches, tilts in his chair and farts.

Right, Danny. Let's see what we can do about Sheamie winning all the money.

Afterwards, Nanny hands us a penny each and puts the rest back in the plastic moneybag for next week. Now, she says, wasn't that great fun altogether?

We all agree it was.

Grandad goes to the pub to play cards and we have our bath in front of the fire in the huge silver bathtub. When we're washed and dried and smelling of talcum powder, we stick forks through slices of bread thick as doorsteps and toast them at the fire and listen to Nanny tell the story of how our father met our mother.

Nanny says our father was the quietest of her fourteen children, hardly said a word. He was always thinking. Then all of a sudden he'd get a notion into his head and neither Hell nor high water would persuade him out of it. Then one day he got into a fight in the school playground in the Christian Brothers. It was the other boy's fault but your father was blamed and beaten half unconscious by a tramp of a Christian Brother. He left school at twelve, barely able to read or write, and went to sea until he was twenty-two. That's where he learned to play guitar.

He was a pirate, wasn't he, Nanny? says Pippa.

That's right. He was indeed.

He had a thing over his eye, a patch, says Pippa.

A black one.

And a parrot, says Pippa.

That's right, Pippa. A yellow one.

Called Polly, says Pippa.

That's right, Pippa.

It sat on his shoulder, didn't it, Nanny? says Pippa.

Shut the fuck up, Pippa, says Mona.

Nanny makes a pretend swing at Mona. Pippa sits back against the brown sofa with her knees pulled up to her chin and a pout on her face but satisfied the story is going to be the same as every other time. The rest of us sit closer to our Nanny's feet, only moving if the heat from the fire gets too much for our backs.

Nanny carries on. Your father's ship worked out of Hamburg in the fifties.

What's the fifties?

A long time ago.

Like once upon a time, Nanny?

That's right, Matilda.

Anyway, that's where he met the Beatles and became friendly with John Lennon. In fact, they looked so alike, your father was often mistaken for him.

The real John Lennon, Nanny? says Sheamie.

The one and only. Of course they weren't famous, then. Anyway, where was I?

Hamburg, says Sheamie.

Now, when he returned from sea and there being no work in Ireland your father went to London with a friend who was starting a showband. I tried to talk him out of it but he said if Brendan Boyer and the Royal Showband could make a go of it, so could he. Even if he didn't, wouldn't it be a better life than standing on North London's Cricklewood Broadway looking for a day's work shovelling cement? One night he was playing in the National Ballroom in Kilburn and your mother was there on a night out from the Nurses Training College. Someone or other introduced the pair of them, they went out together for a year or so, next thing we hear they were to get married. For some reason Nanny gives Mona a queer look and shrugs her shoulders, then carries on, It was all done in a bit of a hurry. Grandad or myself didn't get a chance to go across to London for the wedding.

First time I met her was when your father and herself turned up at door with Sheamie in the pram and Mona barely walking. Said they were leaving for Australia. Your mother was hardly more than a child herself. Now, that's as much as I know. Finish yeer supper and get off to bed.

I don't really want to go to bed. I'm not tired but I climb under the green coat with my brothers and sisters and, when we cuddle together, I fall asleep dreaming about a nurse who falls in love with a prince who plays a guitar.

The door to Nanny's shop buzzes when it opens. It has a wooden floor and a wooden counter with shelves behind. There's a picture of a man on the wall with a grey beard and blue cap and underneath him in big letters it says, Players Please.

Grandad says it's a gossip shop.

I ask him what's a gossip shop and he whispers behind his hand so Nanny won't hear, A place for passin' on everyone's business, girl.

In the shop, I sit on the floor behind the counter eating jellybeans and listening to Nanny gossip to the neighbours, passing on what she's heard from the last customer after promising may the Lord strike her down if she breathes a word.

I love it when it's just the two of us. I haven't had anyone to love me for a long time and if it's just the two of us here she might love me more.

And tell me, Annie, the woman standing on the other side of the counter says, is that one of the grandchildren you were telling me about?

It is indeed. Say hello to Missus Sullivan, Matilda.

Missus Sullivan bends over the counter and looks down at me. She's wearing a red scarf and red lipstick and smiling like she knows me.

Isn't she a sweet child, God love her. And very affectionate I'd say, Annie.

She is, and a quiet poor child. Sure, I hardly know she's there.

Missus Sullivan pulls her head back and I can't see her anymore. I wonder why she doesn't say listen to that accent like everyone else, and what does affectionate mean? It must be something you get instead of an accent.

It's a big change from just having Philip in the house, says Nanny. He's the last of them left in Waterford. John's in the army and the rest of them are in London.

I heard John was in the Congo, says Mrs Sullivan.

He's back a few years from there, says Nanny. His term of service is nearly up.

Will he come back do you think? He must be hitting thirty. Time for him to settle down.

Nanny glares out over the counter to Missus Sullivan. I don't know what he intends to do. It's his own business what he does.

Oh I didn't mean . . . says Missus Sullivan. Tell you what,

I'll have a pound of butter. Well, you're a great woman, Annie, after what you done.

Nanny takes the butter from the fridge and leaves it on the counter.

What could I do after their mother walked out? I'd never forgive myself if anything happened to them way over there. I know the nuns were good to them, but 'tis not the same as a proper home, is it, Hannah?

'Tis not indeed, Annie. Look at them poor children down in the Holy Shepherd convent. Isn't it disgraceful how they're fired in there with the tinkers and the tippers without a mother or a father between them?

It is of course. It's no place for any child.

Did I hear something on the news that the government were talking about improving those places?

Talk is cheap, says Nanny.

And I'll have a pound of cooked ham too, Annie.

A pound of ham, Hannah? A whole pound. Ah here, talk might be cheap but I wouldn't say the same for ham. Have you visitors from America or what?

Well, well, maybe a quarter, Annie?

That'd be more like it right enough.

I better go up and tidy the house before himself gets home or he'll be wonderin' have I anything better to do all day than gossip. No other news I suppose, Annie.

Not lately, Hannah. No.

Oh well, put that on the book for me so, Annie. I'll be in Friday to settle up, as usual.

I will, says Nanny, and she's already licking the tip of her pencil.

When Missus Sullivan is gone Nanny says, The cheek a that one, Matilda. Her and her pound of ham, and asking questions about my John. I don't know what this town is comin' to. Fur coat and no knickers the lot of them, doing their best to gawk down their noses at the rest. They'll get nothing to talk about out of this shop.

Nanny laughs, then I laugh, even though I don't know what she's laughing at, but I'm happy I'm here with Nanny and not down in the Holy Shepherd with the tinkers and tippers and children without a mother or father.

Nanny closes the shop early today. She pulls down the grey blinds. She says it's February, we've had a month to settle and it's time to start school. She's bringing Mona, Pippa and me to enrol in the Sisters of Divinity Girls' School, and Grandad is taking Sheamie to the De La Salle Brothers.

Pippa doesn't want to go to school. We still talk like Australians and everyone will laugh, she says. Nanny says she won't have the school inspector at the door wondering why her grandchildren haven't started school. They take children away for that. She goes to the kitchen for her handbag and Mona yanks Pippa's hair and warns her not to cause trouble. We have to go to school like Nanny said. Pippa says, Ouch! Grandad says, Stop that, stop that for the love a Christ. Nanny screams from the kitchen, Mona, are you tormenting your sisters? Leave those girls alone, you're too bloody big. Mona scrunches her freckles at me to see if I want to complain, but I wouldn't complain to Mona when she's like this, and anyway I'm fed up hanging round the house when it's raining outside and the other kids from the street are in school.

Danny cries to go to school but he's too young. He pulls at Grandad's trouser leg and Grandad pats his head and tells him, Next year, Danny. Danny still cries. Grandad lifts Danny onto his shoulders and Danny claps his hands and smiles down at us with his lovely white baby teeth because he's higher than everyone now and that's better than going to school anytime.

Nanny hurries us out to the car, grumbling at how slow we are and warning Grandad if he sets one foot in the pub this day she'll swing for him.

Sister Gertrude sits behind a desk in a small room with a crucifix on the wall and says sorry, she's full. She holds a black fountain pen in her hand but the pen doesn't move. She turns the pages of her big red book and says, Yes, indeed we are full. Isn't that an awful pity?

Pippa smiles.

Sister Gertrude says Nanny might like to try another school, the Mercy Convent or the Presentation, and stands.

Nanny lowers her handbag to the floor like she's getting ready to fight. Sister Gertrude sits down again.

Well, perhaps, and I'm only saying perhaps, we can fit them in next term, Missus Kelly. Of course they'd have to be Roman Catholics.

Nanny leans back in her chair. Sure, isn't their uncle only a bishop.

Really? says Sister Gertrude.

Really, says Nanny.

Of course, they won't be learning the Irish language because they weren't born in Ireland. Though they will learn the Irish dancing. The jig, the hornpipe and reel. Start Monday.

Monday I'm first into my new blue uniform and yellow socks. In the playground we see other girls come in. The ones with raggedy hair and dirty uniforms sit at the back of the class and have books covered in wallpaper so everyone knows what their sitting room looks like. The girls who have clean uniforms sit in the front and have their books covered in brown greaseproof.

I'm put in the second row beside Natasha White. She has

dimples and wears a yellow hair band and giggles all the time. I tell her my Daddy is in London. She tells me her Daddy went to London once but came back to work in the glass factory. Theresa Flanagan, with the scabby knees and runny nose that she wipes in her sleeve, sits behind us. She says her Daddy went to London too and he came back as well. Her Mammy always says she'd be better off if he'd stayed where he was. The bollox.

Our teacher is Miss Bolger. She has wavy red hair and wears dresses with silver buckles and high-heeled shoes that click when she walks. She likes the girls in clean uniforms the best. Theresa Flanagan invites me to play, but I spend lunchtime sitting against the wall so my uniform won't get dirty.

Saturday morning Uncle Philip minds us while Nanny and Grandad drive to the Cash and Carry store. He sits in Grandad's chair with the hollow and pats his lap and calls to me to sit. He says I'm his special favourite. I'm his pet. That makes me happy because I was never anyone's pet before, but I can't tell anyone because it's our secret and Uncle Philip says you can't tell secrets.

Easter Sunday morning I'm sitting at the kitchen table with Nanny. We're late for mass. Pippa is sitting on Nanny's lap, her bright eyes watery from hay fever and her chest wheezy with asthma. Danny is under the table playing with Nanny's slippers. Mona is walking out the back door in her Sunday frock to call Sheamie from the garden when the front door opens. She stops by the door and we wait for Nanny to say who's there but she's busy telling Grandad to hurry. Grandad is standing at the sink shaving in front of the cracked mirror on the windowsill. The sunshine coming through the glass glistens off his razor as it slides through the lather. He says

24

there was a time he could look in that mirror and see a young good-looking man staring back. They don't make mirrors like they used to. He turns to us with his pink lips grinning through the lather on his round face and I think he wants us to laugh but I don't know why and I don't care why because the kitchen door opens and I know who's here.

It's Daddy.

He comes into the kitchen with the green canvas bag on his shoulder. His hair is longer and there's sweat on his forehead from carrying the heavy bag. I can hear my heart beating, hoping he's found our Mum. I wonder if she's hiding in the sitting room ready to jump out and surprise us.

I look beyond Daddy to the sitting room but there're only the empty chairs and the cold grey ashes from last night's fire.

I think Nanny wants to stand up but she can't with Pippa on her lap.

Well, says Nanny, did you have a good trip, Peter? Have you news?

Grandad doesn't look surprised Daddy's home, but when you have as many children as Grandad you're probably never surprised when anyone turns up. He turns his head to show one cheek shaved and says to Nanny the children shouldn't be listening. Nanny says we have a right, and would you tidy yourself. There's a clean shirt and tie on the ironing board.

A tie, Annie?

Yes, a tie. You're not going to mass looking like the dog's dinner.

There's hardly a need for all that that old nonsense, Annie. Times are changing.

Not in this house, I see, says Daddy. He pats Grandad on the back and tells him put on his tie and do what he's told, like a good boy. Grandad laughs into the mirror.

Mona comes back from the door and runs to Daddy. Pippa climbs down from Nanny's lap and follows her. Daddy lifts them one at a time into his arms and hugs them. Then he lifts me and hugs me. I can feel the strength of his arms at the backs of my legs and the heat from his face, but it's only a little hug and I wonder what that means. Maybe he hasn't found Mum. Pippa sits back on Nanny's lap and Nanny wipes the hay-fever tears from Pippa's pink cheeks. It's like she wants Pippa not to cry if Daddy has bad news. Everyone knows you can't cry twice.

Daddy stands by the sink and lights a cigarette, cupping his huge hand around it so the smoke oozes between his fingers. Mona takes a step closer to Daddy and holds his free hand. You can see Mona's freckles more now that summer is coming. She squeezes Daddy's hand but he doesn't squeeze back. He hangs his head and his voice is sad when he says our mother hasn't been to London.

What about the bishop? says Nanny.

Mona moves closer to Daddy. He lets her hand go and holds her head against his leg and strokes her curly black hair with his fingers. Daddy smiles down at me but I know he's talking to Nanny when he says Uncle Edward has written letters to all the chapels in Australia but he's heard nothing back. The bishop is concerned about the children and asks if you need help.

The children are fine. It's concerned to find his sister he should be, and not worrying about me. I reared fourteen of me own.

Grandad says, Now, Annie, no point takin' it out on the poor bishop, he's only trying to help.

I wouldn't trust the clergy as far as I could throw one of them and the sooner the rest of the country wakes up to that fact the better off we'll all be. Now hurry up and get ready for mass. I wouldn't give the neighbours the satisfaction of saying we didn't go to mass.

Neighbours me arse, says Grandad.

Stop that talk in front of the children.

Looking up from Daddy's waist Mona asks, Will Mum ever come back? Daddy stops stroking her and tells her to sit down. He throws his cigarette in the sink where it sizzles in the water. I reach for his free hand but he tells me to sit too, back where I was beside Nanny. He doesn't sound angry but he doesn't sound happy either. Nanny holds her hand out to me and tells me, Come on, Matilda, sit down here and give your Daddy a chance to catch his breath. He's only in the door. I'm halfway between Daddy and Nanny's chair and I don't know where to go. I don't think Mona heard Daddy because she asks again, Will you find Mum, Daddy?

Daddy doesn't answer.

The sunshine passes from the window and the room turns cool. Nanny and Grandad look at each other and everyone in the room stays quiet except for Danny under the table playing with the slipper. Mona opens her mouth to ask Daddy again but he raises his hand and fires at Mona, Don't ask again. She's gone, she was no good and that's the end of it. Mona's mouth stays open and her eyes flood with tears. But she's too scared to move from the middle of the room. I jump back behind the chair. Pippa gasps and buries her face in Nanny's chest.

Nanny says to Daddy, Peter, the children.

Daddy slams his fist into his open palm.

The sooner they get it in their heads she's gone, the better, he says. I'm sick of it.

Keep your voice down, Peter. There's no need for shouting, the walls have ears.

Sheamie comes in from the garden, looks around the kitchen, turns and runs out again pulling the door closed behind him. I shuffle across from Nanny's chair to Grandad and shelter behind his big bum. I see Pippa's lips tremble against Nanny's apron bib and hear her wheezing grow louder as tears bubble in her eyes. With a gasp she starts to cry, gulping and choking. Daddy brings his fist down again and this time it hits the sink. The board gives out a thump and the cups on the draining board dance.

That's all she's good for, says Daddy, bah, bah, bah. He makes a baby face at Pippa and says, That's all she's good for. She's a big bloody baby.

Nanny turns her old grey eyes to Grandad who turns back to his shaving mirror and scrapes at his face. Nanny rubs Pippa's back and tells her, Do you know what, Pippa, I think there are toys in the attic from when your Aunt Patricia and Aunt Margaret were young. Will we look? Grown-ups hate it when Pippa cries. She gasps like a fish drowning in the air.

Daddy slams his fist so hard on the draining board even the cups in the sink leap.

No toys! he shouts.

The neighbours, Peter, Nanny whispers, I've asked you already to keep your voice down.

Daddy shouts anyway. It's their own fault their mother left. They were brazen. It's the schoolbooks from now on.

Grandad says, Now, son, don't take it out on the children. And don't upset yourself. It's hard on everyone. He turns to us with the razor in his hand and tells us to take no notice. Daddy didn't mean what he said, he has a lot on his mind and he's worn out.

Daddy wipes the sweat from his forehead with the back of his hand.

No point getting yourself upset when you're only in the door, says Grandad.

Danny crawls out from under the table with the slipper in

his hand and gazes up at Daddy with round brown eyes as if he's only seen him now. Everyone stays quiet to see what Daddy will do. He takes off his coat, hangs it on the back of a chair, sits down. He lifts his green canvas bag onto his lap, reaches in and begins to take out Easter eggs, big and small, until he's filled the kitchen table with them.

When the bag is empty he puts it on the ground and lifts Danny onto his lap and presses his lips to the top of Danny's head. Danny smiles with his lovely white teeth and his chubby hands tug at Daddy's long hair. It's grown since the last time he was here and I think Danny wonders if it's real. I'd like to take an Easter egg but I have to wait till I'm told.

Nanny tells Grandad to finish shaving himself and get dressed. She puts Pippa down from her knee and reaches out her hand to Mona and then myself. Daddy's not angry any-more and she tells us, Go to your father. He lifts Mona onto his knee and Mona buries her head in his neck. Then Pippa goes close and hugs him as well. Grandad says, That's better now, and turns to the mirror to shave his other cheek. I move in beside Daddy. There's no room on his lap for me, not with Danny and Mona already there and Pippa hugging his side. But he reaches out his arm and puts it around me. I'd really like an Easter egg but I stay where I am so Daddy won't be angry again. Pippa dries her eyes with the corner of her jumper and Nanny smiles around the room.

Never a dull moment, isn't that what they say? And just look at all those lovely Easter eggs. Can't you see your Daddy loves all of you? You can take one, isn't that right, Peter, can't the children have an Easter egg?

Daddy says yes. We can go to mass later.

Mona takes a big one. I take the nearest one which is small.

I take my egg out into the garden where Sheamie's sitting up on the shed with his thin legs dangling over the edge. It's cloudy but warm. I share my egg with Sheamie and after he's eaten it and wiped the chocolate stain from his mouth he says, Nothing good ever lasts, Matilda, but Sheamie is always saying clever things like that and I never know what he means. I'm sad Mum isn't here and wondering how grown-ups forget arguments so quickly. I wonder will she ever come home. Maybe she'll come tomorrow.

Daddy stays for the week then says he's going back to London. Nanny wants him to stay. There's work in Ireland. New houses being built. It's not like it was in the fifties when everyone had to leave. Daddy shakes his head, no. He could never live in Ireland again. He's been away too long. He has to find our mother. She has to come back sometime.

Grandad is sitting in his chair with the hollow. He frowns but keeps quiet.

In the morning we kiss Daddy goodbye at the front door. He hoists the green canvas bag up on his shoulder and tells us be good for our Nanny and don't be crying. I watch him till he turns the corner and there's a hollow feeling in my legs. Dr Kimble hasn't found the one-armed man. Inspector Gerard hasn't found Dr Kimble. Daddy hasn't found our Mum. I wonder is anyone ever found.

I'm six. My head comes up to a doorknob. Pippa is seven. She's a little higher, but not much. When summer comes the days are long and hot and there's no school and Pippa and me go out in the morning and come back when it's late. We go up the road with the kids from the street and look for rabbits in the Hilly Fields, or play hide and seek in the bucket factory. Today when we come in Sheamie is sitting on the footstool watching the news with Grandad. Sheamie worries about the war in Vietnam, and the Communists in Russia who could kill us all because they have a bomb.

Nanny calls us into the kitchen and when we go in there's a strange man with a shaved head and a square moustache like a razorblade sitting at the table slurping tea from a big red mug. Nanny says he's our Uncle John home from the army. Uncle John asks how we're settling in and we say, Fine.

When I look at him closer I can see he has a hooked nose, thick eyebrows and small round eyes, like a bird. He winks at Pippa through the steam from the red mug.

That's great, he says, and drinks his tea in slurps.

3

Uncle John gets a job on the docks loading and unloading the big container boats from all over the world. He brings home bunches of ripe bananas from Africa, boxes of oranges from sunny Spain and dates from the Mediterranean because he knows Nanny loves dates even though they turn her tongue brown. We can all see how much Nanny loves Uncle John. She tells us, Get out of that chair and let your uncle sit down. Come out of the kitchen and let your uncle have his dinner. Hurry up in that bathroom, your uncle is waiting to go in, and when we come out he's standing there scowling with the newspaper under his wing. He goes out every morning wearing a black donkey jacket with leather patches on the sleeves and comes home in the evening with the smell of whiskey on his breath complaining he has to wait for his tea. Out all fuckin' day and can't get to the table.

Nanny tells him to leave the children alone but he shouts at her and Nanny is too fond of her dates and too worried over neighbours listening to say any more. Pippa backs away when he comes near her and squats in the corner beside the china cabinet. We don't like Uncle John. Uncle Philip is sweet but Uncle John is grumpy and when Nanny and Grandad aren't here you always have to do what he says. The only time he's happy is when he's going to a soccer match with Uncle Philip. The two of them follow the Waterford soccer team all over and last week they were so happy when they won they promised to take Sheamie this week. Sheamie is so delighted he's been tossing around in the bed all night sticking his toes in everyone's face.

Saturday morning Nanny roots around in the closet under the stairs because she's certain there's a blue and white scarf and a hat. She comes out of the closet backwards and fixes the woolly blue hat on Sheamie's head and ties the scarf around his neck and tells our uncles to mind that child and don't let him get lost or crushed in the crowds. I'm warning the pair of you, there's to be no drinking. Not with that child in the car.

Our uncles sit in the front of the car waiting for Sheamie. Uncle Philip is driving. Sheamie is so excited he kisses Mona, Pippa and me and runs next door to tell the Murphys. Mister Murphy is standing on his front doorstep jingling the change in his trouser pocket. He gives Sheamie a half-crown and Sheamie even kisses Mister Murphy on the cheek because that's a lot of money.

Sheamie is waving out the back window as they drive away in Grandad's black Zephyr and we stand at the gate and wave back. Nanny says to Mister Murphy, Did you ever see anything like that in your life, Mossy?

Sheamie's a grand lad, Annie. But he'll feel the cold today.

He will, Mossy, indeed he will. 'Tis a wonder you didn't travel yourself?

Ah, no, Annie, the ban. I'm involved in the GAA, training the young lads with the hurling. I'd be out on me ear if they heard I attended a soccer match. Still an' all, I'll watch the highlights on television tonight. What they don't know won't trouble them.

True for you, Mossy. What goes on inside your own door stays there. Nobody's business but your own, I'm always sayin' it. Not with the crowd of gossipers around this town. Now, I better open the shop before they clamber the door down.

★

The shop is busy. Pippa and me get what Nanny wants from the bottom shelves and Mona gives out the change. Danny sits on the floor behind the counter, his fat cheeks sticky with chocolate, and we wonder how he can eat so much with needles for teeth. Nanny says she can't wait to see Sheamie, but at tea time there's no sign and Nanny is worried. She rattles the cups and saucers in the sink and complains to Grandad, I told them not to be drinking. If a thing happens to that child I'll swing for the pair of them. How will I ever answer to their father? Grandad is warming himself at the fire with Danny asleep on his lap. Grandad says there was a big crowd travelled to the match and the roads are busy, but Nanny is still worried. She brings Grandad his tea on a tray. She leaves it on the arm of the chair so she won't wake Danny and Grandad has to eat with one hand.

We take turns going out to the front door. The street is dark and silent, no people, no cars, and the road glistens with frost under the streetlights. I wrap my arms around myself and shiver and come back inside and sit on the red rug in front of the fire and watch *The Black and White Minstrel Show*. There's a man with a black face and big white lips singing for his Mammy and I know how he feels because I'd walk a million miles for one of my mother's smiles. Maybe she'll come home tomorrow.

The music for the nine o'clock news comes on telly when we hear the car parking out on the road. Nanny makes the sign of the cross and whispers, Thank God. The door opens and Nanny springs from her chair.

Where were yee? My pulse is racing here all night. Ages ago you two should have been here with that child.

Uncle Philip has the black stains on his mouth and Uncle John is stumbling in the door behind him singing, When the Blues go marching in. He marches around the room with his arms in the air. We won again. What a fuckin' team. He catches Pippa's hand and tries to waltz with her but she pulls away and squats beside the china cabinet with her knees pulled up to her chin.

Nanny shakes her head. There's no point talking. Yee're back and that's the main thing. Go out to the kitchen and eat something, yee're a right pair of gawks.

No, we're goin' to the pub.

Nanny says, Not in that state, and pushes them out to the kitchen.

Sheamie is standing at the door with his blue hat on. His glasses are foggy and there are tearstains. Danny's eyes open and shut and he goes back to sleep on Grandad's lap. I want to ask why Sheamie is crying but my uncles scare me with their singing and dancing and bringing Sheamie home with tearstains. I wish Daddy were here. I want my Daddy.

Nanny comes from the kitchen drying her hands in the tea towel. She says Sheamie looks tired and tells him to come out to the kitchen for his supper. It's early to bed for him after his long day. She doesn't say anything about his tearstains but she's not wearing her glasses so maybe she can't see. She says, Mass in the morning, Sheamie. I can't be draggin' you out of the bed at my age.

When our uncles have gone to the pub and Nanny and Grandad are dozing in their chairs, Mona, Pippa and me sneak upstairs. Danny is asleep at the end of the bed and Sheamie is sitting up sobbing. The light is off but we can see him in the dim glow from the streetlights through the gap in the curtains. We ask what happened but he won't say. He's going to tell Nanny in the morning. I sit on the end of the bed just as Nanny comes to stand at the bedroom door.

Out, out, the lot of yee and leave Sheamie alone before I crack yeer arses. Grandad is complaining over the racket and I don't blame him one little bit. Get downstairs the three of yee.

We duck under her arm and run downstairs but when we

hear the bedroom door close and there's no sign of Nanny, we creep back up again, careful because the landing light is on and she'll see us if she walks out. Mona is ahead, three steps from the top. I'm one step below pushing her but she won't go higher. Pippa is where she always is, at the back whispering, This is dangerous. What's Nanny saying?

I hate being in the middle. I'm too far from the door to hear anything and if Nanny walks out I'm too close to get away. Mona can't hear anything because of her deaf ear. Pippa turns to go. Then I hear Nanny.

Orphanage talk! Is that what you learned in Australia? Don't ever say a thing like that again or I won't answer for what happens. They'll take you away and for good this time.

I hear her bare feet moving across the lino and turn to tell Pippa but Pippa is gone already. Mona pinches my shoulder trying to get past but I won't let her. I want to cry out but I don't have time. The bedroom door opens. I spread my arms and jump two steps at a time and somehow we all get to the hallway before Nanny gets to the landing.

In the morning Nanny is quiet. She stares at the dirty cups and saucers in the sink from last night's supper. Her eyes are red around the edges like she hasn't slept and her nightgown is wrinkled down the back like she's been sitting a long time. She doesn't even boil milk for our cornflakes like she usually does when the mornings are frosty. She tells Mona to go to mass with Grandad, Sheamie and our uncles. Pippa and me can stay home. We haven't made our First Holy Communion yet and it won't be a sin. Leave Danny asleep in bed. She lifts her cup of tea and puts the plate with the slice of toast on top of the cup and shuffles back to bed. I wonder is Nanny going to die and we'll be on our own again.

When the others go to mass, Pippa and me go out to play with Toby Murphy from next door. He's seven like Pippa. He has freckles on his nose and a loose tooth in his top gum that he pulls at so it'll fall out quicker and he'll get the money from his mother. He says there's no such thing as a Tooth Fairy and when I call him a liar he says your mother comes in the night when she thinks you're asleep and takes the tooth from under your pillow. It's your mother who leaves the silver shilling, he says, and that makes me sad because now I know why I didn't get any money in the orphanage.

See, says Pippa, told you there's no such a thing as fairies.

Mister and Missus Murphy come out the front door in their Sunday clothes. Mister Murphy wears a black suit, white shirt and red tie. Missus Murphy is wearing a bright yellow hat with a net that covers her eyes. She says Toby can play with Pippa and me but don't go in the house. There might be an accident and nobody would know.

We won't, Missus Murphy.

We play marbles on the pavement until it starts to rain and we stand in the hallway. That isn't really the house and what else can we do when it's raining? We sit on the stairs; that's all right too, that's not really the house either because the front door is open. We sit and watch the rain making puddles on the footpath that runs from the front door to the garden gate till I'm tired from standing. I sit on the bottom step of the stairs. Pippa and Toby sit on the step above me. Toby twists his loose tooth and Pippa puts her little finger in her mouth to see if she has a tooth loose. I don't like them being higher so I move to the step above, then they move to the step above me, then I move and soon we're on the landing and we can see inside Toby's bedroom.

There's a bed by the window and a poster on the wall of men in red shirts. Toby says that's Manchester United and the one with the long hair is George Best and he's the best soccer player in the world. There's a Scalectrix track laid out on the floor like a number eight. It has two cars, one blue and one red. Toby says the red racing car is the best. The blue one gets stuck on the corners and, when you push it, it flies off the track and bounces off the wall.

Toby keeps the red car for himself and Pippa and me take turns with the blue one but we get fed up with it always bouncing off the wall and play Mammies and Daddies instead. Pippa is the Mammy and I'm the baby 'cos Pippa says she can't pretend to be a baby when she's seven. I lie under the bed next to the football and Pippa bends in over me and rubs my forehead. It's dusty down here and there are balls of white fluff in the corners and around the bed legs but I don't mind. I close my eyes and feel Mum beside me. She tells me to sleep now and she climbs onto the bed. I close my eyes and dream of Australia where everything is blue and warm and I don't take any notice of the scream from the bedroom door. I'm at home in my own bed in Australia, my mother is here and I'm safe.

A Scalectrix car comes flying under the bed and I bang my forehead off the edge of the bed when I look out and up at Missus Murphy marching across the floor. Toby is kneeling on the bed with his short pants around his ankles. I can't see Pippa until Missus Murphy drags her off the bed. She's shaking Pippa by the arm and calling her, Bad girl, bad girl. Then she sees me.

What are you doing down there?

I'm the baby. I'm asleep.

Up child. Up out of it.

She drags Pippa and me by the arms to our Nanny's and tells Nanny at the front door, Annie, I found those two up in the bedroom with our Toby and what that blonde one was doing to him a married woman wouldn't do on her wedding night. I know they're young and curious, but there's curious and there's what I saw. You have enough on your plate and

38

not many would take on five young children. But if Mossy finds out there will be Hell to pay.

Nanny's cheeks are pale and she turns her old grey eyes to the doorstep. She clears her throat to tell Missus Murphy she'll get to the bottom of it. She closes the front door and turns her angry grey eyes on Pippa.

Where are you learning that filth? I had Sheamie last night, and now you shaming me in front of the neighbours. Who showed you that carry-on?

Pippa looks at me, then up at Nanny. Pippa's finger is in her mouth and her bright blue eyes flood with tears because she doesn't know what she's done wrong. Neither do I.

Tell me, Nanny says, tell me right this second or I'll slap your arse so hard you won't sit for a month.

Uncle John showed me, Nanny.

Nanny struggles to sit on the stairs. She holds her hand over her mouth and beats her other hand off her chest and makes whimpering sounds that scare us. She stays like that until Mona comes in from mass with her rosary beads wrapped around her fingers. Mona tells Nanny that Grandad brought Sheamie to the pub and they'll be back later. Nanny sends me upstairs until I'm called and tells Pippa to wait for her out in the kitchen. She sends Mona outside and warns her, don't come in unless she's called.

I go to our bedroom and climb up on the bed. Koala is on my pillow and I pick him up because he looks scared. We've always been together. When my mother left, he was there. When I went to the orphanage he came with me and when we came to our Nanny's I carried him all the way from Australia so he wouldn't be alone. He's smaller now and his ear is torn, but only a little.

I carry him in my arms to the window and look for Mona. She's sitting on the footpath in the rain. I press my nose against the cold damp glass and think about calling her but her back is to me and she wouldn't hear. I wish she'd turn around. Mum and Dad said it was an accident. I remember when it happened. Our mother was there. She bent down and covered her head with her hands. I saw Daddy's hand going up, his fingers touching the light bulb. I screamed. Then Mona ran to help Mum and Daddy hit her on the side of the head. Even with my fingers in my ears I could hear the thud. I stopped screaming. Mona was lying on the floor. There was a crooked line of blood from her ear to the corner of her mouth. It was an accident. That's all. Your Daddy didn't mean to do it, Matilda. Everything is all right now. We're moving up north, we'll get a new house. It'll be a new start for everyone and we'll forget everything bad that happened. Don't cry anymore, sweetheart. Mummy hates it when you cry.

I hear Pippa calling and my knees go wobbly. I leave Koala wrapped in Grandad's green coat so he'll be safe and go out onto the landing just as Pippa is closing the front door behind her. I don't want to go downstairs but I hear Nanny at the kitchen door calling me.

Nanny is sitting at the kitchen table. Her two hands are flat on the table with the breadcrumbs.

Close the door, Matilda, and sit down.

She's not barking at me but I jump. I don't want to sit down. The door is a little open. Nanny says to close it fully and sit down. I close it and lean against it.

Sit down, Matilda.

She moves an empty chair from under the table and the scrape of its legs across the floor sends me back even closer to the door.

Sit down, I said.

I was only the baby, Nanny. I wasn't bad. I promise, Nanny, I wasn't.

Nanny slams her palms on the table and the sugar bowl crashes to the floor.

For the last time, sit down!

I creep towards the table feeling the sugar under my shoes. I sit, I stand, I sit again. Nanny keeps her eyes straight ahead at the wall.

I want the truth, Matilda.

Yes, Nanny.

Are you going upstairs to those bedrooms with your uncles, any of them?

I don't know what to tell her. Uncle Philip said it was a secret. Our secret. And you can't tell secrets.

Nanny barks and I hop. I feel my heart racing.

I want the truth! Tell the truth and nothing will happen. Tell a lie and the mark will be on your tongue. Do you understand?

Yes, Nanny.

Are you going upstairs with your uncles?

Yes, Nanny.

Which one?

Uncle Philip, Nanny.

Does he make you do things?

Yes, Nanny.

She springs to her feet and sends me curling back in the chair. I turn away and cover my head with my hands and wait to be slapped but nothing happens. I wait some more and still nothing happens. I take my arm away but only a little. I look back and her brown tongue is in my eyes screaming like she's not my Nanny anymore.

You're a filthy liar! You made it up. Who told you to make it up? Did Sheamie tell you to say that?

I'm not, Nanny. I'm telling the truth.

Sheamie told you to say it. Didn't he?

I'm sorry, Nanny, I'll be good, Nanny, don't send me away. Please, Nanny. I promise, Nanny. I promise I'll be good.

I feel the burning between my legs. I can't help myself. It runs down my legs and makes a puddle on the floor. Nanny pulls her hands down her face and holds them at her chin making her mouth look long. She tells me to stop crying and makes me promise never to tell or they'll put me away for ever. Do you hear, Matilda?

I won't, Nanny. I'm sorry, Nanny.

Nanny sobs in her apron and I don't know what to do. I want to say, I love you, Nanny, so she'll put her arms around and tell me nothing bad will happen, but the words don't come. She dries her eyes on the apron, stoops to pick up the five broken pieces of the sugar bowl and drops them in the plastic bin by the back door before washing her hands at the sink.

Nanny sends Uncle Philip and Uncle John out of the house. I see them through the upstairs window putting their bags in the boot of the car. They're talking to Grandad and shaking their heads, no.

A few days later Nanny closes the shop because she's getting too old for it. Grandad only has his pension and she can't afford the five of us and anyway the house is too small. She's sent for Daddy and she warns me again not to open my mouth. If your father finds out he'll kill you. You know what he's temper is like as well as I do, Matilda.

Daddy comes home. You can see how angry he is when he slams the green canvas bag on the floor and goes out to Nanny and Grandad in the kitchen. Grandad closes the kitchen door but I can hear Daddy screaming, clattering chairs and thumping the table. The five of us stare at the fire, frightened to look left or right. Then the kitchen goes quiet. Danny stands up to go out to them but Mona grabs him by the arm and puts him sitting on her lap. Danny starts to cry and we have to put our fingers to our lips to tell him shush, but he won't shush till Sheamie gives him piggybacks around the room. The voices start from the kitchen again but they're not shouting. First Nanny's, then Daddy's. Daddy walks in and looks down at the five of us but I don't know what that means because you never know what grown-ups mean until they tell you. Daddy asks if we'll go to live with our uncle and aunts in England. Mona asks if they'll take us and Daddy says he doesn't know yet.

Now we're all crying, except Sheamie, who's staring at the floor, and Danny, who's pulling at Sheamie's arm for another piggyback. Grandad comes in from the kitchen and tells Danny, Not now, Sheamie is tired. But Danny cries and tugs at Sheamie's arm again and Grandad lifts Danny into his arms and carries him to the kitchen to make him bread and jam and that makes Danny smile because bread and jam is as good as a piggyback anytime.

While we're waiting for the phone call from London there're more rows out in the kitchen. I think Daddy is changing his mind about us going to our aunts or uncle in England. Nanny screams we're his responsibility and he shouts back she took us and he wants us kept together. I'm upstairs looking out the bedroom window with my fingers in my ears when I see Mossy coming up the front garden path to say there's a phone call.

Daddy goes next door with Mossy and when he comes back he says they'll take us. Uncle James, the millionaire, will take Danny and me. He'd take all five if he could but he has five of his own and his wife won't take any more. Aunt Patricia will take Mona and Sheamie and Aunt Collette will take Pippa, but Patricia and Collette want Daddy to pay. They have children of their own and they're not made out of money.

I never thought I'd have to live anywhere without my brothers and sisters and I start to cry again. Nanny clasps her hands, Thank God it's sorted, and makes the sign of the cross. Daddy says no. He won't pay. He's changed his mind about everything. He wants us where he can get us back. He'll find our mother and he doesn't want us settling into new lives. I don't want them broken up, he says to Nanny. Not like that.

He tells Nanny to get the five of us ready and he leaves in Grandad's car. Sheamie goes out to the garden and closes the back door behind him while Mona sits quietly on the arm of the brown sofa. Grandad lifts Danny into his arms and cries, Ah, no, Annie, the poor children. Nanny waves him away and goes upstairs. Pippa holds my hand and we follow Nanny upstairs.

Pippa cries and I cry too even though I shouldn't because I don't have Pippa's way with tears. Everyone says Pippa has a cry would break your heart. The way her teardrops hang on the tip of her eyelashes is like a raindrop on the edge of a leaf. It's the most beautiful sight in the world.

Nanny is standing in front of the wardrobe putting the little white balls back in the pockets of Grandad's green coat. Pippa is looking up at Nanny with her lovely blue eyes and her teardrops hanging but Nanny won't look at us. My koala is on the bed but I'm not going to take him. Nanny might see him and miss us and say we can come home. I want to say to her, Remember, Nanny, when you said we'd never be left on our own again, and when I sat behind the counter and you gave me jellybeans. But my tongue is tied and the words won't come. Nanny won't kiss us goodbye, either. She turns her back to us and says it's our own fault. She hangs Grandad's green coat back in the wardrobe and closes the door.

4

A small shutter opens in the metal wicket gate. A nun, her head covered in a long black veil set out high over her forehead so only the circle of her wrinkled face can be seen, peers through. I hear the bolt scraping back. The gate creaks slowly open and we step inside to a courtyard surrounded by high stone walls. Away to one side are lawns, a pond, low red-brick buildings scattered in the mist. Ahead of us stands a great building made of stone. Four storeys high, its slated grey roof seems to reach Heaven. The nun grips my wrist with her bony hand. Daddy turns his collar against the October wind and takes Mona in one hand and Pippa in the other and we follow a straight gravel path lined with trees. The pebbles crackle under our feet and the wet leaves stick to our shoes. A door ahead of us in the four-storey building creaks open just enough to let us through and we're in a hallway where holy pictures hang from white walls. Nuns with their arms folded inside their wide black sleeves are waiting. Daddy stays outside the door. We turn back to it screaming, Daddy, Daddy, Daddy, don't leave us, Daddy. But nuns grab Mona, Pippa and me and tell Daddy to leave. There are tears in his eyes and we scream again, We'll be good, Daddy, don't leave us, Daddy, we're sorry, we promise we'll be good.

Daddy kneels with his arms held out and tears running down his cheeks and my heart dances. I pull away from the nun and run to him but the door is slammed in front of me and the hollow sound echoes all around.

We're dragged down long dark corridors through doors

with more dark corridors behind them and all the time getting farther away from Daddy. I scream, Let me go, I want to go home. They keep dragging and saying, Stop that nonsense. Stop it now! I keep looking back. Daddy has changed his mind. I know he has.

We're led to a big room where an old nun sits behind a desk in the corner. Her face is nearly as wrinkled as my Nanny's. Her eyes flecked with yellow in a circle of white. She wears a white habit and veil and twists a walking stick in her hands. We're put standing in front of her and warned there will be no crying and no nonsense in front of Reverend Mother. There's a crucifix on the wall from floor to ceiling and Jesus hanging with a white rag around his waist and the Crown of Thorns ripping his flesh. His face is bloody. The rusty nails buried deep in his hands and feet and his eyes filled with sadness. We're standing on a red carpet. It's as if all the blood from Jesus has dripped into a lake on the floor. Two girls are standing by the door, one big, one small, their faces turned to the wall.

On a glass shelf high up in the corner there's a statue of a woman wearing a blue robe. Reverend Mother points to the statue with her walking stick and tells us that's the Madonna. She makes us walk around the room and wherever in the room we are the Madonna's eyes follow and make the small hairs on the back of my neck stand on end.

Reverend Mother hiccups as she writes our names and ages into the big black book on the desk, and, without lifting her head, snaps at the big girl standing against the wall.

What are you laughing at, Shore? No father, no mother, an orphan like you laughing. Do you suddenly find something amusing in your predicament?

It wasn't me, girl.

What?

46

I meant, Reverend Mother. I swear it wasn't me though. I didn't do that to Sister Ellen's eye.

You know where you're heading, Maggie Shore?

Outside, Reverend Mother.

There will be no outside for you, Shore. The laundry is where you're heading. Get on your two knees and pray to Our Saviour suffering up there on the cross. Suffering for the sins of the world. Suffering for the likes of you, Maggie Shore. I'm sure God had a purpose when he sent his only begotten son to die for us, but when I see the likes of you, Maggie Shore, then I shudder at his wisdom.

Reverend Mother glares at Pippa. Why is your mouth gaping? Shut that mouth. You only open it here for prayer or God's Holy Food and, by the scrawny looks of you, you need plenty of both.

Sorry, says Pippa.

Sorry, what? Sorry, pig?

Sorry, Reverend Mother.

The rubber tip squeaks on the wooden floor when Reverend Mother eases herself up on her stick then rests the stick over her shoulder like a soldier carrying a gun. When she walks across the room it's as if she's gliding over the polished boards. I can tell that stick isn't for walking with. There's a great bunch of keys hanging from a chain that jangles against her thigh. She stops by the door and lashes the younger girl so hard with her stick the girl's eyes water and her knees buckle.

Don't think I didn't see you sniggering, Molly Driscoll.

Sorry, Reverend Mother.

I'm sure you are. Haven't I told you enough times about fighting?

Yes, Reverend Mother.

What did I tell you, Driscoll?

Turn the other cheek, Reverend Mother.

Reverend Mother tells the first girl, Stay on your two knees and pray, Shore. You little gurrier. You're man mad. Any more of your screeching out windows to those tomcats from Trinity Park and you'll do your praying with the nuns in Cork. They'll knock the man madness out of you. You should have been in the asylum long ago.

There's a knock on the door and a rustle of black skirts. A young red-faced nun is here. She's big and looks like she could run with the Reverend Mother under her arm. She has bushy black eyebrows, big red eyes, a stern look and a clean holy smell but no stick to threaten us. I wonder will she listen if I tell her I want to go home. Daddy changed his mind.

Reverend Mother pulls a white handkerchief from her pocket and wipes her sweat from the handle of her stick and the palms of her hands and tells us to go with Sister Gabriel. I look up at Mona, her eyes swollen and red around the edges when she answers, Yes, Reverend Mother. Pippa moves away from me and nearer to Mona. She keeps her hands clasped in front of her and her mouth closed and nods. Reverend Mother looks at me and I tell her my Daddy is coming and she lunges with the walking stick and gives me a rap on the back of the legs and tells us go with Sister Gabriel. But remember, you're being watched. My leg stings and I want to cry out, but you can't cry out when there's nobody to listen.

We follow Sister Gabriel. Her habit puffs around her feet like a black bell when she glides along the corridor. The darkness is falling outside and the corridor lights are on. She leads us up a stairway where girls in scraggy clothes have pieces of torn jumpers strapped to their bums and feet and are bumping down the steps and I wonder are all these girls sent away for doing bad things with their uncle. A skinny girl with a freckled forehead stops bumping and looks up at Pippa and me.

Are yee new? Are yee?

Pippa squeezes my hand and I squeeze back but our hands are sweaty and it's hard to grip. A gang of girls surrounds us on the landing and I feel a pull on my arm.

Where'd yeh get them clothes?

I look up at Mona because she's nine and she'll know what to do, but Mona turns her eyes away and pushes her back against the wall. Pippa lets my hand go and squeezes in beside Mona. Strange faces gather round me and wait for my answer and there's a cry from the cupboard under the stairs, Let me out, Sister. I won't do it again. Ah, Jasus, let me out.

Sister Gabriel tells the girls, These are the Kellys: Mona, Pippa and Matilda. Get on with the work, all of you. I want those stairs to sparkle.

Yes, Sister Gabriel.

The girls move away and we follow Sister Gabriel to the top of the stairs where there's a landing with tall windows rattling in the wind. I can look down to a wet playground and over it to the pathway where we came in with Daddy, but I don't see Daddy. There is a line of trees on this side of the wall; their leaves have fallen away and blow in circles around the playground. The windows have iron bars on the outside and at the other end of the landing there are more stairs like the ones we walked up. One stair must be for coming up and the other for going down. I bite the corner of my lip and look behind for Daddy but all I see are girls bumping.

Through a door and we're in the dormitory. I've seen one like it. I was four and there were beds with curtains around them like white walls. I remember we ran, Mum, Mona, Sheamie, Pippa, Danny and me. We packed our bag when Daddy wasn't there. One bag. Mum said we didn't have time for more. We took a train a long way away and stayed in a big house by a river with other mothers and children who had run away. We stayed there until Daddy found us.

The five rows of iron beds stand head to head and almost side by side, with barely room between them to walk. There must be a hundred of them. Tall windows light the room but it's gloomy from the half-closed shutters. Dark wooden wardrobes as high as the ceiling line the walls and down in the corner a black-haired girl is sitting on a bed. She's my age. Her bare feet dangle above the floorboards and the stained white sheets hang near her by the open window.

Sister Gabriel nearly pulls the scalp off me when she checks our hair for lice. Then she makes us undress. Underwear included. Get on with it. We stand naked in the dormitory while she roots around the wardrobes. I'm cold and I want to go home but I'm in prison because of what I did with my uncle and can't go home until Daddy comes or Nanny says it was a mistake, we never done anything wrong.

Sister Gabriel hands me white woollen knickers that dangle loose and make my bum itch. She puts our own clothes in a cardboard box for the missions. We're given old clothes and with a red marker that she takes from her pocket she writes our initials on the square white tags sewn to the inside.

The three of you get dressed, she says, and don't forget your slips. There's dark corner in Hell for girls who don't wear their slip. It's shameful and a sin.

All I can think of is my new black shoes Daddy sent from London. I hope she doesn't take my shoes.

She shouts to the girl on the bed.

Are those sheets dry, Lucy Flynn?

Yes, Sister Gabriel.

Make your bed and if you wet it tonight you'll spend tomorrow in here as well.

Yes, Sister Gabriel.

Pippa has big tears in her eyes and, when the light catches her soft pink cheeks, you can see how wet they are, and I don't know if she's crying over her clothes or if she's like me, hoping Daddy comes to take us home and frightened she'll wet the bed if he doesn't.

Sister Gabriel leads us downstairs and across the rain puddles of the playground to a room like a shed that smells of stale feet and when she opens the wooden closet I want to cry. It's full of metal hooks and every hook has a pair of worn shoes. Mona has big feet. Sister Gabriel gives her a pair of boy's brown shoes. Pippa's are bright pink and her yellow stockings show through the toes. Mine are black painted, and the straps curl at the ends and don't fit, so Sister Gabriel stuffs the backs with old newspaper but they still clack when I walk. My Daddy will get my new shoes back when he comes. I know he will.

There's a bell at seven o'clock and we follow the other girls upstairs to the dormitory. Pippa and me are given a bed each by the window. Mona is further down between the girls my age and the bigger girls.

Sister Gabriel says we make our own bed, we're not at home now. I'll show you this time but you must learn.

She takes two sets of sheets, pillows and pillowcases from different shelves in different wardrobes and already I can see there's place for everything and everyone. The sheets are stiff and white and when she spreads them they land on the bed like flat pieces of cardboard. She talks and works quickly. You must tuck the sheets in properly, like this, at the top and bottom corners and she shows us how to fold each corner by flattening it with her hand. The top sheet comes in line with the end of the mattress. The blankets go the same way as the top sheet, but not tucked in. Do you see how I'm doing it?

We nod we do, but we don't.

The bedspread is tucked in like the bottom sheet but only at the bottom of the bed. Pull your quilt over the pillow and fold back slightly, then we have this nice straight crease here under the pillow.

Yes, Sister Gabriel.

She hands us white wool pyjamas that zip up the front. They smell like starch and make my skin itch and I wonder am I wearing a dead girl's pyjamas and sleeping in a dead girl's bed.

The dormitory lights go out and we are in darkness when I hear the metal click of the key in the lock. I lie on my back listening to the weeping girls and the movement of bedsprings as girls toss and turn and wait for sleep. I watch the shadows on the wall of girls sitting up in their beds, too scared to sleep. Everywhere there's the stench of pee. I hear the tiptoe of big girls across the floorboards to each other's beds. I hear the moans from under blankets and that means they must be freezing. I want to be home at Nanny's where the five of us slept together in one big bed. Where I could feel my brothers and sisters beside me and we could cuddle together to keep warm and where I had Grandad's green coat with the smell of the ocean to keep me safe.

Slowly my eyes get used to the darkness. I turn to see the shadow of the rusty iron bars on Pippa's soft pink cheeks as she lays on her back sucking her thumb and trying not to cry.

I worry about my brothers, Sheamie and Danny. We left them sitting in the car. Daddy said they were going to a place for boys. A place in Kilkenny. It was thirty miles away. I didn't know how far that was and I didn't care. I just wanted my Sheamie and Danny. I stood on my tippy-toes on the pavement and waved in the window to them. I never had such an ache in my heart not knowing if I'd never see my brothers again. Sheamie was crying in the back seat, he couldn't look at me. Danny was sitting on Sheamie's lap, laughing. He climbed across the back seat and stuck his face to the glass and made a funny shape with his lips. His breath was left on the glass with the shape of his mouth. The window steamed over and I couldn't see them anymore.

When the dormitory falls silent, the only noise is from cars passing on the other side of the high stone wall. Their headlights waltz across the ceiling and the flaking brown paint. Tears run into my mouth. I taste the salt on my tongue like the first day we came from Australia, when Grandad gave us the round crusty bread with country butter. You can taste the salt, he said. I think of our grandmother when she said we'd never be left alone again. I hear her voice in my head when she stood in front of the mantelpiece promising us, making sure we believed her.

This is yeer home as long as I'm alive and there's breath in my body. Do yee hear?

And we nodded that we did.

I want to be angry with her. But I'm scared to in case she finds out and doesn't come for us and then it'll all be my fault again. I want to hate her but I can't hate my Nanny, not when she's all we have.

It's late now. Maybe Daddy will come tomorrow. Maybe even Mum will come tomorrow.

In the morning, the dormitory lights come on and Sister Gabriel is walking between the beds ringing a bell. The stars are still shining in the dark blue sky and the windows are white with frost. We get up and make our beds.

Not like that, child, pyjamas inside your pillowcase.

Yes, Sister Gabriel.

Bottom sheet tucked in, folded at the corner.

Yes, Sister Gabriel.

Get washed and dressed and ready for mass.

Yes, Sister Gabriel.

We line up behind girls pushing and shoving each other away from the big cream washbasins against the wall. We wash and come back to our beds, get dressed. I've forgotten my slip. I don't have time to put it on, so I hide it in my pillowcase and chase downstairs after the other girls. By seven o'clock, the dormitory, stairway and corridors are empty and we're lined up in pairs in the dark icy playground.

A big girl at the front of the line complains to the nun with a black eye, Why can't we go through the corridor, Sister Ellen? It's all right for you out here with them big bloomers. The girls around her titter behind their hands but the nun with the black eye keeps walking down the line counting heads and, when she's happy everyone is here, she rings her bell. A door ahead of us creaks open and the line shuffles forward.

At the chapel door there's an old nun standing beside a brown cardboard box. Bigger girls ahead of me bend down to the box but I can't see what they're doing the way they gather round. All I see are backs and girls bending before they go inside. I don't know what to do. I'm sure they're putting money in and I don't have any. I look for Pippa. I think she's behind me but there're too many strange faces blocking the way. I can't see Mona either. Maybe if I tell the old nun I have no money she'll let me in without any, but you never know what nuns will do. She might drag me before the Reverend Mother who'd stand me in a corner and threaten me with her walking stick. I wonder if I should try and sneak in but if I get caught I'll be in twice as much trouble. I'm cold, but my neck sweats and I try looking for my sisters again but I'm pushed along in the crowd till I'm standing in front of the old nun. She looks down at me. I look up at her with the palms of my hands out straight so she can see I have no money. She looks in the box then I look in the box. The box is full of green pixie hats with spikes like walking sticks on top. I take one and follow inside the chapel but Sister Gabriel rushes across to me wagging her finger, and whispering.

Where's your hat, child. You can't come into church without covering your head.

I put it on.

That's no way to wear a hat, child.

She grabs me by the arm and lifts me so my feet dangle above the floor and when she lets me down again I'm back out in the corridor where Sister Gabriel doesn't have to whisper anymore. Other girls giggle and my cheeks burn when Sister Gabriel warns me, Don't pull your hat over your ears like an idiot. It must sit on top of your head, but tilted to the left.

I put the hat back on but she yells, The left.

Yes, Sister Gabriel.

Get inside and catch Lucy Flynn's hand. She's the girl sitting on the bed when you arrived yesterday.

Lucy Flynn is waiting for me under the balcony with her hat on but mine keeps falling on the floor. Lucy gives me a nod of her head and shrug of her shoulders that I think means don't worry about right or left just stick it on your head and come on. So I do.

Reverend Mother is glaring from the bottom of the spiral stair and I'm sure she'd give me a clatter if we were anywhere but mass.

The chapel is small and has windows with coloured glass high up under the roof. Above the altar angels spread their white wings, and there's a clean holy smell of flowers and polish. The girls in their green pixies sit on the left, big girls at the front. The nuns sit in the middle and on the other side of the nuns, by the confession box, are four rows of older girls and old women in navy scarves. They keep their faces down and Gabriel warns us we are never to look at them, or speak to them. They live in another part of the convent. I wonder are they like me, just older, and will I live here till I'm an old woman in a navy scarf that nobody can talk to. I wonder until the priest with the gold cross on his white robes walks on to the altar and we stand and sing Hallelujah.

After mass, it's breakfast in a big room Lucy calls the refectory. The walls are green. The windowsills are higher than my head but I can still see the iron bars. The girls sit at long wooden tables with benches down both sides. The nuns' table is on a raised platform behind a frosted glass screen. There's a gap under the screen so I can only see their shoulders or the glimpse of a hand moving to pick something from the table, but they can see everything we do.

Mona is sitting at the other side of the room with girls her own age. Pippa is at the same table as me but she's at the other end between two hungry-looking girls. I'm put beside Lucy Flynn and some of the girls I saw cleaning the stairs. We stand and pray when Sister Gabriel stands in the middle of the room and rings the bell for grace before meals.

> Bless us O Lord
> And these thy gifts
> Which of thy bounty
> We are about to receive.
> Amen.

The bell rings again and we sit. The nuns use wooden spoons to fill our tin plates on the table with porridge from great silver saucepans. The room is filled with the smell of rashers, eggs, sausages and toast from the nuns' table but all we have is porridge and lukewarm cocoa. The porridge is cold and I can feel the lumps in my mouth and the back of my throat. I want to be sick but I swallow because I don't want to be in trouble. A girl with foxy hair and a flat nose leans across and asks why I'm here. Is your mother dead?

She's in Australia.

What does she look like?

The other girls around me stop eating and leave their spoons on the table to listen.

She has black hair.

Is it long?

Yes.

Does she look like you, only older?

I think so.

I seen her.

I look at her and she nods. She smiles. She's serious. She looks around at Lucy Flynn and the other girls and they nod their heads and get excited. They've all seen her. They're certain. She was in the hallway a minute ago looking for me!

I leap from the seat and run for the door, but Sister Gabriel catches my arm. I pull at her to get away, but she's big and strong and drags me back to my seat. I tell her my Mum is here and she tells me sit down and finish that porridge and don't move off that seat again until I'm told.

Lucy Flynn and the other girls are laughing and someone has emptied their porridge in my bowl. I want to cry. I want to go home. Lucy Flynn says it's no big deal. We do that to everyone.

I can't eat any more porridge. The clock above the kitchen door shows eight o'clock. I don't know what to do so I just turn my face to the plastic tablecloth and say nothing. Daddy will be here soon. He has to be.

After breakfast we wash the dishes and scrub the floors. Pippa and Mona are ahead of me leaving the room but when I get to the door leading to the playground they're lost in a crowd of girls. Lucy Flynn is standing by the door, her hair damp from drizzle. She says sorry for what happened but that's the way it is. You gets used of it, and don't be standing there, it's dangerous. You have to stay out in the playground till the bell rings. Never mind. It's too late now.

Too late?

Lucy turns away and I feel a huge hand gripping my shoulder. It's Sister Gabriel, and she doesn't look happy.

She hauls me into her office at the bottom of the stairs where there's a tall statue of the Blessed Virgin Mary with yellow roses at her feet. Sister Gabriel lets me down on the floor then lifts me again by the ear and points to the blue slip on the table.

Didn't I tell you there's a dark corner in Hell for girls who don't wear a slip? Not wearing your slip is a sinful, shameful thing to do. Didn't I warn you?

Yes, Sister Gabriel.

And while you're waiting for Hell there's a dark cupboard under the stairs.

She tugs me closer to the table and lifts the slip to show me the leftover bowl of porridge underneath. Do I know it's a sin to waste God's Holy Food? Do I know about the millions dying in Africa and other heathen places? The million dead in Biafra? Poor unbaptized babies who will never see the face of God. Condemned for ever to Limbo.

Where's Limbo?

Never mind where Limbo is. Do you know the effort Sister Marge put into making that lovely porridge? You'll finish it before you leave this room. Now dry your eyes, Matilda.

She sits me in a chair and puts the spoon in my hand and stands over me with her arms folded inside her sleeves. I put the spoonful of porridge to my lips but it's colder than it was at breakfast and the lumps so thick I can't break them with my teeth. My stomach tightens and I puke all over her habit, her shoes and her crucifix. I'm certain she'll kill me. Reverend Mother appears from nowhere, like a white sheet flapping in the wind demanding to know why our hair wasn't cut. It's a sinful length and there's enough temptation in the world and would you tell me, Sister Gabriel, what is going on here? You are responsible for these children.

The child was sick, Reverend Mother.

I wonder why Sister Gabriel doesn't tell Reverend Mother about my slip, which isn't on the table anymore. Reverend Mother orders Sister Gabriel to get this mess sorted. Father Devlin is on his way. Whatever will he think?

Straight away, Reverend Mother.

Sister Gabriel pulls my slip from her pocket and warns me don't forget it again or I'll lament the day. She leaves the room and comes back with a mop and a bucket of soapy water. I get my slip on while Sister Gabriel is mopping. Her face seems kinder now and her voice isn't as angry either.

You should be doing this yourself, Matilda, she says, but I think you've caused enough trouble for one day. Finish what you are doing and go back outside.

Lucy Flynn is waiting by the door again.

See, I told youse not to stand there. Come on, let's go before Father Devlin comes.

Pippa comes over and grips my hand. Her palm is warm but her fingertips are icy. There are tearstains on her pink cheeks and her bottom lip sticks out when she asks why Daddy didn't come. I grip her hand tighter and promise her he'll be here. Pippa says he won't and Lucy says he won't. Lucy says they never do. Lucy says we're in the Holy Shepherd for good. We're Sheps. Get used of it.

5

Friday evenings we're brought to the big washroom at the top
of the playground where the concrete floor is cold and cracked
under our bare feet. We strip naked and fire our clothes in a
bundle in the corner then line up and wait for our turn. I don't
get embarrassed anymore because I'm seven now and I'm
used of it. Along one wall there's a line of ten brown enamel
tubs head high, my head, off the floor. There's a nun scrubbing
a girl at every tub. The tubs are too big to call sinks and
too small to call baths. Cobwebs cling to the corners of the
whitewashed walls and to the rotted wooden beams above
our heads. The summer sun beams through the small windows
above the door making a neat square on the floor and everywhere there's the splashing of water and the stench of green
carbolic soap.

Gabriel lifts me under the arms and plops me in the cold
water. Her sleeves are rolled up and she goes at me with the
scrubbing brush till my flesh is pinky red and raw all over and
all the time she's howling, Sit still and be quiet. Anyone would
think you never saw water. If you don't sit still you'll go
nowhere tomorrow.

Tomorrow?

Your grandmother rang to say she has a surprise and she'd
like the three of you up in the house. If you don't sit still this
instant you'll stay right here. I'll see to that.

It's hard to sit still when tomorrow I'm going home, maybe
for good. I'd like to jump out of the tub and tell everyone that
when I'm big I'll have money and I'll come back with sweets

and clothes and new shoes for everyone. But I can't. There're suds in my eyes that scald and my cheeks are on fire from green carbolic soap. That's how people on the outside know we're Sheps. The raw pink faces we have from carbolic soap. That and the shaved heads.

In the morning Gabriel drives Mona, Pippa and me to Nanny's in the nuns' blue mini-bus. When we get out the kids outside the shop stare at us and I hang my head walking past. A strange man opens the front door and I wonder is this another uncle? He's wearing a white string vest and faded blue jeans. His hair is tied in a ponytail. He has no socks or shoes and Gabriel stares at the man's feet like she never saw a man with no socks or shoes. I look at his eyes and suddenly I know it's Daddy. He smiles down at us and I want to move nearer but Mona grabs his hand first. Mona's coat is open and it's the first time I've noticed the tiny bumps under her jumper and that means she's getting a chest.

Nanny comes to the door in her apron all smiles for Gabriel.

Isn't it a great day altogether, Sister.

God is in his Heaven, surely, Missus Kelly.

And aren't you wonderful yourself, Sister? Look how big the girls are after getting. They're grand and healthy so they are.

Gabriel tells Nanny we're great girls and she's only thrilled to have us and we're excellent at religious instruction. The Sacred Mysteries, the Seven Deadly Sins, the Seven Virtues and the Ten Commandments. Even little Matilda, who didn't know where Limbo was. Gabriel smiles down at me like I'm a great girl altogether but I know she's only doing it because Nanny and Daddy are here.

Daddy wonders what a fine woman like Gabriel is doing being a nun. Wouldn't she be happier getting a good man for herself? Any man? Nanny slaps Daddy on the bare shoulder and puts her hands to her cheeks to hide the blush.

You're awful to be coddin' Sister Gabriel. Take no notice, Sister Gabriel. Full of his fun he is.

Gabriel is as red as a slapped face herself and even though she's smiling I know she's mortified. She covers her mouth with her fingers and tells Daddy, You're an awful man, Mister Kelly. I'm sure now you don't mean a word.

I do. It's a mystery why all those women want to lock themselves away. Can't be natural.

Stop that now, Peter, says Nanny. A joke is a joke.

Pippa steps into the hallway and catches Daddy's other hand. Gabriel says, Well, I'd better be going or they'll have the guards out searching for me.

What's your rush, Sister, says Daddy. Come in and tell me all about yourself and while you're at it you can tell me who's responsible for shaving my daughters' hair.

Daddy leaves Mona and Pippa's hands go, folds his arms and leans against the doorframe, making room for Gabriel to go inside. Pippa moves away from Daddy and comes out and stands beside me on the footpath and that's a sure sign Pippa thinks there's going to be trouble.

Gabriel isn't having any of it. She ignores Daddy like she's gone deaf but nuns are always acting deaf when it suits them. She says, It was pleasing to meet you at last, Mister Kelly, and yourself of course, Missus Kelly.

She hurries out to the footpath and into the mini-bus. Her jaw is dangling as she drives away. I don't think she's met anyone like Daddy before.

You're an awful man, says Nanny to Daddy. That poor nun, she doesn't know if you're blaggardin' or serious.

Won't do her any harm, says Daddy. Bit too good-looking to be a nun. What is she, twenty-five?

If that, says Nanny. Nanny looks down the street after

Gabriel. A nun driving, she says. I never thought I'd live to see the day. Come on. Everyone come inside.

Grandad is sitting in his armchair by the fire. It's July and there's no fire, but he sits there as if there is, warming himself on memories of cold nights at sea in the Merchant Navy. He glances over at us and goes back to reading the newspaper and I don't know what to think. I'm just happy my uncles aren't here. I want to ask Daddy if we're home for good and are our brothers Sheamie and Danny coming home too? But I don't. I don't want to hear him say no.

Nanny stands in front of the mantelpiece and holds her arms out for us to give her a hug. I think she's going to say this is our home as long as she's alive and there's breath in her body. My heart hopes until I remember the last time she said it. Mona and Pippa give Nanny a hug and she kisses them on the cheek. I bend behind the brown sofa pretending to tie my shoelace.

Nanny asks how Mona and Pippa are getting on in school. Mona doesn't hear and Nanny asks again. Mona says she got three gold stars for English. Pippa says she's in the school play.

And what about Matilda? Are you still sitting next to your little friend Natasha? And tell me, what's this I hear from your school about you being a great little Irish dancer?

I don't want to stand up so I tie my other shoelace. I'm ashamed to tell Nanny that Natasha's mother came to the school to complain she didn't want Natasha sitting next to someone from the Holy Shepherd. So now I sit on my own at the back of the class where even girls with wallpaper on their books look down their noses at me.

Daddy goes out to the front bedroom and I follow him because I didn't get a hug yet. He tells me to wait in the hall and when he comes out his yellow eyes are happy and dancing in his skull. He picks me up and when I give him a hug he squeezes like he never wants to leave me go. His beard tickles my face and I laugh. He holds me up to the ceiling, playing with me, but I'm not scared because I know Daddy won't let me fall.

He carries me back out to the sitting room and sits on the brown sofa and lifts his green canvas bag on to his lap. Mona, Pippa and me hold our breath and gather round him while he opens the zip. He puts his hand inside and pulls out a pair of old white socks and hands them to Mona and tells her to make sure they fit before she wears them to mass. Mona takes the socks from Daddy. She stares at them, wriggles them, catches them by the toes and shakes them, opens them at the top and looks inside. She's ready to pout when she catches Daddy winking at Pippa and me.

What did you really get us? No messin' now, Daddy.

Daddy puts his arm around Mona's waist and falls back along the sofa, pulling her to him, laughing and trying to tickle her and it's easy to see Mona is enjoying it the way she keeps jumping on Daddy every time he lets her go. I'd like a tickle too and so would Pippa and we move near Daddy and Mona on the sofa but Nanny cries, Stop. Stop or you'll break the chairs. Daddy leaves Mona go and looks back in the bag. He pulls out two shiny black spud guns with red nozzles for Pippa and me and a watch with a black leather strap for Mona because she's getting big now. We kiss him on the cheek and run straight to the kitchen to rob potatoes from under the sink and for Mona to admire her watch in the cracked mirror over the sink then run out to the front garden so the other kids will see we have something new and won't be ashamed to talk.

The girls stop playing hopscotch on the footpath and come to the gate and stare and sometimes I'm brave enough to stare back. Mister Murphy comes out his door in his train driver's cap and tells us all don't be gawkin' out of our mouths at each other. Go off and play.

I'm happy. We're out of the convent, we're playing with our friends and Daddy's home. If we're good he'll bring Sheamie and Danny home too. We'll have our own home and Daddy will be happy because he has us and that's all he'll ever need. Mum will come back. Maybe she'll come tomorrow.

After tea, Daddy dresses in clean blue jeans and brushes his hair in Grandad's cracked mirror over the sink. Nanny shuffles by him carrying pots with dinner in them. Peter, she says, I hope you're not leaving those children to me while you're off gallivanting. I know about you. You've been out with those Delaney twins from around the corner. I had their mother wailing like a banshee over the back hedge this morning, her daughters were running with a married man with five children in the Holy Shepherd, the cheek of her. Still, she has a point. Taking care of your children you should be, not trotting around like a film star. Is it Hollywood you think you're in, parading up and down with Raquel Welch dangling from your arm?

He could charm her too, says Grandad from the sitting room.

You shut it, says Nanny.

Black cat, black kittens.

Daddy keeps brushing his hair. Nanny leaves the pots on the table and the steam from the bacon oozes from under the lid and up my nose when she reaches up to tap Daddy on the shoulder. Are yeh listening to me at all, Peter?

I am.

I'm getting too old for this. So is your father. The man has blood pressure and has to mind himself. Mind your own children. I'm not responsible anymore what happens.

Responsible? What do you mean by that?

Nanny turns pale and turns her eyes to the floor. I meant nothing, she says.

You should be glad to have your grandchildren up here.

Did I say I wasn't? I'm just letting you know you have responsibilities.

Daddy leaves the hairbrush on the windowsill and swigs cod liver oil straight from the bottle. He kisses Nanny on the cheek and tells Mona, Pippa and me to be good, he'll see us in the morning.

Grandad says, I see he's still wrapping you around his little finger, Annie. Nanny tells Grandad to shut his trap or he'll get no dinner and there's not another word from Grandad.

In the morning Nanny comes in from the kitchen wiping her hands on her apron and tells Daddy, It's a nice day, Peter. God knows how long it will last. Why don't you bring the girls for a spin? Buy them some new clothes; they can't go anywhere in those convent rags.

Daddy is sitting in the armchair in front of the television, drawing with a pencil on a book of plain white pages. I'm sitting beside him on one arm of the chair and Pippa is sitting on the other arm playing with her hair. Mona is asleep in bed. Daddy is drawing a Roman soldier because Pippa asked him to. She saw *Ben Hur* and thinks Roman soldiers are cool, but Pippa thinks everything is cool at one time or another. I think she just likes the word, cool. Daddy can draw anything. It can be yachts with tall white sails, airplanes flying through thunderstorms, houses, big, small or terraced, castles with lakes. And if we say, That's nice, Daddy, he'll say, I'll buy that for you when you're bigger. You have to be happy with a Daddy who'll buy you anything you want when you're bigger.

Well, says Nanny, are you going?

Daddy shoves the pencil behind his ear and looks up at Nanny.

Well, are you?

Daddy brings us to town and buys us bellbottom jeans, T-shirts and runners in Shaws big shop on the Quay. He has a red van he brought from England and the back is filled with cartons of cigarettes, bottles of whiskey and books with pictures of girls in bikinis on the cover. He leaves it all with a man on the Cork Road who owns a green van. He's Umbilical Bill, the man who got Daddy a ride on the cattle ship to London before.

Daddy drives to Tramore. It's teeming with cars but we find an empty parking space by the prom. There's a low wall with a railing on top in front of us and the land stretches out on both sides of the bay like two legs in the bath. At the end of the right leg, sticking up like a big toe, there's a man in a red jacket standing on a high white pillar. He's pointing out to sea. Daddy says he's the Metal Man and he's there to warn the ships away from the rocks.

Is he a real man, Daddy?

No, Matilda, he's made of metal.

Does he get cold?

He can't feel anything.

We walk along the prom in the salty air and I'm delighted with my new clothes and the sun on my face. Soon I'll be sunburned and nobody will know I'm a Shep. I step up onto the low wall and walk along it holding onto the railing. On the strand below us, people lie on beach towels and bake in the sun while kids in swimming togs make sandcastles with their plastic buckets and shovels. There's a man and little girl throwing a rubber ball for their small brown dog. The dog leaps and catches the ball in the air and brings it back and drops it at the girl's feet, barking at her to throw it again. It must be nice to have a small brown dog like that.

Daddy brings us to the skating rink and tells the man at the gate we're from the Holy Shepherd and he's taking us out for the day.

That's nice, says the man.

Daddy takes a step closer and stares hard.

Surely you can let three little girls from the Holy Shepherd in free. It's hardly going to break you. Is it?

I pull at his arm and tell him, No Daddy, don't tell him where we're from but he barks at me, Shut up and keep quiet. He bends down and whispers in my ear that I'll learn more with my mouth shut. Never buy what you can get for free. Free is good. Remember that.

I'm sorry, Daddy.

Mona and Pippa drop their eyes to the ground and move three steps away and I want to move away too, but Daddy warns us, Stay put. Don't move unless I say. The man at the gate tells Daddy he's only working here and it's not for him to let anyone in for free. Daddy carries on pestering him, telling him he has no money and the poor children haven't been outside the convent for almost a year.

There's a queue behind us complaining they'll go elsewhere if the man doesn't get a move on. The man looks down the queue, then back at Daddy who's still staring at him. Daddy winks at the man. Come on, he says. Let the kids in.

The man nods his head towards the gate. Go ahead, he says, go ahead.

The roller skates have black wheels and red straps for your shoes. The skates are heavy and when I try to stand my legs go the wrong way. Mona catches my hand and after a few circles I'm flying around. I'm having such a time of it. With my Daddy watching me I want to be the best roller-skater in the world and with every circle I get faster and faster till I'm going so fast I don't see the little fat boy stopping to lick his ice cream cone. I bang into him and send him sprawling on

68

the ground. He picks himself up and runs bawling for his mother, his father, anyone to pick him up and buy him another ice cream.

I run to Daddy at the gate. His mouth is clenched and I wonder is he angry with the little fat boy. I've fallen and put a hole in my new jeans and grazed my knee and tell Daddy I don't have to go to the hospital. I don't need stitches. Look.

He glares at me and the veins bulge in his temples.

Are you stupid, are you?

But it wasn't my fault.

He mocks me, Wasn't my fault.

The man at the gate is watching. Daddy doesn't care. He squeezes my arm tight and I want to yell out but he screams in my face, Do you think I'm made of money?

People by the gate lift their children into their arms while others move away.

I'm sorry, Daddy. It was an accident.

It was your fault. You weren't watching.

I was watching.

Don't lie and don't give me back-answers. It's the last time I'm bringing you anywhere. You're too stupid for words.

I don't say anymore. There's no use crying and Mona and Pippa are making faces at me for ruining the day and it's my fault Daddy is in a bad mood now.

When we get back to Nanny's, Daddy goes straight into the front bedroom and slams the door behind him. Pippa and Mona run ahead of me into the kitchen to tell Nanny I fell and tore my new jeans. Nanny is sitting at the kitchen table sticking Green Shield stamps in the Green Shield stamp book so she can get a new set of pans. She closes the book and hits it with the side of her fist so the stamps will stick, then bends down to look at my knee.

69

It's only a graze. Go out to play until yeer tea is ready.

We go out to play but when we come back in later Daddy is still in the bedroom. Nanny tells Mona to call him for his tea. Mona looks at her new watch to check it is teatime and goes to call Daddy, he doesn't come out, so we follow Nanny when she goes out to the hall and knocks.

Are you in there, Peter?

There's no answer.

Peter, are you in there?

Peter, will you answer for God's sake?

She turns the knob and tries to push the door open with her shoulder. The door is locked. Then we hear furniture being moved, heavy furniture like a wardrobe being pushed against the door. Jesus tonight, says Nanny. Go for Grandad. He's up in bed.

Nanny sits on the end of the stairs with her head in her hands till Grandad comes down rubbing his eyes. What's up?

That son of yours has himself barricaded in the bedroom. I'm not able for his nonsense.

My son? Oh, yes. They're always mine when they do something stupid.

None of your smart-alec talk. Get him out of that room.

Grandad hammers at the door with his fist, shoves it with his shoulder but the door won't budge and Daddy won't answer.

Nanny says, Let him be for now, he'll come out when he's ready. Maybe it's my fault. Maybe I'm pushing him too hard over the children.

Grandad opens his mouth to say something but Nanny tells him to shut it so Grandad goes back upstairs to bed.

Next morning Daddy still doesn't answer, or the next. Sometimes we hear him mumbling that Satan is in the room and we run screaming to Nanny to tell her Satan is in the house.

She blesses herself at the sink and makes us kneel at the kitchen table saying the rosary till we stop crying.

Grandad wants to send for the parish priest even though Grandad can't stand the sight of him, but maybe he'll be able to talk sense to Daddy. Nanny tells him she'd be ashamed to know the priest or the neighbours knew her business. There'll be no priest, no gardaí. We'll handle this ourselves.

Grandad goes out to the front garden. Nanny, Mona, Pippa and me follow. The sun is bright above the houses and brings the sweat to Grandad's forehead. He rolls up his shirtsleeves and you can see he has big arms with freckles everywhere. He tries lifting the window but it's stuck hard with old paint. He rattles the glass with his fist. Holds his ear to the window and says he hears Daddy singing a song about newspaper taxis coming to take him away. Nanny says, Merciful Jesus, give me strength. She cocks her head to listen. Mona cocks her head. Pippa shrugs her shoulders as if to say cocking your head won't make any difference. I cock my head anyway. Pippa is right. I can't hear anything.

Nanny cups her hand over her ear but I don't copy her. Only old people do that and it makes you look deaf. Even Mona doesn't do it and she is deaf.

Mister Murphy from next door comes to the fence and asks Nanny if everything is all right there, Annie?

Grand, Mossy.

If you need anything, give me a shout.

Grand, Mossy. We're just thinking about giving the windows a new coat of paint.

Mossy goes back into his house and Nanny tells us, Come into the house quick before the world knows our business. Jesus, Mary and Holy St Joseph, can't people keep their noses out of anything.

Nanny and Grandad sit at the kitchen table drinking tea

71

wondering what to do. Pippa sits on Grandad's lap, Mona sits on Nanny's lap and I stand by the sink because this is no time for sitting on laps and anyway there's not enough laps to go round and I worry when Nanny and Grandad argue they'll have to break the glass.

Nanny says, You have to.

Grandad says, My arse I will. And who's going to pay? Your son won't, that's for certain.

I see. He's my son now.

I don't want them fighting anymore and I shout at them to stop. Stop fighting. If they don't stop fighting we'll never get Daddy out.

Nanny says to Grandad, Now look what you've done. You've frightened the child.

It's their father who's causing it. I was mindin' me own business in bed when this started.

Nanny holds my head against her belly and tells me it's all right, don't fret, she'll get Daddy out.

Nanny sends for our uncles and they're here in a few minutes, banging their shoulders off the bedroom door. I don't want to be here with them but I want Daddy to be all right, so I sit on the stairs between Mona and Pippa watching them try to open the door. The door shakes when they push their shoulders against it.

Grandad says, Go easy with that door.

Uncle John tells him, Go 'way and get sense. How else can we open it?

Uncle Philip goes out to the garden shed and comes back with a screwdriver and tries to take the lock off the door. Nanny tells him he's wasting his time, it's locked from the inside and there's a bloody big wardrobe jamming it. Our uncles look at Grandad and he tells them, All right, go ahead. Break it down.

The curtains are drawn and the room is blacker than a nun's habit. Nanny opens the curtains and when the sunlight floods the room we see Daddy lying on the bed in his underpants. Sweat oozes through his forehead and he's laughing at the paint on the ceiling. We hold our noses from the stench of the chamber pot brimming over beside the bed. There's a needle on the floor like the needle I got in my bum and I worry if Daddy is going to die.

Mona, Pippa and me huddle in the corner when our uncles carry Daddy out by his feet and arms to the sitting room and stretch him out on the brown sofa and cover him with a blanket and I'm happy when they leave but worried over Daddy. His eyes are dull and his hair matted with sweat. Why can't Daddy be like that Daddy on the beach with the little girl and the small brown dog?

Grandad leaves the screwdriver on the mantelpiece and collapses in his armchair. That's it now, he says, no more. He wants Daddy gone. He wants the children gone. He wants the house to himself. He never saw the likes in his life. He's seen the world ten times over from the pyramids in Egypt to the frozen Antarctic waste but, Jesus, never did he come across the likes of this. The Wild Men of Borneo frying each other for breakfast wouldn't tolerate the likes of this. No, Annie, enough is enough. Do you hear? Enough is enough. I done me bit, I'm not able for it anymore.

Oh, shut up for yourself.

I'm goin' to the pub.

Go then. That's all you were ever good for.

In the morning, Mona, Pippa and me get dressed and come downstairs early. The cinders in the fireplace are still glowing from last night. Daddy wakes up, licking his tongue over his dry cracked lips. His eyes are long and narrow like grains of rice and he doesn't know where he is. I go to the kitchen to make tea but Mona follows me and says she'll do it. She's ten, I'm only seven and everyone knows you can't make tea when you're seven. I'm to get the cup out of the press. Pippa stays sitting on the couch beside Daddy with her hands between her knees and keeps quiet.

Nanny comes downstairs in her pink nightdress and when she sees Daddy she says, Oh, you're awake. Daddy mumbles something I can't understand and takes a sip of hot tea. Nanny tells him he'll have to sort himself. He's making us a laughing-stock. If anyone hears about this carry-on we'll be the talk of the town and she doesn't want that shame. She takes money from her purse and gives it to Daddy and tells him it's best if he went back to London. I'll have the children up for the odd weekend and a week at Christmas. Get yourself help, Peter, then you might get your children back. Don't come back to this house till you do. I mean it.

Nanny walks us back to the convent and on the way she tells us not to worry. Daddy will get better, and whatever we do, don't say a word to the nuns.

We won't, Nanny.

It's very important. Do you understand me?

We do, Nanny.

She hugs us goodbye at the wicket gate and tells us she'll call for us at Christmas. We can spend the week with her. We turn our faces to the wall so nobody will see our tears when the nun comes to walk us inside.

6

I think Pippa should go first but Pippa shakes her head no. It's early on a June morning and we're sitting on the green roof of the tin sheds, our faces black from the sun and the nuns' garden behind us a sea of bluebells swaying in the breeze. The sun turns Pippa's hair so blonde it's almost white. Pippa says it won't make no difference whether we say it or not. We'll get kilt by big girls anyway.

You go first, Matilda.

You're older, Pippa. I'm not nine yet. You're nearly ten. You're even startin' to get a chest.

Yeah but you're taller, Matilda, she says, as if getting a chest doesn't really count, but all the same you can see how proud she is of her bumps the way she has her cardigan open and the sleeves halfway down her arms like all she needs is a pair of high heels and she'd be pure faintin'.

Pippa shows me the cut on her knee she got when she fell running from a gang of girls. The girls caught her anyway but Pippa bawled so much they got scared and carried her inside to Gabriel.

You're tryin' to get out of it, Pippa. That's the worst excuse I ever heard in me life.

Pippa promises she'll say it after me and makes the sign of the cross over her heart and that means she'll die right here and go straight to Hell if she doesn't say it, only Pippa is always crossing her heart, and she never dies.

Are you doin' it or not, Matilda?

You're some coward, Pippa.

You can't talk.

It was my idea, Pippa.

Then do it, Matilda. I dare yeh. And no whisperin' and no doin' it behind your hand. Come on, you go first.

Will I?

Yeah, go on.

I take a deep breath and put my top teeth out over my bottom lip ready to say it, but not that loud that anyone can hear. Only Pippa.

Fuck!

As soon as I've said it I want to take it back. I hold my breath waiting for a penguin to flutter into the playground demanding to know who said that? But nothing happens, and slowly my heart starts beating again.

Pippa says. What's it like, Matilda?

Do it and find out.

I changed me mind.

I'll kill you. See, I told you you're always tryin' to get outa things.

I'm only jokin'.

Are you?

Pippa puts her top teeth out over her bottom lip then takes them back in again, then out, then in again.

Hurry up, Pippa.

Fuck! she says, and laughs so much she starts to cough but at least she's done it and so did I and I'm pure faintin' because now I can talk like the rest in here. I can say fuck off fuck you fuck her fuck the nuns and never have to say no, twice.

Gimme that.

No.

Give it to me.

Fuck off!

If I can say fuck I can say arse. That's easy. Easier than fuck.

You're a pain in the arse, girl, fuck off. And if I can do all that then I can learn how to stand up for myself in here. I'll learn how to fight. I'll be the best fighter in the Holy Shepherd only I can't do it right now because a strange lorry carrying wheelbarrows, shovels and a big yellow cement mixer that looks ready to topple over is parking in the playground. A hundred children jump in the back, dance on the roof, and climb through the windows yelling to the driver, What's your name? Have you children?

Pippa and me climb down from the roof and run across the playground to ask the driver, What's the wheelbarras for, mister?

For takin' away children who ask too many questions, he says.

The younger kids run away bawling to tell the first penguin they find there's a man in the playground taking us away in wheelbarrows, while Pippa jumps into one.

Gis a spin, mister?

I push Pippa around the playground in the wheelbarrow and a gang of kids take off behind us shouting, Me next, me next. There's a fight. Mona and another big girl are rolling around on the ground pulling what hair they have off each other's heads over whose turn it is and everyone else is still swinging from the lorry.

More lorries come and soon the playground is filled with lorries and workmen in blue overalls and we pester them as to why they're here till there's no use asking anymore. They pull their caps down over their eyes and tell you, Mind yourself there now, we're busy. Stand back, child. Bejasus, if a nail flies you'll lose an eye and what would you do then with a black leather patch over the hole like Long John Silver and not a parrot in sight. Ha, ha.

Pippa wants to ask Doyler and torments me to go with her.

77

That's what we call Missus Doyle, the hairdresser who started a few weeks ago. She was mauled with girls demanding plaits, pageboys, perms, ponytails, curls, bobs, bob tails, rinses and ringlets. All she had was the nuns' electric razor and we still ended up looking like convicts. Pippa said whoever told Doyler she was a hairdresser was either bald or blind or both. One look at Doyler's own hair should have told us. It looks like it was shaped with a piss pot.

Doyler is small. She has a broom that comes up to her chin that she chases us with, but she never catches us. She wears pink and blue aprons and tiny gold-framed glasses with no sides hanging on the tip of her nose. Her voice is the biggest part of her. She's forever booming across the playground, I hear yee over there. I know what yee're up to. We believed her too, till we found out she as deaf as an ear of corn. She complains about her aches and pains, ailments she reads about in medical books, and she has those same symptoms herself, would you believe. Gabriel says Doyler's a hypochondriac but I don't think there's anything wrong with her.

Pippa and me go into her when she's tidying up the refectory. We have to be careful because we know from Mona that people who're a bit deaf can be contrary.

Doyler says, I knew I'd have a delegation in here sooner or later. It wouldn't be up to me to tell yee. Sure I wouldn't have any say in a thing like that.

Pippa whispers to me, What's a delegation, Matilda?

You don't have to whisper, Pippa. She can't hear us.

I hear yee over there. I know what yee're up to.

Doyler runs at us with the broom and Pippa turns on her heel and scatters out the door but I take a chance and hold my ground. There's no point being able to say fuck if I'm going to run from Doyler. I have to start someplace.

Ah, come on, Doyler, tell us.

78

Pippa sticks her blonde head around the door and when she sees I'm still alive she comes back and stands behind me. Doyler leans on the broom and tells us it's to do with the government and isn't it about time too? Mind you, the nuns are none too pleased. They don't tolerate interference. I worked in schools in England for over twenty years and never came across a kip like this. I'd like to do something about it myself and let me tell you two girls there are days when I'm tormented to distraction but daren't open my mouth. Reverend Mother would have me out that door so fast this broom wouldn't touch the floor. And me with my complaints. No, it's best I keep my mouth shut and do what I can behind the scenes. Am I right, girls?

Yes, Doyler.

Who'd cut your hair if I left? It'd be back to the nuns again.

Did you cut hair in England, Doyler? says Pippa.

I did.

I'd say they were glad to see you go.

What?

I said they were mad to let you go.

Doyler smiles at Pippa and goes back to her sweeping.

Pippa and me go out to the playground and watch the workmen come in cars, trucks, on bicycles, their lunch dangling from the handlebars. On the outside of the building they put scaffolding up the three floors. They rip out the crumbling windows and the rusty steel bars, and hack away the old grey dash so rough that, when you fall against it, it reefs the skin off elbows, knees, foreheads. Upstairs, in the dormitory, they build a solid wooden partition that they hammer behind. Our beds are moved to the far end of the dormitory where the big girls sleep. They don't want us here and we don't want to be down here with their bras and stockings hanging from the heating pipes. I have to lie here every night tormented by bras and fights over who robbed the make-up. Make-up is important. If you don't have it you stick a pin in your finger for the blood to rub in your cheeks and use the nuns' black shoe polish on your eyelashes.

A lot of the workmen are young. Doyler says they're apprentices and the big girls are always saying, Look, there he is, and he's gorgeous. There are penguins everywhere, watching everything. I've never seen so many in one place except mass. The tinkers stick their foxy heads out the big holes where the windows were shouting. Hey, mister, any chance of a shag? Hey, mister, she wants teh ride yeh. Hey, mister, are yeh as good as me Daddy? Then hide buckled up laughing on the ground.

Pippa and me ask Mona what shaggin' and ridin' is but she tells us, Stick your nose back on your puss where it belongs, you'll find out when you're older. Mona is twelve and goes to the big girls' school in the Sisters of Mercy where they learn all about shaggin' and ridin' from girls on the outside. Pippa says, Never mind, Matilda. It's letting a boy put his tongue in your mouth. That's how you gets babies. I heard it in school.

Really, Pippa?

And if you wear a black bra you'll have twins. Cross me heart.

The big girls are going mad because the tinkers are sneaking over to the green sheds where the apprentices have their lunch. The penguins hunt them away, screaming, You were told to leave those boys alone, but as soon as the penguins are gone the tinkers are back smoking fags and disappearing to the small toilets under the chestnut trees with the apprentices and soon the big girls are down there too. They say if tinkers can get a ride and free fags down in the toilets then so can we.

Some days I sit up in the chestnut trees watching the big girls and the apprentices. I have to do watch out in case a nun turns up when she has no business and through the broken glass in the toilet window I see them glue their mouths together. And that's only for starters.

At the end of the summer Reverend Mother calls us all together in the common room that we use for the Christmas pantomine. She stumbles as she climbs the three steps to the stage and needs help to get the rest of the way. She threatens us with the walking stick telling us we don't deserve what we're getting, sinners that we are. We'll all end up in the laundry. The room is filled with penguins. They're like wall-paper and all of them waiting for the first snigger so they can hit someone.

Reverend Mother tells us the news: we're to be broken into three groups and each group will have its own section in the convent like three houses on a street with really big families in them. The first group will have my family and fifteen others. Sister Gabriel will live with us and be our mother and that's what we're to call her, Mother.

It's nice to have someone to call Mother again, even if it is a nun.

A week later the bishop arrives for the blessing in a pointy red hat. He showers us with holy water out in the playground. He sprinkles doors, window and walls. The penguins line up in front of him and kiss his red ring and, when he leaves in a long white car with red flags flying from the bonnet, Gabriel trots around the playground tapping everyone in her group on the head to form a line at the door that leads from the playground to where we're to live.

Gabriel tells us we can go in now but there is to be no tearing around or we'll be on our way to Cork where they know how to deal with girls who tear around. Ask Maggie Shore the next time you see her, which will probably be in some dark corner in Hell itself.

Inside, the smell of fresh cream paint is everywhere. The old wooden floors are gone from downstairs and instead we have red tiles with a yellow border. There's a sitting room with a television and a kitchen with a cooker. Proper tables and chairs. A fridge with sausages, butter, not margarine, and a fat blue chicken stuffed to the neck with eggs. Big brown eggs with speckles that you'd need two hands to hold. When I'm shown my own bedroom upstairs I just sit on my new bed with the pink candlewick bedspread and breathe everything in. Smell how fresh it is. The sunshine through the window brightens the room and I never saw anything so fresh or new in all my life. I sit on the bed with my hands under my knees and let my legs swing and look down at my new white sandals and wish I could sit here for ever so they'd never have dirt on them. In the corner I have a wooden locker with a drawer on top and a press underneath. There's a new window with pink curtains and whenever I look out they'll say there's Matilda at her window and when I'm in the playground I can look up and say that's my window and inside is my room with my things in it.

Doyler sticks her head around the door and smiles because she knows how strange I feel with everything, especially after what happened yesterday. I like Doyler. She understands us. I think it's because she has kids of her own. Doyler is to be part of our group, to give Gabriel a hand. And she'll need a big bloody hand with you lot, she says. Doyler sits beside me on the bed and admires my sandals and laughs over the new shoe van that came yesterday.

The new shoe man opened the van doors and the inside was packed to the roof with shoeboxes. Gabriel ran when she saw us coming but the shoe man got trampled in the stampede and we tore the van to pieces fighting over the shoeboxes. Right in the middle of it the nuns' blue mini-bus parked in the green sheds. There was boys in it and we ran to Gabriel complaining we didn't want boys here eatin' our food an' starvin' us all to death and fartin' up our faces and the little pricks needn't think they're gettin' our shoeboxes either.

Then I saw them. I just stood there with the shoebox in my hand. My hands trembled and I wanted to cry but I knew if I started I'd never be able to stop.

The boys, ten of them, walked past with their shaved heads bent down and their shoulders hunched. Sheamie hasn't changed much. Same red hair; he's just taller. Hands down to his kneecaps like they were growing faster than the rest of him. Danny dressed in a little hand-me-down Communion suit. The sleeves were up past his wrists and the stitching torn at the arms. The loose heel of his left boot clacking behind him. He lifted his head and looked straight at me with his round eyes the colour of chestnuts. I smiled at him but I knew he didn't know me. I wanted to pick him up and bring him to the big shops on the Quay and buy him new clothes and shoes so he'd be all cute and cuddly the way little boys should be but all I could do was stand there with the empty shoebox in my hand. When they were gone through the gate we went back to fighting over the shoeboxes. I was so angry I punched the first nose I saw. We left the playground littered with new white sandals. It took the shoe man all day to match them in pairs.

The poor man, says Doyler. Did you ever see the like?

There's a smell of ointment from her elbow when she puts her arm around my shoulder and pulls me to her. I didn't know the boys were coming either, Matilda, she says.

She knows I'm confused because there's so much going on. Confused by bedrooms, bathrooms, baths and brothers, because I haven't had them for so long. It's different when you live on the outside, where you grow up with bedrooms, bathrooms and brothers. But I don't know why I got them. Nobody said I was getting them or how long I can keep them or if they'll be taken from me again.

Doyler leaves and I feel like Cinderella. I sit on the floor in the corner frightened to leave in case everything disappears and I'll have no brothers and a pumpkin for a bed.

Later I go downstairs to watch television just to make sure we really do have one. Gabriel even lets us stay up to watch *The Late Late Show*.

When everyone is asleep I tiptoe down the corridor to the tiny little bathroom that looks out over the playground. I turn on the hot tap and while I'm waiting for the bath to fill I sit on the deep window ledge with my knees tucked under my chin and my cheek pressed to the cold glass. The sky is awash with stars like the eyes of all the mothers in Heaven are watching over their sleeping children. Here, in the quiet darkness, I look for my star. My very own Special Star and think of my mother. If she is in Heaven it will be her star too. Maybe she is alive and if she is maybe she is looking up at my star and thinking of me. I tell her my brothers are with me and we're all together again. I tell her how much I love her. How much I miss her. How much I need her to hold me and mind me and be my Mum again. I wish she would come and take us home. Maybe she'll come tomorrow.

7

Saturday morning there's a gang of us playing down by the pond when Pippa comes running through the gap in the hedge. I'm nine, Pippa's ten. Her cheeks are glowing and I know she's excited because Pippa never runs anywhere. She stops where the ground is muddy in case she dirties her shoes and tiptoes along by the bushes where the ground is dry and cracked making sure she doesn't snag her cardigan on a briar.

Matilda, we're allowed out.

Allowed out? I nearly fall out of my tree. Has our mother been found? Am I going home? No. It wouldn't happen like this. Covered in mud in the Holy Shepherd and Pippa running down to tell me. I wouldn't need to be told. I'd feel it. I'd know. Before I land plop in the muck so close to Pippa I can smell the carbolic on her.

Out where, Pippa?

Outside! Gabriel said so.

To you?

Sheamie told me. And we're getting pocket money too. We can go to Kennedy's shop at the corner on Fridays and we can go to town if a big girl comes with us. I swear it's true, Matilda. She makes the sign of the cross on her throat to prove it, though that doesn't mean anything with Pippa. She wants me to go to the gate with her to see if it really is true.

I search the playground for Sheamie but can't find him. Mona is sitting in the green sheds with the older girls. Her arms are folded under her chest and I know they're talking about boys and don't want to be disturbed about gates. The big girls don't need gates. They just sneak out the bathroom window when the nuns are asleep.

Danny is playing on the fire escape with a bunch of little girls fighting each other over who's playing with him next. The fire escape is mostly white with rust coming through. It runs up the three storeys and there's a pole on the outside running from the top to the ground holding the whole thing together. The little girls tell us Sheamie got in a fight with Mickey Driscoll and Mickey Driscoll gave Sheamie a bloody nose because Sheamie said Pele was a better soccer player than Bobby Charlton. Danny is seven and the youngest boy in the convent so the little girls love him, and even some of the bigger girls love him because he's cute. The nuns love him because he's the best little altar boy and what a pleasure it is to have such a quiet little lad amongst us. If only the rest of you were as quiet as Danny. The nuns love all the boys. The boys can let their hair grow so they'll look like boys on the outside and won't get picked on in school or mistaken for skinheads and wouldn't that be even worse. I think it's a strange world where boys have longer hair than girls even if it's not as bad as it used to be and you can nearly let your hair past your shoulder before the razor comes out.

Danny knows we're his sisters now but it doesn't really mean anything to him and sometimes it doesn't mean anything to me either and that makes me sad. He's just another kid in the convent. He hardly remembers living in our grandmother's house. I tell him I'm going up to the gate and ask him if he wants to come. He sees Doyler coming down the yard with the broom in her hand and he says, Hang on, Matilda. Give us a minute.

Doyler makes a run at him with the broom.

Get down from that fire escape. You were told enough not to be on it.

Instead of getting off, Danny climbs to the first lift and waits for Doyler who's chasing after him but before she can catch him he takes off to the second lift and waits for her again. Danny keeps it up all the way to the top with Doyler getting slower with every step. By the time she gets to the top she's bent over and using the broom to hold herself up. I don't know why she bothers. Maybe she thinks some day she'll catch him. We can barely see them from the ground but Doyler's heading for him with the broom raised ready to clobber him over the head, when he climbs out over the railing and slides down the pole leaving Doyler stuck four storeys up.

Come on, Matilda. Let's go.

Lucy Flynn comes to the gate with us but Pippa won't come past the fire escape. It's early in the morning and the bright September sun slants along the stone wall. Lucy, Danny and me lean against the wall with our faces in the sunlight and our feet in the shade. We wonder. It can't be that simple just to open the gate and walk outside. Can it?

Danny says, What if a penguin that doesn't know Gabriel said we're let out sees us? We'd get killed for nothin'.

Lucy says, So what? We gets killed for nothin' anyway. Come on, Matilda. I'll chance it if you will.

I don't know what to do. I can't ask Gabriel 'cos she'll give me a thick ear for asking pure stupid questions when she already gave everyone the answer. What if someone does see us though? They'd call the gardaí. We'll be handcuffed and carted off in the squad car.

I peek through the rusty shutter in the gate. The road is empty. The footpath is empty. The coast is clear. The squeak when I open the wicket gate sends Lucy running away but Danny stays with me. One scruffy white sandal steps out onto the footpath. The other one has more sense. Danny is behind me whispering, Hurry up, Matilda, before a penguin comes.

The other scruffy white sandal is lifting its heel, then a car comes roaring down the street and I'm stuck, half-in, half-free. Danny is shittin' himself behind me and the driver, a man, is in front. Behind the fire escape I hear Pippa screaming at me to get back. But the car keeps going. Danny says, It must be true, Matilda. It must have been on television. We're free.

The other white sandal is so delighted it follows the first one out. Now there's a pair of scruffy white sandals on the footpath. They go in and out and in and out again tap tap on the footpath like a blind man's white stick. They don't go too far in case the penguins change their mind because the further away from the gate you are the more trouble. But all day Saturday the scruffy white sandals go in and out, and in a week they're across to the houses in Trinity Park where the kids who live there stare at us and sometimes we stare back. The next week I'm at the top of Barrack Street and by the third week I'm pissed off. There's no point going in and out the gate anymore just because I can. I need somewhere to go. I want to do something but I don't know what's out here or even if I'll be let. I never heard of anyone from the convent doing something on the outside. I'll have to ask Gabriel when we get our pocket money Friday.

Gabriel's office makes me knickers stick to me arse. It's small so there's no place to run. There's a narrow wooden table tight against the wall. On the table there's a rusty biscuit tin, without biscuits, and a glass sweet jar, without sweets. Gabriel sits at the table and studies her list of how much pocket money we get. She hands me five pence from the rusty biscuit tin and my other five pence rattles into the sweet jar. Why couldn't she use a wooden box? It had to be glass so I can see my silver five pence lying on its own at the bottom of the jar. Broken plates, cups, dishes. Curses, fights, back cheek.

Not making your bed properly. Sins, mortal, venial, deadly and a host of others all come out of my pocket money. I never know what I'm getting. Sometimes I wind up owing money and that's worse than no pocket money at all.

What's the five pence for, Mother?

She looks at me over her glasses like I've just asked the most stupid question she's ever heard and I better not ask again if I know what's good.

The missions. Offer up your misfortune, Matilda. Think of the starving babies in Africa with their bellies stuck out like black balloons and nothing in their mouths but flies and a set of teeth that's pure useless and don't be sitting there with a mouth like a salmon. You wouldn't have it long in Africa.

She knows that's not what I meant. She knows I was asking why she stopped five pence. I'm sorry for the starving black babies and everything but not sorry enough to give them me pocket money.

What did I do wrong, Mother?

You broke two dishes washing up. You were fighting at breakfast.

I didn't start it, Mother. It was Mickey Driscoll's fault. He hit Sheamie.

I don't care who started it and Sheamie can fight his own battles.

Sheamie couldn't fight his way out of a paper bag.

Fighting with boys. I never heard the like. Now shift yourself or you'll feel the back of my hand. Learn to turn the other cheek.

But everyone'll laugh at me.

She darts a glance over the glasses again but there's a smile in her eyes and I wonder if this is a good time to ask about doing something on the outside, joining something. Maybe not, but you never know when is a good time, so I ask. Gabriel takes off her glasses and fiddles with them on the table while the sweat dries on my palms.

Something on the outside, Matilda. Like what for example? she says as if she never heard of anything outside the convent herself and she's curious to find out.

I don't know, Mother.

We'll see, Matilda.

I know by the way she says it she was hoping I'd have more to say than, I don't know, and I hate it when Gabriel says, We'll see. If I ask again I'll get a clatter on the head. I'll have to wait until she's forgotten I asked and is in a good mood before I ask again, only I never know when that is either. I'm back where I started.

Next Friday Gabriel says I get no pocket money at all for fighting again. She raps her knuckles off my forehead and nearly knocks my head off.

What in the name of Our Saviour is it with you, Matilda? Just look at yourself.

A big girl hit Pippa so I hit the big girl. She gave me a black eye but I don't care. Black eyes are great. Nobody messes with you when you have a black eye. You look dangerous. Then some sneaky girl told Gabriel I was hiding my pointy green boots inside the gate and wearing the new white sandals to school. Gabriel drags me up by the ear lobe and holds the green boots in front of my eyes.

There's the name of ten other girls written on these boots, Matilda. Not a single complaint before you got your feet in them. Explain yourself.

It's a waste of time talking to her. How do you tell someone who lives in black what pointy green boots look like with yellow socks?

The rest of my pocket money is stopped for running from

Doyler when she came at me with the razor. Pippa and me were taking the lice out of each other's hair. We caught and squashed so many lice our fingernails were red with our own blood. Gabriel said our hair was to come off but we complained that girls in school don't get their head shaved when they have lice so why should we? Doyler cut it anyway. I ask Gabriel again about joining something. After what happened to my hair I don't care, she can hit me if she wants. She doesn't. She says she'll have to see Father Devlin about things like that. He's a great man and if anyone knows such things it's Father Devlin. If he says it's safe, then we'll see.

There she goes again.

Saturday morning from my bedroom window I see Father Devlin's black station wagon park in the playground. He walks along the corridor clapping his hands and rubbing the small kids' heads. Where's Matilda? he asks because he hasn't seen me running down the stairs as he was walking past.

I'm here, Father Devlin.

By God, Matilda, look at the height you're getting. I'll have to put a book on your head.

I wonder what he'd want to put a book on anyone's head for but I don't ask because it might be a stupid question and I don't want everyone to laugh.

Will we have a little chat, Matilda?

All right, Father Devlin.

Father Devlin rubs his hands together and looks around the corridor checking for nuns because he likes to bring us to the landing on top of the stairs so he can tickle us when there're no nuns about. He sits on the floor and slaps his lap telling us to sit and I sit, even though at nine I think I'm too old for sitting on Father Devlin's lap, but priests are like nuns and you have to do what they say. And if I don't then he mightn't let me join something on the outside.

I feel his white collar biting into my neck, the roughness of his black pants on the backs of my legs. I say, Stop, because he tickles too rough. I say, Stop, like I mean it. But you always say that and you never know if you mean it or not. He grunts in my ear and says I'm a pretty girl. Stop, Father. I can smell his sweat. I can see it. It's like white rosary beads on his forehead. You're hurting me Father, let me down. His black shoes wobble on the stairs and I know he's getting tired. He stands up and wipes the sweat from his forehead with his sleeve.

Up be God, he says. You have me worn out. Wasn't that great fun altogether? Will we go downstairs to Sister Gabriel?

Yes, Father Devlin.

Father Devlin slips into the bathroom and tells me go on down. I'll be right behind you, Matilda.

Gabriel always makes tea and bakes scones for Father Devlin when he visits. She gets out her best yellow tablecloth and lays it with her best china cups. She pours Father Devlin his tea and spreads butter on his warm scones while she leaves me standing here with my tongue scraping the floor.

Do you like those scones, Father Devlin?

They are only delicious, Sister Gabriel.

He wipes the crumbs from his chin and that takes some wiping when you have a chin like Father Devlin's. He's the only person I know who has a chin wider than their forehead.

Tell me, Father, says Gabriel, have you news of that matter we discussed?

I've started an athletic club with a Mister Douglas. We'll be training Monday night at seven o'clock. How does that sound, Matilda?

Great, Father Devlin. Thanks.

Gabriel says, Now, Matilda, what do you say to Father Devlin? Isn't he wonderful?

I said, Thanks, Mother.

Well, we don't say thanks, we say, thank you. Don't we, Matilda? So I say, Thank you, Father Devlin.

Gabriel says, That's better now, and Father Devlin says, No, no, she's fine, she's fine.

I wonder why I have to say thank you to Father Devlin when in mass we say give thanks to the Lord Our God and if thanks is good enough for the Lord Our God it should be good enough for Father Devlin. Father Devlin says, Don't forget, Matilda. Monday night at the Grotto. Do you know where Our Lady's Grotto is?

Yes, Father Devlin. Thank you, Father Devlin.

If you're half as fast in a race as you are around that playground, you'll have a grand time altogether. And if any of the other kids want to come down, he says to Sister Gabriel, then the more the merrier.

Gabriel holds her hands to her flushed cheeks, Oh, Father Devlin, there's no doubt but you are a marvel. Whatever would we do without you?

Monday night, the green in front of Our Lady's Grotto is bright from the streetlights and Father Devlin is there in his black overcoat. Mister Douglas is writing kids' names in a notebook. Mister Douglas has a long thin nose like looking sideways at a coat hanger and it's like every kid from the Cork Road is hanging from it. He has thin red hair, a lighted cigarette in his hand and he doesn't look like he can run far. The other kids call him Sonny and I wish I were like kids on the outside where you call a grown man you never saw before, Sonny.

Gabriel bought me new runners. She said if I'm going to do it I might as well do it properly. They're not for kicking and climbing, they're for your running, Matilda, and I don't want to see a mark on them. I can't hand out runners right and left. It's not made of money we are. I have to budget.

The runners are smashing. White-white, and there's a lovely smell of new from the inside. I'm pure faintin'. I have my red shorts from school, a red T-shirt, and I look just like the other girls here except for the shaved-up hair and the black eye. There's a girl in a blue tracksuit with three white stripes on the side and you'd hardly get stripes like that unless you were good.

Father Devlin pulls on his cap and tells us Mister Douglas will be taking care of us. He buttons up his overcoat and leaves in his car. I wish he'd stay. Father Devlin is all right when he's not asking us to sit on his lap, but Mister Douglas is a stranger and you never know what strange men will do.

We do sit-ups, press-ups and squats on the green then go on a run out the Cork Road past the glass factory. I look back to see if Mister Douglas is following, but he's sitting on the red-brick wall outside his house talking to his chubby-cheeked wife.

Stay on the footpath, he shouts after us. Stay on the footpath.

After a month of training we're travelling on a bus to our first meet. Sunday morning there're six kids from the Holy Shepherd. I'm wearing handed-in, hand-me-down blue slacks a hundred years old and a green boy's jumper with crazy black zigzags and I'm ashamed. The other kids know I'm from the convent but I hate the world seeing I'm a Shep.

I sit at the back of the bus. I wonder why my father hasn't come home. And about my mother. Where is she now, is she thinking of us, does she miss me like I miss her?

But part of me is excited and I can barely sit still. I'm going somewhere different, seeing new things. I drift away, lost in the mountains and fields. I'm swimming in rivers and diving naked into warm blue lakes, though after a while all the rivers and mountains and lakes look just the same. There's a boy in a field flying a kite, his fingers clenched to the string. That's what I want to be. A kite. A kite without string dancing in the breeze and sun, soaring over forests and cities high up to the clouds away from the convent out over the sea to countries all over the world and never stop till I'm home in Australia where it's blue and warm and the white sand is soft beneath my toes. There's icy lemonade on the veranda and she's there in her bright white uniform like we were never gone, my Mum.

We park in a field and I change my clothes in the bus. The black eye is gone and my hair is almost to my shoulders and I look like everyone else. Mister Douglas has new red tracksuits for us. Real ones. Heavy ones. They make me feel like I'm a real runner. A real person.

The field is filled with people in boots and caps and scarves and kids in shorts and tracksuits. There are mini-buses, big buses, cars and vans parked in a line beside the ditch with their front lights facing outward. The ground is soft and the mud clings to the soles of my runners but the air is fresh and crisp and there's that sweet smell that comes after rain.

Perfect conditions, says Mister Douglas. There's not a cloud. The main thing, lads, is to enjoy it. Do yer best and don't let yourselves down.

I line up with other girls for my race and I have to bend over and put my head between my knees. That's what Mister Douglas says to do.

Relax, girl, relax, sure you'll be grand.

The man with the gun fires and scatters the birds from the trees and I know if I can stay close to the girl who had the white stripes on her tracksuit when we were training, I have a chance. The race is three miles and after two I'm ahead of the girl. She looked really good with the number on her back. I thought she had a plan but now when I glance back I see she's last. Up ahead there're girls in yellow and red and blue tops. Some are so far ahead I barely see them. I pass one girl, two girls. I'm not as nervous now and keep passing girls until there's more behind than in front but the finish is too soon and I'm only fourth but Mister Douglas says I done well.

Did I?

Yes, of course, you're in the final.

I'd like to smile but then he might think that I think I belong here when I know I don't. I turn my face away but the smile comes anyway.

The next race is for boys, then older girls, then it's my turn again. This time I go straight to the front and when I cross the finish line I'm dancing. I'm at the Olympics and the national anthem is playing while they hang my gold medal around my neck. I'm a girl floating up to Heaven on a cloud when Mister Douglas comes across to me smiling and tells me all the running will be like this. Long-distance and cross-country, if I keep it up I'll be very good. He lights a cigarette, coughs, and tells me I have great stamina. I'm eager and never give up and he likes that. I hope you don't smoke. Fags are bad for the running. And eat plenty of raw eggs.

I don't smoke anyway but I don't know where I'm going to get raw eggs. Any eggs. I couldn't tell Mister Douglas I get one egg a year, Easter Sunday. And that's hardboiled. That only the penguins, Doyler, and special visitors get eggs from the fat blue chicken in the fridge.

On the way home the bus stops outside a sweet shop and the kids from the outside go in. There're six of us from the Holy Shepherd sitting together at the back of the bus wishing we had mammies and daddies to give us money when we go away on buses. Mickey Driscoll and his sister Molly sit across from me. Their faces are blotchy like they're going to cry. Mickey won a gold medal too, but my race was over so I won first. I wouldn't tell him that though. I wonder if they'll come next week. I wonder if I'll come next week, until Mister Douglas walks back and slips us money when nobody else can see and tells us not to be shy about taking it.

Us shy? You can tell Mister Douglas never had nothing.

We snap the hand off him. Thanks, Mister Douglas.

Would you lot ever stop this Mister Douglas business and call me Sonny.

We say, Thanks, Sonny, and chase into the shop after the others and it's great to be like kids on the outside where you call a grown man, Sonny.

Gabriel is sitting in her armchair by the sitting-room fire watching Andy Williams on television, while she's embroidering one of those little white pocket-handkerchiefs I often see her with. I'm bursting to show Gabriel my gold medal with the picture of a runner wearing a red top the same as mine but she says, Sit here, Matilda, on the seat beside me, those Osmond Brothers will be on in a minute. I sit beside her and listen to Donny Osmond singing 'Puppy Love'. He's gorgeous and I'm so so gob-smacked when he's finished I have to remind myself what I came in for. I tell Gabriel I won and she says God was running with me and the Holy Spirit was giving me strength. I'm to hang my medal on the board in the kitchen with the holy medals the penguins give for our own sports day but I want to wear it around my neck like girls in school who win dancing medals. I ask Gabriel, Can I keep it for a while, Mother? She looks at me over her glasses and Gabriel has a look would strip the peel off an orange and even though you know you've done nothing wrong you just can't help wondering.

Until tomorrow, Matilda. Not a minute longer.

After school I hang my medal on the board in the corridor

and it's the first medal in the Holy Shepherd won on the outside. Gabriel comes along to check I have hung it there. She stands behind me and puts her hand on my shoulder. Well done, Matilda, she says. Well done indeed.

I don't know what to say when people say, Well done. I don't know what to do, especially now when I hear Doyler screaming from the kitchen like a woman gone mad. Gabriel rushes in and I follow. Doyler's pulling the presses open and slamming them after her, demanding to know where the eggs have gone. The room is full of kids and all of them staring at me and I say, I don't know why yee're all gawkin' at me. By Saturday there's a dozen eggs missing and Doyler sends for Reverend Mother, in case Reverend Mother thinks Doyler is taking the eggs home. She has us all in the kitchen, kids and nuns.

I don't know what's going on, Reverend Mother. There are eggs walking out of this kitchen by the dozen and of course, don't you just know, nobody here knows the first thing.

Now Doyler is gawking at me and I give my best gawk back and I know she'll think I wouldn't be brazen enough to gawk back if I had done it. Not with Reverend Mother ripping the kitchen asunder for missing eggs. Reverend Mother's eyes dart from face to face, the yellow-flecked eyes in a circle of white like two poached eggs in boiling water. I feel my cheeks burn till Gabriel's huge frame moves in front of me blocking Reverend Mother's view. Reverend Mother says she'll be keeping a sharp eye on her eggs and she'll soon discover the thief. We're sent out to the playground but from the corridor I hear Reverend Mother ask Doyler why someone would steal eggs. Are you certain the frying pan wasn't used, Missus Doyle? They're hardly eating them raw. It's only the lowest of the low or the most desperate class of a creature would eat a raw egg.

Next day I get a silver medal and a bronze medal and, by the time the parcel arrives at Christmas, the board is full of my medals.

Up in Reverend Mother's room, Uncle Edward's parcel is on the desk. Mona, Sheamie, Pippa, Danny and me stand in front of the desk. The string has been cut and the Christmas wrapping paper looks like it's been opened and wrapped up again. Reverend Mother has had a good look but she still tries to look surprised when she opens it the second time.

The parcel is packed with toys, games, new clothes and a huge sea chest stuffed with gold coins that dazzle and make us pant, but like every year we can only take one thing each. Sheamie says the coins are chocolate covered in gold paper, Not that it matters, we can't have any, can we, Reverend Mother?

No.

Sheamie smirks.

There's a blue poncho for me and that's what I take. Surely it can't be right that nuns take your Christmas presents. Especially when they came from a bishop but when I complain it's not fair Reverend Mother rants and raves.

You are a selfish girl. That box is going to the poor people who have nothing this Christmas. And you have so much. Look at what's in this box.

Pippa kicks my ankle and tells me to stop causing trouble or we'll all get kilt but Sheamie agrees it's not fair and now even Mona is complaining.

Reverend Mother says she can't have one family swanning around in new clothes while others do without. The Holy Family didn't have new clothes at Christmas. They were lucky to have a roof over their heads.

That's not our fault.

What?

Can't you buy the other kids new clothes too?

I knew before I said it I was saying the wrong thing but I couldn't stop myself.

Pippa mutters under her breath, You're for it now.

Sheamie covers his hands with his face. Danny laughs out loud. Mona didn't hear me; she's still complaining. Reverend Mother is out of her chair, a mad woman from the asylum hopping around the room chasing me with the walking stick. I keep telling her it's not fair, our Uncle Edward sent them things to us, and she keeps telling me, You'll come to no good. You're heading for the laundry, you are. She chases me till she collapses into her chair. Mona, Pippa, Sheamie and Danny are still standing at the desk. Mona is still complaining, only there's no one listening. Reverend Mother gets her breath. She puffs. Well, as it's Christmas, I'll let you have one coin each. Just the one, I said!

She slams the lid down after Danny takes his but she'll be over in the penguins' mansion Christmas night sprawled across the sofa watching Bing Crosby in *White Christmas*, stuffing her puss with Uncle Edward's chocolate.

Christmas Eve the sky flickers with stars. The air is sharp and smells of Christmas. On a radio somewhere in the darkness Louis Armstrong is singing 'What a Wonderful World'. The houses in Trinity Park shimmer with fairy lights and the frosty white roofs wait for Santa. I sit across the road from them on the stone wall. Uncle Edward's blue poncho is soft and keeps me warm. It reminds me of my mother and I wonder if the parcels really come from her.

We've got to know some of the kids from Trinity Park. The others are not let to play with us, and taunt the ones that do.

Indjun lovers.

Mothers point as we come and go and I know they say it's

sad to see those children without a mother or father. I wish I could tell them I lived in a house once, a big house up on stilts, and my mother is a nurse and she loves us and some day she'll take us home. Then they'd know I'm just like them and wouldn't tell their children to keep away.

Beneath me, people struggle up the hill, holding on to the stone wall or just falling down drunk on the footpath. Their caps, scarves and bald heads pass under my sandals and they don't even know I'm here.

I sit here when I feel sad.

Mona and Pippa came into my room this morning.

We'll go carol singing, Matilda. We'll knock on doors and see if people give us money. It's Christmas. Everyone gives money for Christmas.

The old woman in the first house we went to gave us a shilling each and after that there was no giving up, no matter how many doors were slammed in our faces. We had nearly a pound each by the time we got to this one house. I didn't know who lived there and I didn't recognize him until Pippa nudged me.

It's your godfather, Matilda.

I was so happy, I smiled up at him. I hoped he'd smile back. It was a long time since I'd seen him. I was seven and making my First Holy Communion and nobody knew for certain if I was baptized, so I was baptized in the convent chapel. The nuns had everything arranged. A teacher from the boys' school said he'd be my godfather. There we were at the altar, me in my white Communion frock holding my white rosary beads. Father Devlin in his robes with the gold cross. The altar boys in their red tunics and white lace. The nuns kneeling in their pews, the girls wearing green pixie hats kneeling in theirs. Even Sister Pascal sounded good on the organ. I was pure faintin'. A baptism is a huge thing in the convent.

The schoolteacher never turned up and I was left standing on the altar like a fool nobody wanted. Father Devlin told one of the altar boys to stand for me. He was the oldest and the tallest. He was eighteen. I didn't know what was going on when he stood beside me at the altar. I thought I was getting married until Gabriel told me he was going to be my godfather. He'll look out for you, Matilda. He'll mind you. I was happy because I had nobody to mind me.

I never saw him again until today when he opened the door. No smile and embarrassed I was there. His mother came out and stood beside him. She was a big woman in an apron and I could tell she was cooking the Christmas dinner. I could smell the turkey, and we were in her way.

Then Pippa opened her mouth. That's Matilda's godfather.

Who is? his mother said. There're no godfathers here.

She turned to my godfather and sent him inside. I never heard the like. Away from this door, the three of you, and don't come again if yee know what's good. I'll be seeing Father Devlin about this.

I felt tears coming and I felt stupid because I'd smiled up at him and I wanted to die right there on the doorstep. I swallowed my tears because I didn't want him or his mother to see me cry and it was like a lake growing in my chest. Mona stuck her tongue out and told the woman, Piss off you, yeh aul bitch, and leave Matilda alone or I'll get me father. The woman straightened her shoulders and folded her arms and dared Mona, Oh, you will, will you? And tell me now, who might your father be? Or do you know?

Mona put her head down and ran at the door. The woman stepped back and tried to close the door but Mona's forehead rattled the letterbox. The door flew open and knocked the woman back on her arse. Her legs flew in the air and we could see she was wearing thick nylon stockings and knickers thicker than a baby's nappy. Her screams brought her son running from the kitchen, but Mona had kept going and caught him with her head right between the legs. Even on the footpath I could feel the pain. Pippa sprinted out the gate and across the road to the convent. My godfather clutched himself and doubled over. His mouth opened and it was easy to see he wanted to scream but nothing came out. His cheeks went a queer colour before he dropped to his knees and keeled over on his side like a shot buffalo. Mona stepped over him and over his mother, who was trying to pull her skirt down over her knees, and all the time she was wailing, I'll get the priest for you. You haven't heard the last of this.

Shut the fuck up, said Mona.

Mona slammed the door behind her and put her arm around me.

Fuck him, Matilda. If a man can't take a good nut in the balls you don't want him for a godfather anyway.

It was the first time I knew what it was like to have a big sister and I could feel my chest swell and the tears inside me vanish like a rain puddle in the sunshine. But part of me was sad because no one had ever stood up for me before and I wondered if I might ever have that feeling again.

I sit on the stone wall until I don't feel sad anymore. Just angry. At him, his mother, at Gabriel, at Father Devlin. It doesn't last long. What's the use? I'd better go inside. Pippa is calling me to pack for our grandmother's. We're going to her for Christmas because she wouldn't have it said she didn't take her grandchildren up for holidays or the odd weekend. I don't really want to go, not that I have a choice. You'll go where you're told, Matilda. It doesn't feel normal and I wonder, do other girls do that for their uncle? But even saying it I know I will go, and I will do what he wants because he needs me and no one ever needed me.

★

Christmas morning, before our grandmother calls, the playground is cluttered with dolls, prams, bicycles, plastic tractors, roller skates and scooters. One of the big girls is getting in the back door of the nuns' car with her suitcase. I've seen girls sent away to the convent in Cork because they were stone cracked and out of control, but never on a Christmas morning.

The nuns gather everyone together in the common room and lock the doors behind us. There's a shuffle of feet as we kneel to pray the Act of Contrition for the dreadful sins committed within convent walls and I'm certain it's the usual. The mothers have come over from Trinity Park to say we're robbing their children's Christmas toys and could we please hand them back and we'll all stand there bare faced and say, Who us? Wasn't us. Someone musta thrown them toys over the wall.

But it's not over the toys at all, because now we're praying for the salvation of the soul of Patricia Dooley gone away with her suitcase. May the Lord and His Blessed Mother grant forgiveness.

Reverend Mother is at the head of the room in her white habit. She's surrounded by three other nuns standing with their heads bowed and hands clasped in front of them. Reverend Mother is giving us this one chance, only one. All I can hear are girls trying to muffle sniggers and coughing because someone coughed in the corner and when one starts everyone has to do it.

Reverend Mother says there's been carry-on under the chestnut trees. The workmen might have finished their work but the culprits will be located. She blesses herself and rolls her eyes to Heaven and the three nuns beside her follow suit. Reverend Mother points her stick towards the door to tell us Father Devlin is waiting for us over in the chapel. We're to confess we were with the workmen. We're to tell him everything we done to them and everything they done. Hold nothing back. God will know. Father Devlin will know. The Madonna will know. Save your immortal souls. Go and confess.

In the chapel, two of the big girls bawl, But we done nothin'. The foxy tinkers say, Tell Father Devlin yee weren't there den. The two girls say, The nuns told us to tell him we were.

Den tell him yee were.

But we weren't.

Ah, tell him yee had a great time anyway, fuckin' eejits. It's only sex. What's he gonna do?

Lucy Flynn and me are kneeling in the pew behind them biting our tongues and hiding our faces behind our green pixie hats. It's great the way the tinkers keep thumping the two big girls on the head.

When the big girls finish, it's our turn. The confession box has a dry smell and there's a hollow sound when I kneel. There's a crucifix on the wall and a dim light over my head. Father Devlin sits behind the screen, breathing heavy.

Do you know why you are here, Matilda?

The nuns told me to come, Father.

Yes, yes. But do you know why they sent you?

No, Father Devlin.

Any idea at all now, Matilda.

Is it, ah, is it over sex, Father?

That's right, and can you tell me now, Matilda, what is sex?

No, Father.

And what do you think it might be?

I don't know, Father. I just heard the big girls say it.

Try now, Matilda. Think hard.

Is it, is it, ah . . .

Yes, Matilda?

Is it, ah, is it kissing, Father Devlin?

It's a little more than that now, Matilda.

Is it, ah . . .

Yes, yes, go on.

Is it what we do, Father Devlin?

What?

You know when I sit on your lap and you tickle me. Is that sex, Father Devlin?. . . Father Devlin? . . . Father Devlin, are you all right?

Father Devlin is choking behind the screen. He tells me, No, Matilda, no, no. That's a different thing altogether. That's just being friendly. Do you understand the difference, Matilda?

I say, Yes, Father Devlin, even though I don't understand anything.

You must never say that to anyone, Matilda. So you won't now?

I won't, Father Devlin.

Thank God, I mean, good girl, good girl yourself. You can go now so. Remember what I said, won't you, Matilda?

Ah, have I penance, Father?

What? Oh, ah, penance, right. Ah, no, no. Not today, Matilda.

Thank you, Father Devlin.

We come back from our grandmother's the Saturday after Christmas. Father Devlin is in the playground. He hands me a brown paper bag.

Remember what I said, Matilda. Won't you?

I will, Father Devlin.

Sure, you're a great girl. I'll have to put a book on your head and that's all there is to it.

I go to my room and walk around with a book on my head. A thick geography one with floppy covers but it keeps falling on the floor. If I stand still it stays on my head for longer but nothing ever happens. It's just stupid.

I open the brown paper bag full of hard round gobstoppers, reds, greens and blues. I lie on my bed with my feet on the pillow and stare up at the ceiling. I suck and think. I think about why Father Devlin wants to put a book on my head. About the big girls screaming in the toilets. Uncle Philip bringing me upstairs. Sitting on Father Devlin's lap. The big girls sneaking down to the toilets. Patricia Dooley going away with her suitcase. I think when I go to bed, when I go to mass, school, sit on the swings, on the bus and when I'm running.

One summer morning when I'm ten I wake up drenched. Sweat on my face, arms, legs, and bed sheets. I can feel my heart beating against my ribs and it's hard to catch my breath. I know why Father Devlin wants to put a book on my head. At last I think I understand why our grandmother sent us away.

8

Gabriel marches the girls in our group to the church and tells us Reverend Mother has decided we've had too much freedom. The female body is the temple of temptation and can only be saved by prayer. We are to say our prayers and be good Catholics for aren't we Irish and always remember it was the Irish who gave Catholicism to the world. You've made your First Holy Communion, Matilda. You've made your Holy Confirmation. You are a Soldier of Christ.

There are groans all round the chapel but Gabriel waves us away and every Friday us Soldiers of Christ are brought to the chapel for the Stations of the Cross and to listen to Gabriel tell us any time we feel like complaining all we need do is look up there on the wall at Jesus struggling up Mt Calvary with that cross on his back and that will stop our complaining.

We stop at every picture in the chapel and say a decade of the rosary. We pray to all the statues and on the way out we kneel to St Joseph. He wears a brown robe and has a curly beard like a bunch of grapes stuck to his chin. Gabriel tells us to pray to the Blessed Virgin Mary who in turn will intercede on our behalf to her son Jesus who in turn will intercede to God the Father, and on a stifling day in July the chapel is hotter than Hell and, even though it's a sin to say it, the whole thing would bore the arse off you.

Out in the playground I'm covered in sweat and I'm sore from kneeling and bowing and standing and genuflecting and I'm wondering what to do next. It must be at least an hour before the rosary. Mona and me sit on the low red-brick wall outside the door of our group watching the willy-wagtails dance along the roof of the green sheds while we wait for our skin to cool. Mona asks me keep an eye out while she opens the top three buttons of her blouse so she'll get a colour on her chest.

You'd want some sun for that chest, Mona.

She didn't hear me. I'm sitting on her deaf side. She flattens her curly black hair back from her face and lies back as far as she can to catch the sun. She holds her legs out straight and pulls her skirt up over her knees. Birds warble above our heads and the light breeze blowing from the nuns' garden carries the sweet smell of flowers. I watch around the playground for nuns but there's only kids playing on swings and the boys playing soccer using the broken gate on the green shed as a goal.

A blue car roaring like a tank comes around the corner by the fire escape. It's so loud I expect to see a soldier's head sticking out the top. It drives in circles around the playground with a stampede of kids screaming after it.

Gis a spin, mister, gis a spin.

A big girl comes running across to Mona and me pulling at her hair and bawling, It's him, it's him, it's really him. Mona and me look at each other then back at the girl, still pulling out her hair. Mona sits up properly on the wall.

It's who? she says.

John Lennon. John Lennon is after comin' teh see us.

Who? says Mona.

John Lennon.

That's my father, says Mona.

John Lennon is yeer father, Mona?

Shut the fuck up, yeh dope, says Mona.

He parks by the green shed and steps out rolling up his shirtsleeves. His hair and beard are still long and all he needs are those little round glasses and he'd really look like John Lennon. Without them he looks more like Jesus himself. He's wearing Moses sandals, no socks, and he's striding across the playground towards us and I just sit here because when you haven't had a father from seven to ten you wonder if he's your father anymore.

Part of me wonders is he better now and if he's taking us out of the convent. It's not too late to be a family. I know he hasn't found Mum. I'd feel it if he did. Part of me is embarrassed because I don't know what to say to him. He's halfway across the playground now with a gang of kids swinging from his huge arms and trying to jump up on his broad back. He lifts them in the air and swings them around then puts them down and picks up another one.

I turn my eyes down and look at the cracks in the playground. But when I expect him to finally reach us and be beside me and he's not, I worry he's passed by and didn't know me.

I look up and he's sitting a little away from me on the bottom step of the fire escape with Danny on his lap. Sheamie is sitting sideways on the step above them with the sun glistening off his glasses. I don't think Danny knew it was our father when he sat on his lap. Pippa sits on the wall beside Mona and me and I know she's nervous too, the way she keeps tidying her blonde hair and straightening the hem of her frock in line with her knees. Pippa looks at me with her blue eyes as if to ask, What do we do? I just shrug my shoulders.

Gabriel comes to the door to see what the fuss is. Mona nearly shits herself and hurries to close her buttons. She gets away with it because when Gabriel sees my father her eyes roll under her eyelids and she murmurs, Oh, my, like she's remembering the last time she saw him and she's wondering what she's going to say if he starts asking why she still hasn't found a good man for herself. Any man.

My father comes across and bends down for Pippa and me to kiss his cheek, as if he's seen us only yesterday. Mona's cheeks blush when he puts his arms around her waist and bends to kiss her on the forehead. He says he'll be back in a moment and goes inside to talk to Gabriel. We don't know what to think until Gabriel and my father come back out smiling and chatting at the doorway, my father telling Gabriel how he met a man in hospital . . .

Hospital? What sort of hospital? says Gabriel.

Daddy doesn't say. He just carries on about the man he met who showed him where he was going astray with his life. A man who showed him how to put the past behind him and move on. How he reads the Bible and understands Jesus' message. He can even understand Gabriel being a nun even if he's not Catholic himself. That stops Gabriel smiling.

You're not?

She looks down at Mona, Pippa and me, then over at Sheamie and Danny. One of her eyebrows lifts and the corner of her mouth follows, like they're joined by a piece of string. She looks confused. Maybe she's wondering if we've had enough prayers yet to be protected. I'm confused too. I never knew you could be anything else if you were Irish. I thought Catholic and Irish were the same thing.

My father looks out to the playground over the heads of all the kids and talks in a voice I haven't heard him use before. It's calm and sweet and you can't help but listen.

Most assuredly, I tell you, unless one is born again, that person can't see the kingdom of God. Isn't that right, Sister?

Gabriel looks up at him out the corner of her eye, then looks away. Oh, well, she says, as if she's happy that's the end of that particular conversation. She sits on the wall beside us and puts her hand on Mona's knee. She says, You must be delighted to have your father home, Mona. He tells me he's here for summer and he's taking you all out for a spin in the car. Isn't that only fabulous?

Yes, Mother.

And fix your buttons, Mona. You've got them in the wrong holes.

Yes, Mother.

There's a gang of kids standing around gawking and I know they're going mad they haven't a father with a car, a father who can stand up straight.

I run upstairs for my poncho and when I come back my brothers and sisters are already in the car. Mona is in the front seat beside my father. Sheamie, Pippa and Danny are jumping up and down in the back seat delighted to be getting out of the convent. I squeeze in the back beside Pippa. The car is old and you can see the hair-oil stains on the cloth above my father's head and there's a hole in the floor that I can see the road through and smell the fumes from the exhaust. My father wonders if we missed him and we tell him we did. Are we doing well in school?

We all say, Yes, Daddy, even though I never heard of anyone from the convent doing well in school. So long as you can write your name and answer the roll-call every morning, the teachers are happy with that.

I hope yee're not telling lies. I'll find out.

We look at each other before we all lie together. We're not, Daddy.

We drive through town then across the bridge over the River Suir towards the railway station then turn left and travel miles into the countryside. The roads are narrow and we pass men with sticks hunting sheep along the road and when the car slows the sheep gather round us and stick their black faces to the glass and say, Baa.

We stop at a village where there's a shop and people coming out the chapel from evening mass. The men pull their caps from their pockets and fix them on their heads and the women take off their scarves to put into their handbags and all of them blink when they walk out into the sunshine.

My father parks at the shop. There are jars of sweets in the window and I feel my mouth water from tiny springs at the back of my throat. I can taste liquorice already but my father says no. He has food we don't yet know about.

We walk past the shop and stand on the steps of the chapel under the white statue of Jesus with his hands held out in front like he's asking us to go inside. Daddy tells us to gather around and when we do he asks, Why are statues of God always of a good-looking man? We look at each other and shrug our shoulders.

Well, answer me.

Sheamie takes his glasses off and squints up at the statue like some kind of professor.

Because that's what Jesus looks like, Daddy.

God could have been ugly, Sheamie. God could have been a snake or a bird a cat or a dog. Couldn't he?

No.

What do you mean, no?

I mean, that's Jesus up there.

That's not Jesus, Sheamie.

It's not?

That's a big white stone.

But it's still Jesus though. Everyone knows what Jesus looks like.

My father puts his hand on Sheamie's shoulder and tells us it's not Sheamie's fault. The nuns have our minds corrupted and that's one of the reasons he's here. God has spoken to him and given him a mission. To spread His Word and bring people the Truth.

Pippa and Mona have moved to the third step by now so they're a few feet from us. Pippa looks puzzled. Her bright blue eyes keep looking from the statue to my father. I go and stand between them. Sheamie would like to move away too, but my father's hand is on his shoulder and Sheamie isn't going anywhere. Danny is looking up at the statue like he's trying to figure it out but Danny is only eight and you can't figure anything out when you're eight. You're six before you can tie your shoelaces properly.

My father makes the five of us line up on the step facing Jesus and he stands on the step above us, so now we're facing him as well. I feel like we're having our photograph taken. I can see it in my mind. Mona's at the edge, her curly black hair almost to her shoulders. She's wearing a white blouse with the top button open. Her arms folded under her chest. You can see the shape of her bra. She has a pair of black slacks covering her long legs and a pair of green sandals, the ones with the silver buckle that you strap at your ankle. The straps are frayed and she's not wearing socks. Sheamie is standing beside her with his hands behind his back dressed in brown corduroy pants with holes in the knees. Next Pippa, in a dress with a flowery pattern and a white cardigan with the sleeves rolled up to her elbows because the cardigan's elbows are frayed. I'm next, in the blue poncho. Then Danny with his black hair cut in a fringe, brown eyes and scruffy white runners with little laces.

My father is in front of us with the sun shining behind his head like a halo. I can feel the sun's heat on my face. I'm wearing jeans and the sweat runs down my legs. My father swings his arm towards the statue and tells us Jesus is not in lumps of stone. Jesus is in the air and the trees. Jesus is all around us. Jesus is not a lump of rock. Jesus is life itself.

By now the words are flowing from him like water gushing from a fountain. His face is glowing, his hands are waving. It's like he's someplace else altogether. Like he knows everything there is to know. The nuns never told us anything like this and what nuns don't know about Jesus isn't worth knowing. But not even nuns know everything, that's why they have Sacred Mysteries. Anytime something doesn't make sense it's called a Mystery and only God himself understands. There are no mysteries with my father because now he's telling us the Lord saved him from sin. Yes, he was a bad man, yes, he did go astray but the Lord saved his life for a special purpose and he must repay the Lord and where better place to start than with his own children. Don't let me catch yee praying to statues.

Mona says, We have to, Daddy. The nuns will kill us if we don't. They have us doing extra Stations of the Cross and everything.

The Lord, Mona. Pray directly to Our Saviour. I'll sort out the nuns. I won't have my children worshipping false Gods.

I think that might be a good thing but I'm not sure.

An old woman clutching rosary beads comes from the chapel and dips her fingers in the big concrete holy water font by the door. When she walks down the steps towards us Daddy asks her why was she in there praying to statues? The old woman looks my father up and down, then at the five of us. She blesses herself with the sign of the cross and hurries away down the street. I start down the steps towards the footpath, 'cos I'm certain my father's after losing it altogether this time, but he grabs me by the arm and tells the five of us to follow him. We're going inside.

The chapel has a sweet smell of incense and is so silent I hear the candles burn under St Joseph in his brown robe and no beard. The Virgin Mary is kneeling under Jesus nailed to the cross, the blood dripping from the Crown of Thorns. I know he's in pain but I'm angry because God has a mother who weeps and kneels while he gave me no mother at all.

Daddy lets my arm go and we follow him down the aisle

in his Moses sandals past the tired old man kneeling in the back pew with his cap in his hand. My father leads us up the aisle under the stained-glass windows with all the saints in Heaven watching us.

My father tells us that the Catholic church is the instrument of Satan. The priests and nuns are the Devil's own henchmen. Danny asks what henchmen are and Daddy tells him shut up and listen. He'll learn more if he listens.

There's a priest on the altar cleaning the chalice with a white cloth. Daddy stands in front of the altar rail. He points his arm around the chapel to all the statues like he's pointing a rifle. He warns us, in a voice that seems a hundred times louder in the chapel, never to pray to false gods. Pray only to Our Lord.

The priest rushes from the altar. You can hear his footsteps across the marble floor. He has white hair and a white collar and he wears glasses. He tells Daddy to show respect. This is the Lord's House. Daddy tells him he should have every statue down and smashed with hammers. He'd be only too pleased to help.

The priest looks down at Mona, Sheamie, Pippa, Danny and me. He lifts his glass over his forehead and asks Daddy if we're his children. Daddy tells him our mother left and the nuns are rearing us and he's not happy with the notions they're putting in our heads.

Notions? says the priest.

Corrupting their minds with Hell. Frightening them with a vengeful God. God is Just. There's no Hell in the true Bible. It's a Catholic invention to control poor ignorant people and keep the power and the money for themselves. Daddy kneels before the altar with his hands clasped out in front. Look at this, look how they have my children. Praying to that. A great lump of rock.

The priest says, Good God, man, have you no shame? Leave this chapel or I'll call the gardaí.

Daddy's laugh echoes around the church and the priest is worried. His eyes dart around the chapel searching for more like us. He says we have to leave. Daddy stands up and pushes his face close to the priest's and sneers. You hide behind the law of man yet profess to follow the law of God. You're a disgrace. An insult to Our Lord and a betrayer of truth.

I'm sorry. You'll have to leave.

My father turns to us and tells us, See, this is the condemnation, that light has come into the world, but people sincerely loved darkness rather than light because their deeds were evil.

Now he points a wagging finger at the priest and his voice is breathing fire.

Everyone who practises evil hates the light, and doesn't come to the light for fear that their deeds will be exposed. Whoever practises the truth comes to the light to show clearly that their deeds have been done with God.

The priest lowers his head and kicks at the floor like he's trying to poke a hole in it with the toe of his shoe. You can see he's trying to think up something to say. Something that will get my father out of here and keep himself in one piece. Danny sits down in the pew, then the rest of us sit in beside him. It's as if the row is between my father and the priest. It's between grown-ups and it's nothing to do with us, though anyone looking at the way the five of us hang our heads would know we're mortified.

The priest puts his hands in his pockets and says there are many roads to paradise. He's happy my father has found God but he really has to lock up. He puts his glasses in his top pocket and follows us to the door and smiles down when he sees me dipping my fingers in the holy water font. I'm ashamed for my father making a show of us. My father shoves me away and roars in my face. It's water, Matilda. Just water. There's nothing holy about it. He dips his hand in the font and splashes the priest till water drips from the priest's nose then he turns and walks outside into the light and saunters down the steps with his hands behind his back like he's strolling along the beach in Galilee.

The priest makes the sign of the cross over us and says he'll pray for us. We turn our faces away and mumble, Thank you, Father. The priest closes the doors behind us and slams the bolts across, leaving the old man in the pew to find his own way out.

He's what?

Pentecostal, Mother.

Oh my.

Gabriel is sitting at the kitchen table embroidering one of those pocket-handkerchiefs and says she'd better send for Reverend Mother. She can handle the drunks falling in here but she's never heard of a Pentecostal. What is it exactly, Sheamie?

Sheamie straightens his glasses. I don't know, Mother.

Reverend Mother doesn't know either but she's certain it's some class of a heathen and what would you expect from a man who doesn't show his face for four years even to visit his poor mother. She says one thing is for certain, while we're under her roof we'll do as she says and that's all there is to it.

My father stays for the summer and each day he calls to the convent there's an argument with Gabriel over God and our education. We're backward and stupid. We know nothing about the outside world. He wants us to have office jobs when we're older so we can support him in his old age and for that we need education. He makes us sit in a circle in the playground and Mona has to ask us our spellings, but I don't want to think about that now because some days he is good to us. He brings us to town and buys clothes and sweets and gives us money. He even bought us black jumpers with a big red letter G on the front. Reverend Mother had a fit because she thought we were taking God's name in vain till we told her the G was for Gilbert O'Sullivan who is from the Cork Road. I knew she still wanted to take them but she's having enough trouble with my father without fighting over jumpers.

Gabriel never knows what to say to my father. She just stands as far back from him as she can. Some days she sends for Father Devlin but Father Devlin can't handle him. By the time my father goes back to London in September I'm so pissed off with penguins screaming in one ear and my father screaming in the other and making a show of us in chapels I don't know what to think anymore. It seems like everyone is trying to save us. Father Devlin wants to save us from sin. The nuns want to save us from my father. My father wants to save us from the nuns. And all the time we're stuck in the convent.

Sometimes I sit on my own in the green shed and wonder if any of my life is real or is God just testing me. I wonder if the people around me exist when I don't see them and where do they go? Do they just vanish like my mother? Are my brothers and sisters really my brothers and sisters? Do they feel like I feel? Hurt like I hurt? Cry like I cry? When they laugh, do they feel the same way I do when I laugh?

Thinking about it gives me a headache. It's too big for me. It's like trying to think about algebra. Sometimes I think God is like Santa Claus. There's a different one in every shop and none of them ever comes to the convent.

Halloween night, my belly is stuffed with apples and nuts and Pippa gives my shoulder a shake in the bed. Come on, Matilda.

We'll sneak over to Trinity Park to play spin the bottle. You can see her blue eyes twinkle in the moonlight and I know she's excited.

Since when did you start kissin', Pippa?

Never mind.

Come on tell us.

I went with Mona a few times.

Why don't you go with her now, then?

I don't know where she is.

Well, tough. You're not usin' me just 'cos Mona isn't here.

Pippa doesn't answer. She ties her blonde hair in a ponytail and pulls the blankets off me but I tell her I'm asleep and I don't want to go spinning stupid bottles and kissing stupid youngfellas with spotty faces tryin' to put their hands up me jumper.

They won't try puttin' their hands up your jumper, Matilda, 'cos there's fuck all up there. Ah, come on girl, it's only kissin'. Just don't let 'em put their tongue in your mouth. 'Cos I told you already, that's how you get babies.

Don't be so stupid, Pippa. I seen the girls down in the toilets bent over the toilet bowl with their knickers around the ankles and the workmen queuing up outside the door.

Liar.

Suit yourself.

Pippa doesn't want to hear anymore. She just wants to go over to Trinity Park. I pull the blankets over my head again but she still torments me. Come on, Matilda. Don't be a scaredy cat. You have to do it sometime.

I'm not going.

Scaredy cat.

Don't care, I'm not going.

Scaredy cat.

All right. I'll go.

I climb out of bed, get dressed and we creep down the corridor. From the bathroom window we can see bonfires lit all over the city. We climb out the window. A few windows further on the girls from the group next door are swinging from bed sheets tied to the heating pipes. We shin down the drainpipe and climb out over the wall just as the fire truck roars past with its blue light flashing and bells ringing. Across the street, under the yellow light of a lamp pole, a gang of boys and girls from the estate are puffing cheap Albanys they bought in Kennedy's shop after one of them asked a passing grown-up, Hey, Mister, will yeh get us five fags? Some do, others say, Piss off, yeh little bollox.

A boy in a tartan jacket offers me a drag. Pippa says, Go on, Matilda, but I won't because of the running and Pippa doesn't push it. She knows it's a waste of time.

Young kids in masks and costumes go from door to door collecting money and slowly our group moves from the lamp pole and heads for the field behind the houses. There're about ten of us. We strike matches till we get to the top of the lane. The iron gate is cold and rattles under us when we climb and once we're in the field we stand and wait for the light of the moon to come from behind the clouds to show the way to the chapel ruin where the grown-ups can't see us. A dog howls.

I'm goin' back, Pippa.

It's only a dog, Matilda.

I know it's a dog. I'm not deaf. You're mixin' me up with Mona.

Very funny, says Pippa.

Yeah, well you asked for it.

Would you two ever shut the fuck up!

Mind your own business.

The damp from the grass seeps through our sandals and

when we get to the ruin we sit in a circle around a small fire we light from bits of twigs and papers we find.

The empty milk bottle spins and clinks on the concrete floor and I want to go home again but the bottle is slowing. It passes Pippa, her blue eyes glowing in the firelight. Slower again, passing the girl with the ponytail. It rattles a bit, then stops, pointing to me.

I have to kiss George O'Brien. His mother scalps him to save money on haircuts so he wears a wool hat with a pom-pom and he's the spottiest youngfella in Trinity Park. No, the world. He's thirteen and I wonder if you can kiss a boy who's thirteen when you're only ten.

Pippa is laughing her head off telling me, Go on, Matilda.

I'm not kissin' him, Pippa. Fuck that. Take that mask offa your head, boy.

I'm not wearin' a mask, Matilda.

Could a fooled me.

Everyone shouts, Go on, Matilda. My face is on fire. I lean forward and a tongue rushes at me from the firelight.

Put that tongue back in your head, boy. I'm warnin' yeh.

Scaredy cat, scaredy cat.

Pippa says, Thought you said nothing could happen to you over tongues, Matilda.

Something'll happen to him if he doesn't put it back in his gob.

The tongue goes back in his mouth and I lean forward. I close my eyes and my mouth. I feel him close. I hear him breathe. His lips touch mine. They're soft, warm, minty. It only lasts a second. I'd a done it for longer.

9

We've just got back from Christmas in our grandmother's house when a black car with white tyres, a real oldie like you see in gangster films, parks in the green shed beside the nuns' blue mini-bus. A purple-faced man carrying a brown leather briefcase steps out and looks down, checking his shoes haven't been dirtied. He's dressed in a blue suit and blue tie over a yellow shirt and he's wearing gold glasses. Nobody runs over. He doesn't look like the kind of man you run over to. He stands there for a minute watching us play ball, then walks past us and goes inside to the convent. I see him again in the evening walking around the playground with Reverend Mother and Reverend Mother doesn't come to the playground unless there's something big going on.

We're all trying to find out who he is but Gabriel won't say and you'd never know where you'd meet him. At the back of the chapel in mass, walking down a corridor, peeking out a window at us in the playground and then writing stuff into a notebook. I'm certain he's a spy only I don't know who'd be spying on us. The big girls say he's from the lunatic asylum. I don't know what's going on. Every night at bedtime we gather round Gabriel in the corridor and it takes days for her to give in. She's not getting out of here until she does. Even the toddlers are pulling at her black skirts, though they haven't a clue what's going on, but if it's something we want to know then it's something they want to know too, because you can't have secrets in here, even from toddlers. Gabriel tells us the

Purple-Faced man will be here for a week and each of us will see him in her office, separately.

We complain. No way, Mother, you're not puttin' us in a room with a looneytoon.

Stop that silly talk. Mister O'Donovan is a respectable man. Saturday morning, leave your clothes in the kitchen and be ready when you're called.

You mean all our clothes, Mother?

Down to your underwear.

I am scared. I don't want to be in a room alone with a stranger, even if he's not a lunatic.

Saturday morning, I'm sitting at the kitchen table with Lucy, Pippa and Holly Green from the group next door. My jeans are fired over the back of the chair I'm sitting on. There's a pound note in the back pocket that Uncle Philip slipped me getting out of the car when nobody was looking. I wasn't going to take it.

The room smells of washing-up liquid from Doyler clanking cups in the sink. We're wearing knickers and vests, except Pippa, who's wearing a trainer bra and a smile, but she loses the smile when four big girls shout in the window that he's a dirty bastard and he'll make us take our knickers off. Doyler fires her tea towel at the glass.

I hear yee over there. I know what yee're up to.

Pippa asks, Will he Doyler?

Doyler bends to pick her tea towel off the floor. What's that, Pippa?

Make us?

Make you? Make you what? If those girls try making you do anything you tell me.

Not them, Doyler. *Him*.

Yes, Pippa, it would be a sin.

Pippa coughs. The pink going from her cheeks and that

124

grey look she gets when her asthma comes on. Gabriel glides in from the corridor clapping her hands and tells us to wait outside her office. I don't know what to do with the pound. I can't leave it in my pocket or it'll be robbed, or, worse, Gabriel might find it and ask how I got it and why didn't your brothers and sisters get a pound too? Are you doing something you shouldn't be doing? Can you answer me that, Matilda?

Lucy is first in and I lean against the wall with Pippa and Holly Green. Holly is about twelve. I don't really know her that much apart from the playground. She's small and wide and when she walks her knees don't bend. Her arms don't bend much either. She always reminds me of Tin Man in *The Wizard of Oz*. I had a fight with her once but I can't remember why. I think it was just because she was in the group next door and we had nothing better to do. She's making faces at me and if she doesn't stop she'll be in another fight. Gabriel comes out from her office and sits in the chair in the bay window clacking her rosary beads and mumbling her prayers. The watery sunlight comes through the glass and it's like she's sitting in a grotto. The big girls at the window behind her make faces, trying to worry us over knickers. Pippa is behind me snapping her bra straps and there's a worried look on her face. I'd ask Gabriel if we really have to take our knickers off but she'd box me on the head for interrupting the Sacred Mysteries. There's nothing to do but wait and worry until Lucy comes out and Gabriel brings Holly Green into her office. Pippa and me gather round Lucy.

What'd he do to you, Lucy? Pippa asks.

I had to put somethin' in a hole.

That finishes Pippa. She collapses against the wall, clasping her throat and trying to breathe. Lucy runs away down the hall. I want to run for help but Gabriel comes out of her office with Holly Green and the Purple-Faced man. He takes one look at Pippa and tells Gabriel that Pippa is to go straight to the Infirmary. Gabriel brings Pippa down the corridor to find a nun to take Pippa to the Infirmary in the mini-bus and the Purple-Faced man goes back into the office and closes the door. I grab Holly by the arm.

What'd he do to you?

She sticks her tongue out and tells me to mind my own business.

Make me.

She tries to pull her arm away and I tell her I'm not messing.

So?

She knows I won't fight in here. You'd never know who'd turn up when there's nobody to do look-out.

Your father's an alco, Holly Green.

You can't be talking about fathers. At least you don't see my father in here killin' us over spellin's and shit.

He would if he could get up offa the footpath.

It doesn't matter what I say. She has it over me. I let her go because I don't want her to know how scared I am of the Purple-Faced man. She pulls her arm away like she made me leave her go. People are fuckers when they have it over you.

Gabriel comes back and sends Holly down to the kitchen to get dressed and go back to her own group and sends me inside.

The Purple-Faced man is sitting at the polished table reading one of my school copybooks. He has a thing around his neck for listening to my heart but I'm certain he can hear it hammering away in my chest.

I stand in front of him with my arms folded and my legs crossed and Uncle Philip's pound note clenched in my fist. I look over my shoulder. The key is in the lock. Gabriel never leaves the key in the lock! He points to the empty chair in the corner and tells me to sit. I sit facing him and feel my arse clench on the edge of the plastic seat. He stands up and walks towards me and tells me to lift my vest. I keep my eyes to the floor. He lifts it himself. His hands are cold and I grip the sides of my knickers. The drapes are open and a sunbeam lights up the face of the Blessed Virgin Mary praying in the opposite corner.

Breathe in.

Hail Mary full of grace the Lord is with thee blessed art thou amongst women and blessed is the fruit . . .

Breathe out.

. . . Holy Mary Mother of God pray . . .

In again. No, in, I said.

. . . now and at the hour of our death.

And out.

He spreads wooden bricks on the round table, squares, rectangles, triangles and circles.

I'd like you to fit these bricks to the matching shapes on the board here on the table, Matilda.

He takes a stopwatch from his trouser pocket and sits back in his chair looking at it. I won't get off the seat. The minute I touch those bricks he's bound to see the pound note in my hand. He'd ask where I got it. He'd be on to me. I try not to look at the watch. He wants to hypnotize me so I'll tell him everything. I saw it on television.

Come on, Matilda. I don't have all day. There's nothing to be frightened of. Is there anything on your mind? Anything I should know. Have you problems?

Problems? I'm living in here and he's asking me stupid questions like that.

He leans forward on his elbows and I feel the cheeks of my arse stick to the plastic seat and every time I move it's like pulling off a sticking plaster that's been there for a month. I turn my face one way but my eyes glance the other, towards him. He still has the stopwatch in his hand waiting for me to either put the bricks in the hole or talk to him, but I can't talk. My mind is blank. You can't talk to grown-ups. No matter what you tell them it's never enough. Sooner or later I'd end up telling him about Uncle Philip and then I'd really be in trouble. I'd be sent to a reformatory school or out on the street with no place to go.

The Purple-Faced man leaves the stopwatch on the table and writes something in his notebook that's on the desk and tells me to go. Send in Sister Gabriel.

I wait in the hallway on my own until Gabriel comes out. I'm shaking and my legs are stiff and sore. Through the window I see Pippa being driven away in the mini-bus and a crowd of kids tearing after it. When Gabriel comes out she looks disappointed. She didn't expect that. It was only a few bricks, Matilda. Mister O'Donovan is concerned. Your father will have to be told. It'll be up to him to have the final say.

What's my father got to do with it, Mother?

She looks down at me like she's waiting for me to say why I didn't put the bricks in the hole. She looks serious. But the pound is sticking to my palm and I just want to go.

Can I go out to play now, Mother?

She says I might as well.

In a few days the Purple-Faced man leaves. He's left tablets behind and every morning we queue by the kitchen sink so Doyler can check we swallow them. In a week the whole convent has gone quiet. Mona hasn't thrown a tantrum or there hasn't been a fight. I'm sure it's the tablets. They're trying to poison us. Kill us off because nobody cares if we're alive or dead anyway. Every morning at breakfast I put the blue pill under my tongue and when Doyler squints inside my mouth she says, Good girl. We all do the same. Pippa is useless at pretending so she swallows it whole but she's able to bring it back up again, still dry, no missing bits or anything. We flush them down the toilet until Sheamie says he can get twenty pence each for them in the boys' school. He can save to go find our mother.

Twenty pence. That's the new money. Sheamie says it's because we joined Europe. I know nothing about Europe and Sheamie don't know much more.

In a few weeks everything goes back to normal. Mona throws her tantrums, there're loads of fights in the playground and Sheamie is saving for his escape. In a year he'll be fourteen. He'll have enough to go to England where nobody knows or cares where you came from and he'll get a job on a building site where he'll save to go to Australia to find our mother in no time. She's the only one who can get us out of here. I tell him don't be stupid, Sheamie. The gardaí will find you. But he takes no notice. I want to tell him he shouldn't have to look for our mother she should just come back to look for us. Only I don't have the heart to tell him. I'm not even sure I mean it. It's just that I don't want him to leave. I don't want to lose a brother as well.

Holly Green is standing in front of me at Communion and her head is shaking. Like I said, Holly is in Sister Ellen's group so maybe she shakes her head all the time. Sister Pascal is playing the organ like she's Vincent Price in a habit, and the penguins and the laundry women have received their host and are either kneeling in their pews or walking from the altar rail with their hands clasped and heads bowed. I kneel at the altar and watch Father Devlin walking along the rail giving out the host.

Body of Christ.

Amen.

It's nearly my turn when Holly, who's just received her host, jumps up screaming. There's a mouse, look, a mouse.

There he is. Get him. None of us can see a mouse and, even if we could, we couldn't run or scream because we're in chapel and, mouse or no mouse, we finish Communion and the penguins will sort the mouse out later. Two nuns grab Holly by the arms and drag her up the aisle trying to get her outside.

Mouse!

Come along, Holly. Come along.

Mouse!

I wonder why Holly's gone mental. And at Communion of all times. We stopped taking the tablets. Maybe they're putting it in something else? Maybe they're putting it in the host. That's it. They haven't poisoned us with the tablets so now they're putting it in the host.

Father Devlin is standing in front of me with the chalice in one hand and the Body of Christ in the other.

Body of Christ, he says.

Mouse!

I don't want to take the Body of Christ. I don't want to die before I see my mother again. I don't want to end up in the asylum and come back with my jaw wobbly and eyeballs fluttering. I have to do something, but Father Devlin forces the host past my lips before I get the chance to think. It feels round and dry in my mouth. I try to wriggle it under my tongue but I can't let it touch my teeth because that's a mortal sin. I turn from the altar trying to look calm and holy walking back to my seat while all the time I'm begging, Please, God, don't break up.

I get to my pew. I can move God a little with the tip of my tongue. God is loose enough to get my tongue under but He's going to touch my teeth. Just a little, but a little is enough, now there's a mortal sin on my soul but I can't say it in confession because I can't tell Father Devlin, I know you're trying to poison me with the host.

Things are worse. I have to get God out before he melts. I'm not supposed to touch it with my hand but what can I do? I glance around to make sure nobody is watching. Everyone is kneeling, heads bowed. I think Holly is outside someplace. The organ has stopped playing. I cover my mouth and spit God into my hand and make a fist around it and there's two mortal sins on my soul but I burn for eternity with one so one more doesn't really matter.

Now what do I do? I can't drop God on the floor because the penguins will find Him and they'll get the bishop up to bless and lick the floor and there'll be no end to the masses, rosaries, benedictions, retreats and penance begging forgiveness for the Body of Christ being left on the floor where anyone can walk on it and carry it on their shoe. I'll put it in my pocket and do something later, only nobody ever said what to do with God when He's in your pocket. I kneel to pray but I feel like a sinner. I've got two mortal sins and I haven't even left the chapel. Maybe I should pray but I don't know how to ask God how to get his body out of my pocket and anyway I don't think God listens to someone with two mortal sins and then tells them how to commit a third.

After mass the men in white coats come to take Holly away. Holly screaming, Mouse! The men whispering, Shush.

A week later I still don't know what to do with all these Bodies of Christ I'm collecting every morning. I can't ask Mona. Not with the way she comes down to breakfast every morning with a face like a wet week telling anyone who'll listen she's on withdrawal.

A big girl at the table says, That don't work, Mona. Me older sister tried that and now she has twins.

Sheamie has his problems too. He says he's owed a fortune in the boys' school but the boys up there haven't a tosser between them. He should have more than fifty pounds saved by now but he's only got six pounds fifty pence and, to make things worse, the headmaster is suspicious.

Gabriel brings our group in the mini-bus to see Holly in the Red Brick. That's what everyone calls the asylum. The Red Brick. There's never room in the mini-bus for everyone. No matter how much we squeeze there's always someone's foot buried in someone else's jaw. We can see Gabriel's bushy black eyebrows in the rear-view mirror when she shouts from the front seat.

Quiet back there, into your seats.

I can't, Mother. Molly Driscoll's fat fuckin' arse is taking up the whole place.

Who said that? Who's swearing back there?

Nobody.

Is that you swearing, Pippa Kelly?

Pippa ducks down on the floor and hides among our legs.

No, Mother, it wasn't me.

I want to hear it no more. I'm talking to all of you.

Yes, Mother.

There's an empty seat behind Gabriel but nobody dares sit there. That's Reverend Mother's seat. Pippa says, The aul cow, she wouldn't let the Pope sit on her precious seat.

The corridor in the asylum is white. The walls are white the doors are white the ceilings are white the nurses are in white the doctors are in white Holly is in white and the two men holding her up by the arms are in white. If you weren't already insane coming in here you'd go insane from looking at white.

The two men let Holly's arms go and she drops to her knees and babbles like an idiot. We stand and watch her crawl around on her hands and knees. Some girls giggle behind their hands, others stare with their mouths open.

Now, says Gabriel, let Holly be an example to all of you.

Sheamie says, An example of what, Mother?

Never you mind, Sheamie Kelly.

I won't, says Sheamie.

Don't backchat me, Sheamie Kelly.

I won't, says Sheamie.

I won't tell you again.

That's good, says Sheamie.

The men in white coats start to laugh. Gabriel's red face turns redder than ever but even Gabriel will think twice before she'll take on Sheamie when there's anyone around. She can't win unless she clobbers him and nuns won't hit you when there's anyone around.

Sheamie's right. I don't know why Gabriel brought us here but I'm glad she did because now I know Holly isn't poisoned. She's gone mental and there's nothing new about that.

But it doesn't solve my problem. I'm still stuck with loads of hosts in my pocket. It's washday tomorrow and if Gabriel finds out there'll be war. One host on the floor is bad enough. But pocketsful?

I know Gabriel won't look in my pockets. Maybe I'll just say nothing but then they'd just come back next week, only cleaner. No matter where I leave them someone is bound to find them. There's only one place.

Someone is hammering at the door.

I'm comin'. Give me a minute.

I never saw hosts going down the toilet before and they don't seem to want to go down either because they keep bobbing back and I don't know what I'd do if the penguins heard the Body of Christ is bobbing around the toilet bowl.

The door is coming off the hinges and I know it's Mickey Driscoll looking for a wank.

Fuck off, Mickey. I'm busy.

Ah, Jasus, Matilda, I'm burstin'.

Ask Pippa.

She's not home from school yet.

I don't know what to do. Mickey won't leave and the hosts won't flush. I don't mind giving any of the boys a wank. Most of the girls do it for them. It's not like kissing or anything. There're a hundred girls and only ten boys and they always stand up for us if we get in a fight with kids from the outside. I can do it under the breakfast table with one hand while I'm shaking the ketchup bottle with the other. Boys are quicker than ketchup.

What are you doin' in there, Matilda?

Never mind, Mickey. Go away.

Ah, come on, Matilda. Please.

I open the door and Mickey hobbles in with his trousers already around his ankles. I close the door behind him and fire in loads of toilet paper in the toilet bowl, and pray.

Jesus, says Mickey.

Good guess.

The toilet is finished flushing but I'm frightened to look. I don't want to see Christ clambering up the bowl wearing the white toilet seat as a halo telling me he's suffered enough for the sins of the world and do you realize what you're doing to that boy is a mortal sin?

One quick look, the toilet bowl is empty. Mickey's empty. God's gone. Mickey pulls up his trousers and we're out the door and up the corridor just as Gabriel and Doyler are coming round the corner. One big, one small – like Laurel and Hardy.

And where are you two coming from? says Gabriel.

The chapel, Mother.

Praying, I hope?

He was on his knees, Mother.

Oh, really. That makes a pleasant change for you, Mickey.

Sure, I'm doing so much praying, Mother, I don't know whether I'm comin' or goin'.

Sheamie is outside in the playground and he waves me across to tell me the principal of the boys' school has been to see Reverend Mother. He complained there were boys in the school walking around like zombies. The tablets are stopped. I need a new plan, Matilda.

10

I'm eleven. I'm standing at my bedroom window looking down at the empty playground wondering if I should help Sheamie escape. He'll never find our mother and I'll end up losing a brother as well and I'll never have a family. The sky is black. No moon, no stars. The air smells of rain and thunder snarls in the distance. The playground light is on and there's enough light to make out the tin roof of the green sheds and the long shadow of the swings stretched along the ground. My father didn't visit this summer and I don't know how I feel about that. I just know I feel as lost as I did when I first came here.

Somehow, I expect to see my mother coming around the corner. I open the window to the cold September breeze and look down. Sometimes I really see her there smiling up at me and I can't help wondering what it would be like. Would we be strangers or be as if she was never gone? I never let myself think about it for long though. Maybe that's why I'm scared of helping Sheamie. It scares me she wouldn't know me, or wouldn't want me. In my dream I just see her coming to take us home because then I'd know for sure she wanted us. We'd have a house with a chimney and at Christmas I'd pretend I was a child again waiting for Santa. I'd make myself believe in him, just so I'd know what it feels like to try and sleep so the hours will pass quickly but wanting to run downstairs with every toss and turn to see if he'd been. I have it planned. Everything will be simple. We'll have a house on stilts. A sitting room with a glowing fire and a big white shaggy dog called Spot wagging his tail on the rug. He'd roll over when he'd see me and lie at the end of my bed at night to keep me safe. Maybe she'll come tomorrow.

Gabriel comes in carrying a new grey uniform and tells me I'm starting a new school tomorrow.

Why? Where?

Never mind why or where.

But . . . Mother . . .

But nothing. Come away from that window and take that mournful look off your gob. If God sees you with an expression like that he'll make you wear it for ever. Say your prayers, thank God for your blessings, and go to bed. Goodnight, Matilda.

Oh, goodnight.

What?

Goodnight, Mother.

In the morning Gabriel drives me in the mini-bus to this new school on the Mall. It's sunny, just a little cold, and I'd rather walk but Gabriel says she needs to speak to the principal, Sister Joan. This must be her flapping down the corridor toward us like a big black mother hen.

The two nuns whisper to each other in the corner. There's a girl in a wheelchair coming down the corridor and I wonder is she lost? She stops halfway and turns into a classroom and the corridor is empty again. Sister Joan comes bearning over and when she talks she clucks like a hen too.

Oh, Matilda, how delighted I am to have you here. Sister Gabriel has explained everything, but don't worry. I'm certain you'll be excellent now you are here with us. I'm putting you in classroom five. It's the last door on your left at the end of the corridor. Miss Brown is your teacher. Do you know your left from your right yet, Matilda?

Of course I do.

That's a great start. Remarkable. You can go on up on your own so, while I finish here with Sister Gabriel.

When I walk in I want to die. Miss Brown is standing by the window playing an iron triangle. She tells me to come in and close the door. Instead, I turn and run back the way I came. Some of them are in wheelchairs. A boy in the front row has twisted hands and can't wipe the snot that trickles. Some have little bodies and big heads or mouths with thick lips and make gaga noises from the sides of their heads because that's where their mouths are.

I search the corridor for Gabriel, but it's empty. I'm goin' to puke. I try to find a bathroom. I feel tears coming but I have to hold them too because if I let go I'll be sick right here on this empty wheelchair. I run to the front door and bang at the glass to Gabriel as she's driving away. The red lights at the back of the bus come on. I pull at the front door but it's locked. I bang at the glass again but Gabriel drives on; she only stopped to roll up the window. I run again. I find a door but it's a closet with sweeping brushes and a mop in a plastic bucket. I bend over and hold on to my stomach and run again until I find the bathroom door across from the stairs. I close the cubicle door and pull the clasp across. I throw up in the toilet bowl and sit on the floor wiping the tears from my cheeks. My father must be right. I must be stupid. Why else would they send me here?

Sister Joan comes in. I know it's her because I can see her black skirts under the cubicle door.

Are you in there, Matilda? You're not being sick?

No, Sister Joan.

I hear her at the sink washing her hands and humming to herself and I wish she'd go but she raps on the door again.

Don't be long now. Miss Brown will wonder where you are.

Coming, Sister.

I'm afraid to look in the mirror above the sink. Afraid I'll look like them. My hands shake and my knuckles are white when I turn on the taps. I look up a little. I see the grey V-neck of the jumper, the grey tie. I'm wearing them but I don't belong in them. They belong to them. The Mad People.

I wash my mouth out under the tap. The water is cool and takes away the stench of puke. I know I have to look at my face now or I never will again. I look in the basin, white and hollow. The black plug on a silver chain. The plug-hole, where everything washes away and I can believe it never happened. I wash my face and with the water still in my hands I look up. I see my hair on my shoulders. It's black. It's mine. I see my chin, small and dripping wet. My small mouth. My eyes, blue, just like my mother's. That's me in the mirror but there's something missing. This is the worst thing that ever happened to me. Worse than my mother leaving. Worse than our grandmother turning her back on us and being sent to the convent. I can't hide this. I can't say this isn't real. Not when it's staring me in the face.

I go home to the convent and tell Doyler. She turns to the sink and says it's out of her hands. She wouldn't have any say. Gabriel waves me away and says I'm going and that's all there is. You go where you're told. Your father is in full agreement.

What's my father got to do with it?

She doesn't answer.

No matter what I say they won't answer so I stop talking to them altogether.

I pray to every statue in the convent. St Joseph. St Theresa, the Little Flower, St Bridget, the Madonna, Our Lady of Knock, Our Lady of Lourdes, Our Lady of Fatima, Our Lady of the Rosary. I go to the chapel and pray to Jesus suffering up there on the cross for the sins of the world. But the statues aren't listening.

I do what my father says. I stand in the playground looking up to Heaven talking directly to God. I climb the wall to the nuns' garden and talk to the trees and the plants till I realize if I'm seen I'll be carted off to the asylum where I'll go insane from looking at white. None of it matters. God's not listening.

I'm ashamed of the grey uniform. I smuggle my own clothes out in my schoolbag and change in the toilets under the chestnut trees before I go out on the road, then change back to the grey uniform when I get to the Mad School. I sneak to school through back lanes hiding in doorways and behind parked cars so nobody will see me and report me for not wearing a uniform or, worse, figure out I'm hiding it in my schoolbag because I'm a retard, a spa.

I won't do anything for them in Mad School. I won't sing their songs or listen to their stupid triangles. I'll cause so much trouble they'll kick me out and I'll be sent back to my old school. I sit behind Mad Michael in the wheelchair eating his snot from the back of his hands and I stick pins in him because it's the Mad People's fault. If they weren't born then there wouldn't be a Mad School.

I can cut him like two pieces of a jigsaw with the pin. I start behind his right ear then go down in a straight line to the knuckle at the top of his spine. Then keeping just to the left until I'm halfway down his back then out in a half circle to the cheek of his arse. It's a waste of time. I could stick pins in him till I'm an old woman of thirty. He never fuckin' budges.

Miss Brown struts around the classroom with her model walk and her infant teacher's voice wanting everyone to play triangles.

Listen to the triangle, boys and girls. Listen to the different sounds, everyone. And how many sounds did you hear, Matilda?

None. I'm deaf.

Now, now, Matilda, we know you're not deaf.

What?

Matilda doesn't want to play today. All right, Matilda. Maybe tomorrow?

I feel like telling her to shove her triangle up the highest part of her hole but that wouldn't help either. They'd say I was being disruptive, part of my condition. Condition. That's how they talk in a Mad School.

Doyler comes up to my bedroom looking over her shoulder to make sure Gabriel isn't behind her. She sits on the bed with me and asks why won't I talk? She stares at my lips so she'll understand everything I say, but I won't talk to her.

It's a terrible thing what's been done to you, Matilda. That father of yours coming in here complaining about your education every chance he gets hasn't helped. Reverend Mother rang to tell him your bad results and he agreed you needed help.

What results?

With Mister O'Donovan.

The fella with the purple head and the bricks?

That's him. I'm trying my best to get you out of that place but I have to do it quietly. Try and put up with it for now.

I can't, they're all screwballs in there.

I'll talk to Gabriel again. Maybe she'll talk to Reverend Mother. God knows, I can't. No matter what I say she'll do the opposite.

How come you stay here, then, Doyler? Why don't you just piss off? I would.

It's my job.

You could get a proper job. Like in a hairdressin' place.

Hairdressing? What would I know about hairdressing, Matilda?

That's the first sensible thing Doyler's said and I have to

straighten up to look at her. Now we're staring at each other like we're both deaf.

But that's what you are, Doyler. A hairdresser. Isn't it?

What on God's earth gave you that idea? I'm a social worker.

Doyler puts her arm around my waist and I put my arm around her shoulder and it's a strange feeling sitting beside a grown-up smaller than you. We both start to laugh and for a little while I feel better. I don't even know why we're laughing. I ask Doyler what a social worker is and she falls back on the bed rocking and laughing like a woman gone insane and stays like that for five minutes till she can't laugh anymore because of the pain in her back. She sits up, dries her eyes with a corner of the bed blanket and holds her hand to the pain.

Well, Doyler, what is it?

In here, she says, it's someone who cuts hair. She lets out another wail of laughter. At the stupidity of it all, she says.

It's all right for Doyler to laugh, she's not going to the Mad School tomorrow. Still, I'm happy she came to see me. That she noticed me. There are so many nights I wish Gabriel would do that. The nights I can't sleep. The nights there are no stars. Just come in and see how I am. Sit on my bed and ask if everything is all right. Did I need anything? Are you happy, Matilda? I'd tell her I was so she wouldn't think I was a burden looking for things I couldn't have. Maybe she'd give me a hug and say she knows I'm not stupid. I'd hug her back too. Just so she would see how easy I am to love. I know she doesn't notice me. How do you notice one more broken heart in a place like this?

At Christmas, the mother hen herself ambushes me in the school corridor just as I'm coming in the front door. Matilda, she clucks. I hear you're a great one for the Irish dancing.

Would you like to dance for the school in the Theatre Royal? All the school will be represented. Oh, Matilda, I just know you would. I'd really like to put on a play, but, as you might imagine, it's a little difficult this year.

She can't be serious but she is, so I say I will, otherwise Gabriel will keep me locked in till I do and I'll have to give up running and I'll end up with asthma and a big chest like Pippa, getting caught by every spotty faced youngfella in Trinity Park when we play kiss-and-chase and if I ever find the sneaky bitch who told Sister Joan I could dance I'll throttle her.

Four nights before Christmas, I'm in the Theatre Royal with the smell of sweat and make-up everywhere. I'm stuffed at the back of a cramped dressing room with Robin Hood and his Merry Men. Three Blind Mice, all ears and whiskers falling over the Seven Dwarfs singing, Hi ho, hi ho, it's off to work we go. Mother Hen is flapping over me like I'm her little chick. Oh, Matilda, she clucks, your costume is only beautiful. Oh, aren't the colours amazing? Oh, I've never seen a dress like it. You're a credit to the Holy Shepherd and Saint Mary's Special School. Indeed you are. Be sure to thank Sister Gabriel for loaning you that dress.

I will, Sister Joan.

She's off her rocker because she spends too much time around Mad People and that's what happens when you spend too much time around Mad People. But she's right about the dress. It is beautiful. Black skirt cut above my knee and white lace hem. Green lace top with embroidered harps and musical notes of silver and gold that sparkle.

The lights are blinding when I walk on to the stage, the crowd cheering before I even start. I can't see them but I know they're out there whispering along the rows, There she is, there's that little retarded girl now. God love her.

Sister Joan is below me in the pit. She's telling the man with the accordion I'm doing a reel. I stand in position in the centre of the stage. Right leg forward, toe pointed. The audience cheer and when I dance they clap to the music and I'm mortified on the stage of the Theatre Royal. I dazzle around the stage and when I'm finished they go wild. Sister Joan's face is beaming brighter than the stage lights and I'm sorry I ever agreed to come here. I should have let Gabriel keep me in. I should have given up the running, given up the raw eggs and chased every youngfella in Trinity Park myself to save them the trouble, because I know they're not cheering the way I danced. They're cheering that I could walk out here. That I could stand, let alone dance. If I fell flat on my face they'd applaud. If I tumbled off the stage and landed head first on the beaming Sister Joan they'd bring the fuckin' house down.

When the house lights come up I see the Mad Kids sitting in their wheelchairs at the front. Mad Michael is waving up at me and for once managing to clap his hands without poking his fingers in his eyes. I can't help it and I have to wave back because, even though it doesn't help me, at least now I know there are worse things in the world than being an orphan.

Behind the Mad Kids, the convent kids are sitting with Gabriel. If I didn't already know them I'd know they were from the convent. They're the ones without the sweets. Gabriel gives me a wave and I know she expects me to wave back but I pretend not to notice her. Sitting beside Gabriel, fast asleep, is Lucy Flynn and that gives me an idea. I know now I have to get out of this Mad School. I have to help Sheamie find our mother and, if anyone knows how to help Sheamie get money for his escape, it'll be Lucy Flynn.

II

Lucy Flynn is a tinker. Lucy don't look like a tinker though, with coal black hair that shines all the way to her waist and cheeky pink cheeks that always make me think she's hiding something behind her back. She looks really pretty when the penguins finish scrubbing the dirt from her face every time Officer Flannery brings her back in the squad car. Lucy's mother steals Lucy from the convent because she needs Lucy for the beggin' and staelin' and the penguins are always ringing the gardaí to search for her. We all know Lucy was settled once and lived in one of the flat-roofed houses on Hennessy's Road but her mother couldn't stand living in a house so she ran down the street and around the corner to the tinker camp on the Tramore Road, dropping Lucy in the convent on the way.

I tell Lucy out in the playground we need money to help Sheamie escape and she says she'd do anything for Sheamie. She loves Sheamie so she does. She'd love to drag him into the bushes and do dirty things but Sheamie won't go near bush or tree when he sees Lucy.

I hope he's not queer or anything. Do you think he's queer, Matilda?

He's just strange, Lucy.

Lucy says she'd love to run away with Sheamie herself. They'd drive a van around the country gathering copper cylinders, lead, wire and car batteries. They'd make a fortune and have a dozen children for the big children's allowance and live on the dole in a caravan. She's certain Sheamie has a touch of the tinker in him 'cos where else would he get that lovely red hair?

I'd like to tell Lucy my brother isn't a tinker but at eleven you know there're times you just have to keep your gob shut. Instead, I ask Lucy where we can get money and she says we can beg for it.

Beg? No way, Lucy.

Beggin's aesy, Matilda.

I don't give a shit if it is or not.

I just sits on a footpat' outside a chapel or a supermarka with me hand out sayin', Any money, mister? Gis a penny, missus. Ah, Jasus, for the childer, missus. 'Tis better now when I do haves me little cousin wi'me 'cos I waves the empty milk bottle and 'tis faerce hard ta pass a starvin' child tryin' ta get milk for the little shister. You could rob the money but robbin' 'n staelin's different though. Ya hav's to be trained to rob an stael. I can show yeh, but we'll have to go see me mother. If she's in a good mood she'll give us money. We can't go into the shops with nothin' in our pockets 'cos they'd know what we were up to and throw us out. When you have money there's nothin' they can do.

I don't want to go see Lucy's mother in the tinker camp for fear I'll be killed by the tinkers up there and by Gabriel if she finds out where I was. I don't want to steal either. I know it's a sin but I have so many mortal sins on my soul already, from flushing God down the toilet bowl, to not making a proper confession to Father Devlin and doing dirty things with my uncles, a few more hardly matter. When I'm big I'll find a kind priest who'll understand. Especially when I tell him I stole to help Sheamie find our mother.

A line of tinker caravans is parked beside the local tip and a warm January makes the place stink like a blocked drain. The tinkers don't seem to mind because their camp is destroyed with rubbish, drying rags and shitty nappies tossed along the ditches. Lucy runs ahead and leaves me surrounded by dog shit and the mongrels that left it here. They growl and bark and show their teeth and a small girl with a sneaky grin and a dirty face stands blocking my way.

What di ya wants?

I look for Lucy but she's gone.

I asked yeh what yeh wants.

There's a gang of them, with sticks, walking towards me. I want to run but they're all around me now. A big freckled-faced boy leans forward and asks, What are yeh doin' ta me little shister?

Nothin', I'm sorry.

What are yeh sorry for then?

They're going to kill me no matter what I say and I don't know what to do. Then I hear Lucy saying, Fuck off, Miley, and laeve Matilda alone.

Is she with you, Lucy?

That's me friend. That's Matilda. Laeve 'er be.

Lucy walks back and catches my arm. Come on, Matilda. Nobody'll touch yeh.

Lucy's mother is sitting outside her caravan on the front seat of a burned-out car. The car is upside down in the ditch. She's big and bouncy like a beach ball. Her bottom lip juts out to hold the fag that's sticking up from one corner of her mouth and when she talks through the other corner she sounds like a foghorn.

Well, Lucy, she says as if she only saw Lucy this morning instead of the three months since her last spin in the squad car with Officer Flannery dragging Lucy out the back door by the neck saying, 'Tis a good kick in the hole I'd give that one . . . ah, excuse the language, Sister Gabriel.

We climb the three wooden steps of the caravan and inside

147

it's hard to keep my jaws together. It's spotless, cleaner than a nun's arse. Shiny copper pots and kettles hang from the ceiling while brass figurines dance along sideboards filled with cups, saucers and plates painted with white horses drinking from cool mountain streams and a cunning fox grinning as the hounds pass him by.

Lucy says, Yeh looks surprised, Matilda. Didn't yeh ever see inside a tinker caravan before?

For a second I think about it. About the mongrel dogs outside and the cunning fox inside but I don't know what to say to tinkers when they ask about their caravans. I'm saved when Lucy's mother walks in with the fag still dangling from her bottom lip and I wonder how she smoked it all without dropping a single ash and certain if she did she'd puncture herself and squirt around the caravan like a burst balloon. The ash is still hanging when she asks, Will yee have somethin' to drink, girls? And it's still there when she leaves two tumblers of lemonade on the table and wonders who I am.

Matilda, Missus Flynn.

Will yeh get outa dat with yer Missus Flynn and call me Maisy. Dat aul Missus Dis and Missus Dat is only for the settled people, so it is.

She laughs from the guts of her fat belly and blows ash into the air and all over the sheepskin seats. She lights another fag and sits under the copper kettles with her arms folded and her eyes closed and if it weren't for the occasional red glow from the cigarette I'd be certain she's dead. When she finally opens one eye it's to wonder why we're still here. That's what I'm wondering myself till she hands Lucy and me twenty pence each from the silver teapot on the cooker and tells us to don't be sitting in caravans all day with the lovely afternoon outside. And I can't help wondering if it's better to be like Lucy and have a mother like Maisy or be like me and have no mother at all.

Lucy wants to go to Grace's supermarket. They always send us bread they can't sell – brown, white, sliced or loaf. The broken Easter eggs at Easter. Crushed biscuits, broken bars of chocolate or anything bruised or stale in general and it's a known thing in the convent, if you're ever in Grace's supermarket, be sure to break as many bars of chocolate as you can.

We go in past the rattling tin cans of the boy scouts and the machine over the door blowing out air that heats you going in and cools you going out. Past the girl in the magazines booth and the racks of white blouses until we reach what Lucy came for.

Lucy says, Youse don't do nothin', Matilda. Youse just watch me 'cos youse never did it an yeh'll only get cot.

Lucy stands behind a woman with a shopping trolley. When the woman looks back Lucy smiles up at her. Lucy gets to the sweets and slides four packets of Rolo up her sleeve and walks through the checkout as if the woman with the trolley is her mother. I follow her outside.

Now, Matilda, she says, run, and the way she says it I'm sure there's someone following and even though I done nothing wrong I run and we don't stop till we're breathless inside the convent wall and all I want is to go back for more. Lucy says I have to practise stealing sweets for a while but when I get the hang of it we can steal things that we can sell to the traders down in the Apple Market.

The following week I'm with Lucy at the sweet counter trying to look innocent but my heart is pounding under my blue poncho. I feel guilty because it came from a bishop. A holy man. What can I do when it's the best thing invented for stealing sweets?

Uncle Philip's new wife, Rita, works behind the sweet counter and she gives me a pleasant, I-was-almost-a-nun smile.

The poncho is lying over the sweets and I wonder what I'm going to say to her. I only met Rita a few times in my grandmother's house.

Rita glances sideways at Lucy. She knows by looking that Lucy is a tinker and she's probably wondering why we're together, but Rita wouldn't understand what it's like in the convent even if she was almost a nun. She wouldn't understand I don't see Lucy as a tinker. She's Lucy, a Shep like me.

A man in a cap comes to the counter to be served and I wonder will Rita be in trouble if they count the sweets afterwards and find there's fistfuls of jellies missing. I can't put them back because getting caught putting them back is as bad as getting caught stealing them in the first place.

Rita turns to the till and I say, I'd better go, Rita. I'll see yeh.

She gives me a strange look over her shoulder that sends a shiver through me but maybe that's the way you look at people when you were almost a nun. I know all about nuns but people who were almost a nun are a mystery.

Lucy grabs my arm and pulls me away from the counter and we head for the door. When we near the door Lucy says, Remember, Matilda, don't run till we're outside. And don't look back. If yeh looks back they'll know youse was up to somethin'.

I won't, Lucy.

Walking back we meet Sonny waggling towards us on the footpath on a big red bicycle.

Matilda, I'm glad I met you, so I am. I wanted to remind you about the meeting in the park next week. You won't forget?

I won't, Sonny.

I hope you're eating the raw eggs?

I am, Sonny.

No, smokin'?

No, Sonny.

The fags is the worst. Stay away from the fags, Matilda.

I will, Sonny.

Sonny wobbles away reaching in his pocket for the box of fags and all I can think of is I need new runners. These runners are tatty and only the top two holes have laces left. Gabriel already bought me a new pair of jeans at Christmas so there's no way I'm getting runners or anything else for a long time. The meeting in the park is a special meeting and instead of medals you get Waterford Glass and I'd love to see the look on Gabriel's face if I gave her that. Maybe she'd give me a hug and say she was proud of me. Maybe she'd say I wasn't stupid and say she was taking me out of the Mad School. Maybe I should tell her I'd have a better chance of winning if I had new runners but she'll probably tell me Jesus didn't wear runners and Jesse Owens who won gold medals in the Olympics often ran in his bare feet and if bare feet are good enough for Jesus and Jesse Owens then runners with enough laces to tie the top two holes should be good enough for me.

That's the trouble with having nothing. The minute you want something, someone always wants to tell you why you're better off without it.

Gabriel has a small garden in the playground with a low red-brick wall around it and, when she's not talking to Polly the budgie or reading her red pocket prayer book or embroidering those white pocket-handkerchiefs, she grows lily of the valley. They're pinky white and bell shaped and Gabriel says they're holy. My father would say all flowers are holy. I don't bother trying to figure it.

I go over to Gabriel while she's clearing out weeds and dead leaves and hand her the biggest box of chocolates I could fit under my poncho. One with sad-eyed puppies on the lid. If that doesn't soften her up, I'm fucked.

Why thank you, Matilda. Tell me, where did you get the money?

I saved it from me pocket money, Mother.

Did you indeed?

I did.

She must know I stole them, she's not that thick. No one's that thick.

To change the subject I tell Gabriel, The garden looks lovely, Mother, even though there's fuck all in it this time of year, and hope she'll be so happy I noticed that she'll rush to town and buy me new runners.

I never knew you liked a garden, Matilda.

Only yours, Mother.

Isn't that a lovely thing to say?

Ah, Mother?

Yes, Matilda?

There's a race meeting in the park on Sunday and I need new runners.

She holds the chocolates under her arm and looks at me out the corner of her eye.

I see, she says. Tell me, what is wrong with the ones you're wearing?

They're scruffy, Mother.

Now, Matilda, you know pride is one of the Seven Deadly Sins.

But I'd have a better chance of winning if I had new runners, Mother. There's glass and everything if I win. Can't you buy them out of the budget?

The budget is gone for this month.

Gone?

Spent. I account to Reverend Mother for every penny. Reverend Mother accounts to Mother Superior in Dublin. Mother Superior accounts to the Archbishop. The Archbishop accounts to the Cardinal and the Cardinal accounts to the Holy Father in Rome.

I only want a pair of runners, Mother.

Have I ever told you the story of Jesse Owens, Matilda?

Never heard of him.

She stares so long over the sad-eyed puppies I have to turn my eyes away.

Glass, Matilda?

Yes, Mother.

Waterford Glass?

Of course, Mother.

Perhaps we can do something for you so.

Gabriel brings me upstairs to the big shoe closet in the corridor, the shelves stuffed with every size five shoe, sandal, runner and boot that ever passed through the Holy Shepherd. She holds the door open with one hand and holds on to the chocolates with sad-eyed puppies with the other hand and I ask her, Mother, how come you never come to see me race?

Why, you never asked, Matilda.

I'm not supposed to ask, Mother. You're supposed to just come.

Gabriel smiles down at me like I'm a great girl altogether and says she'll come on Sunday, but that only torments me because now I don't know if she's coming to see me run or because I tormented her. Still, she's coming, that's the main thing.

On your own now, Mother. You can't bring the kids.

You know I couldn't go without them, especially the younger ones.

I know she's right. They'd say I was her favourite and she loves me more than them. But, if she brings them, they'll make a holy show of me tearing around the park, like lunatics on an outing from the asylum. It's better if I go on my own, so I tell her, It's all right, Mother. You don't have to come. But she won't hear a bar of it.

No, Matilda. You're right.

No I'm not.

Of course you are.

I'm not. Honest I'm not. I'd know if I was.

I should have gone to see you run a long time ago. I just never realized it was this important to you.

It isn't, Mother. Honest. Well, it is but it isn't. Do you know what I mean?

Of course it is important, Matilda. I insist on going. I'm looking forward to it already.

No, Mother, please, please, they'll make a show of me.

Gabriel's red eyes roll under her eyelids as if she's picturing sixty Sheps going berserk in a park.

Will we leave it so, Matilda?

We will, Mother.

Now, about those runners.

One look in the closet is enough.

I'll keep the ones I have, Mother.

Are you certain?

I'm positive.

Gabriel closes the cupboard and I head down the stairs before she changes her mind. I can't steal new runners. I would if I could but the shoe shop only put one of each pair on the stand outside the door and I'd look a right gawk wearing one new runner. I could steal new shoelaces though. White bulky ones would cover the top and if I put whitening on them before I leave Sunday morning they might look new.

The fat manager in Grace's supermarket knows I'm in here every chance I get stealing right and left with Lucy but today I have Danny with me. I started him stealing in small shops, the stupid ones that keep the sweets and biscuits on our side of

154

the counter. He wants a T-shirt with the Bay City Rollers on the front so I tell him what to do and send him upstairs to where the clothes are. And for Jesus' sake, Danny, don't get caught.

The fat manager is parading up and down the aisle in his blue suit pretending not to notice me. I have a penny in my pocket just in case he checks. Now he's lurking around the washing powder. He knows I don't steal washing powder and he's trying to look like he's not watching me, so to torment him I stand beside him. I pick up a box of Persil and read the instructions. I compare prices with other brands and make tut-tut sounds with my tongue as if his prices are a disgrace and he should be reported to the proper authorities. To torment him even more I stroll towards the sweet counter. I can feel his fat head lifting and his eyes bulging at either the cheek or the stupidity of me stealing from under his nose, then just as I get to the sweet counter I turn away and head upstairs to Danny with the shoelaces already in my pocket.

Danny is in the changing room doing what I told him. Put the T-shirt on under your own shirt. Button your collar and walk out.

We're heading for the front door and I tell Danny, Don't run and don't look back. I want to look back myself and see how close the manager is. I'm not even sure he's following but it's great to think he is and my gut ripples wondering what's coming first, the door or his hand on my shoulder. A woman wearing a scarf pushes a shopping trolley overflowing with bread, cereals, apples, oranges, onions, milk and sugar in our way and we have to stop. I nudge Danny to stop biting his lip, then bite my own to keep the smile from my face at the beads of sweat pouring down Danny's cheeks. I thought he was scared but he's not. He's just trying to keep himself from laughing. The woman moves just enough for us to squeeze between her trolley and the wall and we're at the

Savoy cinema before we look back. There's a queue forming for *The Exorcist*, their faces as white as handkerchiefs before they even get to the woman in the ticket office. Some change their minds and run the other way. I hear a woman throwing her guts up in the lane around the corner and I'm not too happy here myself. The fat manager is at the supermarket door scratching the back of his skull and Danny and me scatter back to the convent before he figures out what we've done.

Sunday morning there's frost on the window panes but by afternoon the winter sun is shining and the People's Park is thronged. Everyone's mother, father, uncles, aunts and cousins are here. Mothers with children in prams and daddies with little girls on their shoulders buy chips and sausages from the vans that came for the day and a man with a blue loudspeaker stands on a platform behind the table with the Waterford Glass.

The narrow racetrack is marked with thick blue ropes tied to trees and wooden stakes and runs right around the park. The track starts at the water fountain then goes past the rusty iron bridge that leads to the old courthouse with its crumbling steps and pillars, then on past the cycle track, past the bandstand and back again to the fountain. While I'm waiting for my race, I stand by the finish line in my red tracksuit watching the others. The crowds line the blue ropes and call out, Come on, Mary, Come on, Patricia, Come on, Louise, Come on, Katherine. I listen to the families calling out the names. I hear how excited they are, whether their children are first or last doesn't matter. They cheer. I'm sorry now I didn't let Gabriel come. There're hundreds here and nobody would have noticed the convent kids.

The man with the blue loudspeaker calls my name. I hand my tracksuit to Sonny and line up with the other girls and wait for the starting pistol. It goes off like a cannon gun and I break out in goose pimples. It's five times around the park but after the first lap I know I could run around it a hundred times and start all over. I hear the families screaming out, Come on Patricia, Come on Mary, you're going great, but I'm running so fast to bring the Waterford Glass to Gabriel for my hug I'm winning by half a lap. I see the finish line ahead and I wonder why everyone is still shouting for Mary and Katherine and Louise. I hear the names going around in my head. Mary, Katherine, Louise, Patricia, and every girl's name I ever heard. No one calls for Matilda. No one shouts, Come on, Matilda. I hear in their voices how much their families care about them and I know no one cares about me. No one cares if I win or lose or never came here at all. And I know I shouldn't be here winning their race from their children and spoiling their day. All they'll say is, That young one from the Holy Shepherd won, and they'll laugh at me and say look at her coddin' herself with her stolen white shoelaces pretending she has new runners. I don't want to be here anymore. I don't belong.

I stop. I just stop and walk away and nobody notices. I bend under the blue ropes and run away and sit behind a tree and cry and wish I was never born. Why did I come? Why was I this stupid? I just want to go home to the convent and never see or hear anyone again in my life.

Matilda!

It's Sonny, and he looks disappointed.

Leave me alone, Sonny. Just let me be.

Why, Matilda? You had it won.

I don't care.

What's the matter? Tell me.

Sonny takes his cap off and kneels on one knee beside me. You're not a quitter, Matilda. Tell me what the matter is.

Nothing, Sonny. I'm just not feeling well, that's all. I want to go home. Will you bring me home?

I like the runners, Matilda. Are they new?

I cleaned them, Sonny.

Jasus, Matilda, they look new.

I feel my tears stopping and a smile coming to my lips and I don't know why.

Sonny stands up and offers me his hand and, when I stand, he puts his arm around my shoulder. I want to pull away but I'd never pull away from Sonny. His fingers are warm when he catches my hand and brings me to a shorter track by the bandstand where girls are lining up for the 100 yards, and he tells me he wants me to run in this race, he'll arrange it.

I can't run short races, Sonny. You know I can't. Just let me go home, please.

On course you can. You're a fighter. You mightn't have much, Matilda, but you have what matters. You've a great heart. Come on, run this race.

Honest, Sonny, I'd rather go home.

Then do it for me. Will you do that, do it for me?

I don't have the heart to refuse Sonny when he's so good to us, so I take a deep breath and tell him I will. Sonny says, I'm going to stand at the finish line and I want you to look straight ahead. Look at me, Matilda. Don't look at anything else, only me.

I won't, Sonny.

Good girl, now dry your eyes.

I dry my eyes and cheeks with my thumbs and line up beside the other girls. Sonny throws his overcoat on the grass and rolls up the sleeves of his white shirt and stands at the finish line bent over with his hands on his knees and when the starting pistol fires, he shouts, Come on, Matilda, come on. I feel my legs stretch from my hips like they never stretched before and I see Sonny getting closer and closer, bigger and bigger, louder and louder, Come on, Matilda, come on, his arms waving faster and faster, Sonny getting closer and closer till he catches me and I knock him back on his arse I'm running so fast.

Oh, God, oh, Sonny. Are you all right, Sonny? Can you get up?

Sonny is flat on his back with his legs in the air. He pokes his head between his knees and tells me, Don't ever do what you done back there again, promise me now.

I won't, Sonny. I'm sorry.

Good girl. Now, give me a hand up.

I offer Sonny my hand and wonder how he knew what was wrong with me.

I'm too excited to wait for a lift home in the bus so I walk the road from the park with the box of glass pressed against my heart. I turn up the Mall, past the wheelchair ramps of the Mad School, past the ringing bells of St John's Church, and the brown railings of the boys' school on the Manor. My feet are bursting to run with every step but I walk so I won't drop the Waterford Glass.

The convent playground is empty and the only sound is from Mickey Driscoll down under the chestnut trees beating a builder's barrel with the handle of a sweeping brush.

Gabriel is sitting at the kitchen table. She lifts her eyes from her prayer book when I burst in beaming and breathless.

I won, Mother.

There you are, now. You didn't need me after all.

These are for you, Mother.

I hand her my prize and wait for my hug. Gabriel slips the prayer book into her pocket and goes to the drawer for a knife to cut the string and when she opens the box there's that little smile for me like I'm a great girl altogether.

Wine glasses, she says, how appropriate, Matilda.

She lifts one of the wine glasses to the window. It sparkles in the sunlight and golden light streaks the room and, when she taps it with her finger, it tinkles like a small brass bell so she knows how good they are.

What about my hug?

There's only the two of us. Nobody would know. Nobody would be jealous. I'd sit on her lap even though I'm too big for sitting on laps, but I'd do it, I would. I wouldn't feel stupid or anything. I'd sit there on her big black lap and feel my forehead against her warm cheek and her arms around me. I'd carry it with me always. It would be our secret. Mine and Gabriel's for ever. And whenever I needed a hug I'd think of it and never need another hug again.

Gabriel leaves the glass back in the box and closes the lid.

We'll keep these for special visitors, Matilda, and won't they be only lovely to have?

What about my hug? She's waiting, that's all. She really wants to give me a hug. She's just not certain of what I'll do when she does. She'll lock the wine glasses away then check we're alone. She wouldn't want anyone to walk in on us.

Gabriel kneels down to lock the glasses in the sideboard under Billy the goldfish, where I know they'll never see light again but that doesn't matter. I won them. I won them for Gabriel.

Gabriel walks to the door and looks outside to the playground. I'm standing in the doorway between the kitchen and the hallway trying to look as if a hug is the last thing on my mind, which is hard when it's the only thing on my mind. Gabriel walks back in and gives me that little smile as if I'm a great girl altogether and I hate it when she does that. She says, I must see Reverend Mother about next week's retreat, Matilda. I'll be back later.

I'm not getting my hug and I feel a fool. I don't even know why I wanted one now. I just did that's all.

12

Mickey Driscoll is fifteen. He's all shoulders and no neck, like his head's been battered into his body with a frying pan. He has ears like jug handles and his face is covered in greasy spots. Mickey heard about Lucy and me stealing and he wants in. I'm sitting in the green sheds with Lucy and here comes Mickey bopping over like Garry Glitter.

You two wanna be in my gang?

Your gang, Mickey? Go 'way and play with yourself.

Ah, come on. Meself and Sheamie started it. There're six of the boys in it but we needs girls as well. We have to have more boys than girls or it'll be a sissy gang and we'll all get kilt. This'll be a great gang, we have rules an everythin'.

Rules, Mickey?

You can't fight with anyone else in the gang unless they become traitors and skin to the nuns if we do anythin' wrong, which we will because there's no point having a gang if you don't. If someone in the gang is gettin' kilt you have to jump in to save them even if there's a hundred against you and you die tryin' to save your own. Oh, and we all have to dress the same.

How can we all dress the same, Mickey boy? We're in the convent, are yeh fuckin' stupid or what?

We're all to dress like Bay City Rollers and wear metal studs in the heels of our shoes. We'll have to rob the studs in Woolworth. The cheap ones with the spikes you stick in the heels of your shoes yourself, we can't afford the real ones in the cobblers yet. That's the boys' job. The nuns have rolls of tartan from the olden times up in the linen room and Gabriel said to take all we need as long as we do the sewin' ourselves, only the boys can't sew. I wouldn't have them in the gang if they could. That's the girls' job.

We'd love to give Mickey a good kick in the arse for thinking girls can't steal and he only wants us for sewing but we decide to join and, like Mickey says, we can't fight with our own.

The linen room is in the attic at the top of a narrow stairway. It was used in the olden times for making costumes for the plays and Irish dancing when the girls who lived here were never let out. The grey donkey from the Christmas pantomime is looking lonely in the corner. Fairy godmothers and wicked witches face each other in centre of the room. Cinderella and Sleeping Beauty lie asleep in the corner while the shelves on every wall are so high that polished wooden ladders slide where leprechauns, elves and hobgoblins hide. The room is bright from the two skylights and even though nobody comes in here much it still smells holy and clean.

Mona wants nothing to do with any gang. She has boy-friends to look after, thank-you-very-much. Pippa says we'll all get caught and end up in Cork, miles from everyone. It's just another one of Sheamie's stupid ideas. Thanks, but no thanks. I'm staying with Mona. It's safer.

Stay with your pal, Mona, then.

Ha, ha, very funny.

You asked for it.

Lucy and me spend days and nights cutting tartan into strips and sewing it on to the sides of everyone's jeans and the sleeves of jumpers and making scarves for our necks and wrists on the old black sewing machine with the push plate underneath, and I wonder what it was like to live here in the olden times when you were never let out, and I feel sad for all the girls who made tartan dresses back then for Irish dancing nobody came to see.

When we're done, Mickey says he should have wider stripes because he's the leader.

Fuck off, Mickey.

We sit in the green sheds and plan our attacks on Grace's supermarket. Sheamie is demented because Grace's have stopped sending us the white sliced bread and he's sick of the nuns' home-made bread. He doesn't care people come from miles to buy it. Sheamie says it's war. If we can't have the bread then nobody else can.

We steal all the sweets we can eat and crush whatever we can't carry so that it will end up in the convent. We stick our fingers through the wrapping on the white sliced bread so it can't be sold and ends up in the convent as well. We're doing so much damage the boys who collect the shopping trolleys tell us the manager is pure demented, tearing the place asunder for mice. He raves all day about mice.

Did you see mice, son?

No, sir.

Keep watching. They're everywhere.

But I'm not happy. What's the use of a manager who is too demented over mice to give you a decent chase and I'm sick of bread. If I eat any more I'll turn into a large sliced pan. This isn't why I joined the gang. We need money for Sheamie and we won't get it like this. I want something big.

Mickey Driscoll says, I have contacts, Matilda.

This gets Lucy excited and she dances round the shed.

Ah, fuck dat. I'm not shootin' anyone. Dat's too much now, Mickey.

Lucy, I said contacts. Not contracts.

Why don't yeh spake proply, den?

In a week Mickey tells us there's a job on. That's how Mickey talks because he watches too much television and that's what happens when you watch too much television. He won't tell us what the job is because we're on a need-to-know basis.

There's a narrow lane at the back of Grace's supermarket where the delivery lorries park. There's the ruin of a castle with weeds growing through the floor. The lane is always quiet, maybe the odd old woman with a wicker shopping bag taking a short cut to town, or kids on the mooch hiding in the castle; but at four o'clock on a cold March morning there's just the ten of us dressed in tartan.

Sheamie tells us we have to wait here on the footpath. I don't ask why because I don't care as long as I get the five pounds Mickey said I'd be paid if we done our job properly and keep stum afterwards.

Keep stum. That's what Mickey calls keeping your mouth shut.

I see the headlights rounding the corner and the green truck pulls up beside us. I know the driver but there's no point running now; he's already seen Sheamie and me. It's our father's friend, Umbilical Bill, and he doesn't have his usual friendly face on. He doesn't even talk as he snaps the lock off the door of the delivery lorry with a crowbar.

I jump in the back with Danny and Lucy. It's dark but we manage to pass the cardboard boxes filled with cartons of cigarettes to the others outside, forming a line to the back doors of the green truck, and in under five minutes Bill is gone one way and we're gone the other way with five pounds each. None of us knows what to do with five pounds. Some of it has to be put away for Sheamie but there's loads left over. At this rate Sheamie will have his escape money in no time. Maybe I'll buy loafers like kids on the outside and get the cobbler to put metal tips in the heels. I'd like that and in a few weeks I'm certain I have enough.

The woman behind the counter in Mark's shoe shop looks

me up and down when I ask for size five loafers. They're nine pounds she says, as if all who ever belonged to me never had nine pounds between them.

Would you wrap them for me, please?

Passing the Apple Market, Umbilical Bill waves me over to his fruit stall. It's cold and Bill is flogging yellow T-shirts that say, Shit Happens, and you can see the tattoo on the back of his hand telling the world, I love Mum.

I like the Apple Market when my father's not around. You can buy anything here from a spanner to a carrot or the shirt off a trader's back. I've seen them do it. Take the shirt off and wave it in the air. I'm not asking five pounds. I'm not asking two. I'm not even asking one. I never know what they're asking, but it's great to watch.

Bill hands me a brown paper bag full of apples and whispers not to mention anything to my father about our, a, well about, you know.

What are you talking about?

He coughs and talks under his breath. About our little arrangement.

I won't, Bill.

Great stuff. There might be another job on this week.

I walk back to the convent with the bag of apples under one arm and the black loafers under the other and it's some comfort to know we're not the only ones worried over my father.

In the morning, the bed sheets are covered in blood and I don't know what to do. I search the other bedrooms for Pippa and Mona but there's no sign. I run downstairs but there's only Gabriel feeding Polly the budgie. She looks at me through the bars of the cage. Her bushy black eyebrows search me from head to toenails.

Bleeding, Matilda?

I'm goin' red, but I don't care. I turn my face away and point, Down there, mother.

Gabriel doesn't look surprised. Oh, you'd better come with me.

I wonder where she's bringing me. Father Devlin for confession? Reverend Mother? Jesus, am I in trouble?

Gabriel brings me upstairs and leaves me standing in the corridor when she goes into the bedroom Doyler uses on the nights Doyler sleeps over. Through the window I can see Pippa and Mona down by the chestnut trees with Sheamie. They're digging a hole to hide our money and I have to move to block Gabriel's view when she comes out with one hand behind her back. She closes the door behind her. She doesn't say a word when she hands me the blue plastic packet and walks away down the stairs.

What do I do with these? I'm left standing in the corridor under a picture of the Blessed Virgin. She's blue, I'm red and I wonder if she ever bled like this.

I run downstairs for Pippa. Grab her by the arm and pull her upstairs and tell her what's happened but she won't talk to me over what I done to her in Grace's supermarket. Shoved all the sweets in her hand and ran off. I thought she'd run too, but she stood there bawling like a baby. She bawled so much the fat manager took pity and let her keep the sweets anyway. Now I have to tell her I'm sorry before she'll take the sulky look off and talk to me.

That's your period, she says.

I know it's me fuckin' period. Do you think I'm stupid or something? I want to know more about it though.

I don't know much more. It's to do with eggs.

That's it. I'm not eatin' any more eggs.

Won't make no difference, Matilda. I never eat eggs and I still gets them.

You get periods?

Ages ago.

Does Mona get them?

Of course.

Some sister yee are, all pally-wally the two of yee with yeer periods. Don't tell me, whatever you do.

Nobody told me before I got them either, Matilda, so don't blame me.

I show her the blue plastic packet and ask her what to do?

Open it for a start.

I rip the packet open and inside there's cotton wool in a net bag with strings at the side. Pippa takes one, opens the strings out, and steps into it over her jeans like it's her knickers.

The strings go here and the pad covers your fanny.

I burst out laughing, but just the same I take off my jeans, put it on and get dressed again.

Ah, Jesus, look at the state of me, Pippa. It sticks out like a willy.

You have to wear a dress, Matilda.

I never wear a dress. How am I going to steal in a dress?

Pippa shrugs.

The bleeding lasts for days and then I'm free and in a few weeks there's almost a hundred pounds buried under the chestnut tree. Sheamie says he'll leave at the end of May, before our father turns up for summer.

This time I think I really do want Sheamie to leave. I know Pippa is probably right and it's all a stupid idea. Sheamie might never find our mother. But it's the only way I'll ever get out of the Mad School. It's the only thing that gives me hope.

13

My father's sister Aunt Margaret is coming from England to get married and the five of us are invited to the wedding. I don't know anyone in the convent who was at a wedding and I'm pure faintin'. Our cousin Jennifer is coming from London with her father, our Uncle James the millionaire, and her mother, Aunt Peg. Jennifer is the flower girl. I'd like to be a flower girl in a long pink dress and being brought to the hair-dresser to have my hair done up in ringlets and the pink ribbons tied in properly. I dreamed about it last night. The altar over-flowed with flowers and the sunlight through the windows turned the chapel into a sea of gold and when the organ played 'Here Comes the Bride' the guests shuffled in the pews turning to look at Aunt Margaret in her wedding gown, all white and smiling, strolling down the aisle on Grandad's arm and me in front with my flower basket, everyone saying how pretty I looked and oh, my, Matilda's hair is only fabulous.

Saturday morning is so warm the tar on the road bubbles. Gabriel drops the five of us up to our grandmother's house in the mini-bus and there's a white Rolls-Royce decked in pink and ribbon parked outside. Another long white car is parked behind, with its windows dazzling in the sunshine. Nanny comes to the garden gate to thank Gabriel for bringing us up but I rush past her and straight through the hallway to the sitting room. Grandad is stretched back in his new green leather chair, which now has a new hollow. The horse racing is on television and there's a glass of stout in his hand and he'd sit there all day by the looks of him.

Well, Grandad, Pippa and me say.

Slow down there now, hold yeer horses the pair of yee. She's in the front room.

Any winners, Grandad?

He doesn't answer and that means he has. We stop running and sit on the new green sofa pushing and shoving each other to torment him.

Oh, here, here. He puts his hands in his trouser pocket and hands us a pound note each. Take that and hide it before anyone sees.

Thanks, Grandad.

We run back the way we came, passing Sheamie and Danny in the hallway.

Grandad has money, lads.

We burst into the front bedroom that smells of hairspray and fresh flowers and there's Aunt Margaret fixing her veil in the mirror. She's even prettier than in my dream. She says she can't remember when she saw us last and look how long your hair is. You were like two boys before.

The penguins don't cut it much anymore, says Pippa.

The women in the room laugh at the way we call the nuns penguins and Aunt Margaret says she's glad she's getting married before you two hit the town. There won't be a man safe. Come over here and give your aunt a hug.

We're careful not to crumple her veil and I'm delighted she even spoke to us with all the women here telling Margaret how stunning she looks. Mona follows us in and the three of us sit on the bed listening to the women from the street gabble on.

Tell me now, Margaret, did you buy that dress in London? Of course you did, I could tell by looking. You wouldn't see the likes anywhere here and isn't it only a fabulous day for you now. You don't always get weather like this in May. Weren't you lucky just the same? God no, Annie, I couldn't touch another drop of sherry. Well, maybe just one more, the blessing of the Virgin Mary aren't you only great now, so you are.

The other women laugh, Don't be talkin' about virgins on a day like this, Hannah. Hannah giggles and offers her glass to Nanny. Just a little more, Annie, a little, that's grand now.

Pippa nods towards the window and squeezes my arm so tight the blood stops flowing. I see them through the netted curtains walking up the footpath. High hats and grey suits. Uncle Philip and Uncle John. For once I wish my father were here.

Nanny goes to the sitting room to tell Grandad Margaret is ready. I don't understand why Margaret and Grandad are leaving first. Why can't we go first and be at the chapel before them? I don't ask though in case it's a stupid question and you can't ask grown-ups stupid questions when they're full of sherry.

Everyone goes out to the front garden. The afternoon sun is high above the red-brick chimney of Denny's meat factory and the sky is blue and clear. The boys are playing football on the street. The girls come to the garden gate to watch Margaret walking out the footpath on Grandad's arm and they say, Oh, isn't she lovely? Pippa and me hold hands by the door because we don't know where the safest place is, the house or the garden. But we agree, no matter what, we're not to take money from our uncles.

Promise me now, Pippa.

I promise, Matilda. You know I wouldn't do that.

Yes, you would.

I know I would but I won't today.

When Margaret leaves with Grandad I watch the second car pull up to the gate. The driver gets out and holds the back door open for Nanny. Uncle Philip and Uncle John are leaning on the garden wall chatting to Mossy Brennan. Pippa tightens her grip on my hand when Nanny tells them to make sure the doors are locked before they leave. Pippa says, Matilda, ask Nanny if we can go with her. But Nanny is already getting in the car with Danny and Sheamie and Mona. We're left at the front door surrounded by neighbours mad to chat because the weather is nice and they're all pissed on sherry and we don't know what to do till Nanny calls to us, Would you two hurry up, there's room for everyone, and I never ran out that footpath as fast in me life.

After the wedding we go to the Bridge Hotel and, even though we've spent all morning getting ready, the five of us look like Sheps. Our clothes are clean, but tatty and out of date. The lobby is full of relations we've never met. The men in suits, the women in long frocks, and they all know who we are. Peter's children, God help them.

Here, girl, put that in your pocket.

Thank you.

Which one are you?

Matilda.

The function room is packed. We sit by the window with Nanny, Grandad, Uncle James the millionaire, Aunt Peg and our cousin Jennifer. Women in dainty white hats and frilly white aprons bring food on trolleys and it never ends until our bellies are stuffed. Roast beef, roast pork, ham, turkey and sherry trifle. Danny thinks he died and went to Heaven. His round brown eyes pop out every time he fills his gob and, if Sheamie ate everything in the Bridge Hotel, he'd still be the skinniest boy I ever saw.

After the meal we move to the bar while the tables are cleared. The bar smells of beer and cigarette smoke and everywhere there's a clinking of glasses. The five of us are standing at the bar with Nanny when Uncle Philip walks in jingling the change in his trouser pocket.

Everyone having a good time, I hope. What can I get you to drink, Mammy?

A sherry. And don't move from here. I'm going to find your father.

Nanny squeezes her way through the crowd. Uncle Philip smiles down at me like he expects me to smile back. I want to run after Nanny but all I can do is gawk around the room like I hardly notice he's here. Uncle James's four sons are standing by the window with glasses in their hands. They're men now and they talk about their careers in the bank, the law, the civil service and a thing called the stock market, where you can make money for nothing. Returns, it's all about returns. Things I haven't a clue about and I think how I was nearly their sister if my father had let Danny and me live with Uncle James when we were young. Would I be like a sister to them now or would they talk about returns while they treated me like a maid in a little white hat, fetching and carrying and wiping their arses in general?

Uncle Philip takes a fistful of change from his pocket and starts sharing it out between the five of us. Mona snaps the hand of him. So does Danny. Sheamie counts his.

Here, Matilda. Put that in your pocket.

No, thanks.

Go on, take it.

No, thanks.

What about you, Pippa?

Pippa's pink cheeks turn scarlet. She lowers her head and her bright blue eyes lift to plead with me for help, but Pippa doesn't need help because Nanny is back with Grandad wondering where can we sit and didn't you get that sherry yet, Philip?

Just giving the kids a few bob, Mammy. I'll get it now.

Oh, says Nanny. There's a surprise. Wouldn't you think he'd have bought himself a suit?

I know before I turn round. One look at Sheamie's long face is enough to know it's my father. Sheamie is fit to cry because he won't be able to run away until my father goes back to London. He'd be too scared to chance it.

Sheamie might be upset but I feel like I've been let out of jail. My father is at the door with Mona. He bends and puts his arms around Mona's slim waist and kisses her on the lips. I run to kiss his cheek and this time I really mean it. I'm safe from Uncle Philip when my father is here. My father isn't that bad and he looks great in his new blue jeans, blue T-shirt and black runners, not giving a shit what anyone thinks. I like that about him and I don't feel different in my blue poncho anymore. My father is here and I'm safe. Nothing else matters.

We move back to the function room. The hotel lights are turned down. Above our heads a great silver ball spins and catches the light like a million tiny mirrors. The tables have been moved back to the walls and there's a space in the middle of the room for dancing. The bar is full all day. Some men never leave it. Uncle James stands there rubbing his fat belly, drinking whiskey soda and buying a drink for anyone that stands near. I hear his deep voice every time I go to the toilet.

Put your money away, it's no good here.

Uncle John is on his own. He's perched, like an eagle, at the end of the bar, surrounded by a cloud of cigarette smoke and the stink of his own farts. His claws wrapped around a fresh pint of stout and his beak stained black from the last one.

White tablecloths are covered with glasses. Empty, half empty, full. Stout, beer, ale, red and white wine. Grandad swirls his brandy glass while he puffs on a fat cigar like a Texan. There's a band, three men in shiny red shirts and black waistcoats playing guitar and a fourth playing drums and singing into the microphone. There's a small black box in front of them with flashing lights that change colour with the music, and all I want to do is dance and dance but I wouldn't dare. I've never danced before.

I'm sitting beside my father. Sheamie is on the other side of him drinking Coke and talking to one of Uncle James's sons about stock markets and stuff, even though a fool could see he's just being nice to Sheamie 'cos it's a wedding and any other time he wouldn't give Sheamie the steam off his piss. Mona is across from me drinking white wine. Daddy said she's old enough. She's almost fifteen. Pippa is sitting beside Mona drinking lemonade, looking around at everyone. Danny is sitting beside Grandad drinking Grandad's stout when he thinks Grandad isn't looking. Everyone stands and cheers when the bride and groom stand up to dance. Nanny and Grandad dance next and before the first song is over the dance floor is covered in suits and frocks.

Jennifer, the flower girl, is dancing with her father, our Uncle James. She looks pretty in that pink dress and the ribbons in her hair. My feet are tapping under the table to the beat and when the music gets faster my arse starts banging off the seat. The chair legs bang off the floor and I'm having a great time till one chair leg lands on my father's foot and, when I look down, his runner is tore. The yellow eyes glare at me. Oh, fuck, I'm dead.

Like dancing, do you, Matilda?

Sorry, Daddy. It was an accident.

He bends down slowly to take off his runners and suddenly dancing doesn't seem such fun. He leaves the runners under the table and stands up over me. The disco lights flickering across his forehead make him look like he's covered in confetti.

Come on, he says, follow me.

I said I was sorry, Daddy. It was an accident.

And I said, follow me.

I know he's bringing me outside for a beating. Making a show, no, an example of me. Making me feel less than I do already in front of our relations with their suits and frocks and talk about returns. He puts his huge hand around my wrist and pulls me across the dance floor and there's nothing for my legs to do but follow.

Nanny is dancing with Grandad and she gives me a wave over Grandad's shoulder when I pass and I wonder is she after drinking too much sherry. When we get to the middle of the dance floor my father stops and pulls up his sleeves. The band start singing 'Twist and Shout'.

He's going to start on me in front of everyone. He catches my two hands and twirls me around. He pushes me out then pulls me back closer and spins me round. Does he want me to dance, or what? I don't know what to think. It looks like he does. I want him to mean it. We dance till the song is over and he never lets me fall and then the band starts again and we're still dancing. He's a good dancer. I know he won a trophy once in the Olympia Ballroom, dancing with my mother. I saw the picture but I can't remember when. The two of them were holding a tall trophy between them with a little dancing man and woman on the top. My parents were smiling, in love, happy. My father was handsome. Still would be if he shaved himself and cut his hair. He wore a white shirt and black tie. His hair was slicked back. Her hair was let down. My mother looked beautiful. It was a black and white photograph but I know her eyes were blue. I don't know what colour her dress was. It was nice. Square-cut collar and no sleeves. I hope it was blue too. That's the way I like to picture her that night.

A circle grows around us in the middle of the floor. Every-one is watching and I know now he's not making a fool of me. He looks great in his white socks, not giving a shit about anyone. This is how to do the hucklebuck, Matilda. He wriggles like a snake and waddles like a duck smiling and clapping his hands pushing his long hair behind his ears while he spins and glides twisting around the dance floor clicking his fingers and three songs later he's still dancing with me showing me how to do the hokey-cokey and telling everyone I'm his daughter. I'm pure faintin', I'm floating over the dance floor when he tells me I'm some mover. I have rhythm. I'm just like my mother. The more he tells me the more I want to dance and make him proud of me because he's changed. He's better because he knows now he has the five of us and that's all he'll ever need. I know he's going to take us out of the convent and buy a house here. We'll have a dog and we'll all be happy and forget everything bad that happened. Our mother might come back. She might come soon.

Everyone is calling for my father to sing and when he heads for the stage Aunt Peg calls the five of us together. Aunt Peg wears a gold bracelet with gold charms dangling from her wrists, gold necklace and gold earrings in loops that jingle when she walks and there's a fur over her shoulders she says is real fox fur. I know she's not lying because the poor bastard's bushy tail is lying on one shoulder while his dead brown eyes gawk at me from the other and you have to wonder why the fuck Aunt Peg is wearing a thing like that with all the money she has.

Aunt Peg says how thrilled she is to finally meet us all. You're lovely children. Your Daddy is really proud of you. I've never seen him this happy. Look at him up there on stage playing the guitar and singing 'Rock Around the Clock' better than Bill Haley himself. It's more like a concert than a wedding.

We turn to watch my father when he sits on a high stool with the microphone to his lips and the guitar on his lap, and my cheeks are on fire because everyone in the room knows he's singing for me and I know I'll never forget this moment if I live till I'm forty. I know the words from when I was little and I remember the song is about a man who would rather die than go to prison. I could never be as brave as that.

> Once a jolly swagman camped by a billabong
> Under the shade of a coolibah-tree
> And he sang as he watched and waited till his billy boiled
> 'Who'll come a-waltzing Matilda with me?
> Waltzing Matilda,
> Waltzing Matilda,
> Who'll come a-waltzing Matilda with me?'
> And he sang as he watched and waited till his billy boiled
> 'Who'll come a-waltzing Matilda with me?'

Now, says Aunt Peg over the music, I'll be going back to England on Monday with Uncle James but we'll be down to see you on Sunday morning. You can spend the day with us.

There's a tap on my shoulder. Uncle Philip wobbling with the drink. The pink shirt open halfway down his chest and the top hat crooked on his head. Daddy is finished singing and he's making his way back to our table.

What about a dance?

I don't want to dance.

That's a nice way to treat your uncle.

He says it loud so my Daddy can hear him and give out to me for not dancing. Uncle Philip knows nobody will believe me if I say why I won't dance. I'll be called a troublemaker and I'll be sent away for ever. But this time it's different. I don't have to dance with Uncle Philip and I don't have to talk to him. My Daddy is here, he's changed, he's proud of me. He's coming home and we're all going to be happy and Uncle Philip can't ever bother me again.

I turn my back and walk away from the table. Nanny stands up to go to the bathroom and I bump against her and knock her back in the chair but I keep going across the dance floor. I want my Daddy to follow and ask me why I didn't dance and I'll tell him, I will. He'll believe me too. He wouldn't have before, but tonight he will. He'll go straight in and kick Uncle Philip all over the Bridge Hotel when I tell him everything Uncle Philip made me do and if Uncle John tries to run we'll jump on him and so will Sheamie and Mona and Danny because they hate him as much as I do.

It's twilight out on the footpath. The night air is sweet and the breeze from the River Suir cools me. If you look hard you can just make out the quarter moon above Tory Hill. The cars are stopped at the traffic lights with their headlights on. The green man bleeps and I cross to the other side of the Quay and wait by the chains along the river. The breeze is colder here and brings goose bumps to my arms. The tide is rushing out. You can hear it gurgle under the bridge on its way to the Atlantic Ocean. This is where I want to tell my Daddy everything because I'm sure that's what girls do. We'll walk along the riverbank holding hands until I'm ready to talk. He'll give me time. We'll sit on a bench. He'll put his arms around me and pull me close to him and tell me he's sorry for everything. He misses us. He loves us. I'll lay me forehead against his chest and feel safe. He'll promise never to leave us again.

I see him coming now through the glass door and he looks angry. He's already guessed what's up. He sprints across the road in his white socks, making the cars stop for him, and stands so close to me I can't see his face without bending back. His huge forehead is wrinkled and the veins in his temples swollen like thick blue ropes.

What the fuck do you think you're doing?

What? I –

Why is he talking to me like this? The words are in my head but they won't come out. My feet that couldn't stop dancing are stuck to the ground.

I feel the back of his hand across my jaw that sends me flying against the chains. The chains sway and I hear the river gushing past. There's darkness and silver in my head like the great silver ball fell from the ceiling and shattered over my head. I'm losing my balance till my father grabs my arm and pulls me back.

Get back in there and tell Uncle Philip and your Nanny you're sorry. Go on. Do it right now. What is it with you? Everywhere you're brought you cause trouble. You're just stupid. That's why you're in that school. You know that, don't you? Now get back in there and apologize.

He grabs my hair and drags me across the road past the cars stopped at the traffic lights. He streals me through the hotel lobby past relations and strangers watching. They turn their backs to us but there's nothing new about that. I don't know which is worse, strangers or relations or the pain in my scalp. I try to yell out but my father doesn't care and there's nothing to do but go inside and do what I'm told.

Sunday morning, my head hurts and I know my father didn't change but I'm used of it. Anyway, Aunt Peg is calling. She'll come along early in her big English car. She'll bring us to Tramore where we'll go on the bumper cars and the roller coaster and spend as long as we like on the slot machines that gobble pennies by the bucketload, but who cares when you have a rich aunt handing out English pound notes. She'll definitely buy the pink ice cream cones and the chips in the Beach Grill, who every fool knows make the tastiest chips in the world. There's nothing in the world like Tramore when you can have chips in oodles of vinegar, cool ice cream at the back of your throat and an English pound to do what you like with. If paradise has a feel, it has to be the feel of an English pound in your pocket.

We're scrubbed and washed. Gabriel is ironing my blue poncho on the worktop by the sink and says she wouldn't know me if she saw me in anything else, although it is getting a little small for you and isn't it time you thought about sending it to the missions, Matilda?

No, Mother.

But surely . . .

No, Mother.

I can't explain to Gabriel how the poncho reminds me of my mother so I wander outside to the playground. Danny is sitting on the swings with Mona and Sheamie. Pippa and me push each other on the roundabout and wonder what time Aunt Peg is coming. The bells for twelve o'clock mass ring out over the city and if she's not here soon she won't be here until after lunch.

We stay on the swings a while longer until Gabriel comes to the door to say lunch is ready, if we want it. She doesn't want to ruin our appetites with the big day ahead but the salt air will take care of that. There's nothing like salt air to give you an appetite.

By three o'clock Gabriel is complaining. Your Aunt Peg is very late. Are you certain she said today?

Yes, Mother.

Gabriel says she'll turn on the television while we're waiting. There's a film she wouldn't mind watching herself. We go into the sitting room and sit and watch Shirley Temple singing and dancing all over the orphanage because she has a rich aunt she never knew she had who's come to take her home.

Sheamie hates Shirley Temple.

Girls' stuff. Come on, Matilda, we'll do something else. Sheamie walks ahead of me out to the playground with his hands in his pockets. Gabriel lifts her head from embroidering one of her pocket-handkerchiefs and warns us not to stray. Stay where I can find you in case your aunt turns up.

Sheamie isn't interested in aunts or anything. He wants to go to the orchard, even though we're not supposed to, and we have to pass the penguins' mansion on the way. Sheamie says they won't see us unless they're looking out windows. It's Sunday and the penguins are too busy praying to look out windows. Sheamie's in such a mood over Aunt Peg not turning up when she should and our father turning up when he shouldn't I think I'd better go with him in case he does something daft.

We climb the stone wall to the penguins' garden then dive on our bellies and crawl through the sea of bluebells. The sun is overhead and we can feel the heat on our backs. When we're through the bluebells we can stand up and run the two fields to the orchard. I look back but Sheamie is gone and I think he's after turning back till his head sticks up from a hole with his glasses still on. He climbs out and runs past me and I wonder what sort of a brother I have trying to escape from the convent so he can go to Australia to find our mother when he can't even get to the orchard without falling down a hole.

The orchard is lovely in spring. The trees are thick with blossom and all round there's a sweet smell of apple. We can reach the bottom branches and pull ourselves up, then climb high into the trees where we'll never be seen. Sheamie jumps up on the big bough, scratching himself under his arms, making monkey noises, but his legs are skinny and he can't hang upside down from the branches and grip on by his knees like I can. He falls and twists his ankle and won't climb back up, so now he wants to do something else.

In the next field is the wooden hut where the pigs are kept. We see them stick their heads in the air and sniff and I wonder how they can smell anything with a flat nose like that. One pig struts around the wire pen with a ring through his nose. Another has baby pigs hanging from a belly full of swollen pink tits. It's sad to see them locked up. Penguins always keep things locked up. Sheamie wonders why they keep pigs at all when he never ate a rasher in his life. Rashers are for Father Devlin and special visitors like the government man who comes once a year to check we're all still breathing, but Reverend Mother has him so pissed on whiskey he never gets past her office. Sheamie smiles when he remembers the pigs eat the blood and leftover bits from the babies born to girls who come to slave in the laundry while they're waiting for their babies to be born.

We sit on the rusty tin roof and lie back with the sun on our faces. Sheamie complains, Grown-ups don't care, Matilda. Even Gabriel was only tormented because she had to get our clothes cleaned for nothin'.

Let's get them back, Sheamie.

Who?

All of them.

The iron gate at the front of the pen is heavy but the two of us manage to open it wide enough to make a gap. We climb back up on the tin roof and sit and watch. But the pigs don't move. Sheamie shouts, Hull, hull, but they still don't move. Sheamie throws a stone and hits the pig with the ring right between the two eyes. It jumps and squeals and sprays shit all over the pen and we have to hold our jumpers over our faces with the stench. The pig with the ring sniffs its way towards the gate and pokes his nose outside. His arse follows. The baby pigs follow the pig with the swollen pink tits. More pigs come from inside the wooden hut till now the field is littered with pigs snorting and spraying.

There's a shout.

Sheamie and Matilda Kelly. Don't move!

I don't believe it. There's a penguin leaning out a window. She's so far away she's like a head on a postage stamp but somehow she's able to see us and soon we're surrounded by penguins. The pigs take off and the penguins take off after them. Sheamie is buckled up laughing on the tin roof. Penguins covered in mud are falling on their backsides, veils over their faces, chasing screeching pigs. By dark we're all locked up, the pigs in the sty and Sheamie and me upstairs. We're thumped, legs, heads, shoulders, and barred from leaving the play-ground. We are to go to Confession. In the meantime, do twenty-five Hail Marys, ten Our Fathers, a good Act of Con-trition and the ten decades of the rosary. Do it in silence on your knees in that corner there, the both of you.

But we'll be here for a week.

Do it!

Sheamie is kneeling beside me. His face is serious but his eyes twinkle at the wall. I'm happy Sheamie is my brother and I know I could never swap any of my brothers or sisters for Uncle James and Aunt Peg or all the stock market returns in the world, whatever they are.

Sheamie whispers, It were worth it, Matilda.

It was, Sheamie.

Are you saying the rosary, Matilda?

It's kinda hard not to when you're on your knees, Sheamie. It's a habit.

But, are you really saying it, Matilda?

'Course not. Are you?

Nah.

14

Gabriel wants to see Mona, Sheamie, Pippa, Danny and me in her office, and when we go in there are five empty chairs in front of her desk. I'm certain there's trouble because Gabriel wouldn't care if you stood through High Mass. She's sitting behind her desk making a little roof with her fingertips, and now I'm not so sure we're in trouble. She keeps her eyes to one side and no way would she wait this long to scream her head off. The room is so quiet you can hear the clock tick on the wall. She fidgets in the desk drawer like she's looking for something important, before closing the drawer and taking nothing out. She covers her mouth with her hand to clear her throat before she tells us she's had a phone call from our grandmother to say we're going away with our father for the summer.

No way, Mother, says Sheamie. He'll drag us to every church in the country. We'll be reading Bibles all day. You can't send us.

Mona stands up and stomps her foot on the floor. No way, Mother, you know what he's like. You can't send us.

Gabriel waves her hand in front of her like she's patting a dog's head. Sheamie, you come with me. The rest of you wait upstairs in Mona's room.

We all complain, But, Mother.

But nothing. Get away upstairs and do what you are told.

Mona, Pippa, Danny and me go upstairs and sit at the end of Mona's bed and stare at the wall because there's nothin' else to stare at except the picture of Jesus and the Apostles sitting at a long table breaking bread, drinking wine and Judas looking over his shoulder as he sneaks out the door, and who wants to be looking at Judas at a time like this.

I don't want to go. The churches and spellings are bad enough but, after what happened at the wedding, I don't want to go anywhere with him. Mona is leaning against the door in her blue school uniform, chewing her thumbnail and not looking at anything in particular. Just to say something I say, This is a nice room, Mona, even though that's stupid because all the rooms are the same but I know being allowed to sit on Mona's bed without Mona going demented means Mona is worried.

Pippa looks over at me.

Do you want to go, Matilda?

Do you?

No. Not for the whole summer, anyway.

Me neither.

Mona flicks her eyes over at us then back to the floor. She's thinking. Apart from anything else, we all know Mona has boyfriends to worry about and she'll do anything not to go.

Gabriel and Sheamie bustle in the door with suitcases and four sets of clothes each. Gabriel tells us to leave the lids open, she'll be back to check we've packed properly. The noise from the road outside comes through the open window so I shut it and the room turns quiet. Mona's room is across the corridor from mine and looks out on to the houses in Trinity Park. I hardly noticed before how every house seems to have a car now and nearly every car a different colour. Sheamie calls them Japanese rust buckets and you can see the rust bubbles eating away at the doors and wings even though the cars are still shiny and new-looking. It seems like everything outside the convent walls is full of colour. Inside, everything is as black and white as the nuns' habits.

I turn back to look at my brothers and sisters and it's the first time for a long time I can remember it just being the five of us together. I try to make myself believe we will have a nice time.

Sheamie sits on his suitcase in the middle of the floor. The sunlight bounces off his glasses and around the walls every time he moves his head to tell us he's running away. Pippa shakes her head at him.

You'd want to leave yourself alone at night-time, Sheamie. You have the brains pulled outa yourself. You wouldn't get as far as the bridge before our father finds you.

I tell Pippa to leave Sheamie alone. Pippa flicks her blonde ponytail and sits back against the wall with her arms folded and her don't-you-dare-talk-to-me-again face.

Still, says Sheamie, we have to do something.

What? says Mona. We can't do nothin'.

Of course we can, says Sheamie. Tell Gabriel we're just not going.

Pippa decides to talk again.

Just like that, she says to Sheamie, say we're not going. That's a brilliant fuckin' idea. I'd say you were awake all night.

I'll say it to Gabriel when she comes back.

Go on, then. I dare yeh.

We pack the suitcases and leave them on the floor with the lids open and sit back on the bed waiting for Gabriel, and here she is already bending down, locking the cases, telling us she never saw five such mournful gobs. We look at each other, nodding, nudging, pointing to Gabriel, but that's as far as it goes till Pippa kneels up on the bed and says, Ah, Mother.

Yes, Pippa?

Sheamie has something to tell you, and sticks her tongue out at Sheamie.

What is it, Sheamie?

186

It wasn't me, Mother. What are you pickin' on me for. I didn't say anything.

Oh yes you did, says Pippa.

Well one of you must want something. What's going on here?

Sheamie's face is as red as his hair and Gabriel doesn't have time to wait for an answer. She has things to do. I kneel up on the bed beside Pippa and ask Gabriel do we have to go on this holiday and Gabriel says it's been decided. Sheamie says, But we don't want to go, and Gabriel says, Well you are going, and that sets Mona off. She stomps her feet on the floor, I'm not going. I don't want to. I'm just not going and that's all there is to it. We'll be kilt. I'm nearly fifteen and you can't make me.

Gabriel snaps up straight and wags her finger at Mona.

I can and I will. And none of your tantrums here, Miss. You'll keep your gob well shut if you know what's good. I don't know what this nonsense is about. There isn't a child in here wouldn't give their eyelashes for even a weekend away, never mind a whole summer. It's on your knees thanking the good Lord for the privilege, you should be.

But she's not convincing us.

It's too long, Mother, says Sheamie. You can say we're only allowed for a week or something.

Gabriel sighs, she sits on the bed between us with her crucifix on her lap and it's the first time I've seen Gabriel sitting on a bed talking to anyone. We gather round her and tell her she knows what our father is like. Sheamie says he'll turn us all into Pentecostals again and for good this time. We'll be brainwashed.

Gabriel draws breath and stares at Sheamie over her glasses.

Do you think so, Sheamie?

Protestants, even. And you wouldn't want that, Mother.

You know how Reverend Mother feels about Protestants. He might even kidnap us away to England to live with him.

There's a lump in Gabriel's throat the size of a doorknob. She lifts her eyebrows and stares at each of us in turn, and we look back with worried faces and nod that Sheamie is right.

I'll ring your grandmother immediately. Don't stir.

We can't laugh. Pippa is sobbing her eyes out till Sheamie tells her she's at it again, wah, wah, wah, does she ever feckin' stop? At least wait till Gabriel gets back. The only one not bothered is Danny. He's lying on the bed with his round brown eyes staring up at the ceiling. Danny is only ten so, no matter what happens, Danny thinks that's just the way things are. I suppose that happens to you when you've been in and out of orphanages since you were two.

Gabriel is back but stays by the door. She says everything is arranged. Your grandmother is coming with you. She's assured me you'll attend mass and receive the Blessed Sacraments. She's mortified enough with your father preaching outside the Cathedral and wouldn't have the shame of a Protestant in the family. You're meeting your Uncle James and your Aunt Peg in Donegal. Get outside the lot of you. That's the end of it.

The end of it?

That can't be the end even though Nanny coming is better than Nanny not coming but no way do I want to be with that Aunt Peg and her dead fox. I'll ask Doyler. I catch her as she's pouring herself a cup of tea in the kitchen but she says it's out of her hands. She wouldn't have any say. Reverend Mother would have her out the door faster than she could bless herself if she attempted to interfere. You know the position I'm in but aren't I doing my best for all of you. Aren't I? Well, aren't I? How dare you walk away from me! Come back here this instant.

Lucy Flynn is waiting for me in the playground with another idea. She's sitting on the swing with her arms wrapped around the chains. Her hair in plaits and her skin blackened from the sun. Lucy says, Me mother is going the live in England, Matilda. We can run away with her and live wi'me relations. Yee haves money, I seen Sheamie hidin't it under the chestnut trees.

I couldn't do that, Lucy.

But you're me friend, Matilda.

I have to stay with my brothers and sisters, Lucy. I can't go. It's not worth running away for.

Suit yerself, don't say I didn't ask yeh.

I won't, Lucy.

Saturday morning, the five of us are sitting on our suitcases out in the playground. We hear it before we see its blue bonnet coming around the corner by the fire escape. It sounds as rusty as it looks and my father's behind the steering wheel with his elbow out the window and the cigarette between his lips. He steps out wearing the brown Moses sandals and the same clothes he wore at the wedding, and fires a fistful of silver coins in the air like thirty pieces of silver dazzling in the sunshine. They tinkle when they land and roll over the ground and set off a stampede of the kids screaming, pulling and pushing each other around the playground. Gabriel comes to the door, all smiles for my father, and it's easy to see she'll be glad to see the back of him and he won't be in here tormenting her.

My father bends for us to kiss his cheek and he tells us to put our cases in the boot and sit in the car. He goes inside to talk to Gabriel and I climb in the back next to Pippa and Danny and Sheamie. Sheamie is sitting behind my father's seat. I'm sitting behind the other seat with Pippa and Danny in the middle. Mona is in the front.

Where's my grandmother going to sit?

Gabriel comes to the door with my father to wave goodbye. Have a nice time and I'll see you when you get back.

There's a dirty yellow caravan with rusty wheels parked outside our grandmother's house. My father hitches it to the back of the car and brings us inside where our grandmother is sitting in the armchair watching the horse racing on television. She has a cup of tea in one hand and her betting docket in the other. My father says, We called to say goodbye, and now we know our grandmother lied. She betrayed us.

She keeps her old grey eyes on the television when she tells us to behave for our Daddy and she'll see us when we get back, if we get back at all with this petrol shortage going on. Cars backed up for miles at every petrol station in the country.

We'll be all right, says my father.

I'm sure you'll manage, right enough. Have a nice time, that's the main thing. She goes to the kitchen to make tea for herself. She doesn't even come to the door to wave goodbye.

No one wants to sit in the front seat. The one in the front seat has to do the spellings. We've all squashed in the back and we're whispering, You get in, piss off, you get in.

Oh, shut the fuck up all of you, says Mona.

Then my father roars, One of you sit in the front!

Sheamie leaps. Everyone else clutches the seat in front of them and when Sheamie lands again he's in the front seat and there are grunts of relief in the back. Soon we're crossing the bridge over the River Suir and I wonder how long before I see it again.

At every garage along the way there's a queue of cars. Each garage will only give five pounds worth of petrol and we have to stop at four garages before the car is filled. We've been driving and stopping and driving on again and it's been hours since our last stop. Mona is sitting in the front seat now. I'm hot and stiff and I'm bursting to piss. I know the others are too, the way they clutch themselves. My father tells Mona to reach under the seat and get the schoolbooks out. We're to do our spellings. Mona can be a bitch with spellings the way she asks the ones she learns in the big girls' school, but today Mona asks the simple ones and, even when we get one wrong, Mona pretends we got it right.

My father winds the window down full and turns on the radio and sings along with the music, 'Seasons in the Sun'. He's in great form. He lets his hand out the window tapping his fingers off the car door and tells us to put the schoolbooks away. We're sweaty in the back so we wind the windows down for the cool wind and if it stays like this things mightn't be too bad.

We stop at a field with hedges all round. Across the road a horse has his head out over a gate. He has a long nose and a toothy grin and I wonder, does he know something I don't? My father tells us to do what yee have to do but hurry. I want to be there tonight.

The field is covered in nettles and great blobs of cow shit. Mona and me run behind a hedge but Pippa won't follow. We hear her through the briars telling Sheamie she has a red blouse on and a bull would attack. Sheamie says bulls don't bother over red, they'd chase anything that moves. They're a bit like Mona.

Mona doesn't hear.

Pippa says, Of course they do, Sheamie. Everyone knows that. Sheamie says, Suit yourself, and turns to the hedge to piss.

When Mona and me come back, Pippa asks, Is there a bull?

No.

Are yee sure?

We are.

We watch Pippa till she gets to the corner of the hedge.

There's two, Pippa.

Pippa puts her hands to her head and screams.

Sheamie is laughing so hard he catches his willy in his zipper. He's bent over and there's water coming from his eyes and I don't know if it's the laughing or if he's in pain. He looks in pain. Oh Jesus, Sheamie, are you in pain? The poor youngfella. Is he in pain, Danny? Stop laughing, Danny, it's not funny. Can we do anything, Sheamie? Are you bleeding? Is he bleeding, Danny? Pippa, are you ready yet? Danny, would you stop laughing.

Mona and me run to the car for our father and tell him what's happened to Sheamie. He jumps out and runs into the field. Mona and me wait by the car.

It's a penis, says Mona.

What is?

A willy.

That's disgustin'.

Why?

Just is.

There's nothing to be embarrassed over, Matilda.

Do you know somethin', Mona. I'd say if you met a boy called Penis you wouldn't think twice about it.

I know plenty of boys called Dick and I don't think twice about them.

Would you say it to Gabriel? Sheamie caught his penis in his zipper.

She wouldn't know what it was, Matilda.

A zipper?

No, yeh fool. A penis.

I was joking, Mona.

You weren't.

I was, Mona.

Mona scrunches her freckles at me. You weren't.

Oh, suit yourself.

I move away to the other side of the car. There are times I'm certain Mona is as crazy as my father there, coming through the gap in the hedge with Sheamie in his arms, Danny still laughing and Pippa pulling up her jeans. Then I remember the day Mona gave my godfather a nut in the balls and I know Mona has a heart as big as the ocean. That Mona is only Mona because of everything that happened. Chasing boys, doing whatever they want her to do, is the only way she knows how to feel loved.

My father puts Sheamie in the front seat and tells him to breathe slowly. That's it now, not too deep. The rest of us are sitting in the back seat trying our best not to laugh. We don't even look at each other because looking at someone who's trying not to laugh is the worst thing you can do when you're trying not to laugh yourself. I can't help it. I have to look. Pippa is sitting beside me, her jaws are blown and there're bubbles blowing from her nose. Mona's face is so straight you'd think it was stitched on but every so often there's a quick turn up at the corner of her mouth. I lean out a little further and try to catch Danny's eye but he turns his head and looks out the side window. Now Sheamie lets out a moan and that sets us off. Even my father laughs and has to pull the car over to the side of the road to calm himself. The thought comes to me that if things stay like this the holiday mightn't be as bad as I thought. Even Sheamie is laughing, only the laughing makes the pain worse and my father says he'll have to find him a doctor. Just in case.

We turn off the main roads on to quiet country roads and search. We're in the middle of nowhere and by now it's getting late. We keep driving till we come to a place called Westport, where Daddy knocks on doors till someone eventually tells him where to find a doctor at this hour.

The doctor lives at the top of a long narrow laneway in a house covered with ivy. He's a small man with grey hair and a stick that he taps on the side of his leg when he talks. He gives us pills for Sheamie and says he'll be right in a day or two. My father says we're going to Donegal and we need petrol. We've gone out of our way and he'll be lucky to get back to the main road. Is there a garage?

Oh, we've a garage right enough for all the good it'll do. Not a drop. Nor won't be a drop for another week. Damn bloody Arabs. If you're stuck, there's a bit of a caravan site over on the island. You're doing a bit of touring anyhow, by the looks of it.

Daddy thanks the doctor who waves us off with his stick as we drive back down the lane. We drive on till we cross over a bridge that creaks beneath us. I can feel the weight of the caravan being towed behind. We're at the top of a hill and in the distance the ocean glints above the treetops. The sun has set but lemon light streaks the water and the sky has turned to gold.

Further on, we drive into a field with a small concrete toilet by the gate. Caravans, some in darkness, others with their windows lit by candlelight, are lined along the hedge. We drive past them and park at the cliff edge like a boulder hanging over a mountain. I'm cramped and I want to get out but I'm on the wrong side of the car. If I get out here I'll end up in the ocean. I wind the window down a little to let out the stench of sweat but have to close it again the way the wind blows my hair around my face. My father says we'll sleep in the car. It's too dark to unhitch the caravan. I want to get out and pee but I'm too tired to care. Sheamie is snoring in the front seat and Pippa is asleep beside me with her head resting on my shoulder. Danny is stretched across Mona, Pippa and me. He's asleep and his head is on my lap. I can't move in case I wake them. Mona moves Pippa's head and rests it on her own shoulder. I roll up my blue poncho and use at as a pillow against the window. There's a dim glow from the dash light on my father's cheek and a puff sound when he draws on his cigarette.

In the morning, I'm stiff and sore and I never had such aches. I'm famished and want to pee and it sounds like there's someone tap-dancing on the car roof. It's raining hard. I wipe the mist from the window with my sleeve and lean my forehead on the damp glass.

There are six other caravans here. Doors and windows closed. Muddy paths run from car doors to the caravan doors. The wet green heads of the trees behind them twist in the wind.

Christ, where did he bring us!

We run to the caravan and wait in the rain while my father pushes the door open with his shoulder. The stench gushes towards us like sour mist and we have to hold our noses before stepping inside.

There's a rusty sink with a broken cup and a cooker that looks like it's glued together with grease. Between the bunk beds there's a red-topped table with iron legs and everywhere is littered with cigarette butts and bread crusts green with mould. My father says we can't eat till it's spotless. He's taking Sheamie and Danny with him for food. Mona, Pippa and me are to have it finished when he gets back. You can get water from the tap outside the toilet over there. There's a sweeping brush in the closet.

When they've gone, Pippa complains, How come we get the shitty work?

Oh, shut the fuck up, Pippa, says Mona.

We pull back the curtains and open the windows for the salt air. We scrub the cooker with balls of steel wool we find in a tin box under the sink. We slap the bunks with our hands sending clouds of dust into the light and sweep it from the worn lino when it lands. The dust gets up Pippa's nose and you can hear her chest wheeze.

We scrape grease, bits of egg, tomato and sausage from the frying pan. Wash the four white mugs, the two cracked cups, the four yellow plates, the two blue plates, the knives, the forks and the spoons. We wipe the table clean then sit and wait for my father.

He has a brown paper bag with apples and pears and another bag with groceries, to last at least a week, he says. It looks a small bag to last six of us a week. He puts one apple and one pear in a wooden bowl and leaves it on the table and warns us not to touch. He leaves the rest in the press under the sink and warns us, don't touch that either. He leaves a box of matches on the cooker and tells Pippa and me to help Mona with the breakfast. He brings Sheamie and Danny to fetch water. I stand at the door watching the three of them hurry across the field and I smile because I know three people going out in the rain for two buckets of water will torment Sheamie to distraction. Especially with his willy the way it is.

Mona lights the gas ring and soon the frying pan sizzles with bacon, sausages, eggs, tomatoes, black puddings and the luscious smell makes my stomach warble.

I hear my father outside the door telling Danny and Sheamie to wash before they come in. He comes in himself and stands behind us drying his hair with a towel. I can smell the rain from his clothes and hear the towel on his hair like sandpaper on wood. He sticks his head in over our shoulders and tells Mona, they're well cooked. Don't you know when something's burning?

Mona doesn't answer.

Well, do you or don't you?

Pippa goes to straighten the knives and forks on the table as if there's nothing the matter here at all. Mona and Matilda have everything under control and I'll just keep out of the way.

Mona keeps her eyes on the pan. If she says yes, she'll get a clatter for not turning off the gas. If she says no, she'll get a clatter for being stupid not knowing when something's burning. I glance over my shoulder. He's waiting with the towel over his shoulder for an answer. I take a chance and tell him it's not Mona's fault. None of us ever cooked before.

Have you a nose? Can't you smell? Wash yeer hands and don't talk stupid. Sit down and read your schoolbooks.

He pulls the frying pan from the gas ring and empties it in the bin and cooks breakfast himself and, when he's ready, we carry our plates to the table.

The food is warm and delicious. Rashers, sausages, eggs, mushrooms. When I'm finished I'm still so hungry I could eat the same again. My father is sitting across from me dipping his toast in his egg and there's one crispy sausage left on the plate between us. I can see him eyeing it but I never wanted anything as much as I want that sausage. I can taste it, cut in little pieces, smothered in salt. It'll still be warm.

Do I act as if, Oh, there's a sausage left, I might as well have it if nobody else does? What could he do if I'm quick enough?

I leave my hand on the table. I'll just let it slide across without looking at the sausage. Sheamie is at the far end of the table still chewing. He's after the sausage too, but he'd have to stand up to reach it and there's still a sausage on his plate. Danny is beside my father, chewing on a rasher. Danny could reach it easily but he'd have to reach across my father. I don't think he'll chance it and even if he does he's only ten and I can tell him to put it back. My fingers are close, touching the warm plate. Pippa is on one side of me, wrapped in a blanket, her chest still wheezy from the dust and her cheeks so pale the last thing on her mind is a sausage. Mona is on the other side of me drinking tea from the cracked white cup. Mona would never chance it. She knows she barely got away with burning the breakfast in the first place, but, even if she does, my hand is closer.

My father goes to the sink to pour tea and that surely means he doesn't want it, so I grab it and put it in my mouth, whole. Jesus Christ, it's scorching. I want to take it out but my father is back. He sits down opposite me again and glares at the empty plate. The sausage is stuck at the back of my throat. If I try to swallow it, he'll notice. He glares over at me with those big yellow eyes then down at the plate. The caravan is silent. Pippa sits back further on the bunk and wraps herself deeper in the blanket like a tortoise hiding in its shell. Danny stops chewing and sits there with his round brown eyes straight ahead and the rasher rind jutting out between his lips. Sheamie has his fork stuck in his last sausage. He brings it to his lips, then stops and looks at my father. What's he doing? If he offers it to him, it's as good as telling him someone took that sausage. Eat the fucking sausage. I can tell by the way my father is looking around he's not absolutely certain there was a sausage. Eat the sausage, Sheamie, I'm choking over here.

My father starts to roll a cigarette with one hand. He licks the paper and puts the cigarette between his lips. He roots in his pocket for a match and strikes the match off the tabletop and lights the cigarette. My brothers and sisters are where they were and the sausage is still stuck at the back of my throat. Mona goes to the cooker for more tea. Danny lets his knife fall on the floor and when my father looks down I cover my mouth with my hand and pretend to cough but the yellow eyes are too quick and he's glaring at me again. Mona is by the sink with the teapot in her hand asking, Would you like more tea, Daddy?

What?

Tea, would you like some more?

Sheamie eats his sausage. My father looks over at Mona and shakes his head, no, and that gives me time to swallow, only the sausage goes down sideways and there are tears in my eyes when my father winks over at me.

Did you enjoy that, Matilda?

Enjoy what?

Your fry, did you enjoy it?

Oh, that. Yeah, it was lovely. Thanks, Daddy.

Can't beat a good fry in the morning.

He drinks his tea from the cracked mug and tells us to clear the table, wash up, and get the schoolbooks out.

But it's our holidays, Daddy. Can't we go outside?

It's raining. We're staying put.

Every day it rains and every day the spelling gets tougher. My father wants them tougher. By the end of the week, Mona is asking words Reverend Mother wouldn't know, but at least we'll be leaving for Donegal soon to meet up with Aunt Peg and Uncle James and my father won't be as bad when they're around.

Some days I see the people in the other caravans. They have children like us. They leave in the mornings and come back in the evenings. They talk to each other and even in the rain visit each other's caravan. At night I hear them singing and laughing and I wonder, would they be singing and laughing if they knew what was happening on our side of the field? It's nearly over though. My father got petrol today so we'll be leaving in the morning.

We're woken in the night by a knock on the door. My father jumps down from his bunk above the back window.

He pulls on his tracksuit bottom and goes outside. Sheamie, Pippa, Danny and me kneel up in the bunk to look out the window. Mona stays in our father's bunk and I'm too embarrassed to look at her. If I don't look at her, I can make myself believe she's not really there. I know they're doing things up there. I hear my father moaning the way my uncles do, but I don't understand why Mona moans as well.

Everything outside the caravan is dark and I can't see who he's talking to. I just hear voices until the moon comes out again, and it's as if my father is standing in candlelight. Now I can make out the two other men. They have long hair and beards like my father. The three of them are laughing and sharing a cigarette. My father comes in and pulls on a jumper and tells us to stay in bed. He'll be back later.

We watch them through the window and in a few steps they vanish in the darkness.

We get up, light the candle on the table and send our own shadows dancing around the walls. We fill cups of water and Mona lights the gas ring to fry sausages and the rest of us laugh when Sheamie tells Mona she can burn them if she wants. Pippa won't eat anything but Sheamie's so hungry he'd eat the handle off the pan. We stand around the cooker and there's a lovely blue glow from the gas ring. We open the door to let the smoke out and the night air in. The rain has stopped and there's a sweet smell from the grass. I sit on the step beside Danny and look up at the moon. The five of us are having such a time of it I could live in a caravan with my brothers and sisters for ever if we had enough sausages.

Oh shit. We've eaten all the sausages.

Pippa wraps herself in her blanket and scurries back to bed. It's nothing to do with her. Danny says we should burn down the caravan. There was a fire and we were lucky to get out with our lives. We'll blacken our faces. Daddy won't know the difference.

We don't take any notice because Danny is only ten so it's bound to be a bad idea.

Sheamie says the trouble with Danny is he don't know there's a hole in his arse.

Pippa sits up in her bunk lifting her eyebrows at me as if to say, Well, don't you learn something new every day?

Mona scrubs the frying pan clean in the sink and says we'll be kilt for sure. Danny is still sitting beside me on the step. He says our father is mad but he's hardly mad enough to count sausages. Maybe he won't notice.

Sheamie says he'd count the hairs on your head if there was money in it. Sheamie leans against the cooker gripping his lip between his thumb and finger telling everyone to keep calm. Get everything cleaned and packed away. Keep calm. For Jesus Christ's sake, everyone keep calm.

15

I'm putting the last mug in the press when he walks in from the dark in his bare feet and starts sniffing the air.

What are you doing out of bed?

I was thirsty, Daddy.

Did you need to get dressed to get water?

I, ah, I thought I might have to walk across the field, Daddy.

He nods. What's that smell?

What smell? I don't get a smell. Maybe it's the candle. I had to light the candle to see what I was doing.

Why isn't it lit, then?

It blew out when you opened the door.

My hands tremble so much I can't get the cup back in the press. My father looks down to the bunks to where the others are pretending to be asleep. He takes the cup from my hand and puts the cup in the press and closes the door. He tells the others to get up and get dressed. I know yee're awake. You don't fool me.

We follow my father out to the darkness where he takes a torch from the boot of the car. We follow its narrow yellow beam through damp fields covered in rocks and hedges and head towards the orange glow in the distance. We creep along a narrow path on the cliff edge where the wind is so strong we have to dig our chins into our chests just to breathe. The Atlantic Ocean howls below us and hurls great chunks of itself four storeys into the air but by the time it reaches us it's little more than a cold mist on our hair. At the end of the narrow path we go through a gap in the hedge. I can feel the briars snapping back on my shins after Sheamie has gone through. We're in a field that slopes upward. We walk along by the hedge till we come to a place with tents and caravans circled around a great blazing fire. The sparks crackle and leap into the darkness and all around us glows orange and black, black and orange.

There are two men sitting against a caravan wheel. Both of them are thin and their cheeks have collapsed. My father sits between them and they laugh and talk and pass a cigarette from one to the other. Pippa nudges me and nods to the man sitting cross-legged by the fire. He has huge round eyes and stares into the flames. Jesus, is he naked? He can't be. He is though, except for the purple beads around his neck. I'm happy the guitar is on his lap.

A pretty girl with lovely white hair tied in pigtails is sitting on a blanket near the fire. She waves to us and calls out in a sweet voice, Don't stand back. Come in from the cold.

She's wearing a long yellow dress covered in flowers and looks about eighteen. She says her name is Sonya. Sonya has a friendly face and a smile warm like the fire, so we sit with her on the blanket. The whole camp seems cosy and warm and friendly, the way a camp should feel.

Are you on holiday too? Mona asks Sonya.

Life is a holiday, says Sonya.

Mona looks at me but I look away. You'd know Sonya was never in the Holy Shepherd after saying a stupid thing like that.

Your Daddy tells me you're only here for a few days. A pity really, we're having a wedding here next month, you'd have had a wonderful time.

She was talking to the five of us but she was looking over at my father warming his hands at the fire.

My father comes across and sits cross-legged between Sonya and me. His eyes are like moons in his skull and he's smiling at the five of us like we done something right for once. He tells Sonya we're his children and he's proud of us. It breaks his heart to see us in that convent. He puts his huge arm around me and tells me he loves me, loves all of us. We're the most important things in the world, after Jesus. He's doing well in London. He's in business with Uncle James, buying old houses, fixing them up and letting them out. He's bought a big house in London for himself and he's taking us out of the convent soon. He'll have a house for each of us for when we're older. We'll be a family again.

Sonya says we're lovely children. We have lovely manners and we're blessed with our Daddy's good looks. She blushes at Daddy and turns her eyes away. Her cheeks are flushed and any fool can see there's more than the fire making Sonya hot.

After a while, Sonya and my father leave us alone. I see them holding hands as they pass on the other side of the fire, then vanish into the night. Mona has a hurt look. Part of me wants to reach over and hold her hand, but I can't. It's like saying, I know. Do you want to talk? There are some things you just don't want to talk about because there's nothing you can do. Mona turns her face away, only for a moment, then turns back to Danny. Danny is excited our father is taking us out of the convent and I feel sorry for him because when I was ten I'd be delighted to hear that too. We try to explain we're in the convent until we're sixteen and can't be taken out unless the nuns and the government agree. He sits quietly by the fire trying to figure it out only you can't figure any-thing out when you're ten and you've never seen anything in your life except walls and nuns. I see the tears on his cheeks but I'm proud of him because, even though he doesn't under-stand, he believes us, and somehow that makes us all a little bit closer.

We sit by the fire until the flames flicker and die and the ashes blacken and there's a cold dawn breaking over the island. The sky is pink around the edges and every shade of grey overhead. The air feels thin and you can hear the birds chirping from the treetops to warm themselves. Sheamie stands up and stretches. He yawns. He has something to do and he'll follow us back.

Mona, Pippa, Danny and me trudge in a single file back through the damp fields where the cattle are stirring from the hedges and the lambs are bawling for their ma.

In the caravan, last night's candle is melted to its saucer. We wrap ourselves in blankets and make tea and toast and sit around the table. We're tired and want to sleep but worried over sausages and why Sheamie isn't back. Pippa says, It don't take an hour to piss. Maybe he's after cuttin' his willy off again.

We laugh. Even Mona laughs, till she says she doesn't think we'll be leaving this place. Not with the way our father was so friendly with the hippies and that Sonya. No way are we going on to Donegal. Forget Donegal.

Pippa glances over at me from inside her blanket. I don't know what to say. I can only worry about one thing at a time.

We wrap our fingers around our warm mugs and sip our hot tea till Sheamie bursts through the door. He's out of breath and littered in twigs and bits of green things.

The father is behind me. I had to cut through hedges to get ahead of him. Look at what I have under me coat. I robbed them offa the hippies.

You can hear the relief. Pippa is so relieved she farts and blushes but nobody laughs. Pippa says to Sheamie, Put them sausages in the press before he comes in. Hurry!

Don't say thanks, whatever you do.

Put them in the press and I'll kiss your arse.

I'd rather keep 'em under me coat.

Would the two of you ever shut the fuck up, says Mona.

My father comes in just as Sheamie is putting the sausages away. He warns Sheamie not to touch anything in there, he'll cook it himself. My father's eyes look tired but the rest of him looks fresh, like he's slept all night in a big feather bed, and he smells like he's just got out of the shower. He opens the door and sends us out to wash. We stink.

It's raining again. There's no point going across the field for water when there's a deluge from the caravan roof. We strip to our underwear and stick our heads under the gushing water and scrub ourselves with the bar of soap. The water is warm and it's like standing under a drainpipe. We're washed in a minute. My father follows out and asks where's the bucket we used and we say we didn't need a bucket. We washed in the rain. He leans against the door and takes a puff of the cigarette. He says if we like rain so much we can wash ourselves in it properly.

We are washed properly.

I'll decide that. Run around that field until I tell you to stop.

The five of us look at each other then back at him drawing on the cigarette.

Are yee deaf?

Mona is, says Sheamie, under his breath.

What?

Nothing, says Sheamie.

So you heard me?

Yes, Daddy.

We run in a group past the other caravans with Terry Wogan on their radios and their doors closed against the rain. I don't mind running. I'm used of it. But I don't know how the others will manage.

We turn at the concrete toilet by the gate and run alongside the hedge by the road then turn again towards the cliff. As quickly as the rain started, it turns to a deluge like tiny pebbles spraying our flesh and the wind so strong it's hard to breathe. We turn at the cliff edge and run towards the caravan. Already Pippa is gasping for air. I can't do it, Matilda. I swear I can't.

Keep going, Pippa. Come on, I'll race you.

She bends over coughing and spluttering and my father is shouting at her from the caravan door to keep going. He'll tell her when to stop. Pippa gets to the caravan door and drops to her knees in front of my father. She tilts forward as if her head is resting on a glass wall only there's no wall and she keeps tilting forward till her soft pink cheeks are caked in the muck and her arms are stretched out by her side like a nun lying before the altar begging God's forgiveness for her sins.

Now, my father says to Pippa, now you're clean.

Danny's jaws are purple and his arms dangle like he's carrying heavy bags and when he's told to get in he falls on top of Pippa in the doorway. There's only Mona, Sheamie and me, and I pity Mona with the soapsuds still in her hair, bits of it flying off or running down her cheeks. The third time around my father calls her in and she collapses beside Danny and Pippa.

Sheamie's legs are like bent spoons stirring in the mud and his bare feet sliding under him every time he turns a corner, and, when he passes the caravan for the fifth time, our father tells him to keep going, but when Sheamie stumbles and falls to his knees my father lifts him by the neck and throws him on top of the others like Sheamie's a wet sack. Now there's just my father and me in this muddy field and there's no way he's doing that to me.

He shouts after me, Keep going.

I wish he knew what a fool he is. Punishing me with my favourite thing in the world. I wish he knew how stupid he looks with his skin showing through his white shirt and rain dripping from his beard. Every time I see the wind blow his hair around his face I know I could run around this field for ever.

I stopped counting laps after ten, and that's a long time ago. I pass him again and turn my face away so he won't see me laugh. The wind and rain have turned his nose red; he looks like a clown. He tells me to get in but I keep going. He shouts after me, I told you to get in, get in now. I keep going past the people in the other caravans who by now are looking out their windows. I see their faces at the glass and wonder why they don't ask, What the fuck are you doing out there in your underwear, girl? Is your father mad? Come in here out of it and we'll call the gardaí.

Does God see me? Is he up there hiding behind the rain clouds waiting for me to give up? I wish I knew so I could ask why we're the ones with a lunatic father. Gabriel would say I'm lucky because I have my faith and that's the greatest gift of all. It doesn't feel like a gift and it's easy for Gabriel to talk when she's not the one running around a field in her knickers.

I slow down by the trees. He'll think I'm tired, think he's beaten me. I speed up along the cliff edge and as I get near him he roars at me to get in. He runs after me and reaches out to grab me but I'm too fast and, when I look back and he's gone inside, I want to sing and dance in the rain, but I only do one little jump and punch my fist in the air. That's enough. I stop running and walk back to the caravan because there's no point running now when there's no one looking. I know my father might kill me when I go in. I don't care. It'll be worth it. I've beaten him.

I do care though when the caravan door is locked. I hear the others pleading, Please Daddy, let her in, and he threatens them to eat their breakfast before he throws it in the bin. I want to knock but if he was going to let me in he'd be out here making me apologize.

It's cramped under the caravan and I have to lie flat. The grass is turned yellow and everywhere smells of wet clay. The only sound is the others washing plates above me. I take off my vest and wring the rain from it but it still clings to my wet skin when I put it back on. I curl up in a ball behind the rusty wheel where the icy wind doesn't blow in my face but it still creeps up from behind clawing the soles of my feet and the backs of my legs and sends a shiver through to my bones and I wonder how long before he lets me in. Did he keep something for me to eat? Did the others hide something? Maybe they'll drop a sausage or a slice of bread out the window. Maybe they already did. I crawl out on my stomach and root between the green blades. I claw, scratch and scrape the wet clay and find nothing and finding nothing I crawl back under the caravan, emptier, weaker and hungrier.

July days are long, longer in the rain, not long enough when you fear being alone in the dark. Sometimes I hear a scream or a cry from one of my brothers and sisters or his feet above my head kicking the table or a chair or one of them. Then the silence when they go to bed that's even worse. I watch the candles being lit in the other caravans. They're having supper, warm tea, toast, maybe a grilled rasher or a scrambled egg. I think about running for help but they wouldn't help. I crawl out and pull down my knickers and squat to piss in the wet grass like an animal. I think about knocking on our caravan door. I'd say anything now. Say I'm sorry a thousand times. Fall on my hands and knees in the mud and say anyone who prays to statues must be a screwball. Please, Daddy, let me in.

I crawl under the caravan again and try to shelter behind the rusty wheel. I've never heard wind so loud. Great chunks of it squeeze under the caravan screeching like a train in a tunnel. I put my hands to my ears and watch across the field as one by one the other caravans vanish in the blackness. I know he'll never let me in. He never let our mother in when he threw her out. That's the last time I saw her. In the back garden. She was naked. Her face covered in shit from where he held her head down in the septic tank. One arm across her breasts, the other between her legs, and in the morning she was gone. Why do I only remember those things now? Remember how he was with her. I was too young, but still I knew. Inside I knew, and I feel a fool for thinking he could ever be different. Part of him is broken and can never be fixed. I know now why my mother left. Why she had to leave. Why she's never coming back. Nobody is ever coming for us because there's nobody to come. Maybe we had to come to this place so I could understand why. I feel angry. And I promise that when we're big and he's old I'll do to him what he's doing to us. I'll make him suffer. I'll stick hot needles in his eyes till he roars and begs me to stop and prays on his knees to statues for forgiveness, but I won't forgive and thinking that makes me warm. My eyelids are heavy but I'm afraid to sleep for fear I'll roll over the cliff. I pray, Our Father who art in Heaven, hallowed be thy name, and God answers me. I drift to sleep with dreams of escaping far from here to a place where there's a warm bed and hot food every day.

In the morning I feel the huge wet hand pulling on my ankle, strealing my face through the grass. My father sticks his beard in my mouth.

Next time I tell you to get in, you'll do it. Stupid bitch. Now get in and eat your breakfast.

I'd like to tell him to shove his breakfast up the highest part of his hole, only I'm hungry and, if we're going to escape, I need to be clever.

Every morning we do spellings. We swim in the ocean because my father says salt water is the best thing for any cuts or bruises we picked up playing.

Playing? Jesus, we haven't played since we got here.

In the afternoons we walk to chapels so my father can scream at worshippers, priests and statues. Some days we get fed, but every day the milk gets a little sourer in the bottle and it's plain to see Mona's right, we're not going anywhere.

Some evenings, when he goes to the hippie camp he leaves us behind and doesn't come back till morning and that's when I tell the others about escaping. But the open roads are too dangerous; our father would find us. We're two hundred miles from the convent, we'd never make it.

We're sitting around the table and suddenly Sheamie's eyes light up. He has the best idea.

Pippa says, You're an arsehole, Sheamie. One day you're planning to escape from the convent, now you're trying to escape back. You're not getting me on a raft. We'll all drown.

She folds her arms and turns her back on us. We tell her she can suit herself. We're going without her.

Yee wouldn't to that to me.

We would.

Pippa pouts.

Stay there, so.

All right, she'll come with us.

Mona fixes her curly black hair behind her ears and goes to fill the kettle.

We'll have tea and make a plan.

On the evenings our father goes to the hippies without us, we roam the island in circles and, as we grow braver, bigger circles each time until we know every inch of the island for miles. We've been at it for weeks. My father hasn't mentioned Donegal or Aunt Peg. We decide to take what we need in the one morning. We'll get up at daybreak and gather everything before our father gets back. Sheamie says that's best because if the islanders start missing things they'll get posses on the look-out all going around in their white wool jumpers and black rubber boots looking for arses to kick because that's what islanders are like. Always looking for arses to kick.

There are mornings I lie in the long grass at the cliff edge and look out at Clew Bay. That's where Sonya told me we are. Clew Bay, off the coast of Mayo. Sonya says it's the most tranquil spot on earth.

Tranquil. Sonya says that means peaceful. She mustn't notice the rain.

On fine mornings, I watch the fishermen from the village carrying their flat-bottomed boats over their heads down the pathway to the gravel beach. They're like giant spiders. I watch them row out against the tide with their lobster pots balanced at the front of the boat. The air around me is so fresh I want to wrap myself in it like a warm blanket. Birds warble over my head and, below me, long-necked birds fly low over water so blue you'd think the sky had fallen on it. I can see why Sheamie finds escaping exciting. It's like ants nesting in my guts.

We rob the gate off the caravan park and hide it in the wood across from our caravan. We know the houses and farms that might have wood for our raft and poles for our mast. We know where there's a cattle trough made of long boards. We know there's no bull. He's in the next field tied with a thick iron chain that runs from his nose to a rock as big as an altar.

We set out early, while the mist is still on the grass and the birds safe in their nests. We have to be careful of farmers with dogs, and women watching from behind lace curtains.

We let the water out of the trough through the plughole at the bottom while the cattle gather round us and moo. They have flies in their eyes and lift their tails to shit. Pippa worries they'll attack us for robbing their trough. No one answers because we're in a hurry, but I can't help wondering if she's right because I've never been this close to a cow unless you count Reverend Mother.

We're heading for the road when we hear the growl of an

engine and the bark of a big dog. A farmer in a tractor is coming over the hill. The big dog is running behind him.

Pippa shouts, Scatter!

We tell her to keep going, he's a long way away.

But he's in a tractor.

Oh, shut the fuck up, Pippa, we all say together.

The farmer is going so fast the tyres stick in the mud. He skids and slides, firing great showers of mud up behind him and we worry he might topple over. He gets out waving his stick and begins to chase us with his dog barking and bounding across the field. We're at the gate by now and we don't know whether to keep going or drop the trough and scatter. It's heavy but we need it. We need it more than the cattle. They're happy with plenty of grass and nobody bothering them over spellings. The farmer is fat and slow in his muddy boots, and he's more worried over his tractor than his trough because now it's after rolling back down the hill, so he's chasing after that instead and we'd be fine only his dog is still coming toward us. It has a head like a bull and chases us up the road till Danny lets the trough go and picks up a rock. He throws it and hits the dog between the eyes. The dog somersaults like he's been shot and we're sure that's the end of him, but when we get back to the wood he's leaping across the field with the rock in his mouth. He's a good dog now because he's pawing Danny to throw the stone again. We call him Blacky and take turns throwing the stone.

Sheamie says we have to break up the trough with rocks and don't crack the boards we need them long to tie to the gate. Pippa wonders what we're breaking it up for? We can use the cattle trough instead. It looks like a boat except it has a flat bottom and all the boats on the island have flat bottoms.

She's right.

We jump in. Sheamie at the front. Danny at the back. Pippa

and me and Mona in the middle and we fit, but Sheamie isn't happy. Sheamie wants to join the Navy some day so he can travel the world and never stay in one place too long. He's forever stealing magazines about boats. He never read about anyone putting out to sea in a cattle trough. That's what it's called. Putting out to sea. It's a stupid fuckin' idea.

Pippa says, They would if they thought of it.

Sheamie says, You're only trying to get out of building the raft. You're always the same, always trying to get out of things.

So? I have asthma, you know.

Yeh have when it suits you. Everything has to suit you, even your shittin' asthma.

Pippa doesn't answer.

Mona complains the trough smells like cow shit and Sheamie tells Mona she's getting as bad as Pippa. Mona scrunches those freckles at him and Sheamie has to tell her, All right, all right, calm down. Danny says, We'll wash it with seawater.

Pippa says, Seawater? I'm not goin' all the way down to the beach getting dirtier than I am already when there's a tap across the field. Sheamie says, There you go again, Pippa. See what I mean? Pippa sticks her tongue out at Sheamie but somehow we all agree. We'll wash the trough with seawater and try to make a boat out of it.

We scrub it clean and head off again. We rob a clothes pole, a clothesline and a blue bed sheet from the house next door to the Gardaí's Barracks after we see the officer wobbling away on his black bike. We steal five boards from the fence of the house next to that for oars. We use rocks for hammers and the nails from the fence to nail the clothes pole to the trough for a mast, and we tie the blue sheet to it with the clothesline.

It looks great. Pippa is pure faintin'.

See, I told yee it would work.

Sheamie has to admit even a blind dog pisses against a lamp pole once in a while.

He says we'll go Sunday morning after the hippie wedding. The father won't come home and a passin' ship'll rescue us. When they see us all bones and our clothes hanging they'll know we're telling the truth.

Will it be an Irish ship, Sheamie? asks Pippa.

It don't matter so long as they get us back to the convent.

What if the people on the ship don't speak English? We'd end up in Timbuktu.

Sheamie says, Pippa, I'm really sick o' you.

Pippa pouts.

The Saturday afternoon of the wedding, Sonya brings Pippa and me to her tent with the two rooms you can stand up in. She dresses us in white lace and brings us to the fields to make necklaces and braids from daisies and buttercups. Sonya skips through the long grass with the sun on her hair and there's something so tranquil about her we just have to skip behind. Sonya says we're hippies now. We don't go to school or mass, we can take our clothes off or leave them on and oh, girls, did she tell us yet how she loves our Daddy. Would we like her for a mother? Our Daddy is wonderful, so handsome, so cool, so like John Lennon and oh, God, Sonya loves John Lennon.

Sonya won't be saying our father is cool when he's swinging her by the hair. Sonya won't love John Lennon when the sight of him makes her piss in her knickers or when she's hiding in bus shelters with her children, afraid to go home.

Sonya is nice and I like her but how can I tell her these things when I'm twelve and she's in love? How do I tell her I don't want her for a mother because I have a mother and I don't want to live in a tent even if the hippies are nice and the only thing bothering them is there are too many trees being chopped down and that's the worst thing of all because trees have feelings, man? That's the trouble with this planet, too many people and not enough trees. And still, there's a guilty part of me wants Sonya to marry my father so he'll just piss off and let the five of us alone. That won't happen. He'd try taking us out of the convent and back to this place I dream of escaping from, and all our work robbing troughs and building our boat will be for nothing.

Sonya lifts her dress by the sides and it opens like a white fan. It's like she's advertising herself for our mother's job. What do you think, girls?

Pippa panics and blows on her inhaler till the pink comes back to her cheeks and all I can do is smile and pray we escape in the morning because, next time Sonya asks, she mightn't take a smile for an answer.

My father says we're gorgeous when he sees us back at the caravan. He's sitting at the table screwing the lid back on the bottle of cod liver oil. And do you know the best thing, girls? Costs nothing. Anything free always looks well on you. Free is good. Remember that. Good, good, good, good, good.

There's a bright August moon floating over the island and smiling down on the white marquee glimmering with candle-light. Two hippies standing by the fire play guitar and sing 'Blowin' in the Wind'. The young hippie bride stands by the fire in a white satin frock, her golden pigtails tied with the red ribbon. I can't understand why such a pretty girl would marry that slob standing beside her. He looks as old as my father and there's enough hair growing from his nose to lace a pair of boots.

We join hands and form a circle around the fire. About fifty of us with flowers in our hair and our faces red and orange in the firelight. No way Lucy Flynn will believe me when I tell her this. She'll laugh her head off. I wonder where the priest is. Will he wear the full robes or just the black suit and white collar? The white collar, I'd say. He'll hardly dress up for a hippie wedding.

Pippa tugs my elbow and says it's over.

Over, Pippa? What do you mean, over?

It is though, Matilda.

It can't be over. There was no priest or nothin'.

Pippa shrugs her shoulders. She can't understand either but we're certain it's a mortal sin till we wonder can you get a mortal sin if you're not Catholic and don't believe in mortal sins and even if you can it's hard to imagine God doling out mortal sins to people who care so much about trees.

Inside the marquee, the hippies puff the cigarettes with the strange smell that makes my eyes sting and my head dopey. There's a table against the back wall filled with trays of fruit – apples, pears, oranges, bananas. Another table is overflowing with hams, cheeses and all kinds of breads. Round, long, short, square and some twisted like braids. Crates of beer, bottled and canned, are stacked against the side wall. There's lemonade, orange and assorted nuts.

Assorted nuts. That's what Sheamie called them.

I thought they were peanuts, Sheamie.

I was talking about the hippies, Matilda.

I wander outside. I'm dizzy. My head feels heavier now and I can't feel my legs. My eyes feel huge and the smile on my face won't go away.

Our father is stretched along the ground beside Sonya. They're sharing a rollie and listening to the two men playing the guitar. I sit cross-legged by the fire. I feel giddy and hungry and I see strange shapes in the flames. Nuns on roller skates, nuns scrubbing floors, nuns disco dancing with Father Devlin. Reverend Mother flying on a broom. Now it's a white goat with horns that curve backward. Can't be. But it's making goat noises and watching me from the other side of the fire.

The hippies shout, There's tomorrow's dinner, don't let it get away.

They chase it through the flames, over my father's legs, in and out of caravans and tents and all around the marquee. The goat rattles pots and pans and knocks naked children on their backsides. The pots clank, the children bawl, the hippies roar and it's the funniest thing I've ever seen until the hippies catch it. They slit its throat with a black-handled dagger and hang it by the back legs from a tree until all the blood runs out on to the ground. They skin it. Stick a pole through its arse that comes out its mouth and burn it over the fire till its skin is roasted.

Sheamie rips a chunk off with his hands and attacks it like a Viking. He licks his fingers and the juice around his mouth glistens in the firelight. His eyes are huge too.

Do yeh want some, Matilda?

That's disgusting, Sheamie. What did that poor goat ever do to you?

I never met him before tonight. Ha, ha.

Don't be a smart arse, Sheamie. You know what I mean.

He's dead, Matilda, and do you know the best thing? It's free. Free is good. Remember that. Good, good, good, good, good. Now, I'm thirsty. See you later on.

Sheamie staggers away laughing and stumbles over Mona's legs and into the marquee looking for something to kill his thirst. Mona is sitting against a caravan wheel. She's talking to a man with a thick black moustache and a silver stud in his ear. I haven't seen him here before. He must have come for the wedding. It's late and I have a bad feeling how this is turning out. Time we went home.

I go into the marquee to look for Pippa, Danny and Sheamie but I only find Pippa and Danny. They're sitting on the floor trying to eat nuts from a bowl on the ground between them.

They're laughing and, when I ask what they're laughing at, they say they don't know. Nuts spew from their mouths and they spray each other with peanuts and laugh even harder and I have to help them from the floor before they'll get up. The three of us fill our pockets with bananas and ham slices and, when we come back outside, Mona is missing.

The walk back through the fields clears our heads. In the caravan we fill empty milk bottles with water and make banana sandwiches to go with the ham slices. Who knows how long it'll be before a ship finds us. We wait at the table in the glow of the candle and the smell of melting wax for Mona and Sheamie. Pippa is frightened Daddy will come home first and make her sleep with him and I tell her he won't. Pippa says he will. She tries to puff on her inhaler but frets so much I have to hold it to her mouth and squeeze when she breathes. She heard Daddy telling Mona it's in the Bible that girls sleep with their fathers.

You're freakin' me out, Pippa.

I heard him. It was all begettin' and begattin', but I knew what he meant.

I know it's a sin but I close my eyes and thank God Pippa is older than me. I hope my father knows it too.

Danny falls asleep on his bunk. Pippa covers him with a blanket and lays his head on a pillow and sits back at the table. We look out the window but there's only darkness. My eyelids are heavy and it's hard to stay awake when all I want to do is crawl into a soft bed with cool white sheets.

The flame is flickering close to the saucer when Sheamie stumbles in the door. His face is black and his knees covered in mud. He points a finger at us and tries to talk but staggers backward and collapses in a heap on the floor. We push him, shove him, kick him, shout at him, Where's Mona? But all we get back is a heavy snore, a fart and a smell of beer.

Now we have to sit and worry over Mona. I strike a match and light another candle. The sleep is gone from me. I just want this night over. I just want to escape and never worry like this again.

Soon the first birds are chirping from the treetops and the darkness is melting in the morning light. It's bright enough in the caravan to snuff out the candle but the flickering flame gives Pippa and me something to stare at.

We both leap from our chairs when we hear footsteps running towards the caravan. Pippa closes her eyes and I know she's praying that it's not our father. It's Mona. Her blouse is ripped down the front and her legs bloody and scrawled with fingernails. She's standing at the door yelling, Daddy told me to go with him. Daddy made me. Pippa and me chase after her when she runs out of the caravan heading for the cliff.

She stops at the cliff edge not far from the caravan. She's looking down and holding her hands by her side like she's standing on a diving board. I hear the ocean four storeys below us smashing against the rocks lifting sea spray into the air. Pippa goes to one side of Mona and me the other. We tiptoe towards her through the long grass in our bare feet till we're only a few feet away.

He made me go. Daddy made me.

Come back, Mona. Come on. Please, just come inside.

Mona lets out a scream that echoes all over Clew Bay and mountains yonder. Trees shake with the clashing of wings and it's like every bird in Clew Bay has taken to the pink morning sky. Pippa puts her finger to her temples as if to say, Mona's after losin' it now. At the opposite side of the field, people are turning on their radios and setting up their plastic tables and chairs for breakfast and hanging their beach towels on the hedge to dry in the sun. They can see us but we're too far away for them to understand what's going on. Sheamie has woken and he's standing by the caravan wiping his eyes with his hands like he's wondering if he's still asleep. By now the sun is bright and Sheamie has to shield his eyes with his hand to see us.

Go inside, Sheamie, I say. Just go back inside. Don't scare her.

Sheamie grunts and fumbles with his shirt buttons and wonders, What's Mona doing? What's going on? He looks up at the sky. Jesus Christ, where did all them birds come from?

I don't answer. Pippa doesn't answer. We wave Sheamie inside and creep closer to Mona. We could reach out and grab her but she's sobbing and shaking and I'm certain she'll pull away if we touch her.

We call again, Please, Mona. Come on. Come in. Yeah, says Pippa. We'll only get the blame if anythin' happens to you.

Mona turns towards us. The sea spray curls itself around her like a white sheet and I can't see her anymore. I wonder if she's jumped and my stomach feels like it's dropped with her till the spray clears and she's still standing there with her arms by her side and water dripping down her face and the front of her blouse. There are tearstains on her cheeks and bite marks on her chest but she still tries to smile and I wish I could hold her and make all the pain go away. But I know I can't. All I can feel is useless.

Pippa and me take her by the hand and walk her inside where Sheamie has warm water and clean rags waiting in a bowl by the sink. We wash the blood from Mona's legs and change her clothes. We try to think of something to say but there's nothing to say. We comb her hair. There's no brush. I want to get a knife and go over there and slit the throat of whoever did this. I want to stick a pole through his arse and out his mouth and roast him over the fire till his skin is crisp and brown and feed him to a goat but all Pippa and me can

221

do is wrap Mona in a blanket and put her to bed and stroke her forehead till she sleeps.

Sheamie groans with the pain in his own head. He sits at the edge of the bunk and, when he looks at Mona, buries his face in his hands. We won't be escaping today, he says. Pippa sits beside Sheamie and Sheamie holds Pippa's hand till Pippa falls asleep with her head on Sheamie's lap.

For some reason our father stops going to the camp and we're back where we started. Spelling in the morning, going to chapels in the afternoon, and a beating or two. It's like this for so long I've lost count of days. I know we'll never escape. That's what I'm thinking this evening when there's a knock at the door. I pull back the curtain and look outside. It's Sonya, black under her eyes, her wet cheeks glistening in the setting sunlight. Our father sits on the chair to put on his Moses sandals and comb his hair. He takes his time and says he'll be back later.

We make banana sandwiches again and run over and back to the toilet filling bottles with water. Pippa wants to go now but Sheamie says it's too dangerous. It'll be dark soon. We'll go first thing in the morning.

We take turns staying awake so we won't sleep too long. First Sheamie. Then Mona. Then Pippa. Then me. We let Danny sleep through because he's only ten and you'd have to be twelve like me to sit awake for hours. Sheamie's watch is on the table. The hands glow in the dark and my brothers and sisters are asleep around me. I sit and listen to the ticking of the watch and the wheezing from Pippa's chest until it's time for us to go.

The dawn is warm and the water is every shade of lemon from the rising sun when we go for our boat in the clump of trees. We clean away the leaves that have gathered inside and drop in the bottles of water and banana sandwiches. The five of us gather round the boat and carry it across the field. Chunks of damp grass and clay stick to the sides and we're terrified our father will come back early and snigger at us for thinking we could ever escape from him. At the top of the narrow path that leads down to the beach we can let the boat slide but we have to get in front to stop it running away altogether and that's even harder than lifting.

Finally we're on the beach. There's nobody around but my heart is banging from the carrying and the worrying over my father and whether the boat will float. We carry the boat over the stones that cut through the soles of our sandals and let it down in the sand at the water's edge. We tie on the blue sheet and let the wind fill it then push the boat into the sea.

The water splashes against the side and it looks a bit wonky but who cares. It floats.

We follow it out. The water is cold but not icy and the sea is calm. The tide is going out. Sheamie says that's good. We won't have to paddle as hard. Mona tucks her black hair behind her ears and climbs in first. She's at the front. Then Danny climbs in. Then Pippa. Then me. As each of us climbs in, the water gets higher and when Sheamie climbs in it's almost coming over the side. The bay is like a horseshoe. Sheamie warns us to be careful, the current might drag us to the left or right. Keep going straight ahead until we're clear of the bay altogether.

We dip our paddles in and row. We keep our heads down like we've seen the island men do and soon we're passing the rocks and heading to the open sea. Our yellow caravan on the cliff gets smaller and smaller and soon it'll be gone and I'll never see the stupid thing again.

A seagull tries to land on Danny's head. Its wings are straight and barely moving and we throw our banana sandwiches in the water to get rid of it.

That was a mistake.

Now there's a flock of seagulls. They've taken off from the rock ledges and follow us like they follow the fishing boats and all of them screeching for bananas and trying to land on our heads. We wave our paddles at them. We throw ham slices in the water but the seagulls ignore the ham. It's bananas they're after. Pippa turns around and screams, Do something, Sheamie. Sheamie throws more banana sandwiches and he tells Pippa just keep paddling an' they'll leave us alone. Danny starts to laugh; he looks up at the seagulls and sings to them. Sorry, we have no bananas, we have no bananas today. Mona tells him, Shut it. Shut it or she'll hit him on the head with the paddle. We keep paddling but we're not getting very far. There's water coming over the side and Mona and Pippa stop paddling and try scooping it out with their hands. The further from the beach we get the rougher the sea becomes. The waves are higher and lift us in the air before slamming us back in the water again. It's like being on a roller coaster and my stomach heaves every time we drop. The seagulls are back screeching over our heads and we try waving our paddles again. It's no use. We're doing so much looking and shouting at seagulls we haven't noticed we're drifting to the left. We're getting too close to the rocks. The blue sheet is breaking loose so now it's more like a flag than a sail. I stand up to grab the sheet to stop it blowing away. Pippa shouts, The rocks, Sheamie. We're going to hit the rocks!

Sheamie jumps in the water and puts himself between the boat and the rocks. His back is against the boat and his feet against the rocks. The boat is too heavy and it pushes him under and we hit the rocks with a thud that cracks the boat's bottom and the white foam gushes under our feet. We shout for Sheamie but we can't see him. The water is too dark and deep. When I stand, the boat rocks and Mona screams at me

224

to sit down, but I dive in and swim down looking for Sheamie.

The water is murky and I can't see anything, only the flat bottom of the boat and the slices of ham the seagulls won't touch. I feel my lungs ready to burst and I come back up and draw air and look around.

Pippa shouts from the boat, Did you find him, Matilda?

I dive back down and the salt water goes up my nose. I can see down to the bottom, rocks and seaweed, but no Sheamie. Then I see his glasses on the bottom and I dive down further and grab them. I feel the current pulling me places I don't want to go but I swim until I can't hold my breath any longer. I swim back up and when my head breaks the surface I feel my ears pop and the wind cutting into my face. Danny shouts, There he is, and points to my right. I see Sheamie's red hair bobbing in the water.

Sheamie swims to the rocks, one hand over the other, and I swim after him. Pippa, Mona and Danny jump from the boat and swim after us. There's nothing to do but sit on the rocks and watch our boat sink. There's nothing we can say to each other that will make it better. I look at my brothers and sisters, their wet clothes, their faces brown from the sun and their eyes white from the salt water, and I wonder what sort of God would give us hope of escaping then send seagulls to destroy it. It's like losing our mother all over again.

It was the bananas, says Pippa. We should have brought more bananas.

Sheamie agrees.

Our father is at the door filing his fingernails. He wants to know why we're wet and we tell him we went swimming but forgot our swimming togs so we went in our clothes. He's not surprised. He always knew we were stupid.

We stay in all day doing spellings hoping our clothes dry

before bed. We know he's going to make us sleep in them. They don't dry and in the morning we're flushed and hot and too sick to eat.

Glugs of sour milk pour out of the bottle over the stale cornflakes. We try to complain but our father says he's not buying milk until what's there is gone. And this is for you, Matilda. He leaves a raw sausage on top of the cornflakes because he knows how much I like sausages.

My brothers and sisters are watching. Pippa throws up on the seat but I'm too sick to care what happens to anyone anymore. My father throws the sour milk and cornflakes in my face and swipes his huge hand across the table sending bowls and bottles crashing against the wall and all over my brothers and sisters and me. He sends us out to wash because we stink and he's sick of the sight of us.

The others are too ashamed to go to the toilets for water so I go, even though it's embarrassing when you're covered in sour milk to stand there behind a woman holding a small child in her arms who has nothing better to do but stand there gawking and telling the child, shush, there's nothing to be frightened of, then hurry away with her bucket half full because she can't stand the smell of me a second longer. It's nearly as embarrassing as waiting for your own bucket to fill while a crowd builds up behind you pretending they don't notice the milk or my hair littered in cornflakes or the stench from me worse than the stale piss along the footpath.

We stay in bed for days with our faces flushed and our throats on fire. Sometimes our father comes back from the camp to check we're still alive and sometimes he even leaves food for us to cook ourselves and the only hope we have is, it's the end of summer.

I know because the geese are flying overhead like a giant V. I'm sitting on a rock wondering if we'll ever leave. The fishermen are coming home for the night in their small boats with their lobster cages stacked at the front. The tide is out and the wreck of our own boat is standing like a tombstone in the sand. I hear Pippa calling me. She comes running along the beach with her soft pink cheeks on fire and sits beside me, panting.

Matilda, we're going home. Honest, he's packing everything away. If we're not back in five minutes, he's goin' without us.

We're back in two.

We're driving out the gate when Sonya comes running towards us in her yellow dress and tears coming fast. My father stops the car and winds down the window but keeps his eyes straight ahead. Sonya begs him, Please, Peter. Don't leave. I love you. You know I do.

I wonder if she's mad. This is the luckiest day of her life and she's trying' to fuck it up for herself. My father looks at her like she's mad too. Grins at her like she's dirt and winds the window up in her face. Something about the way he looks at her reminds me of my uncles. Sonya means nothing to him. My father drives on and she chases the car through the mud, still knocking on the window, begging him to come back. I never knew I could feel this sorry and happy for someone at the same time.

Our grandmother is as we left her. She's sitting in her armchair in front of the television with her racing docket in one hand and her teacup in the other.

It must be Saturday.

When she sees us she leaves her teacup on the floor and her racing docket in her apron pocket and covers her face with her hands and, when she takes them away, you can see the panic in her eyes.

She warns us, You're to tell the nuns I went. Have you got

that? I was there. Never say I didn't go. She looks at each of us in turn and we have to promise before the panic goes from her eyes.

Danny wonders where Grandad is. Nanny tells him asleep in bed. He hasn't been well and she's had the doctor up to see him. Danny can see him another day. She comes to give each of us a hug and I stand behind the others. She hugs Mona, Sheamie, Pippa and Danny and when she comes to me I leave her put her arms around me and when she pulls me close I lean against her belly until she's happy I'm really hugging her, then I push her away. She stands back and stares with her old grey eyes but I turn my back to her and walk out the door.

We kiss our father goodbye in the playground and there's a bitter taste in my mouth. Sheamie says he'll follow us, he's going to check on his money. When we drag our suitcases into the kitchen Gabriel is at the cooker talking to Doyler. I look for Lucy Flynn but there's no sign. Gabriel can't look at us and turns her face to the wall and tells us to put our suitcases away. Doyler stands with her mouth open but from the hallway I hear her saying to Gabriel, Mother of the divine. Those children are like specimens from a concentration camp.

Sheamie is sitting on the bottom of stairs with his head buried in his hands and whimpering. It doesn't take long to figure out our money is missing. So is Lucy Flynn.

16

I'm thirteen. My father didn't come home from London this summer. Not even for the funeral. I'm not complaining, and anyway I've other things to worry about. Mona is missing for the last two days. Gabriel says if she's not here by tomorrow she's calling Officer Flannery. I'd like to ask her, Where the fuck was Officer Flannery when we needed him in Clew Bay? Only I'd get a clatter on the jaw.

Gabriel drags Pippa and me into her office, stands beside the statue of the Blessed Virgin Mary, and wags that finger.

Do you know where she is, Matilda?

No, Mother.

Pippa?

No, Mother.

We can't tell her Mona's been sneaking out the bathroom window for years to play kiss-and-chase in Trinity Park and was always getting caught. She's been caught so often nobody wants to catch her anymore so now she has a boyfriend nobody wanted to be caught by, greasy Pat Murphy who works in a garage selling petrol and fixing tyres. I met my grandmother in town yesterday; she knows all about it because you can't piss in this town without my grandmother knowing all about it.

She gave out, What in the name of God is Mona doing, she's bringing shame on the lot of us and isn't it enough that father of yours and his preaching? The neighbours giving me queer looks, not to mention your poor grandfather above in the hospital after his stroke. And you don't visit your Nanny anymore, alone in that big house with only the walls to talk to.

The walls have ears.

Oh, it's like that, is it? You didn't even come to your Uncle John's funeral. At least Pippa was there, and young Danny.

Uncle John got drunk and fell from the gangway going on to the ship to meet some of his old friends from the docks. They said it was his donkey jacket filling with water that dragged him under. I didn't say anything to my grandmother. I didn't care what she thought so I didn't tell her Pippa only went to the chapel to be certain it really was Uncle John in that coffin, or that Danny only went because Pippa made him go, so she wouldn't have to go on her own.

Next day, a soaking wet Mona walks into the kitchen wondering what we're all gawkin' at when she declares she's getting married. Her long-haired boyfriend is holding her hand and looking like he won't take no nonsense offa no nun. He's here to do the business.

Poor bastard hasn't a clue what's coming.

Gabriel runs at Mona with that finger wagging.

That's what you think, my girl, and you, she says to the boyfriend, turn right back the way you came as quick as you walked in here before I call the gardaí, and if I ever see or hear from you again . . . and the boyfriend who wasn't taking no nonsense from no nuns is out the door and over the wall before Gabriel finishes saying what she's going to have done with him.

Gabriel pulls down Mona's blouse collar.

Will you look at the state of you, Mona. How did you get those red marks?

Mona's neck has been chewed asunder and we're whispering to each other, Will yeh look at the state of her. Jesus, she'll be killed.

Gabriel says, Get down to my office this minute.

I'm sixteen and I can do what I want and there's nothing you can do. I can leave if I want to.

We'll soon find out about that. You can leave when you've a place to go and not before.

They're down in Gabriel's office and a gang of us gathers around Doyler. She leaves her broom by the door and presses her fingers to her lips and tells us all, Shush, as we inch down the corridor. We hear Mona screaming she's in love and she wants to get married and Gabriel demanding to know is she pregnant and did she have intercourse? Then we hear the slap to the side of Mona's face and nearly feel the sting all the way up the hall from behind the closed door.

We're all wondering what intercourse is, and I think Mona is too because for once she's not answering, but we can't ask because Doyler is here and, if intercourse is something you're not supposed to do, it's definitely something you're not supposed to ask about. Instead, everyone will go around looking at each other's neck to see if they've had intercourse so they can tell the rest of us what it is.

Father Devlin arrives in half an hour, shaking the rain from his brolly as if he's the only man who can deal with the crisis. The crisis is over, but any excuse for Gabriel to send for Father Devlin will do. Gabriel has her serious crisis face on but I can see the twinkle in her eyebrows now Father Devlin is here and you can be certain Sister Ellen in the group next door is raging she hasn't a crisis of her own.

Gabriel does her best to keep Mona inside until the nuns get her a cleaning job in a hospital, miles from here and miles from Greasy Pat.

The day after Mona leaves, I come home from school and

Gabriel is sitting at the kitchen table on her own, reading from her red pocket prayer book she must know by heart. She looks up at me from her pages, takes her glasses off and lays them on the table. She says, Matilda, Mona . . . using the same tone of voice as when she says, Matilda, your father . . . I know it means she wants to say more, but I know nuns take a vow of not saying anything bad about people, so when Gabriel says, Matilda, your father . . . I know what she means, so I just say, I know, Mother. And I know if ever a man comes between a nun and her vow of not saying anything bad about people, then it's going to be my father. So when Gabriel says, Matilda, Mona . . . I just say, I know, Mother. Gabriel nods her head, smiles, and goes back to reading her prayer book and I think she's happy someone other than God and Polly the budgie understands.

Before Christmas, there's another crisis. Father Devlin is sent for, again. Officer Flannery is sent for, my grandmother is sent for and she sends Uncle Philip to search every back lane, backyard, alleyway and dockyard in the city, but he can't find Sheamie.

When Officer Flannery calls, the younger kids go tearing up and down the corridor doing the *Hawaii Five O* music and shouting, Book 'em Danno, are yeh putting out an APB, Officer Flannery?

Officer Flannery is a big man with enormous black boots. He pulls his notebook from his breast pocket and brings Pippa and me into Gabriel's office. He sits forward at the edge of the desk with one foot on the ground and the other swaying back and forth like he's telling me, One wrong word and you'll feel this boot up in your arse. He asks for Sheamie's whereabouts and does a lot of staring to see if we're lying. That's what happens when you join the gardaí. You do a lot of staring because you don't believe what anyone says.

Pippa shrugs her shoulders. No, officer. I don't know where Sheamie is.

I don't either, officer.

You wouldn't be telling me lies by any chance, Matilda?

No, officer.

Us gardaí are trained to spot lies.

I know, officer.

And how would you know that now?

I saw it on *Hawaii Five O*.

He throws his cap on the table.

I think you know a little more than you're telling me, Matilda. What would you think yourself?

I put on my most innocent face and bawl like an idiot till Gabriel comes rushing in.

What's up? What's the matter, Officer Flannery?

Well now, Sister Gabriel, I think this one here might know a little more than . . .

I don't, I don't, Mother. Honest, Mother. You know I don't tell lies, don't you, Mother?

There's no way I'm telling the gardaí or anyone else where Sheamie is. He told me before he climbed the wall for the last time, he's sick of walls and nuns and grandmothers who turn their back. He's tired of running with gangs and getting in trouble. If he stays, he'll end up in jail.

Before he left we went robbing in Grace's supermarket. Sheamie in an anorak with a torn shoulder and me in the blue poncho. We didn't even run when we got outside. It wasn't that sort of day. Damp and dull and smelling like rain, and I wasn't in a rush to see Sheamie go. Sheamie said it was the last time he'd rob. That's not what we are, Matilda. It's just what they made us.

It was one of those clever things Sheamie says, but for the first time I kind of knew what Sheamie meant.

233

We went to the Quay and sat on a wooden bench beside the clock tower. It looks like Big Ben shrunk in the wash. It was four o'clock in the afternoon. The Friday traffic made the Quay look like a car park. We kept our backs to it all and watched the big blue Bell Ferry crane on the other side of the River Suir load the ships with the huge metal containers. The tide was turning. We could hear the water gurgle against the wooden beams of the jetty as we fed the hungry seagulls that waddled up to us the dry bread Sheamie had packed for his trip. We talked about the seagulls that wrecked our escape boat and other things we'd done and things we'll do when we're older.

Can't you stay, Sheamie?

I can't take another summer of our father, Matilda.

You can, Sheamie. Honest you can.

I'm not like you, Matilda. You were always the strong one. I knew that the day you kept running around that field. You really pissed him off, Matilda. When you stopped knocking to be let in he sat up all night, waiting to see if you'd do it again. The longer he waited the more cigarettes he smoked.

I catch his eye and the two of us smile at the thought of him prancing around the caravan.

Really though, Sheamie, what if something happens to you?

He laughed and threw a crust of bread on the ground for the seagulls to squab over.

What else can happen? What more can they do, Matilda?

What if you don't find our Mother?

I will.

You mightn't, and what if you do and she doesn't want you? Maybe she has another family. Did you ever think about that? Or worse, what if she only pretends to want you? How do you know you won't wake up some morning and she'll be gone again?

Why are you talking like that?

I just don't want to see you hurt, Sheamie.

Sheamie put his arm around me and I leaned my head against his shoulder and put my arm around his waist. It was the first time I held Sheamie. The first time I felt I had a big brother. He felt so thin and damp. I felt my eyes well. I wanted to tell him I loved him but how do you tell someone you love them when you've never said it before or had it said to you. I whispered it after him when he was gone and it felt strange, but right. I looked around to see if anyone heard but there was only the wino asleep on the next bench. He was wrapped in yesterday's newspaper and I wondered if someone loved him once. Was he born to be like this or is it just what the world made him?

Sheamie would know the answer but Sheamie was already crossing the bridge over the River Suir. I realized how little I really knew him, and how much I wanted to know him and never might.

I watched his red hair disappear through the doors of the railway station and I knew I'd never tell where he was gone. Not if Officer Flannery stares at me all night or handcuffs me and brings me away in the squad car.

That's right, Officer Flannery. Matilda wouldn't lie to the gardaí, so you wouldn't, Matilda?

I sob back, No, Mother. I don't tell lies.

Officer Flannery puts his cap on and stares at me a long time.

Well, if you're certain, Sister Gabriel.

I am, Officer Flannery. Oh, I am indeed.

Gabriel shows Officer Flannery to the door and when she comes back tells me to stop your bawling. The officer is gone. Don't forget Confession this Friday.

I won't, Mother.

Gabriel dips her fingers in the little holy water font hanging on the doorframe and says that in all the confusion she forgot to say there was a phone call earlier and the caller seemed annoyed. I hope you haven't done anything out of the way, Matilda?

17

Rita phoned Gabriel to say she'll collect me at six o'clock Friday evening. I don't want to go. The older I get, the more ashamed I am of the things Uncle Philip makes me do, and I can't understand why it's Rita that rang and not Philip himself. She never rang before. It worries me she's found out, but surely if she had she'd be down here yelling at me? I don't know. I'm scared but I can't think of a reason not to go and if I don't go she'll be down here asking me why. Is there a problem, Matilda? Is there something you'd like to tell me? There's a pain in the pit of my stomach telling me, run, just run anywhere and it'll go away but I can't run when there's nobody to run to.

Uncle Philip lives in one of the big houses on Ballybricken where the cattle mart used to be. Nowadays, there's a wide green with benches for people to sit after the trudge up from town. It's a strange house. The furniture is new. The porch door is new and made with small squares of glass and every square of glass a different colour. The kitchen door is old and has a metal latch instead of a handle. There's a smell of fresh paint from the skirting boards but the wallpaper is faded and the walls are covered in holy pictures and every flat surface has a holy statue on it. Even the mantelpiece has a bottle of holy water in the shape of Our Lady of Lourdes wearing a blue cap for her veil. It's as if they're changing the house bit by bit, only you can't tell which bit they're changing.

Philip is gone for the night and there's only Rita and me. Her Christmas tree twinkles in the front window and her

Christmas cards hang from tinsel above the mantelpiece and along the walls.

Rita puts me sitting in the armchair in front of the blazing coal fire and hands me a packet of salt and vinegar crisps and a can of orange, and when she turns on the table lamp the whole room glows warm and pink. She sits on the sofa against the wall. She crosses her legs and lays her hands on her knees and smiles over at me. Rita has huge teeth when she smiles and you can see her top gum. She looks like she wants to say something, but she just sits there smiling and staring.

Is she waiting for me to say something? The longer she stares the more certain I am she knows everything. I can't keep still in the seat. The harder I try the more I shake. My arse is tight and my face is on fire and I look away. I hold the cool can of orange to my cheeks and hope she doesn't notice. Why doesn't she talk? Why the fuck doesn't she say what she wants to say and get it over with? I know what she's doing. She wants to sit here and watch me sweat until I can't stand it anymore and admit everything. That's why the fire is so hot. She's even got the coal scuttle full. Ready to heap it on the moment the heat begins to fade. Why doesn't she say something? Even the holy pictures on the walls are staring. I want to get up but I wouldn't even get my poncho on before she'd accuse me. Scream at me like my grandmother did because there's no use telling someone who was almost a nun, He made me do it. That he said nobody would believe me if I told because I'm a Shep. Nobody would care. I'd be fired out of the Holy Shepherd and on to the streets where all the men in the world could do what they liked to me.

She wouldn't believe me if I told her how sweet he could be when I did what he wanted. How he told me I was special and how good that made me feel because I was never special to anyone. Would Rita understand if I told her about the morning I woke up drenched with sweat and understood what I was doing was wrong? Would she understand the times I sat in steaming baths trying to scrub him away with soap and water but couldn't because the dirt was on the inside like a mortal sin? She'd never believe that about Uncle Philip. Not her Philip who sits at the front of the chapel every Sunday and receives the Body of Christ. My Philip isn't like that. My Philip is decent, respectful. And what could I say to her? That she's right, he is decent. That he has a good job and nice house and you don't see him hanging around the toilets in the park. How would I make her understand that they done what they done because they could, because we were nothing to them? Because we had no one to mind us, no one to care what happened to us. We're Peter's children, God love them.

Now Rita talks.

It's terrible how things turned out for all of you, Matilda. Philip's heart is broken, but God is good and with his help and the power of prayer everything will turn out right in the end. Tell me, Matilda. Did you see your father lately? He loves you all very much, you know.

I know, Rita. That's all I can say and I feel my voice shudder when I say it.

Have you a boyfriend yet, Matilda?

No, Rita.

A pretty girl like you? The boys must be queuing up.

What she's up to? Why doesn't she just come out and say it? Get it over with. I watch her out of the corner of my eye when she leans forward to turn on the television.

Do you like *Kojak*, Matilda?

When the nuns let us stay up late, I do.

That Telly Savalas is just gorgeous. Isn't he?

He's bald, Rita.

But he's so, so manly. You needn't be shy with me, Matilda.

239

I'd wonder what way is this for someone who was almost a nun to talk but I know she's building up to tell me what she really wants me here for. I can feel it coming. It's in her voice. She moves in the seat and it's like she's winding herself up and I feel my hands grip the arms of the chair. I close my eyes and wait for it but she says nothing and, when I open them again, there she is relaxed on the sofa watching *Kojak*.

Is that it? She hardly asked me here to find out about boyfriends. Maybe my grandmother put her up to it. Especially after all the trouble there was with Mona.

I finish the crisps and the can of orange and Rita hands me more. I say, No, thank you, but she presses them on me.

Thank you, Rita.

You should call more often, Matilda. I don't see much of you these days unless it's tearing through Grace's supermarket like an Olympic sprinter. You spend quite a bit of time there.

Not really, Rita. I . . . I, I'm not let out much.

Doesn't seem like that, Matilda. And now that you've brought it up . . .

Who, me? I didn't bring anything up.

The point is we need to discuss the matter. It's been bothering me a long time and now seems as good a time as any to get it out in the open. Woman to woman, so to speak.

There's a lump in my throat the size of Kojak's lollipop and I feel the crisps jar in my stomach. I'm ready to admit everything when she leans so close to me I can smell her lipstick.

I know what's been going on, Matilda. It's very wrong and your grandmother would be very upset if she knew. She worries a great deal, and if she finds out . . .

I start bawling, for real.

I didn't mean it, Rita. Honest I didn't. I was made to do it.

I jump up ready to run for the door but she tells me to sit down. This must be sorted out before Philip comes home.

He's up in your grandmother's. Your grandfather is ill. They don't expect him to last out Christmas. That's why I wanted to see you on your own, Matilda. We don't want to upset your grandmother, she has enough on her plate.

But . . . I . . .

Rita leans closer and puts her hand on my shoulder.

I know you've been stealing, Matilda. It's wrong and, if you get caught, I could lose my job.

What?

Stealing, Matilda.

Stealing! She's worried I get caught and she loses her job. I'm so weak with relief I don't care what she says now. I tell her, I'm sorry, Rita. I won't do it again.

I know it's not you, Matilda. You're far too nice. You're just mixing with the wrong company in that convent and I know very well they made you do it.

You do?

Of course I do. You must try to find other friends. It's not easy but you must make the effort. Think of your future.

It's no use telling Rita the convent kids are my family. It's easier to agree and go home.

I will, Rita. Thanks for telling me.

Good girl, Matilda. I'm glad we got that out of the way. Aren't you?

I am, Rita, thanks.

Now, would you like tea and toast before bed?

No thanks, Rita. I can't stay. I have a race in the morning.

No, no, you're staying for the weekend.

What?

Philip arranged it with Sister Gabriel.

No one told me, Rita.

Philip wanted to surprise you. I'll be working in the morning but Philip will be here. He'll be delighted to see you.

241

But I can't. I . . . I . . . I have a race. Gabriel should have known. It's important.

Rita stands up to go to the kitchen. She straightens the front of her dress and buttons her wool cardigan.

Of course you can stay, Matilda. I won't hear another word. We can sort something out with the race. Perhaps Philip will bring you. You look pale, Matilda. Are you ill?

I am, Rita. I think I have the flu. I better go home to bed.

Let me have a look at you. Oh, you're flushed and trembling all over. That's very strange. I don't think you'll be racing tomorrow. I'm sorry, but you're staying here.

She unscrews the blue veil from Our Lady of Lourdes on the mantelpiece, makes the sign of the cross on my forehead with the holy water and tells me to sit back in that chair. I'll make you a nice warm cup of tea.

It'd be better if I went home, Rita. If I have the flu, you'd get it.

It's too late to worry about it now, Matilda. Philip has the car and I wouldn't have Sister Gabriel ringing me to say I let you out on a bad night like this, and you as weak as a puppy. You're staying here and that's the end of it.

I'm in bed with the light on, a big sofa feather bed with brass knobs that belonged to Rita's dead mother. There she is staring at me from the wall with her black eyes accusing me. An old woman in a shawl sitting in a wooden rocking chair on Ballybricken in olden days, when men smoked little white pipes and the children had no shoes.

I pull the quilt over my head when I hear the front door open and close. I know it's Philip. I know the quiet way he has with doors. I hear the sitting-room door open and close and Philip and Rita's voices drifting through the floorboards.

What do I do? Do I turn the light out and pretend to be

asleep? No, that never bothered him and I don't want to be alone with him in the dark. I'll lie here until I hear them go to bed. He won't bother me with Rita here.

I hear the footsteps climbing the stairs and I know they're Philip's. I've heard those footsteps so many times on my grandmother's stairs when we've stayed for holidays and weekends. He stops outside the door and I think about jumping out the window or hiding under the bed. I don't have time to do anything. He taps on the bedroom door, then walks in and smiles at me when he sees I'm still awake and I know he thinks I was waiting for him. I feel so stupid.

Philip stays by the door and checks out on to the landing to see if Rita is following. He's wearing a grey suit and red tie. His hair combed back and his face blue from the glare of the lampshade. His shiny black shoes squeak when he moves to the side of the bed.

I told Rita I was coming up to say goodnight and to talk to you again about the stealing. What she doesn't know, won't trouble her.

He sits at the side of the bed and puts his arm around me and there's a strange scent of perfume that isn't Rita's. I look straight ahead at the picture on the wall of Rita's dead mother and I don't know if it's her watching me, or Philip himself making my stomach retch. I watch Philip out of the corner of my eye and, as he opens his belt buckle, my whole body stiffens. Maybe if he sees how scared I am he'll let me alone. Maybe with Rita downstairs he won't go too far. Maybe I should know better. He takes my hand in his, rubbing it.

Do you know how pretty you are, Matilda? Do you know how I feel about you? I know it's wrong but I can't help it. Believe me, I've tried. I just can't help myself.

His hands are large and soft and I pull my hand away but he tells me, It's all right, Matilda. Don't be nervous.

243

I sit up in the bed trying to look like I got a fright.

Stop, Philip. There's someone there.

Then he jumps up. He did get a fright. He goes to the bedroom door and peers outside to the landing and smiles to himself when it's empty and comes back to sit beside me on the bed. He whispers, Shush, Matilda, it's okay. There's nobody there. He's still smiling when he pulls the quilt back but he frowns when he sees I'm still wearing my jeans. He holds my hand again and leaves it between his legs and moans and begins opening my jeans. I tell him I have to go to the bathroom but he begs me to stay.

I'll be here all day tomorrow, Philip. I promise I will. I have to go to the toilet now, honest.

He stands up and straightens his pants and I jump out of the bed and run.

The bathroom is cold and has mirrors everywhere. The walls have green tiles and the floor has white tiles. There're goose bumps on my arms and legs and a hard lump clogging my stomach. I feel tears, loads of them, starting between my legs and gushing to my eyes. Rita is on the stairs shouting, Is everything all right up there, Philip? The green tiles are spinning around me. There's cold sweat dripping from my forehead and stinging my eyes. Oh, Jesus, help me. What am I going to do? Voices in my head. My grandmother screaming I made him do it. My father beating me. Rita shouting, You're a thief, a liar, look what you made your uncle do. My stomach heaves and splashes into the toilet – tea, orange, crisps, toast. I feel my feet running and I can't stop them. Black loafers running on white tiles. The metal tips clicking faster and faster. Please, Jesus. Please help me. I can't live like this anymore.

Rita is here. She has one hand on her forehead and the other holding the open door. Uncle Philip is behind her with his two hands frozen to his face peeping at me between the gaps in his fingers. Rita holds me and I lean against her. There, there, she says like I'm a five-year-old, but I don't care. She strokes my hair and tells me everything is all right. I knew you weren't well. Didn't I say you were pale? Too much orange and crisps, that's what it is. You'll be right in the morning. I rest against her, afraid to let her go, and I promise myself I'll never be alone with him again.

Later, I hear them go to bed and their door close. I'm too scared to sleep. I don't want to wake in the morning with Rita in work and Philip towering over me. I stand at the window and lift up the bottom sash. The icy night air stings my face and turns the room so cold I'm certain even Rita's dead mother has pulled her shawl a little tighter. The hill of Ballybricken is dark and deserted, the only light is from the Gardaí's Barracks on the other side of the hill. There are no stars and no mother to talk to. Just a quarter moon floating above the spire of St John's church. There's no clock in the room, no watch on my hand. The squad car roars out of the Gardaí's Barracks with its blue light flashing and disappears down Patrick Street, then everything goes quiet again. I watch and wait and, when I hear the convent bell ring for morning mass, I run downstairs.

My poncho is hanging in the sitting-room closet. I think about just grabbing it and running, but I'm frozen from standing all night. I pull it on over my head but hear footsteps coming downstairs. Uncle Philip comes in the room in his bare feet and his belt buckle open and tells me to stay. I turn my face from his and try to pass but his arm blocks the door. The veins throb in his arm but his voice is almost sweet.

Come on, Matilda. We'll talk when Rita goes out to work.
I don't want to talk. I have to go, please just let me go.
He takes his arm away to fasten his belt buckle and I try to push past him. He grabs the poncho as if he's playing with me.
Come on. You can stay if you want to.

245

I don't want to. I want to go home.

I wriggle away from him and nearly knock over the Christmas tree. A Christmas bulb falls to the floor and he crushes it under his foot when he moves to block the door again. I can smell that strange perfume from him again that isn't Rita's. I straighten up and try to look at him straight in the eye, but can't. I'm too ashamed. Too embarrassed over things I've done. But somehow I manage to mutter, if he doesn't let me go I'll tell.

I told you already what would happen.

I don't care. I'll tell Rita. I swear I will.

Ha, she won't believe you either. Don't be stupid.

She will. I know she will. I'll make her believe me. And don't call me stupid either. That's what my father calls me. I'm not stupid.

Off you go then, tell Rita.

He moves away and I hurry towards the hallway, but he runs after me and pulls me back by the hair. I grab his hand and look up. I see his face now. It's almost purple and there's spit at the corners of his mouth. He drags me back to the sitting room and I want to cry out with the pain but I don't want Rita to hear. He lets my hair go and sits on the pink sofa with his head in his hands. I wish he wouldn't do that. I don't know what it means. I never know what to do with people when they're like this. He looks up at me like I think an uncle should look at you, but I'm not sure because I never had uncles like that. His voice is trembling and he's not making any sense. I don't know what he's mumbling. His knees are trembling. I'm trembling. I want to get out of here.

I hear Rita's footsteps on the floorboards upstairs and the wardrobe door closing. Philip's pupils are as big as pennies. His eyeballs wide open. His hand reaches into his back trouser pocket and takes out a five-pound note but I don't want money. I don't want anything. I don't feel anything. I just see the front door and dawn breaking through the frosted glass. I need to be on the other side of that door. He's still looking up at me with the money in his hand.

I never meant harm, Matilda. You know I didn't. You're just so pretty.

I have to go now.

Take the money. Please, Matilda. I'd feel better.

What do you mean?

I mean, I'd feel better if you just, you know. Here, go on. Take it.

He'd feel better? What does that mean? Fuck him. I don't know where I get the strength but my blood must be on fire because I've said it before I know I've said it.

Fuck off. That's what you can do now. Just go and fuck yourself.

I turn towards the door without looking back and leave him with his money in his hand and his eyeballs rolling and meet Rita coming down the stairs fixing her handbag strap over her shoulder.

You're leaving, Matilda?

I am.

You must feel better.

A little.

You're certain you won't stay?

I'm positive, Rita. But thanks anyway.

I close the front door and sprint down the street and around the corner. I sit on the doorstep of a house with the porch light on and Christmas lights shimmering in the window. It's barely light. I'm too cold to cry. There's a pain between my ears like my tears have frozen at the back of my eyes. Up the street is my grandmother's house. Across the street there's a hypermarket where Denny's meats used to be.

I sit here watching the sun rise above the chimney pots. The milk float comes down the street and the milkman's helper runs from house to house. I better go home. People are passing on the way to town and I don't want anyone to see me like this.

Back in the convent Sonny is pacing up and down the kitchen with his hands clasped behind his back.

What are you doing here, Sonny? Oh Jesus, Sonny, I'm sorry. I forgot.

Never mind that now, Matilda. Get your stuff, quick. The bus is waiting.

I can't, Sonny. I'm knackered. I'm awake all night.

Awake? Was it the nerves or what? Don't answer. You don't have time. You're here now, that's the main thing. You can catch forty winks on the bus.

Couldn't I just give it a miss, Sonny?

Supposin' I have to carry you to Limerick on my shoulders, you're comin' with me. Days like this are rare. These are the days you can look back on and I won't let you throw it away now. What are you smiling at, Matilda? Did I say something funny or what?

I run upstairs. My bed is made; part of me wants to crawl under the covers and cry but I can't lay down feeling sorry for myself. I grab my stuff from my locker and we run for the bus.

It's my last race under fourteen. It's the All-Ireland finals and we're in the relay. Sonny's daughter, Caroline, Lisa Healy and me. Everyone says St Mary's from Limerick will win because they have the best young runner in the country and she looks it. Tall and lean with a long blonde ponytail, doing little run-ups in her navy tracksuit, knowing the world is watching. Her mother and father are standing at the finish, all wrapped up in their woolly hats and scarves, checking they have enough film in the camera and wondering, Where's the best place to take a picture now, do you think?

Sonny says she's the anchor and that means she's running last and that means I'll be running against her. I know Caroline is fast, maybe the fastest of her group, and Lisa Healy is good too, but I'm petrified. Sonny comes for my tracksuit, looks up at the grey sky, down at the mud, tilts his cap back on his head and walks away whistling. There's a cold wind in my face and fog so thick I can barely make out the hedges. I wish I knew why Sonny was so happy.

I'm standing under a tree with four other girls because there's no point goin' out on to the track, getting wetter, until we see the runners coming through the gate at the top of the field. The girl from St Mary's is standing under another tree, a little away from us, talking to her coach. She's testing the mud with her toe and it doesn't seem to bother her. She looks like she's been getting ready for this all her life and all I want to do is go to bed and cry.

Her coach looks smart in his bright white tracksuit and the gold whistle around his neck and smiling all round him with his big white teeth. You'd never see Sonny in whistles and tracksuits and big white teeth. He wanders around in that overcoat he wears winter and summer, choking on a fag, lucky to have a tooth in his head. Do your best, girl, he says. Don't let yourself down. That's the main thing. Never be less than you are. Still, I see the pride in his eyes when we win. I know it's not for himself and that's what I like about Sonny. Everything is just so simple.

There's a roar. A girl appears at the top gate. She's on her own. I can't see who it is yet. She's too far away and in this fog she'll have to be right on top of me before I know for certain, but I never prayed so hard it's Caroline.

And it is, it's Caroline's red vest coming out of the fog. But there's a girl close behind in blue. I step out onto the track, my heart clattering in my chest and my throat so tight I can barely breathe. Caroline is getting closer, the baton swinging back and forth in her hand. The girl from St Mary's jogs out and stands beside me. Christ she's tall. Everyone says I'm tall but she has legs like a giraffe.

Caroline is closer, so close I can hear her panting and her feet squelching in the mud. She passes the baton to me and I'm off. Go, Matilda, go. I go, but not too fast. There's a long way to race.

I go through the gate at the bottom of the track and into the next field. I hear the cheers for the girl from St Mary's. I'm ahead but not by much and my legs go weaker. There's drizzle blowing in our faces and, when we reach the top of the field, she's right beside me. Though I think I can go faster, I know for certain she can too.

We turn at the oak tree. People are cheering. The ground is heavy, muddy, catching my feet and dragging me in. I slide. I don't fall, but the fright makes me lose stride and I hear her runners squelching in the mud. I feel her beside me, ready to pass. She's waiting her chance, letting me tire, then she'll be gone, the tall girl from St Mary's, the best young runner in the country, against the Shep, the orphan, the retard, and I'm so ashamed. I'll never have what I want. Never have what the girl from St Mary's wakes up to every morning. I'll never have a family. All I'll ever have is a lunatic father and an uncle with a five-pound note.

The tears come to my eyes. Try as I might, I can't hide them. My hand swings back and there's a second when it touches the wrist of the St Mary's girl. We run stride for stride through a muddy lane, people on both sides shouting her on. I could slow down now, let her ahead of me. Let her go so far ahead nobody would notice who was second. Nobody would blame me for losing to the best young runner in the country. We turn at the bottom of the muddy lane round another oak tree; my shoulder touches her arm. She's toying with me, falling back to tease me, pretending to tire, waiting to take the only thing that's mine. The only thing my father can't touch. My running. There's a voice in my head telling me to fight. You have to fight, Matilda.

I hear Sonny telling me not to let myself down and I remember the pride in his eyes when we win. I fight the tears, the hurt, the mud, the five-pound note. No matter how stupid I look trying to beat the lanky bitch from St Mary's, I can't give up. Sonny and the team need me and nobody ever needed me before. Not for real. Nobody else ever wanted me to be just myself. There's strength in my heart and suddenly it's in my legs again and I'm running above the ground, above the mud, above myself. I look back and, Jesus, the best young runner in the country isn't there anymore. I look ahead to the finish line and see Caroline and Lisa jumping up and down cheering. Sonny's cap is covering his face but I know there's a smile inside him that would dazzle you and it's hard not to smile myself. I know I don't have a family like the Limerick girl or any other girl here but maybe some day I will. I might be covered in mud but inside I feel clean and when I cross that finish line I know this must be what it feels like when you've just come home.

18

There's still no word from Sheamie. To make things worse, my father could come home from London soon. If I couldn't tell by the evenings getting longer and the swallows that nest under the convent roof swooping over our heads in the playground I could tell by Danny sitting on the stone wall. If Danny even thinks our father is coming, he climbs that wall faster than a nun's confession. Gabriel is dreading it. She's been praying a lot more lately. Praying is important to the nuns. As important as make-up is to the big girls. They always look so different afterwards, and this morning when I tell Gabriel I'm going for a run she looks badly in need of the blusher.

She's sitting at the kitchen table in her new habit. I took me a while to get used to it. Well, actually, it took me a while to get used to the fact Gabriel has legs. It stops just below her knee. And her new veil is short and sits on top of her head and not strapped under her chin like the old one. Her hair is cut short and has a slight curl to it and it's almost as dark as mine. She's reading her prayer book and from the moment she lifts her head to ask, Is there any news of your father, Matilda? to when I answer, Not yet, Mother, even birds sitting on wires stop singing and are stuck there with their beaks open waiting for the answer.

I'm running along the edge of the pavement by the Apple Market when the hand comes out from the crowd. I know that hand better than my own. I know how the long straight fingers stick together and the thumb lies flat across the palm.

The thick knuckles. The strong, sleeveless arm. The clean fingernails. I know that voice it belongs to. If I didn't know what it could do, I'd want to hear it more than anything. If I didn't know how quickly it can change, I couldn't wait to hear it. I'd dream about it. I'd listen to every sweet and beautiful word and love it more than anything.

I look up. Not as far as those eyes. I wouldn't dare. He'd kill me. He'd say I was challenging him. My eyes stop at the beard. It's longer, scraggier, more grey than black.

Sorry, Daddy, I didn't see you.

You'll never get away from me. Remember that.

I didn't see you, honest.

He bends for me to kiss his cheek and my mind goes blank but I know I've kissed him because there's that bitter taste on my lips. He asks why I didn't write and I tell him I did and he nods like he remembers. It was only one stupid letter Gabriel made me write.

Have you written to your father lately, Matilda?

No, Mother.

Wouldn't it be nice now to tell him how well you're doing in the running and you won the gold medal and had your picture in the paper? I'm sure he'll want to hear all of it, Matilda.

He wouldn't want to hear any of it.

Be sure to say you love him and miss him terribly. I'll post it for you. Wouldn't now be a lovely time to do it, with summer coming.

It wasn't a question. What Gabriel meant by summer coming is, that crazy bastard is going to be here soon, in God's name, do something. I wrote, but I didn't tell him about the running. After what happened in Clew Bay I couldn't, and I hated Gabriel for making me write because I didn't miss him and I don't love him. Now I'm glad she did.

Where are you going now?

I'm off school.

Did I ask about school?

No, Daddy.

I'm caught. I can't tell him about my running. Something new for him to say I'm useless at, but I have my running togs on and the new runners that Sonny bought for my birthday and if he even thinks I'm lying he'll kill me here and now. I tell him about the running and how I got my picture in the paper and, as I'm telling him, I remember how good I felt and for some stupid reason I hope he'll be proud he has a daughter who has more gold medals than the whole Holy Shepherd put together, but it means nothing to him and for a little while it makes me feel nothing.

He sits on a chair with the straw sticking out of its arms and lights a cigarette. He pulls an empty fruit crate beside him and tells me to sit and there's nothing to do but sit here with the cheap clothes, the lousy fruit and the broken records. He asks about Pippa and Danny and I tell him they're in the convent.

Are you visiting your Nanny?

I lie that I called at Easter and he seems happy with that.

It's important to keep contact with the family, Matilda. Family is all you have at the end of the day.

I know, Daddy.

The chapel bells ring for ten o'clock mass and I tell him Gabriel will be waiting, even though he knows she won't and wouldn't give a shit if she was. He twirls the cigarette between his thumb and finger and watches the smoke spiral. Umbilical Bill tosses me an apple.

Thanks, Bill.

I like Bill. I get a kick out of watching him flog the bruised pears he swears he picked this morning, when I know the only thing Bill ever picked any morning was his nose. My father asks how I'm doing with the music and I tell him I can play the accordion and the flute and wonder why is he interested and who told him I'm learning music in the Mad School.

The long thin lips smile to themselves and the eyebrows twitch.

You can go. Tell the others I'll be down. Make sure you're there.

At nearly fourteen you'd think there'd be some sign of a chest. Pippa has the biggest chest in the convent and I can't understand why I have almost none. I sit on my bed looking down the front of my jumper screaming, Come on, come on, for Christ's sake. I pull at my nipples but they only stick out like points and when I let go my skin slaps back flat to my chest and I end up with nipples raw and sore. If I had a bra, I could fill it with stockings and toilet paper, only I'm too nervous to ask Gabriel. She'll say bras cost money and she can't be handing out bras to someone with no chest.

I'm shaking walking down the stairs. I stop on the landing and chew the inside of my lip, wondering if now is a bad time to ask with my father around, but I'll never get one unless I ask.

Gabriel is in the kitchen, her hands white with flour, baking scones for Father Devlin. Hello, Matilda, she says.

Oh shit, she knows.

I run back out to the hallway and sit on the end of the stairs with my chin in my hands. Maybe she doesn't know, maybe she was just saying hello. I walk in and ask straight out.

Mother, can I have a bra?

A what?

A bra, Mother?

She looks at me like I'm demented and wonders, What would you do with a bra, Matilda?

What do you mean what would I do with it? What do you think I'd do with it?

You don't need a bra. When you do I'll let you know.

I need one now, Mother.

Don't be silly. Be off out and play and let me get on with the work.

I feel like crying because she speaks to me like a child, a child with no chest. She wouldn't speak to me like that if I had a bra. Then I could go around holding them up with my arms folded and not have to keep my arms by my side, because you can't go around folding your arms under your chest when you don't have a bra.

Gabriel goes to clean Polly's cage and complains about the kids always sticking bits of weed and leftover corn flakes through the bars. I don't know how the poor little thing survives at all, Matilda. It must be a miracle.

It'd be a miracle if you bought the poor little thing a box of birdseed.

What?

Nothin'.

Gabriel looks through the window and asks if my father plays the guitar and I don't know what guitars have to do with anything.

A guitar?

I run to the window and there he is in the playground with a black leather guitar case in his hand. Pippa is skipping around him like she's delighted he's here. Part of her probably is. Part of her is terrified. That's what happens when you have nobody to love and nobody to love you. You'll look for it from the ones that hurt you most. Even from my father.

He hands Pippa something in a box like a tiny black coffin. It's probably a watch. It is a watch, with a gold strap and clasp.

Pippa kisses his cheek and runs to show the other kids what she's got.

Gabriel goes to the sink, tidying what's already tidied so she looks busy when he walks in all smiles saying, Hello, Sister, nice to see you again.

It's hard not to laugh at the way Gabriel tries to sound surprised when she says, Oh, Mister Kelly, how nice to see you again.

Gabriel smiles at me like I'm a great girl altogether and I still hate it when she does that.

My father leaves the guitar on the table and bends for me to kiss his cheek and there's that bitter taste again. He walks to the window and stands with his hands behind his back and asks where Danny is. Gabriel walks the other way, towards the sink. Have you seen Danny today, Matilda? And she knows he's out on the wall since breakfast and by now he's hiding on the other side of town.

No, Mother. Did you?

Well, I'm absolutely certain he was here earlier but I couldn't say where he is right now. Though I'll be certain he knows you're looking, Mister Kelly.

My father walks to the piano and opens the lid. Plays one or two notes and closes it again.

Did you know Matilda's mother played the piano, Sister?

Did she, indeed? Well, it must run in the family, because I'm receiving fabulous reports about Matilda and her music.

There's a cold sweat soaking through my blouse. He's up to something. By now he's usually roaring abuse at Gabriel about our education and how stupid I am and how it's all Gabriel's fault.

I'd like to see Matilda on her own, Sister. Is that all right with you?

I'm looking at Gabriel, waiting for her to turn around and say we were going somewhere, but she gives me her back.

Go, Matilda, go with your father.

I thought we were goin' somewhere, Mother?

Not that I'm aware of.

I thought you said . . .

You must be mistaken. Go with your father.

The sun is sinking above the chestnut trees and the playground glints orange. There's a crack of wings as the starlings lift from the telephone wires and make great sweeping circles overhead. My father walks ahead of me with the guitar in his hand, through the wooden gate to the nuns' garden full of shrubs and flowers and nuns on their knees with garden trowels digging in the clay.

He kneels beside Sister Rose, who's in charge of the gardens and spends her life on her knees one way or another, and tells her in his sweet, calm voice, the Lord is in her two hands and the garden is an offering to the Almighty and would you mind if we share it with you a while? Sister Rose is so delighted she's offering him slips and bulbs of every hedge, shrub, lily and rose in the garden and the way he's going he'll have her preaching on the side of the road with him if he doesn't stop.

A pleasure, Mister Kelly, why anytime at all. And how is Matilda this evening?

Fine, Sister Rose.

I'm sure you're only delighted to have your father home.

I am, Sister.

Don't let me delay you both any longer. Have a nice evening, won't you. It was a pleasure to meet you again, Mister Kelly.

And you, Sister Rose.

Near a small pond where a family of brown ducks live, my father sits cross-legged on the lawn fringed by shrubs and roses. The ground is hard and the grass is burned in the centre of the lawn and I know the nuns are saying isn't it a wonderful sight to see a man and his daughter on such a splendid lawn on an evening such as this. I tremble when he tells me to sit closer, right here in front of him.

I bought you this.

Bought? My father doesn't buy anything unless he's up to something.

He unzips the black leather case and takes out a shiny wooden guitar. I tell him I can't play the guitar and hope he'll think he made a mistake, but he insists I have the gift.

Huh?

He twists the knobs at the top and listens to the wiry sound of each string, tuning it, getting it perfect. When he's satisfied, he tells me to watch where he puts his fingers and, when he plays, the mother duck quacks. She flutters her stubby brown tail and her five chicks follow her through a patch of ivy to the other side of the garden, where they snuggle in the shade of the wall. He hands me the guitar.

You try, Matilda.

The guitar feels solid and makes a hollow sound when I take it. I sit up, cross-legged, and hold the guitar on my lap the way he did, but I don't know where to put my fingers.

Just let go, Matilda. Be one with the Lord and the Lord will be in your fingers.

What?

The Lord is in every living thing. You must let Him guide you. Close your eyes and breathe the scent of the flowers, hear the birds chirping and be as one with your Maker.

I close my eyes and pray like a lunatic. My father is the lunatic and I'm praying like one. Please, Lord, be in my fingers. I pluck the strings and he screams in my face.

What was that?

I told you I can't play. I don't want to play.

I get up to go but he barks at me to sit, so I sit and try again but this time he doesn't ask, What was that? This time it's, What the fuck was that? You're stupid.

He pulls the guitar from me. This is the G chord, listen to it.

Then he relaxes. His eyelids close and the beard ripples under his nostrils. I look to the other side of the garden to Sister Rose. She glances over her shoulder but, like Gabriel, she gives me her back. The nuns will never do anything. They're too scared of him.

He hands me the guitar again and tells me in that sweet voice to let it all go and be one with the Lord. The Lord has given each of us a gift and yours, Matilda, is music. He told me so. But the Lord expects you to praise him in return.

He sounds so sure, for a moment I can't help wondering if he's right. No, I need him to be right, but when I play the beard around his lips bristles with sweat. He spits in my face. You're stupid. You're a stupid bitch. You're just fucking thick.

I try to wipe the phlegm from my cheek but he forces my fingers on the strings one at a time and squeezes till they bleed. I try again but it's no use and I scream, I'll try, I'm sorry, I'll try again. That's no use either, and I know what's coming. Before I see the long straight fingers curling into that fist. Before I see it speeding over the burned grass, I know it's coming. My head spins and wobbles. Everything is wet and blurry. The roses are turning green and the shrubs are turning yellow and the next thing I see is the bathroom sink running red but it washes away and, when it does, it never happened.

In the morning, Gabriel doesn't ask what happened to my face, she knows.

Pippa is going to town to meet Mona, but I can't go anywhere with a face like a torn sack. Pippa doesn't say it but she's glad I'm not going. She'll be leaving the convent for good next year. She knows the only thing that's going to bother our father for the summer is that guitar, and me. She wants to be well out of the way.

I couldn't go with her if I wanted to. I can't go anywhere until I learn something on that guitar. I'll go to my room and practice the G chord. The God Chord. That's what my father calls it. The God Chord.

Through the open window, I hear the others running out to the playground and I don't want to play this guitar. I don't want to stand next to that lunatic, playing some stupid song he made up himself so I can praise the Lord while he preaches his gospel to the sinners of Waterford or London or wherever he plans to take us. I just want him to leave me alone.

I take the guitar from under the bed and sit on the bed with the guitar on my lap. Maybe if I learn a few chords, that'll stop him hitting me. It probably won't. After the guitar there'll be something else, something new for him to say I'm useless at. There will always be something. I know that now. He'll pick on me until I skip and dance around him in the playground like Pippa, or run from him in terror like Mona and Sheamie and Danny. He'll torment me until he breaks me, until he controls me. I don't know when it was I understood that. I just woke one morning and the answer was beside me on my pillow. It was as if the Tooth Fairy finally found out where I lived.

I'll break a string, that's what. I'll break a string and say it just broke. Who's to say it didn't? I'm sure it happens all the time. Probably did it himself. But no, he'll say, You stupid bitch for breaking the string, because people with the Lord in their fingers don't break strings. I'll say one of the other children broke it, one of the younger kids who won't say I'm a liar. They're always getting at things and breaking them. But I can't do that either. He'll say, You stupid bitch for leaving the guitar where a child can get it. What am I going to do? I'd practise if only my hands would stop shaking. I pray, Please, God, please, Jesus and Holy Spirit who's in everyone. Please help me. I'll be good. I won't curse, I won't fight, I'll do whatever Gabriel says. Please just stop my hands from shaking. But he doesn't answer. He never answers.

I get down on the floor and put my hands under my legs and sit on them. I'll sit here for as long as it takes thinking about good things, but I can't do that either because the only good thing I have is this stupid fuckin' guitar.

I stand at the window watching the others playing on the swings and roundabout and fighting over everything. I'll go outside and walk around for a while. I won't talk to anyone in case they want me to play. I'm just not in the humour for playing. I know they'll say I'm pure faintin' and won't talk to anyone because I got a new guitar, but I don't care, it's better than him beating me.

The sunlight stings my eyes when I walk out to the playground. Gabriel is sitting on the low red-brick wall around her garden talking to Sister Ellen. Gabriel smiles at me like I'm a great girl altogether and asks how the guitar is coming along. I'm sure you'll be a fine guitar player, Matilda. You have the fingers for it.

I don't answer. I'm not in the mood for her. I don't know what torments me more about Gabriel. How she can be so sweet to my father or that stupid smile she gives me, and I don't see what's so special about my bleeding fingers that the Lord is in them and they're so brilliant for playing guitar.

Danny kicks the football to me from across the playground. It lands at my feet and he stands there like he's expecting me to kick it back.

Come on, Matilda, are yeh playin' or what?

I'm nearly fourteen. I'm stuck in a Mad School, my father's

tormenting me with that damn guitar, my brother's tormenting me to play football and I can't get a bra for love nor money.

Gabriel says, Give it a break, Matilda. You've been up there all morning.

All morning and I haven't even held the guitar properly.

There's no use tormenting myself. I'll play ball for a while and maybe I'll feel better later, only we play ball until dark and later never comes.

My father comes to the convent most days now. He takes me to town and we sit in the apple market talking to Umbilical Bill or other people my father knows from when he was young. Those are the all right days. Other days he takes Pippa and me to town to preach. Some days he only takes Pippa. I'm to stay here and practise my guitar.

On a rainy evening in July, Pippa and me are in the sitting room practising disco dancing to the Bee Gees on *Top of the Pops*. Gabriel doesn't mind the Bee Gees and even does a few steps herself. It's like she's just discovered she has legs, and they're not bad either, for a nun.

The song has just finished when I hear Gabriel out in the kitchen telling my father we can use the Madonna's room. I go upstairs and take the guitar from under the bed and, when I come down, my father is sitting in the armchair by the window. On the table beside him there's a bunch of dead lilies in a vase. This is all I need. The Madonna's blue eyes staring at me from one corner and my father's yellow eyes glaring at me from the other.

Come here and show me your fingers, Matilda.

What do you want to see my fingers for?

I want to see if you've been practising.

I have.

Show them to me.

He pulls my fingers closer and I feel his breath on my palm.

Those are teeth marks.

They're not. It's from the strings.

Don't lie to me. Don't lie to your father.

One way or another I'm dead. They are teeth marks but if I tell him they're not he'll kill me for telling lies and if I tell him they are teeth marks he'll kill me for not practising. I'd have practised if I knew what I was practising but there's nothing written down because people with the Lord in their fingers don't need things written down.

He gives me a thump to the temple that drives me onto the floor. I crawl under the table and crouch close to the wall with my hands over my head and he's kicking chairs out of the way to get at me. I see Gabriel's short skirts bustling across the red carpet.

Out. I want you out of here now. Leave that child alone and don't come back here again or I'll call the gardaí.

He's holding a chair – I can see the legs dangling above the carpet. His toes curl tight in his Moses sandals when he turns to face Gabriel. He'd go for Gabriel when he's like this and she knows it. I hear the banging in my chest when he takes a step towards Gabriel. She takes a step back and a bunch of fresh lilies drop from her hand to the floor. I try to find a prayer but there's darkness in my head and the words don't come. A gang of younger kids run in and my father slams the chair against the wall and storms out.

I crawl as far as the leg of the table and look up at Gabriel. She kisses her crucifix, mumbling a prayer. She goes out to the hallway and locks the door and when she comes back she tells me to come out from under there, he's gone. Will you just look at what he's done to this chair? It's beyond repair. I've had enough of him. I really have.

She bends to pick up the lilies when the kids run in yelling, He's back, he's back, he's back, and we hear him banging his fist on the glass. Gabriel goes back out to the hall and I run after her and hide behind her black skirts while she threatens him with the gardaí again. I can't really see him, just the green of his jacket through the wire glass. The younger kids run up and down the hall shouting the gardaí are coming. They're so excited something new is happening, if my father dragged Gabriel and me out to the playground and hung us from a chestnut tree they'd light a bonfire and dance around us like Indians. The bigger kids are gathering around Gabriel, terrified in case anything happens to her. Mickey Driscoll is telling me to hide.

Upstairs, Matilda. Hide under me bed. He won't look there.

Doyler is waving her tea towel. Get away from that door. She runs down the corridor checking the windows are locked. One of the young kids pushes her face up to the glass and sticks her tongue out then runs and hides under the kitchen table. Pippa runs to the kitchen and hides under the table too. I think about following but decide to stay behind Gabriel. I can't run from him if I'm under a table. My father could break the glass but he's doing enough. He's frightening Gabriel and that's what he wants. He's making sure she never interferes with him again.

When he's gone, Gabriel is trembling. She takes out her rosary beads and prays for strength. An hour later, she gets off her knees and puts her rosary beads back in her pocket.

That's it. That's the last time he'll set a foot in here.

Even as Gabriel's saying it we both know it's not true. Grandmother rings Father Devlin who rings Reverend Mother who says, Of course, Father Devlin, I'm certain there's been a mistake, and on a cold Saturday in August he's back telling Gabriel how sorry he is and here's something I thought you'd like, Sister Gabriel.

He's bought her a record player. I know he bought it second-hand in the Apple Market and a cardboard box stuffed with long-playing records and all of them about God.

Gabriel isn't happy with Reverend Mother for leaving my father back in here. I catch her glaring at her behind her back when she thinks nobody's looking. I know there's nothing Gabriel can do and she'll put up with it as long as my father behaves and she's not distracted from putting her feet up with Sister Ellen so they can listen to Elvis Presley blaring out 'Amazing Grace' all over the place.

There's an argument over which group gets the record player. Our father bought it so our group thinks it should be in our group, but the other groups complain that's got fuck all to do with it.

Stop that swearing, says Gabriel.

Sister Ellen says the record player is for everybody.

Gabriel says, Yes, Sister Ellen, it is for everybody. But it's staying in my sitting room.

Sister Ellen puts on a long face but grabs the nearest seat and for a week there're fifty of us cramped in the sitting room until we get so sick of Elvis cryin' and bawlin' in the chapel we go back to the playground, leaving Gabriel and Ellen to argue over who they'll listen to next.

Monday afternoon, he's waiting for me outside the Mad School in his army jacket and Moses sandals. He's leaning against the gate pillar watching the school door, making sure I don't get past. I'm so ashamed, I run out to see what he wants when I'm still wearing the grey uniform. I walk behind him to his blue van parked at the back of the Cathedral where he takes a banner rolled around two long wooden poles from the roof rack. He puts them on one shoulder and a white wooden box he takes from the front seat on the other. We walk to the

Cathedral where the purple banner opens larger than a bed-spread. It has a picture of the Lord standing on a cloud and he has golden light coming from his head. My father stands on the white box, with one hand gripping my wrist and his long hair swept over his shoulders, and in that calm, powerful voice begins to preach.

The Cathedral is on the busiest street in the city and it's throbbing with people. My father preaches to them all. He preaches to the people coming from or going to the Cathedral, lured to the temple of evil by the Catholic Church, the instrument of Satan himself. He preaches to the people who hurry past, blessing themselves, and the ones who just hurry past. He preaches to the ones who cross the street and the ones who stop to listen. He preaches to the ones that laugh and move on and the ones who listen and then move on. He preaches to the ones who stay and hang on every sweet and beautiful word. They've found a Saviour. They found my father.

19

I'm fifteen and still breaking as many plates as I did when I was six, still getting stopped pocket money. I know things aren't as strict as they were but plates still cost money. Sometimes the convent hardly seems like a convent anymore. We still have rules, but I suppose every home has rules. And that's what the convent is to me now, my home. There are barely twenty of us here between two groups. When we're gone, the convent will be closed.

In some ways it's better like this – at least if you leave something down it's still there when you go back – but there's nobody my age to go stealing with and I feel stupid stealing on my own with a blue poncho that's too small.

I've tried to get rid of it. I've left it in rubbish skips and thrown it in the bins covered in banana skins but I always go back. Not because I need it for stealing, well, a little maybe, but because it came from our mother's brother and it reminds me I have a mother and I have to have a mother, even a mother who never came back for me, just so I can feel real. Feel that I belong in the world.

The nuns got Pippa a job in a country house hotel run by Missus Schultz, a fat little Danish woman, who for years has been taking girls from the convent to work as waitresses because the Holy Shepherd girls make the best workers and, Goodness, they're oh so cheap. Missus Schultz lets her stay in the hotel but it's so far away and she gets really lonely and if it wasn't for the Black Forest gateau she'd go demented. I miss her. It's like my family is vanishing before my eyes.

But I'm happy for her. It must be great to be sixteen getting a job and eating Black Forest gateau. I keep asking Gabriel to get me a job, to take me out of the Mad School, but she keeps telling me, no, and today when I come from school she's fuming at the mantelpiece.

Suspended again, Matilda.

Sister Joan found out I was mocking Missus Clancy, the pastry teacher who comes Wednesday afternoon to teach the Mad Kids how to cook a scone without burning the school to the ground. She has a drip at the tip of her nose so big that on a sunny day you can see your reflection in it. It grows until it's so heavy it drops into the pastry and she keeps on stirring. The Mad Kids love it. They laugh so hard, Sister Joan has to douse them with cold water and line them up in the playground to dry in the sun.

Suspended, Matilda. Six times in four months. It's not good enough.

I was trying to get expelled.

I have no doubt about it, Matilda. But it won't happen.

Then get me a job, Mother.

I'm tired of telling you, you go to school until you're sixteen.

Can't I get a job and still live here?

You know you can't. I've told you a thousand times, it's the law. You can't live here unless you go to school!

Well, it's a stupid law. You know I should never have been sent to that school. It was your fault. You should have stopped them sending me.

She folds her arms under her chest and I fold my arms under my chest and we stare at each other across the room. It took me long enough to get a chest and I'm not wasting it now. Gabriel shakes her head as if she's wasting her time but I see the guilty look in her eyes.

She sits at the kitchen table and begins embroidering one

269

of those white pocket-handkerchiefs and I think she's finished but she hasn't.

First thing in the morning you start in the laundry.

What's the laundry got to do with us?

It was Reverend Mother's decision. She has made it clear if there's any more nonsense, you'll be sent to Cork. That'll knock the nonsense out of you. I don't want that to happen to you, Matilda. Miles away from everyone you know. And either do you. Now buck up. It's your last chance.

I know Gabriel thinks she's found a way to get the better of me. She knows the one thing worries me is I'll be sent to Cork.

The laundry is hot and noisy from the big washing machine full of suds and soapy water, and steamy from the big dryers with the glass doors where sheets tumble like dry white clouds. I'm sent to work in the basement where there's a damp smell and Jesus on the cross to keep me company. There's a metal chute where sacks of dirty sheets and towels from the hotels and guesthouses drop from the road above to the cold concrete floor. I empty the sacks into the green bins that one of the old women leaves by the door. Sometimes she nods and I nod back but it's hard to see her face because the room is dim. The sacks are heavy and I have to use my knee to get them to the bin lid and I'm glad when Sister Madeline comes at ten o'clock with warm tea and a ginger biscuit and an elastic band for a ponytail. I sit in the corner on the empty sacks fixing my hair and wonder how Sheamie is. Why hasn't he written? Is he dead or alive? Will he be like our mother and disappear for ever?

All morning, the same old woman comes for the bins. Before lunch, she smiles and I smile back. Sister Madeline brings bread and jam with my tea and biscuit and I sit cross-legged in the corner eating, until she comes for the empty cup and the old woman comes with the empty bin. I asked Gabriel once why the old women are here but she wouldn't say. I've seen young girls come here to have their babies and leave after a year or two when someone might come and sign them out, but the old women never leave. The only thing Gabriel would say was they're Penitent. It must have been a terrible sin if the laundry is their penance.

The sacks tumble from the chute all afternoon and each one seems heavier than the last, and the harder I work the faster they tumble from the chute and I'm happy when it's time to go home. The old woman waves from the front door and it's hard to wave back. My hands and feet are killing me. That evening I can barely walk to Our Lady's Grotto. I don't race anymore. I just like coming down here to help. Sonny only trains the kids up to under-sixteen. He wanted me to join another club. I wouldn't go. It just wouldn't be the same without Sonny. I wouldn't swap Sonny for all the medals in the world.

Sonny sits on his hands and shifts himself on the wall. He takes a long look at me. Them nuns can be villains.

They can, Sonny.

Not to worry, Matilda. One day the world will be your oyster.

What's an oyster, Sonny?

We sit on the wall talking about oysters and everything and nothing. You can do that with Sonny, and the time flies. Sonny gives me a tube of green ointment he says burns like Hell and stinks to high Heaven, but rub it in your knees and elbows and you'll be as right as rain in the morning, Matilda.

Sonny is right. In the morning the aches and pains are gone and it's pissing from the heavens.

The brown canvas sacks are already tumbling when I go in and when the old woman whispers, Good morning.

I say, Hello, but I feel strange, as if speaking to her somehow makes me part of the laundry.

The chute spits sacks on to the concrete floor all morning and I wonder about the rich people in hotels and guesthouses in the world above, eating Black Forest gateau and oysters while their beds are made by girls from the Holy Shepherd or places like it. The old woman and her bin come to the door as if they're a part of each other. I wonder did she ever sleep in a hotel and eat Black Forest gateau and oysters. Is she better if she did or if she didn't? I'd hate to sleep in a hotel and eat Black Forest gateau and oysters then end up in the laundry attached to a green bin all day. Would it be even worse to spend your life pushing bins and never know about Black Forest gateau and oysters? Either way I pity her. To spend your life pushing sacks full of rich people's laundry is no way to live.

On the third day I'm like Jesus. I've risen up from the basement to the laundry itself. The old woman, whose name I now know is Mary, is sent with me to the pressing and folding room. There are three other old women here ironing sheets and they smile when they see me, and I smile back. Great metal pressers along the wall hiss clouds of dry white steam around them and they spend all day pressing sheets and wiping their foreheads with hands wrinkled from years of water and steam.

At the break, I sit on the step with Mary sipping her tea from the little cup and holding the saucer on her lap, frightened in case she spills any. Across from us is a building with yellow brick around the windows where the old women live. It's between the chapel and the penguins' mansion and Mary shows me her window on the third floor where she looks out at the laundry and the stone wall. She knows me from the chapel and asks about my family, because she's missed seeing

Mona and Sheamie and Pippa in mass. It's sad I spent all those years nervous of the old women, and nice Mary knows who I am. I tell her about my mother and how I haven't seen her since I was four. Mary stares at the wall without talking and her tiny brown eyes seem sad and far away. She looks around to make sure Madeline isn't near, then tells me in her voice that's almost a whisper that long ago she met a boy and got in trouble. She doesn't say what kind of trouble but looks at me to see if I understand. I give a look back that I do and I see how easily it happens – you don't have to talk when you do the same thing with the same people all your life and never hear or see anything else.

When Mary is happy that I understand, she tells me how her family sent her to the nuns to have her baby and she could never go home because of the sin and the shame of it, so she's been living with the nuns and doing the laundry since she was a young girl, and I know by the way she can press and fold sheets without looking she's been here a very long time. She ran away once and slept in a ditch, but the gardaí found her and brought her back. The nuns locked her in her room for weeks and I can't help wondering what was so wrong about what she did.

I look at her beside me on the step, her thin grey hair, her face wrinkled, her old eyes turned downward, scared of everything and everyone. I try to take away the wrinkles and the hump from her shoulder and see her as a young girl in love, but I can't. I want to ask about her baby. Was it a boy or girl? Does she miss never seeing it again? About her boyfriend, what did he look like? Were they in love? Did he ever come looking for her? Did she ever see her family again? Or even if she'd like to leave here? But I know by the lines of washing on her wrinkled cheeks, all Mary knows now is the linen and the starch and how many folds go in a double sheet.

★

In the morning Gabriel tells me Reverend Mother needs help and, when Gabriel says Reverend Mother needs help, you don't ask what kind of help then decide if you want to do it. You go straight across to the penguins' mansion and knock on the door of Reverend Mother's office and when she's good and ready to come out you say, Sister Gabriel said you need help, Reverend Mother. And that's all there is to it.

Reverend Mother locks her office door from the great bunch of keys around her waist. I'm not as scared of her now as I was when I was young but she still manages to make me feel small. I follow the swish of her starched white skirts up the grand stairway to the nuns' cells. That's what they call their rooms. Cells. It makes them feel they're suffering.

The cells are small. Small enough for a single bed and a single wardrobe. Reverend Mother tells me the nuns are starting retreat for two weeks. Start in the morning, a spring clean. All thirty cells.

Yes, Reverend Mother.

I start early. Take the heavy drapes from the windows, the sheets from the beds, carry them downstairs and leave them at the door. I get on my two knees to polish the floors till I can see my face. I clean the windows, frames, ledges and sills. I wax the dressing table. The days go quickly, but November mornings can be dark and I don't like it in the penguins' mansion on my own. They have the best of everything but the living rooms are big and hollow and even my own footsteps seem to creep up behind me when I walk down the corridor past the dead nuns staring at me from the wall in their brown wooden frames.

In one of the cells, in a drawer of the bedside chest, there's a photograph of a young red-faced girl with bushy black eyebrows and braces on her teeth. She's standing on a railway platform with a man wearing a sad face and a soft hat, and

274

there's an embroidered handkerchief in his top pocket. There's a bundle of letters tied in a bow with pink string and another photograph of the same girl in a habit. I never imagined Gabriel being anything but a nun. I never imagined her with a family of her own. Her photograph makes me curious. I always wondered what I'd look like in a habit. You can't help it when you live in a convent. Sometimes I look at Gabriel and I wonder if the habit makes her how she is. Her uniform shows she's a Soldier of Christ. Is that all she is? What happened to the girl in the photograph? You'd think I'd know her after all these years. You'd think I could sit and talk to her. Sometimes I think I know Gabriel, then other times I can't figure her out at all. How vows come first. Maybe it's like Sonny would say, maybe she's doing her best.

There's a habit in the wardrobe I could try. It's one of the older ones that come right down to the floor. I take it out and leave it on the bed; that way if someone comes in I can say it was in my way cleaning inside the wardrobe. There's a girdle in the drawer and a bra so big that, if I catch one end, I'd have to stand on the bed before the other strap cleared the floor and the cups are so huge Mona and Pippa together wouldn't fill them. I'll try that on first. No one will come in. The nuns won't leave the chapel when they're on retreat but I'll peek outside, just in case. The corridor is empty, only the dead nuns staring at me from wooden frames.

I have to wrap the bra straps around me twice. Maybe if I try the pink girdle it'll fit better. There's a pair of frilly pink bloomers. Might as well keep going.

I get everything on and look in the mirror. The skirts are bunched on the floor, my hands have vanished inside the wide black sleeves and my face is lost inside the crooked veil, yet for some reason I feel strange. The room seems peaceful and holy. The habit is heavy, responsible. You could see yourself running around trying to save souls, tearing off to Africa and countries all over the world.

How simple everything would be if I became a nun. I'd have no father tormenting me, no worries about how I'll live when I leave. I'd be taken out of the Mad School. Danny would be certain of a good job; the nuns would see to that. I'm just going to see what the habit looks like from behind when I hear the clank of keys. I stop and listen but there's only that peaceful silence. I imagined it. No, I didn't, there it is again. The door opens and the crackle of white skirts is gliding towards me looking an awful lot like Reverend Mother. It has me by the neck, down the stairs and in her office before I'm certain it is Reverend Mother. She stands me in the corner beside the filing cabinet while we wait for Gabriel. There's a painting over the mantelpiece of a nun in a habit from olden times. There's a plaque on the picture frame telling you she's the Founder. She has a face that would crack eggs. I can feel her black eyes on me and all I want is for a slit to open in the carpet so I can slide down into it.

Gabriel is here flicking snowflakes from her shoulders. One minute she's staring at me like she's trying to be certain it really is me in the habit. She peeks, blinks, peeks a little closer, then turns her face to the wall. Reverend Mother's face is a flame. She barks at Gabriel, Is this how you're rearing your children, Sister? Will you just look at this specimen?

Then she turns on me. What have you to say for yourself, rooting through Sister's drawers?

I wasn't at her drawers, Reverend Mother.

You were.

I was at her bloomers.

She springs from her chair holding the stick over her head warning me, Don't you be cheeky with me.

I wasn't cheeky, Reverend Mother, honest. I ah, I just wanted to, ah . . .

Stop blabbering. Stop looking to Sister Gabriel. She can't help you now.

I was thinking about becoming a nun. And I wanted to see what I'd look like in a habit.

Gabriel lets out a scream and collapses against the table holding her hand over her mouth. Reverend Mother tells her, Compose yourself, Sister Gabriel. Compose yourself. Perhaps this child has had the call. She sits down again and she's nearly smiling at me while she wonders if I've had the call. I look at Gabriel and she looks back as if to say, You're the one who said it. I can feel the Founder's eyes all over me. Like I'm being measured for a habit. Reverend Mother spreads her hands on the desk.

Well, child, have you received the call?

I didn't hear a voice now, Reverend Mother, if that's what you mean.

You wouldn't. That would be the Carmelites. She smiles, telling me what wonderful times lie ahead. I look over at Gabriel again. She's looking straight ahead but I know her ear is cocked and loaded underneath the veil.

Did *you* get the call, Reverend Mother?

Of course, Matilda.

Matilda? She never called me Matilda before. What the hell's going on here?

The Lord called me when I was eleven. I'm surprised it's been so late in your case. But, it seems God has chosen you, Matilda. You will take your vows here with us. Do you know the most important vow, Matilda?

Ah, keepin' away from men?

Reverend Mother gasps and falls back in her chair clutching

her throat. Out the corner of my eye I see Gabriel's hand going up to her face. I don't know what to do. I try folding my arms but the sleeves of the habit are longer than my arms and they flop like flippers. I feel like a fuckin' seal.

Reverend Mother composes herself and sits forward in her chair and knits her fingers together under her chin.

Tell me, how old are you now, Matilda?

Fifteen, Reverend Mother.

She stares right at me and I turn my eyes down to the table.

The Lord moves in mysterious ways his wonders to perform, surely. The most important vow, Matilda, is the vow of obedience.

You mean do what I'm told?

At all times.

Even if I think something is wrong?

Especially if you think something is wrong. That's why it's called obedience. Don't worry about it now, it will all become clear in time. But, tell me, did you find yourself being drawn, Matilda?

Drawn, Reverend Mother?

Like a thirsty man crawling through the desert is drawn to water?

All the time she's talking, she's closing her open palm, slowly, carefully making a fist. It's as if she's crushing a flower.

That's it, Reverend Mother. I was drawn.

Towards God, Matilda?

Towards the wardrobe, Reverend Mother.

Reverend Mother bangs her fist on the table so hard the typewriter clacks. She moves books, papers, pens, rosary beads around her desk and finally lifts the Bible, ready to throw at me, till she realizes what she has in her hand. Now she's screaming at me to leave that habit and veil on her desk. She never saw such a sacrilegious act. Now, here I am standing in bra and girdle and pink bloomers and that's more than she can take. She tells Gabriel she wants my case packed. That girl will be on her way to Cork within the hour. I'll make the arrangements personally.

Gabriel's face is redder than I've ever seen it. Her mouth tightens and her eyes narrow and she stares hard at Reverend Mother. She puts her arm around my shoulder and walks me to the door and tells me to wait outside.

What about the bloomers, Mother?

Later, Matilda.

I'm out in the corridor in the pink bloomers, where passing nuns lift their eyebrows and cup their hands over their mouths before slipping into a side room each one telling the other, Wait till I tell you what I'm after seeing outside in the corridor, Sister. Every time the door opens I see them rocking back and forth on the sofa, tears running from their eyes. Helpless with the laughter.

Through the window I see Sister Rose in the garden burning weeds and twigs. Raised voices come from behind Reverend Mother's closed door, but I don't know what they're saying. I don't even have time to worry. Gabriel comes out and closes the door gently. She stands in front of me like a woman who's just gotten something off her mind.

What's happening, Mother?

Nothing, Matilda. Nothing at all.

Will I come back in the morning, Mother?

Do. But for God's sake, Matilda, try leaving things alone.

I look up at her and smile. All right, Mother.

There's a smile on Gabriel's lips because, this time when I called her Mother, she knows I meant it.

She cradles my face in her warm hands and kisses my forehead. She puts her arms around me and hugs me tight. I hug her back and it feels right. I feel like I imagine any girl with a mother would feel. I know Gabriel isn't my real mother but right now that doesn't matter. She's the only mother I've known, and for that I love her.

Later, I go to my room and take the blue poncho from my locker and walk over to the nuns' garden. The garden is like a Christmas card, snow on the tree branches and the window-sills. Sister Rose has gone inside but the bonfire is going strong and the heat dries the tears on my cheeks.

I leave the poncho burning on the flames, and walk away.

20

I've never been this scared walking through the wicket gate. I'm in a world I know nothing about. Cars seem to pass quicker than before. They honk their horns and screech their tyres when I cross the road with my empty suitcase. People on the pavement hurry past with their umbrellas up. They stare at me, walking along with the suitcase over my head, trying to keep dry. Their eyes say it all. You don't belong out here. Go back where you belong.

Sister Kathleen is the matron in St Mary's Hospital. My hands tremble knocking on her office door, while an old man with a walking frame shuffles down the corridor. The nurse beside him tries to hurry him.

Come along, Brendan. We don't have all day.

The old man shuffles over to me. Where's your ticket? Who left you in here?

The nurse tells me to take no notice and rolls her eyeballs under her eyelids as she leads the old man away by the elbow.

That girl should have a ticket. This place is gone to rack and ruin.

It is, Brendan. Now come along, there's a good man.

Matron calls me into her office. It's a strange office, but then it's a strange hospital. It's small and gloomy with just a crack of light through the yellow Venetian blinds and smells of old leather shoes. I expect to see Humphrey Bogart sitting there in a hat, smoking a cigarette and calling me Punk. There's a picture of Jesus hanging on the wall, his heart pumping red and his head tilted to the side so you pity his sad face. Sister

Kathleen is sitting behind the desk in a navy uniform. Her eyes dart from me to the empty suitcase.

I hope you appreciate the opportunity we've given you. I've told Sister Gabriel I'll take you for the summer. On trial, so to speak. If you work out I'll consider making you permanent.

Yes, Sister. Sorry, Sister. I mean Matron, Sister.

You are sixteen, I take it?

I am, Matron.

I don't know what to do with the suitcase. Leave it down or hold on to it. If I leave it down she'll know it's empty and think I'm a right oddball walking around with an empty suitcase and send me back to the convent for being demented.

I hang on to it and lean a little to one side and put on a painful face as if the thing weighs a ton and hope she doesn't ask me to leave it down or say, Oh, that suitcase looks terribly heavy, give it to me. Then what would I do?

You start at seven and finish at four. Under no circumstance bring anything from outside to any patient. It's a rule.

Yes, Matron. Already there're rules. I should have known.

Wages are paid on Thursday. Fifty pounds a week, less ten for your keep.

Thank you, Matron.

What size are you?

Five feet seven.

I meant your clothes.

Sorry, Matron. Size eight.

She hands me a blue smock from the drawer under her desk that she tells me belonged to the girl had the job before me. Another hand-me-down.

Change it in the laundry for a clean one every Tuesday.

Yes, Matron.

You're a religious girl. You say your rosary every day, do you?

I did in the convent, Matron.

Just because you're out here with the rest of us is no reason to change. Now come with me.

I follow her flat white shoes moving quickly up the corridor. Her arse is wide in the navy uniform and the cheeks sway from side to side but she walks straight and swings her arms like a soldier and moves as silently as the tick of the silver watch pinned to her breast pocket. She leads me to an old dormitory in the attic. Another dormitory. I should have known that too.

The room smells of stale cigarettes. It has five iron beds along the wall and it's just bright enough to see mine in the far corner, where the roof slopes to meet the wall. There's a girl sleeping in the first bed but the others are all made, white, neat and tidy. Matron tells me to unpack; I can have the rest of the day to myself. Start in the morning.

The mattress is thin and the bed squawks when I sit down and I get such a fright I jump up, so the sleeping girl won't wake up roaring abuse and what the hell do I think I'm doing causing a racket at this hour?

I don't know what to do with myself. There's a small locker on one side of my bed and on the other side a wooden press with three drawers. The bottom drawer is mine and even on my own I'm embarrassed I have nothing to put in it. A window above the bed is big enough for my head to fit through. I can reach out and touch the red-brick wall in front of me and look down to the narrow alley from where the smell of cooking drifts up from the kitchen below. Cigarette butts parade the sill like toy soldiers. I find out later, Mags Riley, who sleeps in the next bed, never uses an ashtray. She doesn't even put them out and I spend half my night jumping up to check if the bed's on fire. But I'm frightened to say anything. Not because she's older and bigger and has arms like a man. Not because she's rough or tough. I was reared with the roughest and toughest. It's because she's from the outside and everything out here is new and frightening. Even the old patients are new.

I wonder if I've made a mistake.

There are four wards in the hospital, two for old women and two for old men, with twenty iron beds, all numbered, in each ward. I have a mop, a bucket and a bottle of lemon cleanser and every morning I mop and clean. Polish the wooden lockers and shine the windows. I change the sheets with Nurse Agnew. She has a shiny round face and wears a blue plastic apron so the shit won't stick to her bright white uniform.

The old woman groans when we turn her over in the bed and Nurse Agnew roars at me, Don't let that pan drop.

But it drops with a clatter on the tiled floor, sending piss and shit hopping off the walls.

Nurse Agnew calls after me. Come back here. Come back this instant. Matron!

Matron chases me into the bathroom and yells to the back of my head I'll have to get used to it. I'm stuck to the floor of the cubicle and she tells me there's no room here for weak stomachs. Up out of it. She pulls the chain and the spray goes in my eyes, up my nose, and I'm puking in the bowl again.

Then I help with the breakfast and medication.

The medicine is on the trays in clear plastic thimbles. The trays are numbered and there's a number for every bed. I found out after I gave number seventeen to number twenty-seven and had the old woman in seventeen asleep all day and the old man in twenty-seven singing, 'I'll Take You Home Again, Kathleen' to Matron and wouldn't stop for two days.

I pity the old people, like the bald Missus Sutton in number thirteen. I know how broken-hearted she is over her wonderful daughter and son-in-law who came to take care of her. She

284

boasts how they never missed a day taking her to hospital after she broke her hip, and how they wheeled her to chapel every Sunday. She insisted they wheel her to the solicitor, so she could sign over the red-brick house, and how the very next week they sold up and moved to London and left her here to die. She begs God to take her so she can be with her dead husband who stands at the end of the bed each night, telling her it won't be long.

Mister Phelan in bed twenty has a purple nose full of holes like a sponge and tells everyone he's going to marry me. I turn red every morning when he almost tumbles out of bed trying to peer down the front of my blue smock when I polish his locker. He laughs, Christ, if I was twenty years younger, we'd make a fine couple. What would you think yourself?

Mister Stacey with the white hair in the next bed says, You should have been dead twenty years ago.

Let me outa this bed. By Jasus, Stacey, I don't need to be twenty years younger for you, yeh aul bollox.

Walking sticks rattle the iron beds and wheezy chests laugh and croak till Matron with her navy uniform and Sergeant-Major walk barges in.

What's this ruckus?

The old men lie back and rest, their eyes blind, their ears deaf, while she parades up and down looking for someone to pick on. She stops at Brendan, sucking an orange in number seven. The other old men say he worked in the Coliseum picture house that's closed now, which is why he's tied to the bed at night. Sometimes he escapes and goes around the wards with a toilet roll for a flashlight, waking everyone, looking for tickets.

Matron pokes him in the ribs with her bony finger. What's this? We have a bin for orange peel. Haven't we?

Brendan jumps up in the bed.

Tickets, please. He glares at Matron. Who left you in here? Then whimpers when Matron takes his bag of oranges away.

You can have them back in the morning, if you behave.

She fixes Brendan's sheets. Checks the green tubes coming from his nose and tells him, Sleep now till we call you for the late show.

Two days later, Brendan is dead. Matron closes his eyelids and bends over him with her rosary beads in her hands whispering an Act of Contrition in his ear, and I look around the ward, wondering who'll be dropping off next. I'll miss Brendan and hope he's in a place where cinemas never close and batteries never die.

I know Matron said not to bring anything for the patients, but it's hard to refuse after Brendan is carried out white and stiff and Mister Phelan with the purple nose leans out of his bed. Matilda, would you do an old man a kindness?

I will if I can, Mister Phelan.

Don't mind that Mister Phelan. Call me, Frank.

I will, Mister Phelan.

Do you ever go to town, Matilda?

I do on my day off.

He whispers behind his hand. Can you get me Jack Daniels, Matilda?

What bed is he in, Mister Phelan?

Oh, Holy Jesus. He rolls back on the bed with the tears and laughter coming so hard he has to beat his hand on his chest but that only sets him coughing. He rolls to the other side of the bed and churns up ropes of green phlegm into a hankie he keeps under his pillow. He wipes his mouth on the bed sheet, rests back on the pillows and you can hear his chest wheeze every time it goes up and down. Wait till I draw breath. Christ, you're a tonic. Better than any doctor.

He reaches under the mattress for a ten-pound note and

tells me call to the off-licence on the Quay. Tell them it's for me and you'll have no bother. There's two pounds change. Keep it.

I couldn't, Mister Phelan.

Take it and don't have me to get outa this bed to you.

Thanks, Mister Phelan.

I'm delighted with the two pounds. I'll give it to Danny for pocket money so I can get him away from stealing. After all, it's my fault he's doing it.

Next pay day, Matron wants me in her office. I feel like I'm back in the convent with Gabriel taking money for curses and broken cups, the way she dangles my wage packet between finger and thumb because she knows I need it. She wouldn't do it to Maggie Riley or any of the other helpers, but I'm a Shep and I have to be grateful when she tells me I'm to do the night shift. Without a job she knows I have no place to go but back to the convent. All I need do, she says, is sit in the aisle between the beds and call the night nurse if a patient tries to escape.

Escape?

She says it happens.

She doesn't say at ten o'clock when the night nurse gives out the medication the lights go out and the hospital is a different place in the dark. That all you'll see are shadows you don't understand and only the faint light from the nurse's station tells you where to run if you feel a hand on your shoulder. She doesn't tell me about the wailing groans and heavy farting smells of old people, or when I'd look at my watch at four in the morning it's only midnight, that there's only two hours gone and six to go and not the other way round. She never said I couldn't get to the canteen because I'd have to pass the dead Mister Sutton telling his wife it won't be long. She never told me about rattling beds or how helpless

I'd feel when they want to scratch but can't because their hands are tied. She never told me I'd stick my fingers in my ears so I wouldn't hear the screams brought by bed sores or how I'd hold my nose to block the stench of piss and shit from overflowing bed pans. She didn't warn me how stiff I'd be, or say how happy I'd be to hear the first bird singing because a new day was beginning.

Slowly, the darkness melts and shadows become curtains and beds again. Strange sounds become old people with names. Mister Stacey wheezing in his ventilator mask. Missus Sutton waving goodbye to her dead husband and Mister Phelan sucking his tongue when he slips me ten pounds.

Would you like a glass of water, Mister Phelan?

Water? Is it trying to poison me you are?

The Matron marches around in her soft white shoes counting beds and patients and I wonder why she has to count beds and who'd want to run away with a hospital bed. Maggie Riley and the other cleaners come in their blue smocks while the nurses put on the blue plastic aprons and untie the patients' hands.

Matron says, You look thin, Matilda. Pale even. Maybe this night work doesn't agree with you.

I'm fine, Matron. Just tired.

Go to your dormitory and sleep. You must have your rest, Matilda.

Yes, Matron.

Back in the empty dormitory I toss and turn, but how can I sleep when I've been reared to live by the ringing of a bell and to ask permission to go to town or make a slice of toast? Suddenly I'm awake all night and supposed to sleep when I should be getting up for mass. I can't lie in bed all day. It might even be a sin. I have to stop thinking like that.

★

288

The town is deserted at seven o'clock in the morning. There's only yesterday's newspaper and last night's fish and chip wrapping blowing along the gutters waiting for the street cleaner to come along. I wander in circles and end up at the far side of town by the industrial estate. I think about going inside one of the factories and asking for a job, but I don't know how to ask for a job, and I'd have to tell them I was in the Holy Shepherd and the Mad School and that would be the end of that. I wander back through the empty streets again. The street cleaner strolls by and tips his cap at me. I'm sure he wonders why I'm here every morning but he just keeps strolling along, sweeping the papers onto his shovel and tossing them into his bin before moving to the next pile, pushing his brush ahead of him as he walks.

By ten o'clock, the middle of town is teeming with people and I know nobody. In Kelly's shop window on the Quay there's a blue dress I'd like for Mona's wedding, but it's not the same when there's nobody to say, Yeah, that's nice, Matilda, and help me find a pair of shoes to match. Someone to have fun with trying on clothes. Someone to have coffee or tea with instead of feeling embarrassed because I'm sitting alone with an empty cup. The waitress clears the table and asks if I want anything else and I politely move on to stare in another shop window, feeling strange and alone because I think I must look strange and I am alone.

Mona managed to get herself pregnant. It was always going to happen to her. Always going to be her way out. At least he's stood by her and they're getting married in a few months and living with her boyfriend's parents until they can afford a house. I ring Pippa. I imagine her on the other end of the phone in the hotel lobby up to her knees in carpet.

Missus Schultz doesn't like anyone from the Sheps ringing, Matilda. I'll get in trouble.

I'm your sister, Pippa.

Doesn't matter. I can't meet you, Matilda. I won't go near town when our father's around. Anyway, I'm meeting Mona. We're going to Kilkenny to pick out the wedding dress.

Don't ask me, whatever you do.

I didn't think you'd come.

That's the trouble with you, Pippa. You never think, unless it's about yourself.

But . . .

Get lost, Pippa. Just get lost.

I slam down the phone. I don't know when my sisters became so selfish or if they were always that way and I just didn't notice. Maybe it's the way you become when you live on the outside, and maybe that's the way I should be myself. They should know how I feel. They're my sisters, my family. They should understand how someone who's been locked up all their life and suddenly has their freedom can be the loneliest person in the world.

I wander back to the convent. Men with bulldozers are knocking down the stone wall and I think of all the nights I sat there and wept to be on the outside. Now I don't belong here either and I wonder if I ever will. I still see the convent as my home but I don't go in. Reverend Mother doesn't like you coming back. She thinks you're looking for something. All I'm looking for is a home. Someplace to belong. I know I have to leave all this behind me now, but it's hard. I think about going inside the chapel but I don't pray anymore.

In Patrick Street there's a sign in the cobbler's window: *Room to Let*. I worry he'll know I'm from the convent and make some excuse but there's nothing I can do. There's a jingle when I open the door and the shop smells of glue. I hear the cobbler hammering out in the back room but he stops when he hears me come in. He's old and wears a black leather apron and when he comes to the counter I look at him straight in the eye because I'm tired of not being able to look people in the eye. The sweat is thick on my palms when I ask about the room and all I need to do is turn my eyes away to make it stop, but I keep looking.

He studies me closely.

You're a bit young to be out on your own.

A woman needing new soles on her platform shoes comes to the counter and the cobbler serves her before handing me the key.

You seem like a nice girl. Take a look at the room and let me know what you think. I can't come up with you. I'm stuck here for a while.

The room is small but warm and clean and has a tiny little bathroom with a hand basin and a shower and a small window that looks out to the lane behind the Regina cinema. There's a single bed, a table and chairs, two armchairs, a cooker. Knives, forks and spoons in the drawer under the sink; cups, saucers and plates on the dresser.

In the morning, I take a taxi with my suitcase from the hospital and move in. Unpack my two dresses, my two pairs of shoes, one black, one white, three jumpers and other odds and ends. I have a black-and-white photograph of Mona, Sheamie, Pippa, Danny and me that I had framed. One of those cheap silver frames from Woolworths was all I could afford. I found the photograph at my grandmother's the day of Grandad's funeral. I decided to go to his burial. He never did us any harm. I know, he never did us any good either. The photograph was on top of the wardrobe covered in dust, with the photograph of my mother and father holding that trophy with the little dancing man and woman on top. I thought about taking that too, but what's the use? Koala was trapped in the space between the wardrobe and the wall. He must have fallen down there years ago.

I hang the photograph on the wall and sit in the armchair by the window. I remember the photograph being taken. It was the day we left Australia. My father held the camera to his eye.

Say cheese.

Pippa and me were at the top of the slide in blue cotton frocks with short sleeves. I was looking off to one side. Danny was sitting at the bottom smiling at the camera with his little baby teeth. Mona and Danny were standing. Mona in another cotton frock and white ankle socks. Sheamie was looking serious. The sky was clear and blue. The kookaburras were screeching from the treetops and the sun glistened off the metal chute of the slide. I was looking off to the side watching the gate. I was certain my mother would know we were leaving. That she'd feel it. Our suitcases were piled together behind my father and, at the other side of the lawn, a nun was trying to tempt a snake into a plastic sack. It was supposed to be a new start but there's no such thing. Not until my father is out of our lives.

The room feels strange after sharing my life with hundreds, but if I can stand a night in the hospital, I can stand anything. I get an extra ten pounds in my wages because I'm not paying the hospital for my keep but I have to buy food now, especially on the evenings when Danny calls, and I can just afford to hire a television and for a few days I feel like a millionaire with buttons and knobs I never had before. I can turn it on or off or turn the volume up and down and move the TV from this wall to that wall but I've never felt so lonely, and moving the television around is a sure sign of it.

I buy a book. It's big and blue and has a photograph of a

pregnant woman holding her belly on the cover and it's all about women's bodies. Even though I live on my own I can't stop myself from hiding it under the mattress. On my nights off I sit up in bed reading about clitoris and uterus and think, don't they sound like sisters. Good morning, Sister Uterus. Sister Clitoris.

It says here the clitoris is located, ah hardly, oh . . . ooh . . . ooh . . . oh that's definitely a sin.

One night I'm in the dark. No light. No television. No book.

In the morning, the cobbler comes up to show me where the electricity meter is located under the sink and where I'm to put fifty-pence pieces in the slot.

You mean I have to pay?

Did you think it was free?

I never thought about it at all. I thought it was just there.

You mean like air?

Something like that.

He went downstairs chuckling to himself, Christ, that's a good one. Wait till the wife hears this.

I can't go through the world not knowing electricity has to be paid for, wondering what else I don't know. I'd like a job, a decent job in a factory where I can meet people who won't drop dead right and left, people who are more than likely to show up in the morning. People who know about electricity meters.

21

In the morning, Mister Phelan slips me ten pounds for Jack Daniels and I ask him if he knows anything about getting a job?

I should. I had enough of them. What do you want to know, Matilda?

Mister Phelan knows my grandmother from the shop. He knows I was in the convent and he knows without me telling him that nobody will give someone from an industrial school a job. He calls to Mister Stacey in the next bed, Hey, Stacey, didn't you work in an office?

Forty years.

Mister Phelan tells me to get an application form and bring it here. We'll handle the rest.

Thanks, Mister Phelan.

You must tell your grandmother you were talking to me. Frank Phelan. Tell her I was asking for her.

I don't see her anymore, Mister Phelan.

Oh?

These things happen, don't they?

Mister Phelan must see from my face I don't want to talk about it. I wonder can he see from my face that I hardly think of her anymore unless someone mentions her name. That she's gone from my life for good and that's the best place for her.

He nods and changes the subject.

Try one of those big American companies, Matilda. Never work for an Irishman. The minute an Irishman gets his foot on the ladder, he'll use the other foot to kick the next man back.

I'll try, Mister Phelan.

A week later, Thursday, I'm getting ready for work when the doorbell rings at the same time as the bells for seven o'clock evening mass. I know it's not Danny because I gave him a key. Someone must have made a mistake. I look out the window but I don't see anyone. The last of the shoppers are heading home and down the street there's already a queue outside the Regina cinema for *Kramer vs. Kramer*.

Downstairs there are two letters on the hall floor addressed to me. This is definitely a mistake. I start to open one at the same time as I'm opening the door and there he is on the footpath, carrying a guitar in black leather case and bunch of withered flowers I know he picked from someone's garden. The beard is gone but the hair is as long as ever but thin and wispy on top. He takes a step forward so I can't close the door. His huge shoulders spread wide across the doorframe blocking the light.

He's polite when he talks. He heard I had my own place. He's disappointed I hadn't invited him for dinner. Daughters should invite their fathers for dinner. Aren't you going to ask me in?

I can't do anything but stand aside. I bring him upstairs and make an excuse about not inviting him for dinner. I meant to invite you, Daddy, but I work nights and I haven't been around much.

He hands me the flowers. I leave them by the sink that somehow doesn't seem like my sink anymore. I leave the letters in the press that doesn't seem like my press. The wooden chair groans with his weight when he sits at the table. He leaves his canvas knapsack on the table and the guitar on the floor beside him and all I'm wondering is, what's he doing with that guitar?

He folds his arms and lies back in the chair. He looks strange without the beard. His face looks bigger. His cheeks red and raw as if he's just shaved with a blunt razor, but he's still a handsome man and I can see what my mother would have seen in him.

You're seeing me now. What would you have for dinner? Ribs and cabbage would be nice. Ribs, cabbage and boiled potatoes.

I'll get them.

When?

Saturday. I'll make dinner this Saturday.

What time?

Six o'clock.

Where's your guitar? I don't see it.

I left it in the convent. I didn't have anywhere to put it before.

You'll go back for it.

Of course.

When?

I'll go tomorrow. Look, I'm late for work, I'll have to rush.

He ignores me and tells me to sit across from him. He even points to the chair. I sit but I don't know where to look or what to do with my hands. I lay them on the table. I can feel my pulse beating off the wood. He rumbles through his knapsack for the little pamphlets he hands out when he's preaching and his voice is sweet and calm.

Here's one about Elvis Presley, Matilda. Elvis was given his voice to praise the Lord but, when he turned his back on the Lord and lived a life of sin and gluttony, the Lord punished him. Just as he punished Jim Reeves in that plane crash. Pat Boone, on the other hand, turned to the Lord. He gave away the wild life and the Lord has repaid him with a good marriage of forty years.

He lets the pamphlet on the table and tells me to read this later. He has another pamphlet, about giving and receiving. It is better to give than to receive but you must give with a good heart. You'll read this too.

Yes, Daddy.

I've done the wrong thing living on my own. He's going to spoil this too. The flat feels cramped. My legs feel cramped. I find it hard to breathe because he knows where I live and he'll be back.

I'm getting nervous all over when the door opens and Danny walks in with the front-door key in his hand. I can see the way my father looks that he didn't recognize him straight away. He's grown since last year. His shoulders are bigger, rounder, and there's a wisp of hair above his top lip that teenage boys get. I can see in his eyes, he's surprised my father's here but tries not to show it.

Danny takes his coat off and leaves it on the back of a chair. He kisses my father on the cheek and sits in the armchair by the window under the photograph of the five of us as kids, his body shaking, and if I can see it my father can too.

My father takes the shiny wooden guitar from the black leather case and hands it to Danny. Danny's wearing clean pressed black pants and shiny black shoes. His hair is shiny and brushed across his forehead, so I know he's just come from serving as altar boy.

I bought you this for your birthday, Danny. You'll learn to play.

Thanks, Daddy.

How are you doing in school?

Danny's round brown eyes stare down to the floor and his cheeks turn pale. The heel of his shoe starts tapping on the wooden floor. The light of the evening sun through the window catches the glass frame of the photograph. I look at myself, a little girl's face in a head of black hair trying to understand what was happening to her. We were going to Ireland to live with our grandmother. Our new beginning.

My father stands up and pulls his chair across and sits in front of Danny. Danny's eyes plead with me over my father's shoulders and I can't just sit and do nothing.

You leave him alone. Can't you see he's terrified? I've said it calmly. I didn't want to provoke him. Maybe I should have said nothing.

He turns around and there's that glare. I'm sick of people looking at me like nothing. Sick of my father thinking he owns us. Anger drives me out of my chair. He stands up to meet me and we're so close I can smell him, soap and cod liver oil. I was never this scared but I can't stop my finger pointing to his face.

Leave my brother alone. He's not doing anything to you.

Sit down and mind your own business, Matilda. Don't back answer your father. Don't be stupid all your life.

I know what you're up to. You're not doing to him what you done to the others. And don't ever call me stupid again.

He snorts, grins, talks to me like he's giving me this one chance because I'm stupid and don't know any better.

I won't warn you again, Matilda.

Good.

I feel his whole body stiffen. Whiff that cod liver oil. My eyes are in line with his chest. The plain white T-shirt ripples across it like a flag. My toes touch the leather tip of his Moses sandals. I want to pull back but if I do I'll lose. Surrender before I start. I'm tempted to look at Danny, but I won't take my eyes off my father's hands. They're by his side but I know how dangerous they are. I feel his toes tightening; even his toes are solid. His huge open hand reaches up almost touching the light bulb. Ready to strike. Ready to beat me again. The light bulb sways and I yell, Hit me. Go on. Do it. I look him straight in the eye. I dare you.

I hear the cobbler downstairs pulling the metal shutter down over the window, locking up for the night. I feel my throat tightening, drying, ready to let me down just when I need it more than I've ever needed anything in my life. I keep staring straight into his yellow eyes; my eyes are still with me. My eyes won't let me down. I'm daring him and, for the first time, I see something I never saw in his eyes before.

He's thinking. He's thinking what he's going to do next. Wondering if I'm still afraid of him and what does he do if I'm not.

His eyes narrow; his cheeks lose colour. I can feel his rage. I hear him breathe. I've gone too far. My legs feel hollow and my head heavy with blood, but I've been here before. I've been kicked and punched all my life.

I point to the floor.

This is my floor. Mine. And I want you off it.

The veins in his temples are swollen and purple. His mind is made up and I know what's coming. Even before I see those long straight fingers curling into that fist, I know what's coming. I feel it before it lands. I see everything as clearly as I see the guitar on Danny's lap. The yellow eyes, the long narrow eyebrows, the long straight fingers curling into that fist, the photograph on the wall, the smell of cod liver oil. I take a step back and duck.

His fist swipes above my head. I pull the guitar from Danny's lap and crack it against the side of my father's head. I feel the sting shoot through my arms like I've hit an iron pole. He hardly budges. There's a blunt pain in my side but I blank it out. He caught me with his other fist under the ribs. I can't think about it. If I think about it I'll feel the pain and I can't afford to feel anything. I swing the guitar again and smash it against his temples. The strings twang and snap. His head wobbles. There's no look on his face. It's as if all the muscles have gone limp. His face sags. His body sags. He drops to his knees in front of me like he's praying to a statue and I still see everything clearly.

I see the five of us as kids being torn from each other's arms outside orphanages and I hit him.

I remember how close the five of us were and I hit him.

I remember caravans, nuns, beatings, nights of terror and I hit him.

I remember Danny jumping off the convent wall and hiding in terror and I hit him. I remember a little girl being led upstairs by her uncle and I hit him.

I remember Mona's legs covered in blood and I hit him.

I remember Pippa falling on her face in the mud and I hit him.

I feel a hand tearing at my arm. I hear Danny yelling my name and dragging me away.

Stop, Matilda. Jesus Christ, will you stop.

My father is lying on the floor covered in chunks of guitar and the stub of the handle is still in my hand. Danny pushes me against the wall and pins my arms to my side. My father's satchel is at my feet and I kick it towards him and yell at him.

Get out and don't come back. Tramp.

He groans and crawls along the floor by the wall. He reaches for the doorknob and pulls himself up slowly. His fingers leave a trail of blood on the door. I don't want him to get up but I don't want him to lie there either. I pull away from Danny and make a kick but Danny pulls at my arm and I kick at fresh air.

My father stands at the door rubbing the blood from his forehead with the back of his hand and there's a blood smear across his face. He stares at his hand. He stares at me but I don't care because I've been here before. He stares at Danny who's still pulling at my arm. My father could kill me now. We both know it. But when I look at him now, there's no fear. Just pity.

He stays at the door a while. Should I give him another chance? We'll start again, Daddy. I should say something. I can't just leave him standing there.

Get out. And shove your pamphlets up your arse.

I walk to the corner and take the sweeping brush and begin sweeping the floor as if everything is finished and there's nothing more to say.

He lifts the strap of the canvas satchel over his shoulder and turns and closes the door behind him leaving his blood on the doorknob.

I wait and listen to his footsteps fading down the stairs. The whirr of traffic as the front door opens, then silence when it closes.

I send Danny out on to the landing to check he really has gone and I collapse onto the chair. I'm shaking all over.

I won't cry, but I can't go to work like this. Danny comes back to say our father is gone and I send him to ring the Matron that I'm sick. When he goes, I don't know what to do. I sit down, then stand up, walk around the room. I have to do something. Do anything, keep going, wash cups, saucers, plates. Clean away the blood. I open the window and take deep breaths. The evening air is warm and sweet and down the street the queue for *Kramer vs. Kramer* has gone in.

I take the letters from the press and sit at the table. The first is from Sheamie and my heart nearly leaps out the window. He's working on a building site in Manchester. He's been offered a job as an apprentice electrician and he'll probably take it. The wages are poor to begin with so he'll need to have savings. He spent enough nights on park benches when he came here. He's put off the idea of finding our mother. He needs to find himself first, but he'll be home for Mona's wedding. He's happy she's not inviting any of my father's family, otherwise he wouldn't come, even for Mona.

I smile. It sounds just like Sheamie.

PS Mickey Driscoll turned up here and stayed a few days before heading off to look for work in London. He says he has contacts. By the way, it was Mickey who robbed our money. He told me when he was drunk. Hardly matters now.

Love from Sheamie.

I leave the letter on the table. I'll read it again when my head clears. The second letter is from the factory. Would I please call for an interview at ten o'clock in the morning.

Interview? What's an interview? No one ever told me about interviews.

Mister Phelan's unopened whiskey is in my press and he'll hardly mind if I take a sip. I drink it straight from the bottle and it's like lightning through my body till my toenails feel on fire. One swig becomes two and then three till I don't care about interviews anymore, but in the morning the inside of my mouth feels like it's grown a beard. I'm on the floor wrapped in a blanket and Danny is laughing down at me from the bed. He lifts himself up on his elbow and does an impression of Gabriel wagging her finger.

How many times have I spoken to you about fighting, Matilda? How many times have I told you to turn the other cheek? What am I going to do with you? By the way, that Matron said she wants to see you today.

I jump and, Jesus, there's pain. Like hot coals on my forehead.

Am I in trouble, Danny?

Don't know. I told her you were sick last night and couldn't work.

And?

And what?

And what else, Danny?

Nothing else. Just call to see her today.

I get showered and there's a bruise the size of a saucer under my ribs. I get dressed ready for the interview and, as I'm walking out the door, Danny sits up in the bed and calls me back.

Matilda, thanks for standing up for me.

I feel embarrassed and I don't know what to say, only, Go back to sleep, Danny. I'll see you later.

The man in the factory wears a suit and tie and a bright yellow shirt. He has an office as big as a field with three phones on his desk. All red. He says they're a big American company making games and jigsaws and my application was excellent, the job is mine. Machinist. All I have to do now is see Mister O'Leary through that door there and if I come through that test I'll be sent for a medical.

Test? No one told me anything about tests.

Mister O'Leary wears a white coat and has a stopwatch in his hand. He tells me I'm to put those different-shaped bricks there in the matching holes on that board on the table.

More bricks. I should have known there'd be bricks.

Matron is sitting behind her desk when I go in and she's not smiling, but there's nothing new about that. She leaves me standing while she writes what she has to write and phones who she has to phone then looks me up and down and tells me I look pale. Are you ill, Matilda? We don't want you carrying infection in here. Now, I've been giving some thought to your position. As you know, I only took you on trial, however I've decided to make you permanent. She's certain I'm pleased. Make the most of this opportunity and who knows how high I can rise. In a few years I might even be in charge of my own vacuum cleaner.

But, Matron . . .

Not now. I'll speak to you tomorrow.

I get to the ward and Mister Phelan's bed is empty. Sheets stripped from it and lying in a bundle on the floor, and I know I could never work in a hospital. Seeing people you've come to care about die. Even if my mother was a nurse, this could never be for me.

There's a cough from behind the screen and I think I'm seeing things when Mister Phelan pulls back the curtain and walks towards me pulling up his trousers. He has one sock on and the one in his hand he leaves on the bed.

Matilda, he says, they told me you wouldn't be in today. Isn't it grand now you're here? What's up, girl? You look like you've seen a ghost.

Mister Phelan. I thought, ah, I thought you were dead.

By, Jasus, no. There's fight in this dog yet. Mind you, if it wasn't for yourself I'd a died a thirst, ha, ha. Tell me, do you have that message?

Of course I do.

Slip it in under the mattress there before that bitch turns up.

Are you going somewhere, Mister Phelan?

A walk. Can't a man go for a walk in this place without twenty bloody questions? Tell me, did you get any news?

I did, Mister Phelan. I went for an interview this morning.

Out with it. Are yeh listening there, Stacey?

Mister Stacey sits up in the bed and fixes his pillow behind his head. I am, he says.

Go on, Matilda. What happened?

By now, all the old men are sitting up in their beds listening and my face is as red as a slapped arse in the middle of the ward.

I had to do a test, Mister Phelan.

And?

They said I had the fastest hands they ever saw.

Of course they did. And did you get the job?

What did you say in the application form, Mister Phelan?

Ask Stacey there, he's the expert. He might be half-dead in the bed but the brain is still operatin'. Isn't it, Stacey?

What did you write, Mister Stacey?

Mister Stacey beckons me over with his finger. A bit closer, girl. A little bit more. I don't want the world to know our business.

Tell me, Mister Stacey.

I done what everyone else does, Matilda.

He laughs out loud and calls me closer till his mouth is almost touching my ear. I can feel his breath in my ear-hole. Then he shouts so the whole ward can hear.

I lied!

The ward is in uproar when Matron with her Sergeant-Major walk barges in. What's this ruckus? Then she looks at me. Why are you still here?

The ward is silent. The old men lie back in their beds, their ears deaf and eyes blind. Mister Phelan, who was doing a jig between the beds, is frozen. One leg off the floor, the one without the sock.

I need to talk to you, Matron.

I told you already, tomorrow.

I won't be here tomorrow.

And why not?

I'm leaving.

What do you mean you're leaving? You can't leave. You can leave to go back to the Holy Shepherd for yourself and work in the laundry till someone feels good and ready to take you out but that's about as far as you'll be travelling, young lady.

I got a better job.

Oh, you did, did you? We're not good enough for you now. Is that what you're saying?

It's not like that, Matron. I wouldn't do that.

We were good enough to take you out of the Holy Shepherd but we're not good enough for you now. Is that what you're telling us, Miss all-of-a-sudden-high-and-mighty?

I'm really sick of people who think they have it over me. I'm ready to give her an earful, that I'm leaving and that's all there is to it, but there's a roar from Mister Phelan that makes me smile. He's fired up and ready to go, so I just leave him to get on with it.

Bollox this, he says. He stomps his foot on the floor, the one without the sock, and tells Matron to leave that girl alone. Do you want to keep her here till she's dried up and withered like the rest of us, you included, and only fit for a bed herself? She's seen enough misery in her life. Then he looks at me. Well, Matilda, haven't you?

I suppose I have, Mister Phelan.

You're to call me Frank.

Oh, says Matron, so it's Frank now, is it?

Mister Phelan shoves his big purple nose close to Matron's face.

It's still Mister Phelan to you.

Matron pulls her head back. Well, she says, backing down, I wouldn't have it said I stood in anyone's way, but I do have people to answer to, as well you know. I have my orders.

By now, the ward is silent. You can hear the rustle of starched sheets as Mister Stacey sits up in his bed to listen.

Matron pulls back from Mister Phelan's nose and straightens her blue skirts and tidies her hair. She nods her head that I can leave and turns on her heel and heads back up the ward in her soft white shoes, while she's reaching into her pocket for her rosary beads.

There are tears behind my eyes and I don't know whether to laugh or cry and even Mister Phelan's purple nose sniffles when he tells me, Call up an' see an old man sometime, Matilda.

I say I will, and try not to let it show that some day I'll call and they'll tell me he's gone for good.

He sits on the edge of the bed and puts his sock on, then slips his feet into his shoes. He bangs his heel on the floor to make sure they're tight then stands up and pulls his braces over his shoulders. He offers me his hand, but I kiss his cheek instead and, as I'm walking out the door, I hear him tell the other men, By Jasus, lads, I never lost it.

Walking back to the flat, I feel strange. I don't know if something is over or something is beginning or is it just another day? Danny will be out in a year or two and he'll need a place to live. I don't want him coming out to nothing. I walk past the Infirmary where my father carried me in his arms to have stitches in my leg.

I have time to kill, so I walk out the Cork Road past the green in front of the houses where I trained with the other kids before I raced. It's empty, bar a little girl in a summer frock playing with her doll and pram. I stand beside a wooden bench at the edge of the green and watch her play, trying to imagine what that feels like.

I walk towards town past the convent then past the Apple

Market. Umbilical Bill waves to me and I wave back from the other side of the street. I'm walking against the crowd but hardly notice them. It's like back-walking over my life, trying to make sense of everything, but I could walk for ever and never make sense of it.

Back at the flat, Pippa is waiting by the door with her hands in the pockets of a shabby brown coat with a cheap fur collar. The crowds are passing by and I walk up behind her and tap her on the shoulder.

You'd want to be careful, Pippa. You never know who you could run into.

She lifts her head. Her cheeks are pale and she looks fed up.

I hear your flat is the safest place to be these days, she says.

I knew there had to be a reason you were here.

Ha, ha. Very funny.

You asked for it.

Sorry, Matilda. Don't be like that. Mona was here. She's sorry too.

Mona was never sorry for anything in her life.

She waited for ages.

What for?

She wants the three of us to meet up tomorrow to pick out her wedding dress. We didn't go to Kilkenny. We wouldn't go without you. You know that, Matilda.

Do I?

We're just not used to you being out. That is, I'm not. Everything's a mess. I don't know where I belong. I rang the hospital and they said you left hours ago. You're my sister, Matilda. I don't have so many I can afford to lose one.

I take the key out of my jeans pocket and slip it in the lock and, when I open the door, the sunlight stretches along the hall floor. I walk to the end of the stairs and call back, Are you coming in or not?

She comes in and closes the door behind her and follows me upstairs. Danny locked the windows before he left and the room feels stuffy. Koala is sitting on the window ledge.

Pippa waits by the door of the flat like she's not sure whether to come in or not.

Come in, Pippa.

She takes her coat off and sits at the table and fumbles for a cigarette in her purse. I fill the kettle and plug in the flex and lift the bottom window sash. The fresh air seeps in with the beeping of a car horn and the garble of the people below me on the street. A light breeze gently lifts the netted curtains and lets them drop. Pippa lights a cigarette and drops the burnt match into the saucer on the table. She looks at me with her blue eyes and the teardrops on her eyelashes hanging like raindrops on a leaf. You just couldn't be angry with her. How can I blame her for wanting to feel safe?

Aren't you talking to me, Matilda?

I move back to the window and sit on the windowsill with one foot on the window ledge and the other on the floor. Koala is in my arms and my chin resting on my knee and I'm looking out on the traffic and the people heading home with their parcels and carrier bags. The world is getting ready for the weekend. I've never had a weekend. One day has always been the same as another.

Pippa says, I like the flat, Matilda. You've done well. I'm stuck with that Missus Schultz. I'm fed up living in the country. And she keeps calling me Vippa. Vippa, have you the brekvest ready? Vippa, vare are you now? I swear, Matilda, she's driving me veckin' vonkers.

I was thinking of getting somewhere bigger, Pippa.

Really? Can you afford it?

I thought you'd like to share.

Me?

No, the koala. Yes, you.

I have no money.

You could get a job in one of the factories. It'd be a lot better than where you are. Then we'd have a place for Danny to live when he gets out. I don't want him coming out to nothing.

I look back and her face is brightening. We can be a family, Pippa.

The pink glow comes to her cheeks and that makes me feel good. I could never be angry with my brothers and sisters. They're the most important people in the world. The past doesn't matter now. I won't let it.

The kettle boils and Pippa takes the mugs from the press and I turn back to look out the window.

The sun is setting and the clouds are a lovely shade of pink. There's a warm breeze on my skin that lifts my hair and lets it drop.

Pippa wants to talk and make plans. But there'll be time enough tomorrow. Today, I just want to be a girl having a cup of coffee with her sister.

Acknowledgements

Thanks to my reading group of one, Olivia Hamilton, who read an early draft and waved it through. To Edel Coffey, for her solid advice on hard necks. To all the staff at Penguin Ireland, but especially to Patricia Deevy for having the gift of second sight. Above all, I am indebted to my dear friend Kate Walker, a wonderful writer, who took me under her wing and taught me never to use a cliché. My heartfelt gratitude, Kate.